FOR THE GOOD O

BY THE SAME AUTHOR:

THE LABYRINTH MAKERS
THE ALAMUT AMBUSH
COLONEL BUTLER'S WOLF
OCTOBER MEN
OTHER PATHS TO GLORY
OUR MAN IN CAMELOT
WAR GAME
THE '44 VINTAGE
TOMORROW'S GHOST
THE HOUR OF THE DONKEY
SOLDIER NO MORE
THE OLD *VENGEFUL*
GUNNER KELLY
SION CROSSING
HERE BE MONSTERS

FOR THE GOOD OF THE STATE

A Novel

by

ANTHONY PRICE

LONDON
VICTOR GOLLANCZ LTD
1986

First published in Great Britain October 1986
by Victor Gollancz Ltd,
14 Henrietta Street, London WC2E 8QJ
Second impression October 1986

British Library Cataloguing in Publication Data
Price, Anthony
For the good of the state.
I. Title
823'.914[F] PR6066.R5

ISBN 0-575-03901-9

Photoset in Great Britain by
Rowland Phototypesetting Ltd, Bury St Edmunds, Suffolk
and printed by St Edmundsbury Press Ltd
Bury St Edmunds, Suffolk

For Fiona Barling

It is by my order and for the good of the State that the bearer of this note has done what he has done.
3 December, 1627 *Richelieu*

(From *The Three Musketeers* by Alexandre Dumas)

PART ONE

The Gentle Art of Shibbuwichee

IN THE EVENT, it was not Henry Jaggard himself but Garrod Harvey who connected the fate of the Department of Intelligence Research and Development with the projected British Museum Exhibition of the Treasures of Ancient Scythia. However, the Foreign and Commonwealth Office had in some sense already pointed the way in its latest signal on the subject of the exhibition, in which the curious request of the visiting Third Deputy-Director of State in the Ministry of Culture had been passed to Jaggard for his attention; and it was Garrod Harvey's private opinion ever afterwards that Jaggard had already decided to do what he suggested should be done, and had merely been waiting for him to speak up . . .

"So it was that fellow Audley who dropped the word to the Prime Minister?" Typically, although he was far more worried about the situation in the Soviet Embassy, Jaggard embarked on the less pressing matter first. "Are you sure, Garry?"

"Absolutely certain." In his role as 'Creature to the Duke', Garrod was accustomed to his master's oblique approaches. "But he didn't do it personally of course. So we'll never be able to prove it."

"Why not?"

"Because he's no fool. He's an interesting man, in fact—I've been studying his *curriculum vitae* for a couple of days, actually." Garrod was well aware of Jaggard's view of the Research and Development Department, so this piece of anticipation had come all too easily. "He's quite a distinguished scholar in his own right, did you know? Apart from his money and his connections—"

"Damn his money and his connections! Are you saying that I can't go and read the riot act about him to Jack Butler?"

"Yes, I am. Exactly that." The good thing about Jaggard was that he expected straight answers to straight questions. "It's his connections which add up in this case. He's got a great many of them, going back over nearly thirty years, Henry. Both sides of the Channel, and the Atlantic—the Americans think the world of him."

"And the Russians?"

"And the Israelis." Harvey knew then that Jaggard had seen the FCO signal. "But in this case it was a woman named Deacon. Laura Deacon, Henry."

"Laura—" Jaggard frowned at him. "Laurie Deacon's daughter—?"

"MP for North Wessex." He knew also that Jaggard would be making all the necessary connections now. "She inherited her father's safe seat when he went to the Lords. And Audley's always been very thick with the family: it provides his local MP . . . and one of his routes into the Commons back-benches, when he wants to have questions asked." He couldn't risk a smile with Jaggard in his present vengeful mood, so he shrugged instead. "Perhaps we should be grateful he didn't do that in this instance."

"Oh yes?" The mood hardened even more. "So it was Laura Deacon who spoke to the PM, you're saying?"

"They met last Friday. Laura Deacon dropped a name, and she also said that Colonel Butler would know all about it. And the PM summoned Butler directly."

"And he spilled the beans directly, too. Why the hell did he do that?"

Harvey rejected the temptation to agree with him. "It was his duty, Henry—be fair!"

"His duty?"

"His duty." Harvey agreed whole-heartedly with his master about the Research and Development Department. But he also liked and respected Jack Butler as an honest and devoted officer. "The PM has the right to go direct to the head of R & D, Henry. And the Head of R & D has direct access the other way—that's how old Fred Clinton constituted it, from way back."

"I know that." Jaggard gestured dismissively. "But he also has a duty to *me*. And there was no reason why he shouldn't have told me first—" He stopped suddenly as he caught the expression on Garrod Harvey's face. "Or was there?"

"He didn't have time." It was one strike to Jaggard that he also respected Jack Butler. "Audley deposited his report on Colonel Butler's desk about five minutes before the PM's office rang. So my guess is that he'd planned everything to the minute, practically: that the PM would hit Butler at once, and then the Minister himself immediately after that. He knew what *everyone* would do—maybe he even knew that the PM would be so pleased—at being able to catch the Minister on the hop, as well as being able to suppress the leak—that there wouldn't be anything we could do against him even if we could trace it all back." He watched Jaggard look in vain for loopholes. "Because the PM *is* pleased. So R & D is riding high at the moment, Henry. Because they came up with the information in time, just when it was needed."

Henry Jaggard scowled at him. "But the Minister *isn't* pleased."

"Ah . . . yes, I can well imagine that, Henry." And so he could. (Another leak in the Minister's department—albeit plugged in time, but not plugged by the Minister's own expertise, only by the PM's superior intelligence.) And he could also see why Henry Jaggard was incandescent with rage, too. (The Minister was a good friend and ally of his when cuts and economy were the order of the day.) "It's unfortunate."

"It's more than that, Garry. He's been made to look a fool. And so have I." Jaggard's better side showed as he grinned at Harvey. "I can survive that, but this makes him a two-time loser at No. 10. And now I've got to tell his Special Adviser in fifteen minutes that I can't give him the scalp he wants, so this sort of thing won't happen again." The grin evaporated. "Is there no way I can give him a scalp, Garry?"

"Audley's?" Harvey knew what his master wanted. But for what he planned to propose he needed more than that. "Colonel Butler will never give you Audley, he'd resign first." He shook his head. "Offering hostages isn't his style. Besides which, R & D is too busy with Gorbachev at the moment. And Audley's too valuable—he's right at the heart of the work."

"Yes." Jaggard well knew what R & D's main present preoccupation was. "But . . . this wasn't any of Audley's damn business."

"That's not the way David Audley would see it." He had to lead Jaggard on, evidently. "Clinton gave them *carte blanche* from the start—as well as direct access to the PM—remember?" He knew that Jaggard remembered, even though R & D had been born—born by Caesarian section—long before their time. "He gave them '*Quis custodiet ipsos custodes*' as their motto. And he always said they were his Tenth Legion, Henry—remember?"

"Huh! More like a Fifth Column now!" Jaggard's nostrils expanded. "Audley isn't even the real problem—R & D is the real problem, itself—no matter how important the work." He shook his head slowly. "It's not '*Quis custodiet*' now—it's bloody *Imperium in imperio*! It's become a state within a state—and it's got to be cut down to size, Garry. For the good of the state it was founded to protect, in fact."

They were almost there. "I agree." But he needed some reassurance, nevertheless. "But with reservations, Henry."

"With reservations?" Jaggard gave him a fierce look. "What are you driving at?"

It wasn't the moment to make some submissive animal-signal: Jaggard was almost as intolerant of yes-men as he was of R & D. "Their research is first-rate—particularly their analytical advice. And they're coming up with first-rate stuff about the Gorbachev appointments right now, Henry—the Americans are trading us all manner of things in exchange for it. So there's no way we can abolish them—they're far too useful."

"Who said I want to abolish them?" The fierceness amended itself. "All we need is to *control* them, so that they don't cause trouble on the side—" Jaggard raised a slender hand. "—and I don't mean that they're not damn good at covering up the trouble they make . . . and their mistakes too . . . because they are—I know that—you know that." The hand clenched. "But they *do* cause trouble—and they *do* make mistakes—every time they go into the field on their own account." The fist unclenched, and Jaggard tapped the file on his desk. "Even, for example, God only knows what sort of mayhem might result from this FCO signal if I let it go any further. Which, of course, I won't—that, at least, I can stop, anyway."

They were there at last. But Harvey craned his neck, as though attempting to read the superscription. "Which is that—?"

Jaggard covered it. "Audley's too busy with the Gorbachev work. Apart from which he'll only cause more trouble in this case, if he runs true to form."

"Which was that?" Harvey stopped pretending to read through Jaggard's hand. Because Jaggard was going to tell him anyway.

"Apart from which the KGB is undoubtedly up to mischief." Jaggard gave him an unblinking stare. "And since the FCO processed the signal they'll also want to know what the outcome is. But I shall say 'no'."

"Ah!" Harvey let the light dawn. "That'll be that odd communication about Professor Panin, I take it—?" After letting the light dawn he let himself relax. "I was thinking . . . it's a curious coincidence, isn't it—eh?"

"Curious?" Jaggard stopped covering the file.

"Well, there's obviously no connection between what Audley's just done and whatever Professor Panin and the KGB may be contemplating." He let that out as an arguable statement, because they both knew who Panin was, beyond what the Soviet Embassy and the FCO alleged he was. "So it is a pure coincidence, Henry. There can be no question about that."

The stare cracked, and Jaggard flipped open the file. "'*Professor Nikolai Andrievich Panin. Third Deputy-Director in the Ministry of Culture: one of the foremost authorities on the archaeology of the royal tombs (6th and 5th century BC) in the bend of the Dnieper, the districts of Poltava and Kiev, and the Crimea*'?" He looked up at Garrod Harvey, then down into the file again. "'*Dr David Longsdon Audley. CBE. Ph.D. MA (Cantab)*'—" He looked at Harvey again "—'*distinguished medievalist*'?" This time he didn't look down again. "Have you seen this SG?"

That wasn't a trick question. "Yes. My name's on the list, Henry."

"Yes?" The nostrils blew out again. "But I've also got a clever-dick note from some wag in the FCO—did you get that too?"

That wasn't a trick question either. "No."

"No?" Jaggard looked down quickly to refresh his memory. "I've got: '*1. Isn't Panin one of theirs and Audley one of yours?*' And '*2. What has 6th–5th century BC Scythia got to do with Medieval History?*' And '*3. Are there any Royal Scythian tombs on Exmoor?*'" Jaggard considered Harvey dispassionately for a moment. "And then they advise me that Professor Panin is to be given all reasonable help and consideration, because HM Government is concerned to improve Anglo-Soviet cultural relations, pending projected diplomatic and cultural exchanges running up to possible East-West disarmament talks later in the year." He gave Harvey another couple of seconds. "Are there any Royal Scythian tombs on Exmoor?"

"Not that I've heard of." That was the moment, as the full awfulness of the FCO advice registered, when Garrod Harvey began to suspect that Henry Jaggard had been there ahead of him, thinking the same wicked thoughts. "Prehistoric ones, maybe—or Neolithic. But that could be Dartmoor, not Exmoor . . ." He let Jaggard see that he had something else in his mind.

"Yes?" Jaggard paid his penny cautiously.

"I was just thinking." On second thoughts it would be better to be honest—or fairly honest, anyway: that usually paid better with Jaggard. "Or . . . I *have* been thinking."

"About what?" Jaggard hadn't got his pennyworth yet.

"About Audley. And Panin." He gave Jaggard a seriously questioning glance. "I take it the FCO doesn't really know why Panin is here? That he's General Zarubin's Number Two, I mean?"

"They certainly do not." There was a metallic curtness about Jaggard's reply: it was the sound of the penny dropping. "Nobody knows except the Viking Group. You know that."

"Yes. So that's just you and me, and de Gruchy." Garrod Harvey deliberately thought aloud. "But the Americans also may have an inkling, we decided."

"They may." Jaggard accepted the thought. "They've almost certainly got someone of their own in the Soviet Embassy. So it's just possible they've also picked up a hint of the Polish operation—agreed."

"Yes. But their man is at a much lower level than our Viking." Harvey could see that the very mention of Viking, the highest-placed contact they had ever had in the KGB's London Station, made Jaggard cautious. Yet he still had to push matters further. "So the Polish operation is the one you want us to leave well alone."

Jaggard stared at him. "The one we *have* to leave well alone, Garry." The edge of his patience was beginning to fray. "We've been through all this."

"Even though we know that Zarubin—Zarubin and now Panin . . .

even though we know that they're up to some bloody mischief." Harvey nodded, noting the shift to 'we', even though the emphasis had been on 'have'.

"Yes." Jaggard knew that it had been his rank-pulling decision over their indecision which had swayed the vote. But, to his credit, he had never been afraid of responsibility. "Viking's worth more to us than any bunch of miserable Polacks. And they must be damn close to him already—in fact, I'm not at all sure that this whole Polish thing hasn't been dreamed up just so that they can pin their leak down. Because we haven't had a whisper about these so-called 'Sons of the Eagle' from our people in Poland—they've never even heard of them. But whoever they are, and whatever the KGB's doing, Viking is just too valuable to risk, that was the decision. So what are you after, then?"

The moment to break cover had arrived. "Maybe we don't have to risk Viking, Henry. Because, according to the FCO, it's Panin who wants to meet Audley. And Audley doesn't know anything about Viking—it's just that he and Panin are both 'distinguished scholars'—" He remembered Audley's file "—and old friends too, maybe?"

"'Friends'?" Jaggard tossed the question aside contemptuously. "I thought you said you'd read Audley's file? Back in '70—remember?"

"Yes." Panin had got exactly what he wanted in '70. But Audley had totally humiliated him in giving him what he wanted, and that would rankle forever afterwards. But, much more to the point, Jaggard had read that file too. "So Panin hates Audley. But then Audley also hates Panin, Henry: he's an old Clinton recruit. And old Fred Clinton always made a point of recruiting on the KGB principle of good haters—'cool head, hot heart', and all that." He watched Henry Jaggard accept the statement. "True?"

"True." Henry Jaggard nodded, out of his recent scrutiny of the Audley file: over the years, others before them had crossed swords with David Audley (and had come out of each clash-of-steel with scars, and the wiser); but no one had ever even remotely hinted that his hot heart wasn't in the right place, though he was a Cambridge man. "But Panin is a very dangerous old man, Garry. And—"

"And so is Audley a dangerous old man, Henry." Now they were only negotiating the fine print of the agreement. But they had to go through it line by line, for the record on the tape under Jaggard's desk. "It's a toss-up which of them is the more dangerous. But I agree that there'll be trouble when they meet." The thought of the tape concentrated Garrod Harvey's mind. "Only my bet is on Audley—like last time." There was one more important thing to put on the record. "Old Fred Clinton must have made the same bet back in '70." Not that the tape mattered, really. Tapes could be edited, but editing tapes wasn't Henry Jaggard's style any more than throwing his subordinates to the wolves was Jack Butler's. "You're quite sure that Audley doesn't know about Viking, I take it?"

Jaggard shook his head slowly, without bothering to answer what wasn't even a question.

"What I mean, Henry, is that he doesn't know—*and we can't tell him, not even if we wanted to, can we?*" Harvey paused deliberately. "Not even if he asked us about Panin. Which he won't in any case, because that isn't his way of going about things, you see."

Jaggard leaned forwards. "Just what exactly are you proposing, Garry? To let Audley go in blind?"

"David Audley never went into anything blind in all his life." All Jaggard wanted was a little reassurance. "One of our problems with him in the past has been that he knows too damn much, not too little. So he'll know Zarubin's in London for sure—you can bet on that. And he'll know who Zarubin is, too."

"But Poland isn't his field."

"*Everything* is his field. He's a Clinton-vintage R & D man born and bred, Henry." Harvey briefly considered the possibility that he might have been wrong about Jaggard's intention, but rejected it. "He's an interesting man."

"'A distinguished scholar'—so you said." Jaggard knew there was more to come. "'A medievalist'. But I would have thought the sixteenth century was more his period. The treachery was more three-dimensional then, if I remember correctly."

"Yes." That was Henry Jaggard's period, of course. And, as a devout Catholic, Jaggard had equivocal views on it which were well known. "But did you know that he's also a recognized authority on Rudyard Kipling?"

Jaggard nodded cautiously. "Kipling is down as one of his hobbies, in his file."

"It's more than a hobby." Harvey silently blessed the young Garrod Harvey junior's stuffiest godfather, who had given his birthday presents with such old-fashioned seriousness. "He's just written a series of articles in the *Literary Journal*. Which are going to be turned into a book, I believe. He believes that Kipling is our most underrated author—and our most misunderstood one."

"Indeed?" Jaggard's politeness was strained to breaking-point, like the window of the de Havilland Comet which Garrod Harvey's own godfather had trawled up from the sea-bottom off Elba thirty years before. "So what?"

"The most recent one was on Kipling's children's stories." Harvey gauged the moment when Jaggard would explode, as the Comet window had exploded. "You know, my wife tells me that 'We are what we eat'.

But it seems to me that, more accurately, 'We are what we read'. Or . . . in the present generation what we *don't* read—I suppose it's what we *see* now, on the television. Which is a truly dreadful prospect—"

"*Garry*—" Jaggard controlled himself with difficulty. "I have to see the Minister's Special Adviser in about two minutes. And I don't think I'm in a position to stretch his patience—do you?"

It was time to lower the pressure. "I think we might have something to offer the Minister. At least . . . if he's prepared to cover our flanks, if anything truly unpleasant occurs." Garrod Harvey couldn't bring himself to recall 'the good of the state' as an ally, even though it had to be their only true good, for what he envisaged; because the Minister's Special Adviser would only be concerned with the good of his Minister. "Because Audley's most recent article was on Kipling's children's stories, as I was saying—"

It was to Jaggard's credit that he merely opened his mouth and then closed it without exploding, like some of the Comets which had managed more flights than others.

"There's this passage he quotes—" Harvey held Jaggard's attention "—which just about sums up the way he operates, on the rare occasions when he goes out into the field. Because when it's all over he always says 'I didn't do anything—it just happened that way. It wasn't my fault.' It's called '*shibbuwichee*', apparently."

"It's called *what*—?"

"'*Shibbuwichee*'. Which Kipling thought was a form of Japanese wrestling." Nod. "My elder boy was given a complete set of Kipling by his godfather last year, so I've been able to look it up: *'These wrestler-chaps have got some sort of trick that lets the other chap do all the work. Then they give a little wriggle, and he upsets himself. It's called "shibbuwichee", or "tokonoma", or something'*." He blessed old Hetherington again, and his own memory too. "And that's how Audley operates. So what I thought was that we might do the same to him now, Henry."

"How?" Jaggard was there, ahead of him.

"If we tell him Panin wants to see him, he won't be able to resist that—"

"But if he does?"

"We'll make it irresistible. Leave that to me." Part of their usual accord was that there were some things which Jaggard didn't need to know. "But I don't think he'll want to miss Panin for a return game. And that could solve our Polish problem without the need to risk Viking. Because he's never going to let Panin outsmart him. So you can be sure that whatever Panin really wants, Audley will find out what it is. And he won't let Panin get away with it."

"But . . . if it goes the other way—?"

"Then there'll be a scandal." Garrod Harvey shrugged. "But if we leave Zarubin and Panin to their own devices there'll be a scandal *anyway*, most likely, Henry. But *this way* . . . this way it'll be a Research and Development scandal. Because Audley will never come to us for help—it's not in his nature to come to anyone, not even Jack Butler if he can avoid it. And certainly not when someone like Panin is involved. He'll want to *shibbuwich* the man, like last time, Henry: David Audley's whole psychology is dedicated to *winning*, not to Queensberry Rules games-playing. But if he loses this time . . . then you can blow R & D wide open, Henry."

"Yes." That enticing possibility plainly captivated Jaggard—as it had from the start. "But if he *loses*, Garry—Panin's a murderous swine . . . and Zarubin—" He fixed Harvey coldly "—Zarubin's worse than Panin, in so far as that's possible, Garry."

That was the good Catholic speaking, echoing generations of good Catholic Jaggards from the Reformation onwards, who had sweated and suffered for their Faith then, and had been disadvantaged even in liberal England for the next three hundred years afterwards, down to the living memory of Henry Jaggard's own great-grandfather. "So?"

"I can't risk Audley." The cold look became deep-frozen. "Bringing R & D to heel is important. But what they're doing at the moment is important also. And Audley's done a lot of good work, over a lot of years, Garry. So risking him now just isn't on."

"I agree—I do agree, absolutely!" Harvey understood the complexity of his error and Henry Jaggard's dilemma simultaneously: the professional and patriotic ninety-nine-hundredths of Henry Jaggard wanted what they both wanted; but the hundredth part of Henry Jaggard was old Catholic and very different—what it wanted, that hundredth part, was either Major-General Gennadiy Zarubin on his raw knees in front of the High Altar, praying for the forgiveness which the Holy Catholic Church never denied sinners . . . or Major-General Gennadiy Zarubin broken and bloody, and turned over to the Civil Power for appropriate final punishment, like in the old days.

"I do agree, Henry." Garrod Harvey kept his face straight. *Because what Henry Jaggard wanted was for Audley to win and lose at the same time; and that was exactly what he was now about to offer to Henry Jaggard, and the Minister's Special Adviser, and the Minister, and the Prime Minister, and Her Gracious Majesty, Queen Elizabeth II!* "But my money's on David Audley—I think he'll screw Panin into the ground, and General Zarubin with him. But I also think we have to give him a bodyguard, to watch over him—"

"A bodyguard—"

"That's right: a bodyguard." Nod. "I've taken that for granted."

Another nod, for good measure. "Not just to look after him, but also to keep us informed as to how he's breaking all the rules in the book. Because that's what he always does—he doesn't even pay lip-service to the rules, Henry. So if he screws Zarubin—Zarubin and Panin . . . then, even then with a bit of luck, we can still make a scandal of it—if we have someone on the inside beside him, watching him—?"

Jaggard frowned, as though some long-outdated moral scruples were attempting to skirmish with pragmatic experience, like bows-and-arrows against machine-guns, which was no fair contest.

And yet (as though the longbowmen and crossbowmen were cheating, by capitalizing on the silence of their weapons), Jaggard was still frowning at him.

"We have to have someone alongside him, Henry." He had to press home his technological advantage. "Otherwise he'll weasel out of it somehow, like he always has before."

"He'll never accept anyone." Jaggard left his moral scruple behind. "Or he'll want someone he can trust, like Mitchell or Andrew from R & D, Garry."

Garrod Harvey shook his head. "They're all too busy, with their own Gorbachev work. And they don't fancy minding Audley, at the best of times." He made a face at Jaggard. "Minding David Audley is a thankless task. And in the past it's also been rather dangerous. But, in any case, R & D hasn't got the manpower for it. Or the womanpower."

This time Henry Jaggard knew better, and merely waited for enlightenment.

Garrod Harvey turned the shake into a nod. "I fed a few notional facts into the computer this morning—profile facts."

Henry Jaggard looked at him, trying to pretend that he knew 'notional facts' and 'profile facts' from the double yellow-lines on the road outside, far below them in Whitehall. "And—?"

"I think we've got just the man for the job. At least . . . he's a medievalist, of a sort. And he also speaks fluent Polish." Garrod Harvey smiled invitingly.

Henry Jaggard was so relieved to have left the computer behind that he accepted the invitation. "And—?"

They had passed the point where Jaggard might have said 'What you're proposing is monstrous, Garry', even though what he was now proposing was just that. "He isn't Audley's son, Henry. But he could have been. Audley will never be able to resist showing off in front of him."

PART TWO

The Man for the Job

I

TOM MOISTENED THE end of his stub of indelible pencil and wrote '1025' beside the line of the bailey ditch on his sketch-map.

If Willy's measurement of the *motte* ditch was about 500 feet in circumference, then the whole *motte-and-bailey* was a dead ringer for the Topcliffe castle in size, if not in date—obviously not in date, because Topcliffe was an early post-Conquest castle, and this was as yet not anything at all except an anonymous 'earthwork' on the ordnance survey map. So it just could be Ranulf of Caen's adulterine castle, which certainly should be somewhere hereabouts if his calculations were right.

On the other hand, it was certainly not much of a *motte*, he thought doubtfully, looking up into the impenetrable undergrowth above him and trying to estimate the height of the mound. These were undoubtedly Ranulf's lands, *de facto*, if the local bishop's *de jure*, in the mid-twelfth century; and both Ranulf and the bishop had changed sides in the civil war, several times and not always at the same time. But the Norman barons—even a two-timing (or ten-timing) jumped-up shyster and petty hedgerow mercenary knight like Ranulf—had thrown up more impressive earthworks than this in a hundred other places, with little time and their enemies at their backs. So it still could be merely a fortified manor, a hundred years or more away from Ranulf's brief medieval gangster flowering during the years of anarchy. So, allowing for the wear-and-tear and the wind-and-rain of all the 800 years afterwards, it all depended on Willy's measurement, which should establish the circumference and diameter of his hypothetical *motte*, with its stockade and tower, which could perhaps be proved during his next leave—

The sound came from behind him—above and behind him, in the undergrowth which hemmed in the edge of the *bailey* ditch, at its junction with the *motte* ditch (if this really was a genuine *motte-and-bailey earthwork castle*, he thought pedantically)—and he accepted that it had to be Willy, because the *motte*-ditch was all thorn-bushes and brambles, even worse than the tangle above him, from which Ranulf might once have defied the might of King Stephen (or maybe the Empress Matilda, according to which side he'd been on at the time)—

So he would have to apologize to Willy (Willy would never give him the benefit of the doubt, after that last unfortunate slip on the edge of the moat at Sulhampstead, which had not *really* been his fault—but *poor old Willy)*—

But it wasn't Willy: it was—he dropped his pencil as he stuffed the sketch-map into the back-pocket of his jeans, and automatically reached down to find it, but then stopped just as automatically in mid-fumble, half in nothing more than surprise, but then half in momentarily irrational fear, at the glimpse of a uniform.

Then the fear was subsumed by self-contemptuous irritation with himself, for letting the sight of an ordinary British policeman frighten him—not a Mister-Plod-PC-49 fatherly copper in the dear old high helmet admittedly, with red face and button nose and bicycle-clipped trousers, but a young copper in a flat cap, and no older than himself; yet a young copper who seemed just as surprised at the sight of him, and who was even now more concerned with extricating himself from the trailing bramble-sucker from last year's blackberry growth which had snagged his uniform.

The trouble is, he justified to himself quickly, *I have met too many other sorts of policemen, of the shoot-first and who-cares? variety, these last two years, and that's a fact!* But the conditioned reflex was still nonetheless strong enough to make him pick up the stub of pencil slowly, and to hold it up between thumb and forefinger for inspection, complete with an ingratiating smile, as he straightened up in slow motion to match the gesture, as if to say: *'Don't shoot, officer! This is just me—Tom Arkenshaw . . . And this is just my stub of pencil—not a grenade or a pistol!'*

But the young policeman only stamped down on the ensnaring blackberry thorns, innocently oblivious of his gestures of submission; which gave him time to come fully to his British senses, to wonder aggressively *what's a bloody copper doing here, sneaking up on me on the edge of old Ranulf's ditch?*

One final trample. And then the young policeman sucked his finger, where a thorn had caught it, before looking down at him again. But it was a damned hostile, suspicious look all the same, thought Tom.

"What are you after, down here?" The policeman frowned at his finger again, and then gave it another suck.

Tom's hackles rose. This was old Ranulf's ditch, or near enough—not somewhere beyond the Green Line in Beirut, or a poxy Third World slum within mortar-range of a British consulate. But then he thought *maybe I'm trespassing—?* But there were no peasants in these coverts, so far south of Watford Gap, surely?

"What—?" Caution inclined him towards a show of ignorance, to probe the question further, before he pulled rank and privilege. But then a crunching-and-crashing sound, emanating from the floor of the ditch, away to his right, diverted the policeman's attention.

Other sounds accompanied the crunching-and-crashing, which Tom could guess at, but which he didn't want to interpret as he bent down to look for their source and prepare for the emergence of their author.

"What's that, down there?" The policeman assumed—assumed all too correctly—that whatever Tom was 'after' was related to the sounds.

Tom peered uneasily into the tangle. At the very lowest point of the ditch, which was probably all of six feet higher with in-fill than when Ranulf had forced the local peasantry to dig it, there was something like a tunnel. But, although it might be sufficient for the local *fauna*—foxes for sure . . . and maybe even badgers, if there were still badgers unpersecuted here—it was hardly enough for Willy, surely—? Because, for one thing, it was muddy—

"Have you seen a gentleman hereabouts?" inquired the policeman, obviously despairing of any other answer, and not expecting it to issue from the bottom of the ditch, anyway.

It was Willy: Tom's ear, attuned to the worst, caught a word—two words, more precisely—from the other sounds which marked Willy's passage, exactly according to his orders, with two-yard measuring pole in hand.

Tom turned towards the policeman. Perhaps it was just as well that he had a policeman in attendance, he decided. So the important thing now was to keep the man in attendance, to protect him from physical assault.

The crashing became louder, and the words—good old Anglo-Saxon words, echoing the sentiments of the original ditch-diggers—became clearer.

"Eh?" He encouraged the policeman to repeat the question.

"Have-you-seen—" The policeman took him in with a despairing glance "—a-gentleman—a-*gentleman*—round-here?"

"No," said Tom truthfully. "Why?"

The direct question, following the direct answer, was just the right one for the situation, Tom decided. Because it detained the policeman for another moment; and, if Willy didn't arrive in a moment after that, he could always try the next question—a good late Medieval question, which had been John Ball's question—

When Adam delved, and Eve span, Who was then the gentleman?

"You haven't seen anyone?" Now the poor devil was caught between the suspicion that he had an awkward customer on his hands and the final arresting vision of Willy's emergence backwards from the thorn-and-blackberry tangle; and the adjective was strictly accurate rather than Freudian, because Willy's designer-jeans-encased backside was without doubt a vision sufficient to divert any man from his proper duty, thought Tom.

"Only her," he answered again truthfully, but this time more doubtfully, as he observed the condition of the jeans.

"*Seventy-six—*" She still held the measuring pole in her hand as she broke free from the tunnel "*—seventy-seven—*"

But that wasn't the whole circumference of the castle mound, thought Tom quickly. He had taken the longer line of the *bailey* ditch in all innocence, not knowing about the tangle on the far side of the mound which she must have had to fight her way through, which had left him time to measure that part of the mound's circumference which fitted into the *bailey*. So that meant 77 plus 25, multiplied by six. Which meant that Ranulf's castle was slightly bigger than Topcliffe, but not significantly so; which might mean that Ranulf had been building under the pressure of hot civil war, where William's man in Yorkshire eighty years earlier would have been throwing up his defences against the sullen pressure of a largely unconquered but disorganized and leaderless Anglo-Saxon population. So that evened things up. But . . . but, at the same time, it firmed up his theory that this couldn't actually be Ranulf's headquarters in Sussex. Or . . . if it was his HQ, then that might mean—

"You *bastard*!" exclaimed Willy, sitting on her heels in the mud. "Look what you've done to me!" She surveyed herself. "Christ!"

The designer-jeans were certainly not what they had been before he had sent her out to measure the castle ditch. And her hair had come down at the back—and at the front, too.

"Christ!" She let go of the measuring pole with one hand, in order to examine the other hand. "I'm *goddam* hurt!"

That would be the dead blackberry suckers from last year—or maybe the thorn bushes in the tunnel. It was much too early in the year for stinging nettles, certainly. Because there had been no stinging nettles at Sulhampstead last week, nor within the old Roman walls at Pevensey, the week before.

Willy was busy sucking her finger—

Stinging nettles were interesting, thought Tom. They were always to be found in association with agricultural activity, rather than military or monastic work—was that true or false? There had been sheep at Sulhampstead, and cows at Pevensey. Or had it been the other way round? But, either way, there might be room for some intriguing research there—

"*Tom!*"

Tom experienced momentary irritation—he had never really thought about the incidence of *stinging-nettles* before—but then he realized too late that what was expected of him was regret and guilt, and tried to contort his features appropriately. "Willy-love, I am *sorry*—"

"*Bastard!*" Her voice fell from self-pity to cold anger: she might well be remembering her experiences at Sulhampstead.

"I said I was *sorry*—"

"I'll give you 'sorry'!" She picked up the measuring pole with both hands and jabbed it at him like a spear. "I'll *make* you sorry—"

"Now, Willy—don't be like that." Tom skipped sideways as she jabbed at him again. He was just out of range, but she had risen to one knee and was aiming dangerously low, towards parts of him which he would undoubtedly be sorry to have injured. "*Willy*!"

"Don't you 'Willy' me—" Just as she was rising from the other mud-caked knee, pivoting on it at the same time to reach his new location, she saw the policeman on the edge of the ditch above and behind him.

The policeman cleared his throat nervously, otherwise evidently struck dumb by the intended act of Grievous Bodily Harm he had been witnessing. Or it might be just the sight of Willy herself, thought Tom with proprietorial admiration.

"Gee!" In the instant of recognition the wide snarl had turned to jaw-dropped surprise, but in the next instant she had re-arranged her expression so that now it merely registered interest. "Well, hi there, officer!"

Tom's admiration increased, and he felt that same curious twinge of an emotion he had experienced several times just recently, but hadn't taken the trouble to explore. Or maybe didn't want to risk exploring—was that it? he wondered, shying away from a traffic light in his mind which shone red and green at the same time.

"Good morning . . . madam." For a moment the policeman seemed undecided as to how to address her. But that would be as much because of the rich mid-western American accent—foreigners were always tricky—as because of the contradiction between her dishevelled appearance and her abundant self-confidence, Tom estimated.

"He's looking for a gentleman, Willy," he advised her.

"Uh-huh?" She didn't even look at him as she stood up, using her ex-deadly-weapon to help her. "Well, I guess he better go look somewhere else—" she smiled her sweetest smile at the policeman "—because there's no gentleman here."

Tom knew then what he knew he had known from the moment the young policeman had materialized out of nowhere, which he had only been resisting because he didn't want to know it; because, when a man was more nearly happy and carefree than he had any right to be, he also had the right to resist the inevitability of a 99-per-cent certainty, just in case that last one-per-cent was on his side. But he turned back towards the policeman, hating himself because he was suddenly even happier—no longer carefree, but excited now, and utterly consumed by that old addictive drug—because they wanted him this badly. And it still fed his happiness, as their eyes met, that the policeman knew too . . . although with nothing like that 99-per-cent certainty even now . . . that this unlikely gipsy-looking non-gentleman was nonetheless his *gentleman*—just his *gentleman* being awkward, no more.

The policeman struggled for five seconds against his remaining doubts, but then surrendered to the slightly higher odds. "Sir Thomas Arkenshaw?"

Tom sympathized with him. Half his stock-in-trade was derived from the wild accidents of twentieth-century history, which had crossed unlikely genes with a different environment; and also he knew that it was always painful for such a good solid Englishman as this to throw a 350-year-old baronetcy on such a questionable product.

"I am Sir Thomas Arkenshaw." As always, the foreign half of him threw down the Anglo-Norman half contemptuously: the Dzieliwskis had ridden in a hundred battles before the low-bred merchant Arkenshaws had made enough money to interest any *parvenu* Stuart King of England. "Yes."

"Thank you, sir—Sir Thomas." The policeman stumbled slightly over Debrett's Correct Form of Address, one part of him obviously still unwilling to accept the identification. But then he squared his shoulders and gave Tom the full benefit of the doubt. "I'm sorry to disturb you, Sir Thomas—" with an effort he didn't glance at Willy "—but there's . . . there's another gentleman who wishes to see you . . . urgently. He's waiting for you back in the lane, by the gate."

Now it was Tom's turn for disbelief. "Here?"

"Yes, sir—Sir Thomas. By the gate."

That changed matters. Being sent for was one thing: by routine they knew where he was shacked up with Willy, and the hotel people knew where he was to be found this morning. So, despatching the nearest policeman to find him was the simplest and quickest way of effecting his recall. But this automatic assumption had been wrong, for the mountain had come to Mahomet. And that was another thing altogether.

"Right. I'll come at once—" He had started to move before he remembered his manners, and turned back to Willy "—if you'll excuse me for a moment, Miss Groot—?"

"Be my guest, *Sir* Thomas." As a good servant of a great republic Willy accepted the call to duty without demur, only with a proper disrespect for the undeserved and unrepublican title he bore.

"Thank you, Miss Groot." Tom threw the words over his shoulder as he scrambled up the side of the ditch towards the policeman.

(Sending someone down to scoop him up, and presumably to brief him on the spot . . . that might mean a panic, minor or major—)

His foot slipped, and he slid back half a yard—

(How *exactly* did they build their ditches? Revetted with turf or with wood?)

(Alternatively . . . whoever it was who'd pulled rank on the local police —*another gentleman* suggested rank, so it could even be Phillipson—)

The policeman observed his problem, and extended a helping hand.

(Did Norman ditches differ from Anglo-Saxon works? Or from Roman ones—had their expertise been passed on? That sounded unlikely—in England anyway, if not on the continent . . . But what about the pre-Roman ditches of the great hill-forts—?)

The policeman hauled him up the last few feet, catching his sense of urgency as well as his hand.

(There must be some specialist research on ditch-digging somewhere —just as there had to be something on the incidence of stinging nettles; that was always the way of it, simultaneously enlightening and frustrating: there was always someone who had got there, or been there, before, asking the same questions—)

"Thank you." He made his peace with the policeman with a smile. He must stop thinking about old Ranulf's adulterine castle now. It might not be a panic at all, but just Phillipson (or whoever) pulling rank unnecessarily, for any one of a thousand footling reasons, to pick someone else's brains. Or even to take a look at Willy, maybe—

No, it could hardly be that. Willy was a known quantity, and he had registered his friendship with her, as the rules required. So they couldn't read the riot act over her.

He lengthened his stride. Only another few yards and he would be able to look down on the lane which had once briefly been the busy road to Ranulf's illegal strongpoint, but which must just as quickly have degenerated back to the mere farm track it had become forever after, under Henry Plantagenet's iron-fisted rule. Poor old Ranulf—

Poor old Tom! He amended the thought instantly as he looked down on the gateway, and saw Henry Jaggard. *Poor old Tom!*

Jaggard? Christ! When he'd thought of the mountain coming to Mahomet, he'd only thought of Snowdon or Ben Nevis, not Mont Blanc or the North Face of the bloody Eiger!

"Sir?" At least he didn't need to pretend not to be astonished. Even if he'd been wrong about Willy—even if Willy had been a KGB major in drag—that wouldn't justify the presence of Henry Jaggard here in Ranulf's lane, just by the opening in Ranulf's *bailey* ditch.

"Tom, dear boy!" Henry Jaggard surveyed him with fleeting distaste. "I am sorry to come upon you like this—" He looked around "—in the middle of nowhere." He came back to Tom with a basilisk smile. "What on earth are you doing here?"

The middle of nowhere was right, thought Tom with sudden insight: Jaggard knew exactly what he was doing, and why he was here—and who he was with, down to the room number in the hotel. Because it was Jaggard's right and business to know that. But it was still the middle of nowhere.

"I'm just doing another *motte and bailey*, sir." Tom accepted the fiction, and played up to it deliberately. "I think it's one of the illegal castles Ranulf of Caen built during the reign of King Stephen—mid-twelfth century. But no one's ever done precise measurements on it." Time for a disarming grin. "It's down as a late 13th century fortified manor in Herrick's *Medieval Earthworks*, actually. But I don't think Herrick ever took the trouble to look at it."

"Is that so?" Polite lack-of-interest in exchange for disarming grin. No one was fooling anyone. "That's rather interesting, I should think." Jaggard took another survey of the middle-of-nowhere. "But I can perhaps understand why he didn't—Herrick, was it?" Jaggard had plainly no more heard of Professor Albert Herrick than he had of—of, say, Ranulf himself . . . or of Ranulf's contemporary, King Boleslas III of Poland, whom Tom's Dzieliwski ancestors had served. "It is rather inaccessible, isn't it!"

Yes, thought Tom. *And as good a place as Henry Jaggard could hope for, to meet poor Tom Arkenshaw unobserved and off-the-record!*

Jaggard cocked a knowing eye at him. "And Miss Wilhemina Groot doesn't mind braving the wilds of the English countryside with you, then?"

"No, sir." The bugger didn't need to throw Willy into the conversation so crudely. "Her ancestors built forts like this in Iowa and Minnesota, against the Sioux in the 1860s, so she tells me—" Tom gestured towards Ranulf's ramparts "—not the same design, of course . . . but the same general defensive idea, more or less—just earth and timber-work and man-hours—*plus ça change*, and all that."

"Is that so?" Henry Jaggard opened his mouth to continue, but Tom owed him one for Willy.

"If you've got the time I can show you how it works. *Motte and bailey* is pretty much a standard Norman design, with minor variations. It's a bit muddy and overgrown on the other side, but—"

"Thank you, Tom! But . . . in the circumstances . . . *no*, I'm afraid." The very slightest edge of Henry Jaggard's dislike broke through the surface of his confidence, like a shark's fin in a smooth sea, warning Tom that whatever he had in store wasn't going to be one of those plum diplomatic sinecures in safe East European communist countries where the food might be bad, but the scope for terrorism was limited to the point of boredom. Besides which, of course, with Tom's well-known maternal background he knew himself to be automatically *persona non grata* in most of them, anyway.

And, also besides which, he had already pushed his luck as far as it was safe to do. So a bit of proper departmental enthusiasm was in order now. So . . . *although this particular son-of-a-bitch will never promote you, Thomas Arkenshaw-Dzieliwski . . . show proper dutiful-enthusiastic-interest, damn your eyes!*

Although, Henry Jaggard was a shrewd operator, who didn't generally let his prejudices interfere with his duties, to be fair. So maybe he'd been a bit naughty, thought Tom, half-repentantly. "Yes, sir?"

Jaggard estimated him for a moment. "We have a little bit of a flap, Tom. And . . . I'm genuinely sorry for descending on you, believe me . . . but you've got the exact profile for it, you see. So your leave's cancelled, as of this date."

"That's all right, sir." Tom waved his own olive branch back. "This earthwork isn't going to go away."

"And Miss Groot?" In victory Jaggard was suddenly generous. "Senator Groot's daughter, would that be? Or grand-daughter?"

"Niece, actually." No, not generous at all. Merely politic—politic with Miss Groot, not *Sir* Thomas, whose true measurements were precisely known, and who was plain *Tom* in consequence. But he shrugged dismissively, nevertheless. "But I don't think she'll go away either. Not that it matters." Oddly enough, it was beginning to matter; though this was hardly the moment to admit it to himself, never mind to Jaggard. "A flap, you said?" And it was even less the moment to pretend that he wasn't surprised to see Jaggard in a flap in the middle-of-nowhere: with Jaggard he not only had no need to play stupid—he positively couldn't afford to do so. "What sort of a flap?"

Jaggard looked past him, to make sure Senator Groot's niece was not materializing inconveniently on the horizon. But the young policeman appeared to be doing his duty in detaining her where she was, for that one glance was enough. "Tom . . . when did you last have dealings with Research and Development?"

Tom was just about ready for any question but that. It could have related to anything from Beirut to Managua, by way of Belfast; or from

Black September to the Red Brigade (as recently reconstituted), by way of the IRA. But . . . it was one hell of a sight closer to home than that. "R & D?" But Jaggard would know bloody well when he'd last consulted R & D: it was a suspiciously unnecessary question. "Not for ages . . . apart from their routine briefings—the ones I'm cleared to receive, anyway—?" he was entitled to end the statement on a question.

"I mean face to face. Not the briefings."

"Hell!" Tom concentrated his memory. "One of them chipped in his piece at that seminar . . . He'd been over in Dublin—*Field Research*, he called it." Memory etched the face and the facts. "Mitchell was his name —'Source PLM' in the briefings . . . He was into the IRA and the KGB, by way of ancient history. We got the Irish foreign connection from the Fenians in America backwards, all the way through Napoleon and Louis XIV to Philip of Spain. He's a historian—a published historian, too—" The etching included the man's recommendations on the best Irish whiskeys into the bargain; but that wouldn't do for a teetotaller like Jaggard, by God! "—a military historian—?"

"Who else?" Jaggard crossed out Mitchell. "In R & D?"

Caution engulfed Tom. But he mustn't show it. "Well—Colonel Butler runs their show, of course—" But that was mere banality, insulting to both of them "—who else *what*?"

"Who do you know in R & D?"

The caution became murkier. "Who do I know? No one, really." It wasn't that he had any particular loyalty to Colonel Butler's band of brothers, who seemed to live in a world of their own, pursuing their own ends (but which ends had so far mercifully been different from his, as it happened); but, in any case, before he admitted that he wanted to know why Jaggard was quizzing him now. "I've met Mitchell. And I know *of* Colonel Butler—who goes way back, of course—" He couldn't leave that *of course* to be questioned, because although Colonel Butler must go *way back* to be Director of R & D no one knew anything about him—any more than they knew anything much about anyone in R & D; so he must throw in some more names as ground-bait, and quickly "—and Macready, the economist . . . and they've got a Special Branch man, who's an expert on trade union leaders—or rather, the young fliers who dropped out of circulation to learn their business over there, like—"

"Andrew." Jaggard nodded, rising to Tom's desperate indiscretion quickly. "Ex-Superintendent Andrew." He nodded again. "And I think you must know Commander Cable—socially, perhaps?"

Now he must be close, thought Tom: to throw in James Cable as a *dyed-in-the-wool* R & D man, and not just a temporary attachment—

"James, of course," agreed Tom. So James really was Research and

Development's Society contact, not just a Royal Navy man waiting for his Trident appointment, in succession to his father's original nuclear command.

"And Audley?" Jaggard relaxed enough to check that Miss Groot had not yet broken through their defences.

"I've heard of him, of course." *Who was it going to be?* wondered Tom. The genuine 100-per-cent truth was that he didn't know much at all about R & D: they were reputedly a bunch of weirdos who produced good material by questionable means known only unto themselves, but who seldom issued out of their ivory Tower into the real world; which (rumour added, he thought uneasily) was just as well, because they only took jobs which no one else wanted, which ended in tears for someone.

But Jaggard was watching him very narrowly now, and that jogged his memory disturbingly, after the thought of Willy somewhere out there, behind Ranulf's earth ramparts: R & D always liked to have an obligatory woman or two on their strength, someone had said. And once they had had a little beauty, whom they had lost in particularly harrowing and incompetent circumstances; so now they had another one, whose intelligence was said to be only surpassed by her ugliness, which was altogether exceptional.

"Yes?" An old fox watching a young rabbit sitting just inside its briar patch, that was what Jaggard reminded him of, thought Tom.

"I don't really know anyone else." *Oh no, Brer Fox!* Whatever Jaggard might know about Willy, or any of Willy's predecessors, she and they were strictly extra-mural activity. So if the man had any ideas about the Sycorax of R & D, he had another thought coming. "I really don't know any of them—I told you."

"You don't *know* David Audley?" Jaggard sketched mild bewilderment. "Now . . . that *does* surprise me, rather."

Audley? Tom frowned. "Why does it surprise you?"

"I thought he was an old family friend. In fact, I'm sure he is, Tom." Jaggard exchanged suspicious disbelief for mild bewilderment. "Of your mother's, as well as your late father's—eh?"

"My—?" Tom floundered for a moment, unable to bring up the shield of truth quickly enough "—my mother? Well, if that's so, it's news to me—" The sudden doubt in his voice only made matters worse. *Audley?*

"Not to say an old admirer, indeed." Jaggard agreed with himself smugly. Then he caught the look on Tom's face. "Failed admirer, of course—*proxime accessit*, but failed—*also ran, but unplaced*, that is to say . . . and a long way back—" Now he was actually attempting to extricate himself "—your late father and he were both rugby players at Cambridge, Tom."

Oh—*shit!* thought Tom, momentarily ignoring his master. Mother's admirers had been legion, long before Father had cashed in his baronetcy for another set of wings but still within the scope of his own childish memory. So it ought not to be any surprise to him that there had been other and younger moths singeing their wings on her flame in her salad days—*shit!*

"It was long before your time." Jaggard's agreement with himself was no longer smug: it was insultingly apologetic. "I should have realized that." Then he recalled himself to his duty. "But he is an old friend, anyway."

Tom was saved just in time by the same imperative from snapping back *How the hell do you know?* Because that was really only professionally interesting—because it was Jaggard's business to know, was the immediate answer; and he could tax Mother with that question later, at his leisure, some other time. All that mattered now was that it was almost certainly true.

"At Cambridge?" He got his voice back to the level of professional interest. "That would be rather before my time." But . . . *Audley*, of all people—the name hit him again: Audley was . . . a *bête noire* now, or at least an *eminence grise*, as well as an elder statesman and something of a legend, rather than a *proxime accessit*—so . . . *trust Mother!* But Jaggard was here, in the meantime. "I'm afraid you've had a fruitless journey."

Jaggard took another look at his surroundings, for all the world like one of King Henry II's men come to make sure that Ranulf of Caen was no longer occupying his illegally-constructed strongpoint. "Not fruitless, Tom."

No? "I mean, I can't tell you anything about him . . . that I'm sure you don't already know—"

"About him—Audley?" Incredulity. "My dear Tom, I know all I need to know about David Audley already. He's a very old colleague—not to say old friend." Jaggard half-smiled. "David and I go back a long way, almost into pre-history." The half-smile evaporated. "Of course, it would have been a bonus if you had been acquainted with him. But only a small bonus—it's of no great importance."

"Importance to what?" Tom couldn't keep the suspicion out of his voice.

"To what I want you to do."

A flap, Tom remembered. "I'm due in Athens on Friday."

"That's all taken care of. Frobisher has agreed to lend you to me for the time being." The half-smile began to condense again. "He said you'd be pleased—that you don't like dealing with the Greeks."

"I don't." Frobisher himself would not have been pleased: Jaggard would have had to pull rank to obtain that 'agreement'. "But we're going to have a problem there—"

"Then it will be someone else's problem." Jaggard sliced through his half-hearted protest abruptly. "As of this moment your problem is Audley."

Being sliced like that irritated Tom. "But there's no one else who can deal with it as I can. It isn't a problem of protection—it won't be a diplomatic hit next time, it'll be a British tourist. And it'll be a bomb. So someone's got to galvanize the Greeks into pre-emptive action—". The thought of Bill Bennett arguing with Colonel Stamatopoulos through an interpreter irritated him even more "—and I can do that. Because . . ." He caught his big mouth too late: he was not only kicking against the cut-and-dried inevitable, he was also devaluing Bill, who was not only better than he was in Africa and Central America, but a good bloke into the bargain. But that was too complicated to explain here on the edge of Ranulf's ditch, with the first drops of today's rain spotting his face.

"Because you're the best?" Jaggard ignored the rain.

"Because I speak Greek." Bill's solution to Anglo-Greek relations would be to restore the Elgin Marbles, as though they were the same as General Wolseley's Benin rubbish, from West Africa.

"Because you're the best, Tom." Jaggard ignored his answer. "But, as it happens, this isn't so very different from what you're accustomed to do. In fact, the only difference is that it should be easier—the protection I want."

It was time to stop arguing—or pretending to argue, thought Tom: it was time to find out what Jaggard actually wanted. "But Audley's not diplomatic—" But there was a short answer to that, he realized "—not over here, in England—?"

"I don't want you just to protect Audley—" Jaggard stopped suddenly, and stared at him for a moment, his spectacles rain-blurred. "Of course, I do want Audley protected—not just because he's an old friend, either . . . Because what's locked up inside his head is probably of more value to us than anything Jack Butler's got in his computer records."

That was Research and Development in a nutshell, thought Tom: the only reason it still existed was that it had its own top secrets, which it played like cards close to its chest in spite of all orders to the contrary.

"It's a Russian he's meeting, Tom." Pause. "It's a somewhat fluid situation at this moment. But you may be able to solidify it for us, is what I'm relying on."

A Russian, thought Tom. And then . . . *a Russian in the UK*—Jaggard had implicitly said as much, in answer to his question about Audley, after suggesting that it wasn't so very different from what he was accustomed to do. But what did he mean by 'solidify'? "A Russian diplomat?"

"A diplomat." But Jaggard's face did not confirm his words. "Name of *Panin—Nikolai Andrievich Panin.*" He met Tom's questioning expression without any sign of surprise. "Professor of Scythian Studies—or maybe it's of Scythian Archaeology, I don't know . . . But for our purposes he has diplomatic status, as an umpteenth cultural attaché, to discuss the possibility of a Scythian exhibition at the British Museum the year after next."

"Uh-huh?" Even without Jaggard's deadpan expression Tom had his own experience of certain Russian cultural attachés in the Middle East, who had looked—and behaved—as though they could have set up prehistoric exhibitions from first-hand experience. "Which directorate would that make him? KGB Archaeology—is there one for that?"

Jaggard looked up at the rain-clouds above, which still couldn't make up their minds whether to drop their full load here, where there was no shelter, or further east, where there were more people. "Actually, that wouldn't be wholly inappropriate for Comrade Panin, you know." He took a handkerchief from his pocket and began to dry his spectacles. "He really was a professor once upon a time, and an archaeologist too." He held up the spectacles to the sky. "But he also goes back a very long way in State Security—pre-KGB, pre-MVD even . . . possibly NKVD, early 1940s, in the War of Liberation—God knows, perhaps even before that, for all we know." He settled the spectacles back on his nose and looked at Tom again. "That makes him even older than David Audley—his old friend David Audley."

"Old . . . *friend?*" As Jaggard seemed to be waiting for him to register surprise, Tom obliged him dutifully.

"Old acquaintance." Having published his libel Jaggard carefully retracted it. "Old adversary, of course." He smiled at Tom. "David will tell you a lot about Comrade Panin, if you ask him nicely. He's by way of being an expert on the subject. And . . ." He trailed off deliberately.

Old, thought Tom. *Old adversaries—old acquaintances . . . old friends —old family friends . . . even old admirers. Maybe not quite as old as old Ranulf and his adulterine earthworks, but old, old—*

"And?" Jaggard hadn't come to the point yet, but was waiting to be prompted.

"Yes. I was just thinking . . ." Jaggard pretended to be just thinking a little longer ". . . if you want to know about Audley, you could do worse—a lot worse—than ask Comrade Panin. It's quite possible that he knows more about David than we do."

That couldn't be the point. "I'm going to meet him, am I?"

"Panin?" Jaggard wrinkled his nose as a large rain-drop spattered on his newly-polished spectacles. "Oh yes . . . In fact, you're going to meet both of them—and very soon, too." He nodded. "This is a time for meetings, Tom: Comrade Panin is soon to meet David Audley—by request, and with our agreement, naturally . . . And you are going to mind them both, when they meet. And then you are to stay with Audley, like a limpet. Because we don't think Panin has come over here for old acquaintance's sake. We think he wants more than that."

Tom was aware that he'd got more than he'd bargained for in answer to a simple question, and reeled slightly under the pressure of the disorderly mob of questions which crowded his mind. But better to let another simple one through, while he imposed discipline on the big ugly ones. "What's my authority for this, if Audley asks?"

Jaggard looked disappointed. "My dear Tom—aren't you Diplomatic Protection? Panin has diplomatic status—"

"But I only protect our own people overseas." Tom shook his head, even though he knew that he was nit-picking. "That's bloody thin."

"But your section advises the Special Branch and the Anti-Terrorist Squad." Jaggard shrugged. "Use your wits—tell him whatever you think he'll believe, for God's sake!"

Actually, it wasn't such a silly question, because a man like Audley wouldn't believe any old rubbish. But that was his problem now. "Who can I call on for back-up?"

"That depends on what Audley wants." Jaggard gave Tom a shrewd look, as though he'd seen more in the question than had been intended. "But if he wants anything, then you deal with Colonel Butler—you deal with him, but you report to me. And I don't want my name mentioned. You just stay with Audley, and keep me informed as to what he's up to. Right?"

It wasn't at all right. "You want Audley *watched*—as well as protected?"

"My dear Tom—not *watched*!" Jaggard registered mild outrage. "Of all people—not *watched* . . . if that's what you're suggesting—?"

It was beginning to rain: the clouds had come to a decision at last. But Jaggard seemed oblivious of it.

"I'm not suggesting anything." To his annoyance Tom found himself thinking of Willy, out there in the rain behind him somewhere. "I just want to know what the hell you want me to do."

"Of course." All Jaggard saw was his annoyance, not the reason for it. "David is a difficult man . . . opinionated, arrogant—not to say eccentric. But his loyalty is above question—don't even think about it . . . And quite outstanding in his field, Tom—quite outstanding." Jaggard nodded to emphasize the accolade. "We *need* him. And we need him *now*, with Panin on the premises."

Tom could see the rain running down Jaggard's face, and could feel it running down his own. And he thought *if Jaggard's a liar, then he's a good liar. But then—*

"And we need him kept alive—*alive*, you understand?"

"Yes." *But then he would be a good liar*, Tom's train of thought reached its terminus. But he didn't think the man was lying now. "Keeping people alive is my business." He nodded back at Jaggard. "So what?"

"So . . . Research and Development undertakes field-work occasionally. And I think this will be one of those occasions. Because whatever Panin gives Audley, David won't pass it on—he'll do it himself." Another nod. "But . . . he's old, Tom."

Old—

"He always cut corners, and took risks—even in the old days—"

The *old* days—

"I don't so much want him *watched*, as watched *over*. So I want to know what he's doing—and preferably before he does it. And I want to know why he's doing it, and how he proposes to do it—I want to know every last damn thing that's happening. Do you receive me?"

Tom had seldom been given more equivocally unequivocal orders. "Loud and clear." All that remained was for Jaggard to explain what was actually happening, which required such precision. "And Panin?"

But Jaggard was looking past him, at whatever he could see through his rain-distorted lenses.

Tom turned, although he already knew what he would see.

"Make your farewells to Miss Groot," said Jaggard. "There's a car down the bottom of the lane with a man in it who'll tell you about Panin —or why we think he's here, anyway. His name is Harvey—Garrod Harvey."

In this downpour it would have been unreasonable to expect the young policeman to keep Willy in polite conversation. Short of physical restraint he could hardly have restrained her, and even as it was her hair was plastered close to her head.

"You can keep the man and the car for the time being. He'll explain who he is, but he can pass as your driver. Miss Groot can take your car. I'll give you time to collect your gear from the hotel." Jaggard's voice came from behind him. "Go and say goodbye to her—*now*."

Tom had already raised his hand. There were too many questions still unasked, but an order was an order. But—

"Harvey will tell you what to do, in the car." Jaggard filled the essential gap in his knowledge. "*Go on, man—*"

Tom launched himself up the rampart, his feet slipping and sliding in the grass. *Equivocally unequivocal orders was right!* he thought.

It all depended on Harvey, whoever Harvey was—

"Willy! I'm sorry, darling—" She looked even wetter than he felt, with her shirt outlining her shape agonizingly "—I'm sorry!"

"Duty calls—huh?" Her lip drooped on one side.

Her understanding only made it worse. "It does. But I'll call you myself as soon as I can. This may not take long."

"And then more *mottes* and more *baileys*?" She adjusted her unhappiness with an effort. "I can't wait—" The effort produced a grin "—at least it probably won't be raining on you back in the Lebanon, I guess."

Tom blinked the rain out of his eyes. "I should be so lucky!" In front of Jaggard all he could do was touch her wet shoulder. "Take the car—I'll call you soon as possible. Maybe this evening, maybe not. Okay?" The thought of *this evening* without her was loss and desolation. "Goodbye, my love—"

"Goodbye, my love—" She echoed him "—take good care, Tom."

He slipped and slid back, down past Jaggard and through the open gateway. There was a car far down the lane, already facing outwards, on to the main road. But, of course, they always turned round for a quick getaway, like adulterers parked in secluded driveways. That was the rule.

So it all depended on *Harvey* now—

Before the high hedge cut him off he turned back towards her: she was standing just as he had left her, on the edge of old Ranulf's rampart, like a statue.

Take good care, Tom, he thought.

II

THE JOURNEY'S LAST hour, after he had divested himself of Harvey at a convenient railway station, was curiously disquieting, even a little frightening.

If there was one thing Tom prided himself on, it was the ability to concentrate his mind on what was important, to the exclusion of all minor matters, however gratifying and pleasurable. But now, when . . . after all Henry Jaggard had said (and not said), and with what Garrod Harvey had added . . . when that concentration should have been on *Panin, Nikolai Andrievich* and *Audley*, *David Longsdon*, and the web of circumstances which hypothetically bound them together . . . but now—*now*—he was faced with a damned, bloody mutiny of his thoughts against the direct and legitimate orders of his mind.

It wasn't even as if they were merely wandering away into the countryside on either side of him, alerted by sign-posts which pointed towards early Norman castles known to him, or even to places adjacent to such castles—*Aldingbourne, Arundel, Bramber, Cadburn . . . Ashley, Barley Pound, Basing, Bishops' Waltham, Castle Redvers*—the counties' roll-call came to him automatically and geographically as he drove westwards, as it did all the time, wherever he was, whatever he was doing elsewhere—*Alton Charley, Eccleshall, Litchfield . . . Ascot Doilly, Ascot Earl, Bampton, Banbury*—it would have been the same in Staffordshire or Oxfordshire; and he had walked them all anyway, or nearly; and even if an odd name had registered it would still only have been in passing and a minor matter; because (as he had already thought about old Ranulf's almost forgotten *motte* only this morning) what had outlasted eight or nine centuries' decay would still be there waiting for him another day, another time.

But Willy wouldn't—

He shook his head at another approaching signpost—*Branding 4*—he didn't want to go to Branding—

Or *Willy might not be, anyway*—

Then he caught sight of the place-names on the other arm of the sign-post: *Upper Horley 5 . . . Steeple Horley 6½!*

And, by God, *Steeple Horley* was *Audley, David Longsdon*—and he'd hardly even thought of Audley since he'd deposited the wretched Harvey on that damp station forecourt, protesting only half-heartedly that this wasn't what *Mr Jaggard* had intended. But at that moment it had been exactly what *Sir Thomas Arkenshaw* had intended, Tom had thought with obstinate satisfaction at the time. Because he wasn't going to turn up at Steeple Horley, to beard Audley in his den, with a driver who quite obviously wasn't a driver (in both conversation and driving-ability) because the man drove like a spavined cart-horse but talked too casually about old treacheries, and dropped old names with them, as though he knew it all, had seen and met them all.

But that was where it had all gone wrong nevertheless, as he'd parked on the forecourt, with Garrod Harvey still talking—

There had been a girl—a very pretty girl, with a tip-tilted nose and breasts to match, such as he loved, and all the confidence of all three—there had been this girl about to cross the station forecourt entrance—*God damn! he had stopped the car automatically, just to look at her . . . but, when he had looked at her, he had thought of Willy instead!*

Only six-and-a-half miles—and he was still thinking of *Willy*. And, what was worse—what was much, much worse—he wasn't thinking about the next time, if there was a next time: he was cursing Jaggard—Jaggard, and Garrod Harvey, and Audley, and bloody Panin—and wondering what Willy would do now, with the rest of her weekend—now *this evening*, now *tonight* and now *tomorrow*—

But this was foolishness—mere schoolboy foolishness—thinking about . . . not Audley, not Panin . . . but what Willy *might* be doing tonight—

But she had said *'Goodbye, my love—take good care!'*

The road curved more sharply than he had expected, and there was a great high downland ridge swinging away from him as he twisted the wheel, then swinging back into view, stark against the confused sky, which didn't know whether it was winter or spring.

How much emphasis had she put on that? Had it been no more than a casual goodbye—a warning not to drive too fast? And why should that matter to her, anyway? Or to him?

Even the bloody sun had come out now, suddenly hot through the windscreen, making him blink—when it had finally pissed down out of dark clouds over Ranulf's bloody little ditches, and she had stood there watching him leave her in the lurch, and—

Oh *shit*! thought Tom. *He had forgotten to pay the bloody hotel bill!*

And there was another sign-post: *Upper Horley* that way, and *Steeple Horley*—

He had left her in the lurch, and soaking wet, and with the bill. And there was that naval attaché, clean-cut and crew cut, and a good Anglo-Saxon Protestant out of Annapolis and Polaris—or Trident—

whose father was a distinguished professor of something at Harvard, or Yale—

Of Scythian Archaeology, maybe—?

Tom gritted his teeth and jammed his foot on the brake simultaneously as he realized he was over-shooting the sign he'd been looking for, which was half-hidden in an overgrown tangle of hedge.

The car bucked and skidded slightly under him, on the loose gravel of a road which was only half-a-car's width wider than a track. But mercifully there was nothing behind him to slam into his backside, only a distant cyclist he'd overtaken half-a-mile earlier. But . . . it had said *The Old House*, hadn't it—?

It was very quiet, as much in the middle of a sudden sun-lit nowhere as he had been so happily this morning with Willy, under those rain-clouds. *'Rain at first, followed by bright periods spreading from the West'*, the weather man had said on the radio this morning. But the truth was that 'bright periods' were all in the mind, not the sky.

He engaged reverse gear savagely, scattering the gravel again for an instant before remembering the lone cyclist and jamming on the brakes again in panic, gripping the wheel convulsively as he squinted into the mirror.

But there was no cyclist in view now—

Tom frowned into the mirror, first relieved, then angry with himself for his carelessness, and then mystified, in quick succession. Where had the cyclist gone—?

He lowered the driver's window and poked his head out of the car. The high curve of the downland was still there, sharp against an outrageously blue sky—the last rearguard of this morning's clouds were far to the east now. But . . . if this was *Steeple* Horley, there was bugger-all to it—not a roof in sight, let alone a steeple.

Then he saw the cyclist, watching from a gap in the hedgerow on the other side of the road, fifteen yards back, peering from behind a blackthorn tangle and a large pair of spectacles.

"Is this—" As Tom took a second breath to pitch his voice louder he couldn't honestly blame the cyclist for taking cover from such a lunatic driver "—is this Steeple Horley?" Manners! "Could you tell me, please?"

The head vanished instantly, but the rear wheel of the bicycle came into view just below where it had been, as though the cyclist—it had been a boy in an American baseball cap—was readying himself for instant flight.

"Steeple Horley, is this?" Tom addressed the rear wheel.

The head appeared again, hesitantly and partially, and then nodded. "Yes."

About ten years old, estimated Tom. And, as small boys must not talk to strange men, needing encouragement. "Where's the steeple?"

The boy drew breath. "Sixteen-thirty—it fell down then."

And 'sixteen-thirty' would be in the reign of King Charles the First, not at 4.30 yesterday afternoon: the spectacles somehow suggested precocious erudition to Tom, and encouraged him towards precision. "I'm looking for 'The Old House'—where Dr David Audley lives—?"

The boy stared at him for a moment. "Why?"

That wasn't at all what Tom had expected. But a straight question required a straight answer. "I have an appointment with him. He's expecting me."

"Oh!" The boy rose up on one tip-toe to apply his other foot to its pedal. "In that case . . . *follow me!*" Then he vanished again.

Tom backed the car obediently, until he reached the hedgerow gap again, and saw that he had been right the first time: the overgrown legend on the sign did indeed indicate that *The Old House* lay somewhere down the equally overgrown lane down which the boy had invited him. But of the boy himself, and the bicycle, there was no sign.

Twenty yards down the lane there was a gap in the great tangle of thorn and blackberry bushes on his left, revealing a tiny brick cottage surrounded by apple-trees and an immaculately-tilled vegetable garden. But there was no boy and no bicycle waiting for him at its picket-gate. And there wasn't any garage, or even a break in the brief ramshackle fence, and the lane continued beyond the gap; so did Audley have a son, then—and a wife—in this *Old House* of his? Harvey hadn't said—Harvey must simply have taken it for granted that he knew, or that it was of no importance; or maybe Harvey had left him to stew in his own juice, on being dismissed; but he hadn't thought to ask, anyway.

He accelerated cautiously. If the boy was Audley's . . . allowing that he might be a spindly-twelve, home from some expensive local prep school . . . that would predicate a much younger wife, or an elderly mother—?

He was in the midst of an annoyingly ill-founded and inadequately-based hypothesis when the hedge fell away abruptly, and he saw what was undoubtedly *The Old House*, on his right—old stone and buttressed—an ancient roof, with an early sixteenth-century pitch: as a house it hardly made sense in its lack of coherent architectural purpose, with what looked like a barn abutting it—a buttressed barn also, without windows, but with a fine arched doorway wide enough for a loaded wagon, and built of fine ashlar much too good for any barn in a countryside where worked-stone would have been at a premium, with no quarries handy, or rivers up which such stone could easily be brought.

He had to swing the wheel hard again as the lane ended while he was making nonsense of what he saw, to bring the car round into a wide square of gravel, in the L-shape of the eccentric house and the impossible barn: stone like that was like gold-dust—or gold-blocks—like the high-cost outer skin of castles designed to resist rams at close quarters, or petraries and mangonels and trebuchets at a distance, in siege warfare; or to impress the neighbours when English life became more settled and civilized . . . but not for a bloody *barn*—not stone as beautiful as that, for God's sake!

But there was a ditch, right in the middle of an expanse of rough-cut fieldgrass—

Tom got out of the car, frowning. It didn't look like a serious defensive ditch, for there was no sign of berm or rampart. But maybe there'd been a palisade—it could have been a pathetically-defended manor house, or even an Anglo-Saxon site . . . compared with Norman works, domestic Anglo-Saxon work was a joke, mostly. And it was undoubtedly a very old ditch—

"Can I help you?"

The question caught Tom between the shoulder-blades, at his greatest disadvantage, back in another time.

"Yes—" He swivelled in the gravel "—I'm sorry—"

"Sir Thomas Arkenshaw?"

"Yes." Tall, thin, blonde—slightly faded blonde—fortyish, and well short of pretty, but not uninteresting, Tom registered in quick succession: typical well-bred English stock, perhaps a shade over-bred.

"Yes." She agreed with him coolly. "My husband's office phoned."

"Yes?" There was something not quite right about the vague, haughty stare of hers. Tom was used to people staring at him unbelievingly—as the young policeman had done at first this morning, before the penny dropped; never mind his unEnglish face, few people knew what a baronetcy was, and expected an elderly knight, dubbed for long years of distinguished civil service or exuding commercial power and prestige. But, although this woman wasn't the type to make that mistake—and wasn't *quite* staring unbelievingly, anyway—there was still something wrong. "Yes—" He smiled hesitantly. "—I'm not late, am I?"

"No." She ignored the smile. "But you do have some form of . . ." she extended a long thin-fingered hand on the end of a matchstick arm ". . . of identification—?"

"Oh—yes!" The extraordinary thing was that she was somehow rather sexy with it—matchstick arms, vague expression and ash-blonde hair so pale that no one would know when she went off-white, thought Tom professionally; only the recent memory of Willy, as bouncy as a squash ball and as wholesome as her own proverbial blueberry pie, relegated the woman to the second division.

"Thank you." She fumbled his identification, like the Tsarina accepting something rather nasty from a flea-ridden *moujik*, which she had to take but would have preferred not to look at before she passed it to someone else. "Why were you sorry?"

"Why was I—?" Now he was behaving like a *moujik*, damn it! "I was captivated by your beautiful house, actually—craning my neck like a tourist, when I should have been knocking on your door, Mrs Audley."

"I see." She waved his identification card briefly and very closely in front of her face, but then smiled at him, displaying fetching dimples. "It is rather beautiful, isn't it? We're terribly lucky to live in it, David and I."

"But I didn't understand it." Tom knew when he was on a winner. With some women it would be their children—or their diamonds, or their dogs, or the expertise of their dress-maker. But with this one it was her home.

Nikolai Andrievich Panin, KGB and all the way back to the NKVD of the 1940s, he thought: *that was as far back as he wanted to go. But, for this moment, Panin would have to wait!*

"The house—?" She tried to take another look at his picture, but it didn't seem to do her any good. "Or the barn?" She abandoned his identification in favour of the barn. "David loves the barn—he says there's nothing like it in the whole of Southern England." She favoured him with another loving smile. "You know about architecture, do you, Sir Thomas? But, of course, you must do, mustn't you—in order not to understand it, I mean?"

He had to say something intelligent now, for God's sake! "All that fine ashlar . . . better than the house itself!" That was a fact, anyway: the porch in which Mrs Audley was standing had been added at a later date, but there was nothing unusual about that. But such stonework as he could see behind the wisteria which covered the house was far rougher than that of the barn. "But it's that archway to the barn I really can't understand, Mrs Audley."

As he gestured towards the barn doors, one of them quivered, and then began to swing outwards towards them.

"The archway—of course!" Mrs Audley gave him another tick, quite oblivious of the opening doors. "That's what all the experts notice first —the man from *Country Life* was very taken with it, last year—particularly with the defaced stones on each side, where the coats-of-arms have been cut away. He thought that might have been done not long after the battle of Bosworth Field, in 1485." She blinked at him, with sudden embarrassment, as though aware just too late that she had insulted him by unnecessarily adding the date to the battle. "Henry Tudor gave the Honour of Horley to the Wilmots, after the Stokeseys had been killed at Bosworth. And the Wilmots had always hated the Stokeseys—at least, since Barnet and Tewkesbury." This time she didn't supply the date, but offered him the names of another two battles from the Wars of the Roses with another blink, as though they were two recent parliamentary by-elections.

"Is that so?" Tom was torn between the barn doors, which were now just outside his range of vision, and the dates of Barnet and Tewkesbury, in a civil war which had never particularly interested him, because it had not been distinguished by any good sieges. But it wouldn't do to disappoint her—

Damn! he couldn't resist those barn doors anymore (which had to be not later than mid-fifteenth century now, and were even more inexplicable)—

The same small boy was poking his head out of the gap between the heavy doors, only now he could see that little face more clearly: enormous horn-rimmed spectacles, metal-braced teeth, and head encased in its baseball cap, which bore the legend '*Forget—Hell*', superimposed on the red-white-and-blue starred flag of the Confederate States of America; and, as he observed the tiny apparition, it succeeded in squeezing itself through the gap only to trip on its own feet, to sprawl in the gravel.

Barnet . . . and bloody *Tewkesbury*—?

"What is it, darling?" Mrs Audley addressed her son, at her feet, as he searched blindly for his spectacles, which had jumped off his little nose, to fall just short of Tom's feet.

"Here—" Tom bent to retrieve the spectacles, but failed to complete his sentence as he observed the long blonde plait which had fallen out of the baseball cap. Instead, he thought *Christ! I'm slipping! I can't tell the little girls from the little boys now!*

"Thank you." Little Miss Audley pushed her spectacles back on to her face quickly, and gave Tom half-a-second's half-blind acknowledgement before offering her mother another pair of spectacles, which she had been carrying in her hand. "Your glasses, Mummy."

"What, darling?" Mrs Audley gazed vaguely at her daughter for another half-second, and then accepted what was being offered to her. "Oh—thank you, Cathy dear!"

Miss Audley turned back to Tom. "Thank you."

"Not at all." Tom searched for something to say. She might be anything from eleven to fourteen, but now that they were both wearing spectacles each was a dead ringer for the other, straight up-and-down and flat as a board, and blonde, yet wholly feminine with it: *how could he have failed to see!* "Miss Audley—?"

"My daughter, Sir Thomas," answered Mrs Audley. "Cathy." She nodded at the child. "Sir Thomas Arkenshaw, Cathy."

Cathy Audley gave Tom a fearsomely precocious doubting frown, as baffled as any of her elders and betters, as she offered him her hand.

Smart girl, thought Tom. "Miss Audley." But to hell with her. "Your husband is expecting me, Mrs Audley, I believe?"

After having re-examined his identification through her thick-lensed spectacles, Mrs Audley looked at him properly at last. "Yes, Sir Thomas . . . Cathy, go and tell your father that Sir Thomas has arrived."

"Yes, Mother." Cathy focused properly on him again also, but again registered doubt. "Sir Thomas . . . Ark- Arken-?" She began to retreat backwards towards the gap in the barn doors. "Arken-what?"

"*Shaw*," completed Tom. "Like in 'certain'."

She grinned at him as she slid into the gap. "Or 'George Bernard'? Or 'Tripoli'?"

Tom frowned. *Tripoli*—? But by then she had vanished again.

"I'm sorry, Sir Thomas," said Mrs Audley, shaking her head. "Sometimes she's grown up. But sometimes she says things no one but her father understands—I'm sorry!"

"Don't be." *Tripoli?* wondered Tom. "She's delightful, Mrs Audley—like your house." *Tripoli?* he thought again. Exactly like the house! "But what did she mean by 'Tripoli'?"

She shook her head again. "Heaven only knows! I certainly don't!" She laughed, half-regretfully, half-proudly. "But please—it's 'Faith', not 'Mrs Audley', Sir Thomas." She gestured towards the porch. "Do come inside—David will be with us directly."

"Then it's 'Tom'." The thought of Audley—not *David*, and a world away from *Father*—dragged Tom back to harsh reality. And not *Tripoli* either—Tripoli was a damnably nasty Libyan memory: he had been scared stiff that one time he'd been in Tripoli, sailing under false colours on a dangerous coast—once in Tripoli was enough, and he was glad that he could never go back there. "Please lead the way . . . Faith."

He followed her into what seemed for a moment like cool darkness, smelling of furniture polish and the old-house-damp which so often rose from deep cellars beneath. Then he was at the foot of an oak staircase, looking up towards a window ablaze with stained-glass sunlight.

And *Panin*, he thought—*Nikolai Andrievich Panin*—who was another world away from David Audley here and these two females-of-the-species, but also in the same world that he and Audley both inhabited outside it.

"Tom—" Faith Audley accepted the diminutive as of right, having been quite properly unimpressed with 'Sir Thomas' even before she'd had a clear view of him "—we have to go through the kitchen because we've lost the key to the french-windows in the dining room. David says he hung it up, for the winter . . . but heaven only knows what he actually did with it . . . It'll turn up one day, of course . . . He's down in the orchard making one of his bonfires—making a bonfire is one of the two jobs he's good at . . . the other is making compost heaps—" She threw her domestic prattle over her shoulder as she led him down a short passage towards a stone-arched doorway "—bonfires and compost heaps are major scientific operations, according to him, and I'm not allowed to touch either of them—" Beyond the door lay a huge kitchen, dominated by an equally huge table, scrubbed pale with time and elbow-grease "—which is ludicrous really, because I'm the scientist in the family, and David doesn't really know why one wire must go on one terminal—"

She was already opening another door while Tom was still taking in the kitchen's weird mixture of ancient-and-modern, between its smoke-darkened beams and stone-flagged floor, and the gleaming plastic gadgetry of electric cooker and microwave and dish-washer, via a middle-aged solid fuel Aga stove, with a museum-array of copper saucepans and a blackened fireplace furnished with an iron turning-spit which could have roasted a whole pig to celebrate the news of any battle of the Wars of the Roses, if this household had been on its winning side.

"Tom—?" Faith Audley's voice issued from the half-light of another passage.

"Coming!" *Damn the Wars of the Roses!* Tom shook his head.

Another short corridor, with a laundry room on one side and a larder on the other, and other doors—for the extremes of boiler and freezer, maybe—?

Tom blinked as the light streaming through the last door hit him, and stepped out of the house in Faith Audley's wake, following her under another stone archway which had never started its life in a kitchen garden wall, its crudely defaced heraldic shields reminding him of the bigger arch above the barn doors.

Then the full sun hit him as he emerged from the archway into a little courtyard at the back of the house, with a stone well-head in the centre of it and a fine view of the high downland away across a coarse winter lawn in the foreground.

But no sign of Audley—? He frowned towards the man's wife.

"This is the first good day we've had, when it hasn't rained much—" She wasn't looking at him, but at the grass "—but does he prune the roses? *Oh no!*" She turned to him at last, sniffing the air as she did so. "*He* has to make a *bonfire* . . . and if the wind stays in this direction . . .

we shall get the benefit of it—" She swung round to look at the house "—in fact, I'd better go and close all the windows before it's too late—excuse me, Sir Thomas—*Tom* . . . But I'll put the kettle on for a cup of tea while I'm about it. David will be here directly." She indicated the nearest of a group of dirt-stained white ironwork chairs. "He knows I was bringing you here."

Tom wondered what Research and Development had passed on to Audley about him, in preparation for this meeting. Whatever it was, it ought to be about him, not Panin, because Jaggard had indicated that the Russian had arrived unobtrusively, by agreement with the FCO. But R & D had ways of knowing things, Harvey had warned; and it would certainly know all about one Thomas Arkenshaw, Harvey had added nastily: "*He probably knows more about you than we know—and maybe more than you'll find comfortable, old boy!*"

So what? thought Tom, considering the grimy seat of the chair. It looked as though it hadn't been sat on since last summer, and although he might have parked his castle-exploring denims of this morning on it he wasn't about to mess up the good suit he had packed for tonight's dinner-with-Willy that would never take place. Instead, he sauntered across the yard—it was more a terrace than a yard, separated from the lawn above it by a low stone wall—until he reached the well, which was completely equipped with a rusty winder and an antique wooden bucket on a chain. Idly, he picked up a small piece of flaked stone from the rim and dropped it in.

One, two—plop!

"Hullo, there! Arkenshaw, I presume?"

Tom controlled his involuntary start of guilt at being caught throwing something into another man's well: there were parts of the world where that rated a bullet in the back. Also, he had somehow expected Audley to come from the direction of the lawn, rather than from behind him.

A slow innocent turn was required, anyway.

"Good afternoon, Dr Audley." *'Big, ugly old devil'*, Harvey had said off-handedly, and all those adjectives filled David Audley's bill exactly: in his gardening clothes, which had not seen better days for many years, he resembled nothing so much as an ageing Irish navvy who had done his share of fighting for pounds and pints on the old fairground circuit of his native land. *So that makes two of us*, thought Tom, *who don't look like themselves!* "I'm sorry to descend on you like this." That was what Jaggard had said to him; only this time it was no lie. "But you've had a phone-call, I gather."

"I have." Audley advanced across the terrace in his enormous navvy's gumboots, which looked as though they had steel toe-caps, until he was able to look down on Tom from close quarters from his six-foot four. "But I won't shake your hand."

"No?" What confused Tom was that the big man's intense scrutiny of him was nevertheless not in the least hostile—if anything his expression was as innocently friendly as his battered features allowed. "Well, you don't have to—" He stopped as Audley's hands came up, palms upwards.

"I've been making a bonfire." Audley presented two massive, dirt-encrusted paws. "So I'm not really fit for decent company—my wife won't even let me in her kitchen. She says I'm like 'Pig-pen' in *Peanuts*." He grinned a huge grin. "Charlie Brown—? She's a Charlie Brown addict, is my wife." He chuckled. "I see myself rather as Schroeder, the intellectual one—with her as Lucy, because she packs a mean right hook. But she sees me as 'Pig-pen'—we never see ourselves as others see us, do we?"

Tom struggled against an enveloping sense of unreality. The idea of the willowy, blue-blooded Mrs Audley, pale and fragile, packing any sort of punch . . . the idea of her in those huge hands, bear-hugged . . . was incongruous to the point of disbelief. And there was also the unlikely offspring of this unlikely union, and *Tripoli* too, in the back of his mind.

But there was another explanation to all this, which was tripping him before he'd started to move: one thing Jaggard and Harvey and rumour were agreed on was that Audley was tricky. So he had to be tricky too!

"Your daughter packs a mean punch too, Dr Audley." He grinned back at the man.

"She does?" Audley hadn't expected that reply. "She does—yes." He cocked an eyebrow. "Yes?"

"Yes. She had me with a reference to 'Tripoli'—in relation to George Bernard Shaw and Thomas Arkenshaw. But I shall have to work it out before I take you away from your bonfire, anyway." Another possibility opened up. "And I suppose I should be glad that it was a bonfire and not a well-rotted compost heap—?"

Audley stared at him, momentarily off-put. Then his eyes softened, and he smiled the ugly man's smile—the legendary smile Tom had heard of, which had softened women down the ages according to Willy.

"Ah! *Now* I see it!" Audley nodded at him. "I didn't see it at first . . . and I don't really *see* it now—the resemblance. But it's there in the mind —Danny—and now *Tom Arkenshaw*!"

"It?" Tom realized that Audley had been too quick for him. "What resemblance?" The second question came out before he could stop it. "Danny?" The third was too closely-coupled to the second, damn it!

"Danuta—*Danushia* . . . or *Danka*—?" Audley closed his eyes for an instant, and when he opened them again he wasn't looking at Tom at all, but at someone else who wasn't on the terrace with them, but in another place and another time. "But *Danny* to us, Tom Arkenshaw—*Danny Dzieliwski*—" He pronounced the name better than most Englishmen did: *Den-chev-less-ka*—"your mum, Tom Arkenshaw—Diana, Lady Arkenshaw, dowager baroness, I suppose that would be now, eh?" Suddenly Audley's face was an inscrutably battered mask, like the defaced coat-of-arms on the archways of his home. "Now that she's sailing under British colours? And whose colours are yours this afternoon, Tom Arkenshaw, I wonder—eh?"

Bloody Jaggard had miscalculated! was all Tom could think for a moment. *If he'd thought that Audley wouldn't see through this, by God!*

"You know my mother, sir?" He felt dreadfully young now.

"I did." Audley's face was no longer inscrutable—it was brutal now. "Don't mess with me, boy: you may not know that as well as I know it, but you know it well enough. Because that's why you're here—because someone thinks I'll treat you better because of it . . . Baynham, it could be . . . It wouldn't be Jack Butler—he doesn't play games like that . . . Or it could be Stacey—or Jaggard . . . Or, most likely, because he's inclined that way, it could be Garry Harvey—" All the time he'd been building his bonfire, out in the orchard since that phone-call, Audley must have been going through the possibilities, against what Research and Development would have told him; but, although he'd got some of them spot on, he hadn't had enough information for certainty.

"That isn't why I'm here, sir." That was all Tom could manage as he thought *I should have phoned up mother—I'm an idiot!*

"No?" Audley grasped the winding handle of the well, and swung it as idly as Tom had thrown the stone into the well, making the chain squeak. "But . . . the bugger of it is that I *will* treat you better. So whichever of them it is, he's no fool!" He dropped the handle. "'Tripoli', she said, did she? Well, you'll have to work that one out for yourself, I'm afraid!" Then he frowned at Tom. "But as for your long-forgotten—long-forgotten, but never-forgotten—mother, Tom Arkenshaw . . . how is the dear girl . . . after longer than either of us would care to remember? She's well, I hope?"

That was more than Tom cared to think about. "My mother is very well, sir." He had to buy time to think about that, although thinking about Mamusia as a 'dear girl' was altogether too much to think about. "And my job now is to keep you in the same excellent state of health—that's why I'm here, Dr Audley."

"Me?" Audley sniffed the air suddenly, and Tom was aware that he'd caught the same smell, of that distant bonfire taking hold. "What's that supposed to mean, may I ask?"

They had come to the point. And it was mercifully a world away from Mother. "It means Panin, sir—Nikolai Andrievich Panin."

"Panin?" Audley sniffed again, and then relaxed. "Well, he doesn't constitute a health warning, I wouldn't have thought—?" Then he frowned at Tom. "But you're diplomatic protection—overseas protection—? How does Nikolai Panin concern you?"

"He's here in England." As Tom nodded he smelt bonfire smoke again. "And he wants to talk to you."

"He does?" Audley was unrelaxed now. "Then he's your problem, Tom Arkenshaw—not me." He sniffed again, and turned suddenly towards the house, as though he had realized what his bonfire was about to do. "*Damn!*"

"No, sir—" Something cracked sharply inside and outside and above Tom's head, and the French window behind Audley simultaneously exploded into fragments—

Audley started to jerk back against the splintering window as Tom's conditioned reflexes reacted out of Beirut experience: *with a car bomb when the world fragmented you were already too late—but with the bullet you heard you had one fragment of time before the next one, which you wouldn't hear, arrived—*

He grabbed the man by whatever he could take hold of—which stretched under his hand for one agonizing delaying instant before taking the strain as he dragged Audley down with him on the stone-flagged terrace, behind the pathetically inadequate protection of the wall, before the next bullet arrived.

III

FROM WHERE TOM finished up lying behind his own stretch of wall, he found himself looking directly at Audley across a gap through which three or four stone steps connected the terrace with the lawn. But although they were thus facing each other at about the same distance as a moment before, the unnaturalness of ground level seemed to bring them much closer together, so that he was quite irrelevantly aware first that the big man hadn't stood very close to his razor before breakfast.

But then the features beneath the grey stubble annexed all his attention: as he watched them they were contorted into even greater ugliness by what Tom thought for an instant might be a mixture of surprise and fear —but which he knew in the next instant was red, blazing rage, only half a second away from an irrational explosion of movement.

"For Christ's sake—*keep your head down, man!*" What lent urgency to the command was the inadequacy of the wall. "Unless you want your great brain spread all over the terrace?"

Mercifully, the old ploy of the crudely descriptive warning, which he had used in far less desperate circumstances on far less imaginative men, worked well enough with Audley: the glare in his eyes flickered, but then faded as he subsided physically, shrinking down like any sensible man who had suddenly realized what the smallest piece of nickel-plated steel could do at high velocity to flesh and blood and bone. And with Audley there ought to be recollection as well as imagination: it might be half a lifetime or more since he had been under fire, but he had once been in a real war, Tom remembered.

"All right, all right!" The features twisted again, and then Audley showed his teeth like an old wolf. "You think he'll try a second shot?"

"I don't know." Tom shifted his position slightly, to get a view of the terrace and the house. The well-head offered secure protection not far away. But where could he go after that?

"Aren't you supposed to be the expert?" Audley had his second wind now.

"I don't know where he fired from." Tom estimated the distance from the well to the French windows (but they might be locked) . . . and then to the archway leading to the kitchen passage (but that was too far for safety). "You were looking down the garden, weren't you?"

"I was looking at you, actually. You were telling me how you were going to protect me, as I recall—" Audley stopped abruptly. "I'm sorry! I'm not in practice for this sort of game, Tom Arkenshaw—forgive me!"

Tom concentrated on the damaged French window. There were two steps up to it, from the terrace, and the bullet had struck high up, at the exact junction of four small lead-lights, driving the lead inwards and cracking others below them. So—

"A long shot," said Audley. "It was a long shot."

"How do you know?" But he was almost certainly right, thought Tom. "Or are you trying to reassure me?"

"I'm trying to reassure myself, more like! I don't *know*—" Audley checked himself again, but only for a fraction of a second. "*Stop there! Not another step, Cathy!*"

Tom shifted his gaze from the smashed window, and saw half of what Audley had seen from where he lay, which was framed in the arch.

"But, Father—"

"Not another step—understand?" Audley's voice steadied. "Do you hear me?"

"I hear you, Father." The visible part of the tea-tray quivered. "But I don't understand you. Is there something—" The tray lurched slightly "—Father . . . what on earth are you doing?"

"Where's your mother?" The man's voice was almost conversational now. "Not another step—remember? And I mean that. Where's Mummy?"

"She's shutting the windows," Cathy snapped back irritably. "To keep out *your* smoke, Father . . . And I think she's just broken the one that sticks, in the little bedroom—I heard the glass go . . . So she's not going to be very pleased with you, because she's been asking you for ages to make it easier to close." She paused only for an instant. "Is there something I can't see, that I'm about to step on? Because this tray weighs a ton!"

"Go—" Audley choked slightly on the word, and Tom sympathized with him as he cleared his throat "—go back to the kitchen. Don't . . ." He trailed off, as though he was thinking again, and drew a deep breath. "Someone's just taken a shot at us, love—from somewhere up on the hillside. What you heard was the bullet hitting the window—okay?"

For a moment of disbelief the tray was steady as a rock. "Yes, Father?" Then it trembled. "Now?"

"Wait!"

Tom stared at Audley, aware irrelevantly that he could now smell the bonfire against which Faith Audley was closing her windows.

"There's my good girl!" said Audley softly. "Go back and find your mother. Keep away from the windows. Find her . . . and say to her 'Limejuice'—*'Limejuice'*—got that?"

"Yes, Father."

"Repeat it—" Audley held his voice so unnaturally steady that the steadiness somehow emphasized his urgency "—repeat it, love, please."

"'Limejuice'." Cathy sounded slightly offended. "'Limejuice', Father."

"Jolly good!" The false encouragement sounded equally unnatural. "Off you go then, love."

But that wouldn't do for Cathy Audley—Tom wanted to shake his head at the man, but he was staring too fixedly at the archway.

The edge of the tray stayed in view. "But . . . but . . ."

"*Off you go!*" Then Audley looked at Tom, and understood the limits of obedience belatedly. "I've got Tom Arkenshaw here to protect me, Cathy love—that's what he's here for." He grinned hideously at Tom. "Isn't that so, Sir Thomas—?"

Tom smelt the bonfire again, and thought that he would never smell a bonfire in the future—if there was a future—without smelling his own inadequacy. "That's right, Miss Audley," he agreed.

"*What's this?*" Another voice from somewhere behind the child startled him just as the tray, and that part of her which he could see, disappeared. "Have you broken something, Cathy—?"

"'Limejuice', Mummy—" The child cut through her mother's angry question "—Father says *'Limejuice'*!"

Tom strained his ears to catch the woman's reaction, but there was only a moment's silence hemmed in between the wall and the house, against the distant drone of a faraway aircraft. Then there came a clink of teacups on the tray followed by the sound of the backdoor closing. So . . . whatever it meant exactly, that codeword, it was a Word of Power—and Audley was blessed with intelligently obedient womenfolk, young and old, when matters came to their crunch.

"As I was saying . . . I don't know." Audley attended to him again. "But . . . he missed, anyway."

Tom felt the hardness of the flagstone under his hip-bone. "You also said that he fired from somewhere on the hillside."

"So I did." Audley sounded curiously relaxed now. "Because from the bottom of the garden he couldn't have missed—I also made that assumption."

Tom frowned at him, trying to remember the bottom of the garden. There had been a hedge—? He couldn't remember, damn it!

"It's a bare hundred yards." Audley shook his head. "I think the bullet went just over my head, maybe a bit to one side . . . It's a long time since

I've had that disagreeable sensation—or I suppose it could be called 'agreeable', relatively speaking . . . But then, again, I wouldn't have imagined that I heard it if it hadn't missed, would I?"

How could he be so damned cold-blooded? thought Tom irritably.

"Thirty-nine years, to be exact." Audley's eyes glazed at the memory. "And I was also sniped at several times in Normandy, the year before—Jerry loved to pick off silly fools who poked their heads out of their tanks . . . But, of course, I never *heard* a bloody thing—*no*—there was *one* time . . ." He focused on Tom, and dropped the rest of the irrelevant anecdote instantly. "About a hundred yards, the end of the garden, anyway. So if he had a Brown Bess, and this was Waterloo, that's about what I'd expect. Because the French skirmishers shot at Mercer in front of his battery for about half an hour—and from considerably less than a hundred yards, too—also without hitting him." He nodded at Tom, as though childishly pleased with himself at the thought. "'So long as they were aiming at me I wasn't worried'—didn't he say something like that?"

Tom smelt bonfire again. And now there was a wisp of smoke to go with the smell. But, much more confusing, was the thought that any competent marksman, let alone a *professional*, could have missed anything, at any practical range, with a modern rifle; or . . . had Audley *moved*—or *had he himself moved*—at that precise instant, when the finger had squeezed so gently—?

"You said . . . from the hillside?" Tom felt his anger well up. "And bugger Waterloo!"

"Yes—quite right!" Audley mistook anger for urgency. "My dear boy—I'm only talking because I'm shit-scared—I'm sorry! You may be used to this sort of thing, from the Lebanon, or wherever . . ." Audley closed his eyes and screwed up his face. "I'm only trying to reassure *myself* . . . that he isn't coming down the garden right now, to spit in my eye, for God's sake!" He kept his eyes closed. "But . . . there's a track up the hillside—it goes diagonally from left to right, with bushes on the outer edge for cover . . . And that would give him a nice clear long-shot on to this terrace . . . God only knows the distance, downhill—more than a quarter of a mile, but less than half, so say about six hundred yards." He opened his eyes again. "Easy access from the road down the bottom—quick getaway. The bugger must be kicking himself now, missing at that range, whether he's still there or not—eh?" He watched Tom. "But how long do we wait for him to get cold feet? Until I get rheumatism?"

"No." At that range the man *shouldn't* have missed, thought Tom. But he certainly wouldn't miss twice, if he got a clear shot.

A clear shot! he thought suddenly, staring upwards.

"No," he murmured, twisting himself off his hip on to all fours.

"So what—" Audley's mouth opened as Tom raised his head above the parapet "—for God's sake, man! *Get down!*"

Tom studied the view gratefully. If there was a hedge at the bottom of the garden he couldn't see it, never mind the hillside beyond. What had deceived him had been Faith Audley's estimation of the direction of the wind: it wasn't blowing directly towards the house, but more diagonally, so that they were only on the edge of the thick clouds of smoke which were now billowing from the orchard across the lawn.

He got to his feet. "Your wife said you were good with bonfires." He grinned happily down at the big man. "I can see that she was right."

Audley stared at him for a moment, then raised himself quickly. "Ouch!" He rubbed his hip fiercely. "Damned old bones!" Then he considered his handiwork. "Ye-ess . . . I'd forgotten about that." He nodded at Tom. "That'll be the damp stuff on the top catching—smoke . . . The trick is to get the driest material underneath, with an access for air to windward—that makes for a hot heart, and then you can burn anything if you've graded it properly. But you must get the ash straight on the flower beds, when it's properly cooled, and before it has a chance to rain—it's useless once it's been rained on, you know." He climbed stiffly to his feet, to tower over Tom.

"Is that so?" said Tom politely.

"Yes. The rain washes out the potash." Then Audley gestured towards the archway. "Do you think it might be advisable to run like hell now, while we can? Before I exhibit unbecoming twitches of fear—?" He started to move before Tom could reply. "In fact, I think I'll lead the way, just in case you've forgotten it."

Tom followed him back into the kitchen passage, and watched him lock the back door and shoot a massive iron bolt.

"There now!" Audley turned to him. "I observe that you are unarmed. But I take it that you have your armament in your car?"

"As a matter of fact . . . no, Dr Audley."

"What?" Audley started to move again. "But I thought you fellows were all armed to the teeth—" He flung the words over his shoulder "—apart from which, I had the impression that *you* said that you had come to babysit *me*—?"

"Yes—" Tom had to trot to keep up with him as they reached the kitchen "—but we weren't expecting—"

"Not expecting?" Audley cut him off as he prised a 12-bore shotgun off two wooden pegs on the wall above the fireplace. "Now where the hell are the cartridges—?" He frowned around the enormous kitchen.

"They're on the table," said Tom, pointing.

"Ah!" Audley broke the 12-bore and loaded it. "That comes of having a good wife, by God! Not that she isn't going to give me hell for this!" He snapped the gun together. "Not expecting? I thought that was what girls say, whose mothers didn't teach them the facts of life, Sir Thomas Arkenshaw." He thrust the gun into Tom's hands. "Here—you take it—you're the ruddy expert! And your reflexes are evidently better than mine. And so they should be." He waited while Tom examined the weapon. "Do you think he'll have another try?"

It was no good saying that he didn't know, so Tom shrugged. "I wouldn't have thought so. But if he's stupid enough to miss, then perhaps he's stupid enough to try." But first things first. "I don't want to wait for him on the ground floor, anyway." He looked around. "And . . . where's your wife—and your daughter?"

"You don't need to worry about them."

"I'll be the judge of what I'll worry about, Dr Audley. Where are they?"

"They're safe. That's all you need to know." Audley made an obstinate face. "This is an old house. It's got nooks and crannies in it that it would take you hours to find. You let *me* worry about *their* safety, Tom Arkenshaw—you just worry about *me*. Because that's who I'm worried for."

So that was what 'Limejuice' had signified—*Take cover!*—thought Tom. And that was why Audley had relaxed once the family codeword had been transmitted, and his family was safe. "Very well, Dr Audley. Then I want to get you one floor up. And I want some back-up before I get you away from here. So I need to make a phone-call."

Audley shook his head. "You don't need to worry about that, either. Faith will have made that call. That's the first half of Limejuice—she knows what to do." He pointed towards the door through which they had first entered the kitchen. "I'll lead the way—"

"No." Tom pushed past him. "Which way at the top of the stairs?"

"Right." Audley nodded submissively. "The door at the end of the landing is the one you want."

"Close all the doors behind you as you go."

"Okay—I know the rules." Suddenly there was a note of weariness in Audley's voice which made Tom pause. The man might know the rules, but it was probably a long time since he had had to apply them, so there were allowances which had to be made. Indeed, he had said as much—*'I'm not in practice for this sort of game'*, he had admitted.

He grinned at the big man—big *old* man, was what he had to remind himself: considering that the last time Audley had been shot at (or the last time he was admitting to it, anyway) had been before he, Tom, had been born . . . and considering also that the man had now just been shot at with his family around him and his garden bonfire smouldering peacefully—considering all of that . . . he could have been a lot more troublesome. "It's just a precaution, Dr Audley," he said reassuringly. "Almost certainly quite unnecessary. Because I think he's long gone. I wouldn't have put my head up if I'd thought otherwise."

"Aye." Audley gave him an old-fashioned look, as though he understood exactly what Tom was doing. "And you'd never be able to face your dear mother if you'd lost me, would you?" Then his expression hardened. "So let's get on with your unnecessary precautions, shall we?"

The old house was wrapped in stillness ahead of him, so that every sound he made echoed for an instant and was then extinguished as the silence damped it down. But at least that made their passage easier, the more so since the man at his back really did remember the rules, standing still whenever he stopped, and moving again only when he signalled, until they reached the room at the end of the landing.

Suddenly the carpet was thick underfoot, after the stone flags of the ground floor, which had seemed to have the whole world under them, and then the solid oak of staircase and landing, with only the occasional rug from Bokhara or Tabriz which (with everything else around him) had served to remind him that Audley did not depend on his pay for his lifestyle.

This was the master bedroom, with a duvet-covered bed tailored to Audley's size and the loneliness of the long-distance runner before finding any other occupant. But, more importantly, there were windows on three sides of it, with views of front and back.

"Wait!" Audley's voice had recovered its note of command during their journey.

Tom watched him fumble beside the bed, observing his bedtime reading at the same time with a sense of unreality: on the oak table in the hall below there had been the whole morning's take of newspapers, from the *Sun* to *Pravda*; but here was Patrick Wormald's *Festschrift* for his old tutor, Wallace-Hadrill, of early medieval fame; and *Ideal and Reality in Frankish and Anglo-Saxon Society* somehow weakened his hold on more pressing matters.

"What are you doing?" He forced himself to check the terrace first, through an arrow-slit window alongside a very twentieth-century *en suite* bathroom which had been built into one corner of the vast bedroom.

"I'm . . . I've just switched on the bloody alarm system—" Audley straightened up cautiously, as though he well knew how close his head came to the beam directly above him "—is what I've just done. So now . . . any exterior visitor will be welcomed with a klaxon loud enough to wake the dead."

Tom commenced the long walk to the dormer window at the other end of the bedroom. "So you're used to this sort of thing, then?"

"No—" Audley followed him with his eyes "—no, we damn well are *not*!"

The sweep of gravel at the front, with his black Rover in the middle of it, was equally empty. But *Ideal and Reality in Frankish and Anglo-Saxon Society* had hardened Tom's heart. "Then why such a sophisticated alarm system?" He turned back towards Audley, setting the butt of the shotgun on the carpet.

Audley's face became brutal. "There are such people as burglars—they wear masks and striped jerseys, and have bags over their shoulders labelled 'Swag'—don't you have them in London?" Audley paused. "Or Beirut? Or Athens? Or Cairo and Alexandria and Khartoum?" Another pause. "Or is your brand of security purely political, and not capitalist?"

Tom admired the view from the third side, across open fields in which sheep were busy recycling grass on the edge of the downland ridge for half a long mile, up to a fence beside a road which climbed the ridge. That would be the road which connected with the track . . . but there was nothing on it now, of course.

"I used to keep geese, to do the same job much less expensively. And I ate the ones I didn't sell at a profit," said Audley bitterly. "I rather like geese. They treat human beings with proper contempt. But Faith doesn't fancy them—either as geese or goose. And . . . she's a scientist by training, so she has to believe in electronic gadgets."

Tom thought of the Persian carpets, which would roll up very easily, and of some of the other objects he'd seen. So *burglars* was fair enough—except for one thing. "And what is 'limejuice', then?" He tore himself away from Audley's rural tranquillity. "And why 'limejuice', anyway?" He injected pure curiosity to soften the sharpness of the question with a half-smile, remembering that he must make allowances.

Audley blinked. "I once had the doubtful honour of serving with an armoured regiment which couldn't really protect itself properly when it ran into Germans." He blinked again. "In great big tanks."

Tom waited. And then restrained himself, and continued to wait.

"Eighty-eights were fortunes of war—misfortunes, rather . . . And Mark IVs were about even-steven—" Audley looked clear through him "—the only trouble was, the Germans were *better* than we were, like the First XV playing the Second XV . . . On a good day, with the wind in our favour, and some of them sick, we could maybe take them, with a bit of luck—like, if we mixed up with a good infantry battalion, who had things under control . . . and a couple of 17-pounders to blunt Jerry's enthusiasm—" Suddenly he was looking at Tom. "But T-Tigers—*Mark*

VIs—and especially *King* T-Tigers . . . that was like playing the All Blacks—we really couldn't handle them at all. You just had to hope that you were in the reserve troop that day, on the touchline cheering the team on." He nodded. "Because then—then if you were lucky, and spotted them first . . . then you could call up your little spotter plane, who was stooging up and down in the clouds up above, trying to be unobtrusive at about the speed of an invalid tricycle, and hoping *he'd* be lucky too . . . And then, if it really *was* your lucky day and his, there'd be a squadron of rocket-firing Typhoons within call." He drew a long breath. "Some days there wasn't—or not quickly enough for the lead troop . . . Some days the spotter bought it . . . But that *was* Limejuice, anyway: it was there to protect us from our just deserts."

And genuine history it was, too, thought Tom—like Mamusia remembering dead Uncle Henryk; and, also, perhaps not something Audley was normally so garrulous about, except that now he was in mild shock from the terrace. It was a phenomenon Tom had observed before, and most recently on the part of an elderly Palestinian Arab, who had regaled him with his memories of the King David Hotel bomb in '46, in gory detail, after that last Beirut massacre.

"But Limejuice now—" Audley caught his expression "—our duty man will pass it on to Special Branch liaison. Which means we'll have the nearest police unit in the first instance. Then an Armed Support Group —or whatever they call it now—"

"The police arrive unarmed?"

"God knows!" Audley had evidently accepted his 'merely a precaution' reassurance at face value. "But it's certainly an 'Approach with extreme caution' job . . . And finally, in God's good time, a couple of our own people will appear—it's all laid down in the Contingency Book . . . Which Jack Butler updated not long ago, as it happens." He sniffed. "Which is why I've got it all off pat—I had to sign that I'd read it . . . You don't think this is an everyday occurrence, do you?"

Tom had drifted back to the front window. "I was beginning to wonder."

"Well—you can stop bloody-wondering. It isn't. At least, not to me, by God!"

The square of gravel was still empty. "Not ever?" He turned towards the open field with the sheep, deliberately not looking at the man.

Audley didn't reply to the question, and Tom remembered his Arab again as he crossed to the arrow-slit window. "Not ever?"

"In twenty-five years . . ." Audley spoke against his better judgement, just like the Arab ". . . I've had trouble three times here."

The old Arab had had constant trouble since the 1930s. So Audley had been damn lucky, thought Tom: he was still living in the same house. And the terrace was as empty as the forecourt, so he was still lucky. "Three times—?"

"Only once . . ." Audley searched for the right word, committed now to his indiscretion ". . . genuinely."

Now what the hell did he mean by that? wondered Tom.

"The other two were illegitimate intrusions. And heads rolled because of them, on the Other Side, I can tell you!"

"They did?" Tom was disappointed in his man suddenly.

"They did." Just as suddenly all the heat went out of Audley's voice. "You think I'm bull-shitting you, Tom Arkenshaw—I can see that. Right?"

"No—"

"If you want to think that, then you do that. And if you think I'm trying to impress you . . . well, you can think that too." Audley paused. "The last time was ten years ago. And I was in Italy at the time. It was about the time your section was formed." Another pause. "And if you care to check the record you'll find that it was formed on my recommendation. You were in your second year at university at the time. You were secretary of the Anglo-Polish Club and treasurer of the Wine and Food Society, which must have been a lot more enjoyable." Another pause. "And would you like me to give you the name of the woman who recruited you?"

Harvey had been right—*sod the bastard!* "Not especially, Dr Audley. But I would like to know why you're assuming this is the Russians."

"I'm not assuming any such thing. And for God's sake call me David—otherwise I'll have to call you 'Sir Thomas'. It's bad enough that I've had to explain to my daughter what a baronet is, without having to do that."

"Yes?" Tom grabbed the diversion gratefully. "What did she say?"

"She was quite relieved." Audley fell for the diversion like any doting father. "You had confused her somewhat, I think."

"If it's any consolation to her, she'd confused me too, you can tell her—David."

"Yes?" Then Audley saw through him. "I'm not assuming any such thing."

He'd better not go on underrating Mamusia's old admirer. "No?" Besides which, he had to keep checking the windows—not so much for some mad bugger with a rifle as for some poor devil of a policeman saddled with an 'extreme caution' order. And that meant the forecourt again. "Then who else could it be? Who have you offended?"

"Nobody—that's the trouble, Tom." Audley's frown indicated that he had already tackled the problem, but in vain. "I'm not into Irish matters nowadays—I'm not reliable there . . . And the same applies to Arab-Israeli business—no one trusts me with them either . . . except the Arabs and the Jews themselves, that is—and they don't matter . . ." He bit his lip.

"But you're a Soviet specialist—aren't you?"

"Supposedly . . . sometimes." Audley bridled slightly.

"Like now?"

Audley chewed at his lip, as though he didn't like its taste. "In so far as it's any of your business—yes . . . But nothing contentious . . . Interesting, maybe—*bloody fascinating*, if you like—" But then he shook his head decisively "—only I don't see how it could be them—not this time . . . if ever."

Tom felt reality slipping again. "You're sacrosanct, are you?"

"What?" Audley focused on him as though he hadn't heard.

"Where I come from they aren't above hitting people, David."

Audley stared at him for a moment. "But you aren't where you come from. And I'm not 'people', Tom." Now Audley was focusing exactly on him. "No, don't get me wrong, my lad: no one's sacrosanct, I agree . . . But at my level, over here and over there, there are a few unwritten rules, Tom."

"What rules?"

"What rules?" The brutal look returned. "In theory the rules exist at two levels—at least, according to Jack Butler, who's a great man for rules —'Rules of Engagement', as he puts it—okay?" But then he read Tom's face. "You're used to terrorists, boy—uncontrolled ones and Soviet-controlled ones—*I know!* But that's not what I'm talking about now."

"So what are you talking about?" The fact that Audley knew the score made it more confusing. "What two levels?"

"Okay!" Audley nodded. "There's the gentlemanly level—which Jack truly understands. Which is like Wellington at Waterloo, when this artillery officer comes up to him, and says he's got a clear view of Napoleon and his staff, and a battery pointing in that direction, and he's ready to fire. But the Duke says 'No! no! I'll not allow it. It is not the business of commanders to be firing on each other'. *Okay?*"

Tom felt he had to argue. "But what about us trying to hit Rommel in North Africa—the Keyes commando raid? And the Americans killing Yamamoto with that aerial ambush, after they'd broken the Japanese naval code?"

"That was different." Audley waved a vague hand as he peered out of one of his own windows, across the pacific sheep. "That was hot war, not cold war."

"Wasn't Waterloo hot war?" That had been the second time the man had mentioned the battle of Waterloo, which fitted neither what Harvey had said about him nor *Ideal and Reality in Frankish and Anglo-Saxon Society*.

The hand waved again. "That wasn't disgusting twentieth-century war—it was *gentlemanly* . . ." Audley gave him a cautious sidelong look ". . . at least, it was on Wellington's side, anyway—if you are about to throw Sous-Officier Cantillon at me, eh? But then Bonaparte was no gentleman—he was just a National Socialist born a century too late—" The sidelong look suddenly became sardonic "—although I suppose you, of all people, wouldn't admit that, eh?"

Bloody hell! thought Tom: what was *'You, of all people'* meant to mean? "Who?" And this wasn't either the time or the place for such games. "Why—*who*?"

"Didn't Bonaparte pretend to be nice to the Poles? Apart from fathering a child on Marie Walewska?" Audley circled round him, to take a view of the terrace on his own account. "Count Walewski—Napoleon III's ambassador in London, to Queen Victoria, wasn't he?" He concentrated on the terrace for an instant. "All clear this side."

The conversation was taking an unreal and tangential turn, reminding Tom of his earlier passage of words with the elfin child on the forecourt. But then the wife had warned him that they were like each other; and everything that had happened here had been unreal—even the house itself was unreal, and this sudden unseasonable outburst of sunshine and blue sky, when he'd left grey clouds and rain in the real world.

"Hadn't you better keep an eye on the front?" Audley chided him gently. "The police will come up the drive, like Christians. But they'll be scared, so I wouldn't wish not to welcome them—you understand?"

Audley was quite matter-of-fact, but somehow that only made it worse, projecting Tom's memory back out-of-reason into his own childhood, when *Mamusia*, beautiful and sweet-smelling, had read him to sleep with some silly story about *the Elf-King and his daughter, who lived Under the Hill, half in their world, and half in our world, where the flowers were brighter but the dangers were more dangerous* . . . and this was under a hill, or nearly, and there was an equivocal daughter—and an even more equivocal father, who'd known *Mamusia* herself, too . . . and where danger was undeniably more dangerous than it ought to be on a quiet afternoon in England!

"Yes." He pretended to scan the empty forecourt again. The trick in Mamusia's story was to hold on to something from his own world: the boy in the story had held on to his penknife: all he had to feel the shape of in his coat-pocket was the little wallet with his credit-cards in it; but then nothing could be more *real world* than credit-cards, after all. "Who the hell is—or was—'Sous-Officier . . . Cantillon'—?"

"Cantillon?" Audley seemed to expect him to know who the man was. "Why—he was the Napoleonic veteran who tried to assassinate Wellington in Paris in 1814, dear boy." He paused interrogatively. "And the unspeakable Bonaparte left the fellow 10,000 francs in his will—*not* the sort of thing a gentleman would do, as I said—did your dear mother never tell you that story, Tom?"

"My mother?"

Audley gazed at him for a moment, reflectively. "No, I can see that she didn't—perhaps understandably, in the circumstances."

Tom was beginning to feel foolish. "What circumstances?"

"What circumstances?" Now Audley seemed surprised. "My dear boy, your mother—*my* Danny Dzieliwski—*your* dear mother was—and presumably still is—quite devoted to Napoleon Bonaparte. And all things French . . . quite uncritically, if I may say so. The dreadful Corsican was one of her great heroes—after Marshal Poniatowski, of course. 'The epic of Napoleonic Poland' was one of her favourite themes . . . I won't say that I learnt all my Polish history *from* her—rather, I learnt it so that I didn't have to sit listening to her without being able to argue back, when she swept her generalizations halfway across Europe. In fact—" Audley raised a large dirty finger "—in fact, I became quite an authority on Casimir the Great and Jadwiga of Anjou in my own right, thanks to her. But I never really got beyond the medieval period in any detail, to be honest—modern history is mostly far too complicated for me."

It was happening again—

"So don't get the idea that I'm an expert on Bonaparte—"

"No—" It must be stopped, thought Tom desperately.

"No, indeed! I just happen to be reading this book my wife gave me, about Colquhoun Grant, who was Wellington's Head of Intelligence in the Peninsula—brilliant field operator, quite brilliant . . . And I had an ancestor who was killed there, you know—on my mother's side—charging with Le Marchant at Salamanca in 1812. So she's always on the look-out for books on the Peninsular War—Faith is, I mean, not my mother—"

"*David!*" Tom finally cracked. "For Christ's sake—I don't want to know about your mother—or my mother . . . Or Casimir the Great and Napoleon, for Christ's sake!" And what the *hell* had the child meant by *Tripoli*? "Somebody just took a shot at us, David—remember?"

"At me, dear boy—not you. How could I forget?" Audley screwed up his ugly features. "I'm only talking because I'm frightened—I told you. It's a reflex in some people. But at least it's preferable to other physical reflexes I've encountered—" He stopped suddenly. "You don't think he was shooting at *you*, do you? But . . . he would have had to be a *very* bad shot, surely—?" He stopped again, and frowned at Tom. "But then, he *was* a very bad shot—wasn't he!"

Audley had got there at last, however belatedly. "Yes."

"Yes . . ." Audley's frown deepened. "A sitting target—or a standing-still one, anyway . . . And he would have had plenty of time to sight-up, and make all the necessary allowances, too . . ." He stared clear through Tom.

But that had been one of the problems. "He would?"

"Oh yes." Audley nodded through him. "He would have spotted me in the orchard. But I was moving around, and the trees wouldn't have given him a clear shot." He drew a breath. "Only, after we had word of your impending arrival, and the sun came out . . . after that Faith got the chairs out and put them on the terrace. So then he would have known he'd get a clear shot." He focused on Tom again. "But then he missed—eh?"

"Yes." That was one problem solved—which only left another in its place. "Yes?"

"So it can't have been the Other Side?" Audley cocked his head. "But . . . they have been known to miss, Tom."

"Not often." It was time to push the old man. "And not when someone of Panin's seniority is involved, David. He wouldn't have used Sous-Officier Cantillon for the job."

"No . . . no, that's true." Audley drew another breath. "But this isn't Nikolai Panin anyway." He shook his head. "No."

They were back to Jack Butler's 'Rules of Engagement'. But, whatever Jack Butler and the Duke of Wellington might believe, there were no rules that couldn't be stretched and broken outside the playing fields of Eton—the small print of military and political necessity legitimized every successful action retrospectively—that was why the *Belgrano* was at the bottom of the South Atlantic.

"He's a gentleman, is he?" But Audley had referred to *two* levels, he remembered. "Or is it that you're old friends, and he's sentimental?"

"Huh!" Audley didn't mind being needled, Tom realized in that instant; or being *Danny Dzieliwski's boy* maybe did confer an advantage, as Jaggard had calculated? "Old Nikolai's no gentleman, that's for sure! He's a true-red child of the Revolution—*homo Sovieticus Stalinus*—he may have been an old-time cool-head, hot-heart patriotic Russian during the war—the 'Great Patriotic War'—and afterwards, for a time . . . But surviving the last thirty-five years has surely corrupted him into a cold-hearted bastard who knows exactly which side his fresh white bread is buttered, by God!" He shook his head at Tom, almost sadly. "That's the bugger of their system, young Tom—it corrupts ordinary decent men more efficiently and comprehensively and quickly than ours does . . . apart from bringing the absolute shits to the top even more quickly than we can manage—eh?"

Interesting, Tom began to think, when a slight sound from outside broke the thought suddenly. "So Panin was an ordinary decent man once upon a time—?" He turned towards the window casually. "Was he?"

"I think he might have been. He was certainly a damn good archaeologist once upon a time, by all accounts. And he's undoubtedly one of their best disinformation men."

"And you know him from way back?" He was torn down the middle between what Audley was saying and what had just come into sight, down the track from the road.

"Not from way back. I first met him fifteen years ago."

Tom held his face rigid. The measure of Audley's intelligence memory was that *fifteen years* wasn't *way back* to him. And the measure of the difference between Nikolai Panin's world and their own was what he was watching now, outside.

"I did him a good turn . . . after a fashion—" Audley was slightly thrown by his failure to turn back from the window this time. But, for the life of him, he couldn't tear himself away from what he was seeing "—and he returned the compliment, a few years later . . . after a fashion."

"Yes?" What that meant was that self-interest and co-operation had briefly coincided for David Audley and Nikolai Panin, no more. But also that those two occasions had been the beginning of some sort of relationship between them over fifteen years, nevertheless.

But he couldn't go on watching. "Yes? What was his fashion, then?"

"None of your business—" Audley read his face. "What's the matter?"

"Now he wants to meet you again, is what's the matter, David."

"And now *I* want to see *him*." Audley frowned, dissatisfied with that explanation. "What were you looking at, Tom?"

"The police have arrived, David," he admitted.

The old man relaxed slightly. "They have?"

"Not 'They', David—it's just one policeman." Tom turned back to the window, inclining suddenly towards cruelty. "He's just taking his bicycle clips off his ankles now. And he doesn't seem very scared, either—he's just parking his bicycle alongside my car . . . and he's looking around as though he owns the place—six-foot-plus, slim build . . . about forty, forty-five . . . fair complexion—red weather-beaten, or a Winter holiday on the Costa del Sol, or regular visits to your local pub—I don't know which at this distance."

"Yes." Audley took one step, but then stopped. "That'll be Alan—

Constable Grant . . . Does he have a carrier on the back of his cycle?"

"Yes—" Tom stared at the bicycle "—he's got some vegetables in it —or something green—?"

"Bedding plants, most likely," agreed Audley. "Alan knows just where to go in the village, to fill his garden in the spring. That'll be him, right enough. So . . . Faith will have to give him some of her plants, from the greenhouse—"

"*David*—for Christ's sake!"

Audley stood where he was. "It's all right. She planted far more than we need for bedding-out . . . And no bugger's going to shoot a village policeman, Tom—not at 600 yards, in default of me—or you." He shook his head. "Not even Bonaparte would pay him 10,000 francs for that."

Harvey had said that Audley wasn't popular in certain quarters, and Tom could see why that might be true. "So you're not scared any more?"

Audley swayed, and then steadied himself. "Oh . . . I'm still scared—"

A heavy front-door-knocker banging echoed in the distance, from somewhere in the depths of the house.

"That's Alan." Audley nodded. "There's an electric bell, and a bell on a chain, out there. But Alan always uses the door-knocker. He doesn't believe in gadgets."

The echoes died away, but now there was another sound—of tyres scattering gravel, and then of a car coming up the drive from the road.

"I'm about as scared as Nikolai Panin should be," said Audley. "Because Fred Clinton laid down a sanction—oh, about twenty years ago, after some rogue East German tried to do for him what Sous-Officier Cantillon tried to do for Wellington, without KGB clearance . . . And Fred wasn't going to have *that* game played with impunity by all and sundry, with apologies afterwards." He gave Tom one of his brutal expressions. "Fred was no more a gentleman than Bonaparte was—or Nikolai Panin is, you see, Tom."

Tom heard the police car scatter gravel again, as it reached the forecourt. But that was no longer important.

"So he invented *MAD*—or his version of it—long before the Pentagon did . . . '*Mutual Assured Destruction*', eh?" Another nod. "Only his version wasn't a general holocaust—it was much more precise . . . But not *exactly* precise, in case one particular KGB boss wanted us to take out one of his rivals—you understand, Tom?"

He had heard of this, although almost as a legend rather than the truth: the *life-for-a-life* concensus in the intelligence community, which constrained and inhibited them from killing each other at the higher levels.

"You know what I'm talking about?" Audley had heard the doors of the police car slam, but he ignored the sounds.

"Yes." The revenge-names were pricked at the highest level, the word was. And Research and Development was the highest level.

This time the electric bell pealed out, from down below and up above simultaneously, halfway to the sound of the burglar alarm.

"So if I'm taken out, then Panin can't expect to celebrate this Christmas either. Because he's my exact opposite." The bell rang again, and Audley waited for the echoes to die away. "So the sooner we meet now, the better for both of us."

IV

To Audley's scrambled phone Tom said: "*Would you hold for a moment, sir*", as the door of the study opened; and then, to the Special Branch man, "*What is it?*", holding his temper in check as he heard the sound of Audley's voice approaching, through the open door; and then Faith Audley's voice too, raised in protest—so she had been retrieved at last, from her bolt-hole, wherever it was—

"Sir—" The Special Branch man also heard the approaching voices, and paused understandably—but then jinked strangely, as though something unexpected had touched him from behind, lifting his left arm and looking down into the gap at the same time.

"Sorry!" Cathy Audley's little face, eyes magnified behind their spectacles, and teeth metal-braced, appeared alongside him. "Hullo, Sir Thomas!"

"What's happening?" said Jaggard in Tom's ear. "Are you there?"

"I know what a baronet is," said the child earnestly. "Father said to look it up. So I did—in my *Everyman's Encyclopaedia* . . . That's what he *always* says: '*Look it up*', he says. So I took *BAR* to *CAM* into the hole. And—"

"*Cathy!*" Faith Audley bulldozed the Special Branch man out of her way. "That's enough!"

"Are you there?" repeated Jaggard.

"But I didn't tell him where the hole was, Mummy," the child protested. "I was just talking about *baronets*—"

"Be quiet!" Mrs Audley concentrated on Tom, ignoring her daughter. "Sir Thomas, will you please tell me what's going on in my house?"

"Yes," said Tom into the receiver. *Come back Beirut, come back Tripoli!* "Would you hold for a moment, sir." He frowned at the child as she squeezed past the Special Branch man: *Tripoli?*

Audley appeared behind his wife. "Faith love—for God's sake!" he caught Tom's eye. "I'm sorry, Tom—"

"Sir!" The Special Branch man tried simultaneously to hold Tom's attention while giving ground to Audley and his wife and avoiding a rather fragile table piled high with books. "Sir—?"

Come back Athens, come back Nicosia, come back Tel Aviv! But at least Jaggard was quiet now, in his ear—

"Sir Thomas—" began Mrs Audley again.

Tom held up his free hand. "Just a moment, Mrs Audley—" He nodded at the Special Branch man "—yes?"

"The hill is clear, sir." The man took a deep breath. "There's no one up there now—" He rolled his eyes sideways "—but . . ."

"Yes?"

This time the man swallowed. "It was a high-velocity bullet. It went through the window, and then a lampshade on a table, and then into the panelling on the wall, on the far side. But we'll have to wait for forensic to recover it. They should be able to tell us a lot more."

"Thank you." Properly speaking, there was nothing else Mrs Audley needed to know—properly speaking, she had already heard more than she was entitled to hear, even. But in her own house, and since she was David Audley's wife, it might be prudent to entitle her to more than that. "So what else are you doing?"

"Tom—" Audley's mouth opened. "Who's on the phone?"

"It's okay, David." It would never do for Audley to know that Jaggard was on the other end; it was bad enough to know himself that Jaggard was quite remarkably laid-back with this hideous turn of events, almost as though he'd expected them; or, at least, that they didn't surprise him. "Just the duty man—" He turned back to the Special Branch man quickly "—Well?"

"There'll be more support manpower here soon." The man didn't know quite what to say. "It's almost too late for road-blocks—we're very close to the motorway here. And we're almost into the Gatwick radius, anyway . . ." He shrugged ". . . we can't inhibit traffic inside that without Home Office clearance, sir."

So much for *Limejuice*, thought Tom: if someone in Athens had taken a shot at Colonel Stamatopoulos, or one of his friends, then half of Greece would have ground to a halt. But in the Home Counties of England, and with no blood spilt, the traffic had to get through regardless.

"David—" Mrs Audley addressed her husband, failing Tom.

"I told you, love—some fool has got his lines crossed, that's all."

"You also told me that *Limejuice* was just a precaution, after last time—"

"That was . . . that was ten years ago, love."

"I don't care if it was a hundred years—"

"Mrs Audley—Faith—" Obligation and self-interest suddenly coincided: he needed Audley to himself and he had to get the man away from her and here as soon as possible. But now he had a chance to cement a relationship which Mamusia had begun before he had been thought of "—your husband's right, actually." He remembered the Special Branch man. "Thank you, Sergeant. I'll come back to you. But we'll want an escort vehicle—"

"And a car for my wife," said Audley. "I don't want her here tonight."

"Right—that too." Tom nodded the Special Branch man out of the room before turning back to Faith Audley. But then he also remembered Jaggard. "Hullo?" There really wasn't anything else that he wanted to say to Jaggard, the bugger seemed so remarkably laid-back in the circumstances of their high-velocity bullet. "I'll call you again when I'm free."

"Don't bother, Tom. I've got the general picture well enough. You just watch over Audley and his old friend, that's all. Just get Audley to the rendezvous first—then I want to know what he gets up to—where he's going, and who he's talking to. And preferably in advance—do you understand that?"

"Yes." It took no effort to slam the phone down. *Come back Beirut . . .* but, most of all, *where are you now, Willy?* "I'm sorry, Faith—"

"No." Some of the fire seemed to have gone out of her, damped down under the fine drenching spray of cruel reality. "I can see that I'm getting in the way of more pressing matters." She gave her husband a weary little smile. "There's a right time for being difficult, and this isn't it." She bit her lip. "I'll go quietly, Sir Thomas—in fact, I'll just go and pack my toothbrush. All right?"

"No." It was working out so well that Tom was almost ashamed. "What I meant was that some fool *has* got his lines crossed—and I am the fool. So your husband was really just protecting me." He knew that he mustn't look at Audley, for fear that she might do the same. "The bullet was for me, Mrs Audley, you see. Not for him."

"What—?" The lie caught her in the act of turning away. But that, most annoyingly, left her half-facing her husband. "David—?"

"Ahh . . ." A lifetime of dissimulation had greased the big man's mental reflexes. "Well . . . to be fair, that's for the experts to say, Tom."

"It was for me, David." He could only admire the crafty way Audley had fixed the lie, with so little warning. "But . . . you understand, Mrs Audley—Faith . . . that I can't tell you what I usually do. But, in any case, I'm not doing it now—" *True, Tom Arkenshaw, you lying bastard!* But what could he say next "—so I trust it won't happen again—" *Not good enough!* He could see that in her face "—but I'll keep an eye on him now, I promise you, anyway." *True again!* he thought. *But what a fearful promise!* But, for better or worse, it was made now. And that sort of promise couldn't be unmade, which was worst of all.

"Huh!" Audley chuckled obscenely. "Just keep away from me—that's all!"

"*David!*" She gave him a broken look. "You look after yourself too, Sir Thomas." She drew a breath. "I have to believe that my husband is indestructible." She took another breath. "I'll go and find my toothbrush, anyway."

Tom watched her depart, chin up.

"I shall get hell in due course," murmured Audley. "But, in the meantime—"

"No!" All Tom wanted to do was to think in peace for a moment, before they all came back to him again: to think about what Jaggard had said, and hadn't said; and about what Harvey had said, and had hinted at; and about Audley too; and maybe even about Mamusia. "You just go and pack your toothbrush too, David. We can talk in the car—okay?"

At first Audley didn't reply. Then, when he did, he sounded as though his gratitude was already being stretched. "I was only going to thank you for that little white lie. But . . ." he shrugged ". . . if that's the way you want it, you're the boss." He turned in the doorway. "For the time being, anyway."

Tom waited for a moment, then turned back to the huge cluttered desk, staring for another moment at the red phone among the tower-blocks of books and magazines and buff folders, and the scatter of notes and notebooks and photo-copied newspaper cuttings, which together left no square inch of its surface free.

Jaggard had not really been surprised, he decided—

Places in the books—and in the magazines—were liberally reminded with numerous slips of differently coloured paper, pale pink and green and blue; and there were passages marked in the newspaper cuttings too, Audley-interest-stained with broad soft-felt pen-ink of similar colours, like cross-references.

It was always hard to tell for sure on the phone, a practised liar always had the edge on the phone—he could deceive anyone except Mamusia on the phone—

The whole room was full of books: books shelved from floor to ceiling of every wall, books crammed between the shelves laterally where there was room, books in ranks and piles on the floor; there was only that one little dark gap behind the high-backed oak chair, to the right of the door, where that tall grandfather clock ticked away now in the silence like a monstrous death watch beetle, which had no books, apart from the leaded windows with their fringes of wisteria.

So . . . because he had already decided that Jaggard had not told him everything, or even half of it . . . that was a subjective conclusion—

He turned back to the desk. There were books on it which didn't fit among their fellows—or, even more, among the pink-stained names in the topmost cuttings from a wide range of Soviet and American specialist publications: *Chebrikov* from the Politburo, and *Aliev*, from the KGB . . . and the geriatric *Lomako*, who was (wasn't he?) a survivor from the prehistoric 1940s . . . and . . . *Shevardnadze*—who the hell was he? But there was that bastard *Shkiriatov*, anyway, from his own recent Syrian experience—

So this was what Audley was doing right now: trying to pick this year's Kremlin Grand National winners—or at least fix the odds!

But then . . . where did Kennedy's *Revised Latin Primer*, and Cassell's *Little Gem Latin Dictionary* (the former old and ink-stained, the latter brand new) fit into this field? Or, right in front of him, on top of a pristine copy of yesterday's *Izvestia*, this antique little blue Volume IV of Caesar's *Gallic Wars*, open at that point where *'Caesar's arrival encourages his men —acting on the defensive he retires—stormy weather prevents further action— large forces swell the enemy's camp, confident of victory.'*

There still wasn't a sound from that interesting little book-free gap, behind the chair, where there were four framed sets of campaign medals on the wall beside the grandfather clock, and darkness below.

Quibus rebus perturbatis nostris novitate pugnae tempore opportunissimo Caesar auxilium tulit—God! he couldn't make sense out of that! But instead he addressed the shadows behind the chair. "So what do you know about baronets then, Miss Audley?"

No sound. *But Jaggard had not been surprised*, and Tom was ultimately convinced by his own instinct. "King James I—1611?"

Infinitesimal sound, less than the scuffle of an October field-mouse refugeeing in the house. "For the defence of Ulster—?"

"That's right." Tom was torn between his memories of Caesar, and more recent ones of Arkadi Shkiriatov, and the presence of Miss Audley, never mind Jaggard and King James I. "To raise money for the defence of Ulster in 1611—go on!"

"People who had enough money had to become baronets. And they had to pay for thirty soldiers, at eight pence a day, for three years." The voice strengthened. "But Scottish baronets were different. They paid their money for the colonization of Nova Scotia. You aren't Scottish, though."

"No." So Jaggard must have a damn good idea what Panin wanted, even if he didn't know for sure. "Tell me more?"

"Do people often shoot at you?"

That was the point: if it wasn't Panin (and, even apart from that MAD sanction of Audley's, Panin would hardly have the man he wanted to meet shot before the meeting) then someone else knew about it, and had done it. "Does your father often do your Latin prep for you?" He turned towards the chair.

"No." The pale little face barely topped the chair-back. "Only when I'm really stuck." She blinked behind her glasses. "Do you shoot people?"

That was also a point, thought Tom. Terrorist groups the world over, from his own Mediterranean to that same Ulster which had forced a title on the original Sir Thomas Arkenshaw . . . terrorist groups shot people without a second thought. But the agencies of the First Division players, the sovereign states, only resorted to violence when they were really stuck—that was also very much the point.

"No." It wasn't funny, but he must smile at her. "Only when I'm really stuck, anyway." But Audley would have worked all this out much more quickly. "I think you ought to go and get your toothbrush too, oughtn't you?"

"Mother will do that. What I want to know is—" She stopped as he raised his hand "—what—?"

"I also think she'll be looking for you, Miss Audley." *What I want to know*, thought Tom, *is what you meant by 'Tripoli'. But I don't think this is the moment for asking!* "And then she may remember where she last saw you—?"

The little hand, with its long thin fingers, covered the braced teeth in sudden consternation. At this stage, thought Tom professionally, it was a toss-up whether she'd flower into the slender beauty of her mother or merely end up thin and plain. But either way she would be an interesting young woman one day, for the young man who could match her spirit.

"Golly—you're right!" She ducked out from behind the chair, but then halted in the doorway, just as her father had done, but with her chin up, like her mother. "You will look after Father, won't you?"

What Jaggard had ordered, and what he had almost unthinkingly volunteered to obey in order to get rid of this child's mother, came home to him again. "I'll do my best. But I rather think he's quite capable of looking after himself, you know." He grinned at her reassuringly.

But she was totally unreassured. "No, he's not." She shook her head almost angrily. "That's what everyone thinks—they think he's *so* clever, and so does he. But he isn't at all—he really isn't."

"He isn't—?" Tom was totally taken aback.

"Oh—he *knows* a lot—" She caught his thought in mid-air "—he knows everything about everything—" She had to be quoting someone, thought Tom; and most likely it was her mother "—but when he wires up a plug he fuses everything, and when he cuts anything he usually cuts himself too—honestly, he does."

Definitely, this was Faith Audley overheard; and this child had already proved she was good at overhearing; and yet . . . in a curious way all this echoed what Harvey had said about Research and Development, too: its unmatched intellectual performance was seldom matched by its performance in the field, whenever it strayed out of its back room.

"He does need looking after, Sir Thomas." The little serious face matched her earnestness. "So you *will* look after him, won't you? *Won't you?*"

He had to get rid of her, for his own peace of mind. But only one answer could do that. "Yes. I will look after him."

She gave him one dreadful signed-and-sealed nod, and then vanished. But then, just as he was starting to heave a sigh of something less than pure relief, her face appeared again, suspended halfway up the edge of the door.

"I bet you don't miss!"

Miss? "Miss . . . ? Miss Audley—?"

"When *you* shoot at anyone—you don't miss!"

Nothing less than a categorical answer was again required. So he turned his hand into a pistol. "Never, Miss Audley." He pointed the pistol-finger at her, knowing that he mustn't smile. But that wasn't difficult because it wasn't a smiling matter—indeed, it was doubly not so, he thought grimly, because he would need to carry a real gun now, just like in Beirut. And there had been nothing remotely funny about that. "Never. So off you go then." This time he wanted to smile, but couldn't. The Special Branch unit would have a couple of revolvers, most likely those "safe" Smith and Wessons they favoured but he didn't like: he could certainly pull enough rank to get one of those. But meanwhile she was still staring at him fixedly through her pebble spectacles. "Otherwise your mother *will* miss you, Miss Audley. And I don't think that would be healthy for either of us."

As he sighted his finger on her she vanished, and a moment later he heard her whistling in the passage with all the preparatory innocence of an old lag who knew just how to answer the question "Where have you been?" with a calculated half-truth. And that would be a Greek-meets-Greek situation, if ever there was one—

But he mustn't waste his thoughts on women and children—even *Audley* women and children (who both agreed that their man couldn't look after himself!)—

He was looking at his pistol-hand, which was still pointing at the half-open door, out of which that shrill, tuneless whistling still issued, far off now—

He turned back to the desk, to the red phone among the cuttings from *Soviet Review* and *Izvestia* and *Études Russes*, and *Caesar's Gallic War*.

What was that tune? It ought to be from *Anna and the King of Siam*—

He needed a hand-gun. And with all the havering that request would occasion he ought to go and ask for it now. But—

What it ought to be was *'Whenever I feel afraid/I hold my head erect—And whistle a happy tune/So no one will suspect/I'm afraid—'* But it wasn't—

But he wanted to phone Jaggard again, and ask him what the bloody hell was actually happening.

But it sounded curiously like the proud battle hymn of the United States Marines—

But Jaggard already hadn't admitted that he had any idea what Panin wanted, so he was unlikely to admit more than that now. And, for that matter, Audley hadn't even bothered to ask that same obvious question. So . . . either he had guessed correctly that Sir Thomas Arkenshaw was not privy to its answer . . . or he already knew that answer, and therefore didn't need to ask the question—?

The sound faded into the otherwise-silence of the crazy old house, with its newly-broken window. But it surely had been that old US marine threat: *'From the halls of Montezuma/To the shores of Tripoli/We will fight our country's battles/By the land or by the sea—'*

The whole Audley family was getting its tooth-brushes, and Tom Arkenshaw needed a gun—that was the long-and-short of it, he thought.

But . . . *Tripoli*, again?

He didn't like guns. The theory with guns was that they settled all arguments finally, of kings and cowboys as well as terrorists. But that was as facile as *'the best things in life are free'*, when Willy (and his best suit, which had not been tailored to suit a Smith and Wesson five-shot hammerless) certainly didn't come without a credit card or a cheque-book —*guns*, experience warned him, were never the end of things, but only the beginning of other things, more complicated and embarrassing first, and more unending afterwards.

But, in spite of all of that, he still needed a gun—

Finally, he got the show on the road, more or less.

There were cases in the hall, with Mrs Audley and Miss Audley beside them, and a plainclothes man beside them.

The front door was open, and he could see Audley himself in the porch, talking to one of the drivers, who had an Ordnance Survey map in his hand.

"Not outside, sir—if you don't mind," said the plainclothes man as Tom gestured to Mrs Audley, after he had just failed to stop her husband.

Tom dearly wanted to hear what Audley was saying, but there were limits to what he could achieve, with another Special Branch man—the sergeant, no less—striding towards him now.

"Mrs Audley—" He had promised her to keep his eye on her husband, and he couldn't escape her now.

"Sir Thomas." Unlike her daughter, she wasn't whistling. But she was still chin-up. "Thank you, for all your help."

The sergeant coughed politely, and offered him a completely-holstered Smith and Wesson, with the good grace to be embarrassed in front of Audley's family.

"Thank you, Sergeant." What made it worse was that he would have to put the damn thing on here and now—*what the devil was Audley doing, pointing to the map, when he didn't even know where he was going?*—because the other SB certainly wouldn't let him outside carrying it like a pound of sausages.

"Let me hold your coat, Sir Thomas," said Faith Audley.

"And I'll hold the other—" Cathy Audley seized the weapon and its harness before anyone could stop her while Tom himself was trying to catch what Audley was saying. So all he could do was to give his coat to the wife and recover 'the other' as quickly as he could, but much too late for his peace of mind.

"Ah!" Audley returned to them, eyeing him critically as he put his coat on again. "'Arma virumque cano'—'forced by fate, and haughty Juno's unrelenting hate'. . . But I fear it would break your tailor's heart—it doesn't sit at all well under that good worsted, Tom. Makes you look like a soldier from Chicago, rather than a soldier of the Queen—what d'you think, love?"

"I think you're being your usual self, David."

"There now!" Audley plainly couldn't see that his attempt to lighten the occasion was only making it worse. "All the sympathy she can spare from herself, she freely gives to you, Tom. Which is probably not a lot."

The Sergeant coughed again. "If you would care to sign for the . . . equipment, Sir Thomas. And we would like it back when you've finished with it, if you don't mind."

"Well, love . . ." Audley drew a deep breath ". . . after we've made ourselves scarce the Sergeant here will take you both to your mother's. And he'll leave a man with you, just for form's sake . . . And he'll also leave someone here too, just to mind the silver—you do know how the burglar alarm works, don't you, Sergeant?"

"Yes, Dr Audley." The Sergeant recovered his requisition form.

"Thank you." The weight of The Thing reminded Tom how much he hated guns. But it would never do to admit that he didn't want to start with it, never mind finish. But what he wanted to do most of all was to get at the police driver whom Audley had briefed. "Mrs Audley—"

"Sir Thomas—" She wanted to say more. But at least they both knew what couldn't be said "—perhaps we shall see you again some time? I gather my husband was at Cambridge with your mother—?" That was the most she could manage.

"Yes—yes, I'm sure we shall . . . in much more agreeable circumstances." That was all he could manage in reply. "Miss Audley—" But he had to do better in her case, so he patted the Chicago bulge before he offered her his hand in farewell "—goodbye, Miss Audley."

Miss Audley opened her mouth, but then she caught her mother's eye and all the things she wanted to say remained mercifully unsaid, so she didn't say anything at all by way of farewell.

"I'll see you in the car, David." He transferred his serious smile from the daughter back to the mother without looking at Audley, disliking himself for taking the credit for his delicacy when all he really wanted to do was to talk to the police driver outside.

Outside, there were visible evidences of *Limejuice*, in the form of his own car now very close to the door, sandwiched between two police cars, and with armed men on the gravel beyond who were not in the least interested in him.

The man he wanted must be in the lead car—

"What was that you were discussing with Dr Audley?"

"Sir?" The driver blinked at him, then recovered. "Dr Audley was giving me a route to the main road, sir."

"Yes?" That was logical, because Audley obviously knew the country roads in his own territory. But then so did the police driver. "Show me."

"Show—?" The urgency of the order overrode the man's surprise, and he reached for the same map which he had consulted in the porch. "We're *here*, sir—" he crinkled the map towards Tom and stabbed it with a blunt competent finger "—and we go as far as . . . *there*, sir. Right?"

There was out of the spider's-web of minor roads around Steeple Horley, along a main road. But it was well to the west of the direct line towards London, which Audley should have presumed was his direction—unless he knew better . . . But he bloody-well *couldn't* know better—could he?

And there was something else, by God! "As far as you go?"

The man looked questioningly at him. "As far as you want us to go with you, sir . . . is what I meant . . . sir?" He wasn't sure now if he'd got it right.

"Ah . . . yes." Tom nodded, and straightened up. If that was where Audley wanted to go, then it suited him very well, because it gave them good access to the westward motorway, so there was no need to countermand it. And once they were on that main road their escort would be superfluous, anyway.

But now he heard the front door slam behind him. So the old man—once Mamusia's *young* man, but his *old* man now—*the old man, who knew where he wanted to go*—had made his proper untearfully stiff-upper-lipped farewells, and they were going at last. But now going, it seemed, to two different destinations—

"Well, thank God for that!" Audley stretched the seat-belt wide with relief, and then fumbled incompetently but quite happily to find its anchorage.

"You don't mind abandoning your family?" Tom slammed him back into his seat with a clear conscience as the car ahead accelerated: the rule was to keep tight and fast, risking collision rather than a three-second clear shot for any potential sniper along the way; but it was Audley who was taking him for a ride now, not vice-versa, anyway.

"Not in the very least—quite the opposite!" Audley let the strap wind itself up again. "The further I am away from them, the safer they are—huh!"

"Huh?"

"Huh!" Audley settled back comfortably. "Having a large policeman in the house—in my esteemed mother-in-law's house . . . that'll poach the old haybag to rights, by God!" He twisted suddenly towards Tom. "In fact, I do her an injustice: she's a dear old bird—and a tough one, too . . . But having a policeman there will flatter her, so she won't quarrel with her daughter, she'll be too busy making him endless cups of tea, and generally making his life a misery—" He concentrated on Tom "—or . . . what would your dear mother do, if she suddenly found a large policeman in her parlour, because of you—?"

The car in front swung out of the drive into the road, much too fast for safety and taking Tom by surprise until he saw the uniformed man who was waving them on. "I've never bothered her that way, David."

"No? Mmm . . ." Audley trailed off, evidently summoned again by rose-tinted recollections of his undergraduate past. "Mmm . . ."

Well—damn his memories! "Where are we going?"

"Where—?" A particularly deep pot-hole in the uneven surface of the road helped to shake the old man out of his *temps perdu*. "Ah . . . now, I was meaning to tell you about that. A minor detour, no more."

There was no point in protesting. "Yes?"

"I should have told you." Audley suddenly sounded contrite. "It was remiss of me—I'm sorry, Tom."

"It's okay." The trouble was, contrition didn't suit the man, it just wasn't his style; which, if it was because of those ancient memories, would very soon become irritating if it wasn't nipped in the bud at once.

"It's hardly out of your way. We can still pick up the London road . . . oh, in just a mile or two from there." Audley got in before he could start nipping. "We may even save time, in the end."

Unless the old liar had discovered a shorter line between two points than a straight one, they were going in very nearly the opposite direction, that was the truth of it. "Just tell me what the hell we're doing, David."

"Yes." Audley's meekness was as bad as his contrition. "Well . . . we're going to talk to someone—someone I need to talk to. So when we get to the main road . . . we bear left there, until we come to the Three Pigeons—which is a big pub with coloured lights . . ."

Left would be even further to the west, or at least north-west. "Yes?"

"And then, about five miles further on . . . there's another pub—just by the church . . . the Bear and Ragged Staff. You turn sharp left there."

That would be due-bloody-west. Which was fine for Nikolai Andrievich Panin, who would probably be already within sight of the Bristol Channel by now, speeding down the M5. But for a man who ought to presume that he was going to London it was a bad joke.

"Yes?" Tom stifled the temptation to ask Audley whether he habitually navigated across England from pub to pub, with the occasional church thrown in.

"Yes." Audley nodded. "It really will save us time. And maybe not time alone, Tom."

"Yes?" But pubs didn't matter. What mattered more was . . . *who the hell did Audley want to see, who mattered more than Panin, who wanted to meet him so urgently on Exmoor?*

And, come to that—*Exmoor!* Because the Russian would have needed Foreign Office dispensation to go so far. But—never mind the Foreign Office!—he would have required Moscow Centre dispensation too, to swan off into the far unexplored West of England, to meet his old friend, and Mamusia's—

"I'll tell you where to go then. But it's only a step or two from there."

A step or two to the west, near another pub? The Red Lion, or the Eight Bells, or the Vine, or the George and Dragon—or the Old Castle, where even now, in a better world, Tom Arkenshaw ought to have been drinking champagne cocktails with Miss Wilhemina Groot, in the privacy of the bridal suite? *Bloody hell!*

"Who are we going to see then, David?" He thrust Willy out of his mind, back to London where Audley thought he was going, but wasn't.

"Ah . . ." Audley jerked forward as the police car in front illuminated its hazard lights, and then slowed; and then signalled left, as it drew aside on to the grass verge by the side of the road. "You go ahead here, Tom."

Tom drove ahead into the first beginnings of evening, unsure whether he was glad or sorry as he lost sight of the flashing lights behind him. He didn't know where he was, because he'd never castle-hunted seriously in Hampshire. Somewhere to the north of this, or more like north-east, Henry of Blois had thrown up one of his 1138 strongpoints at Farnham, certainly. And there were other 1138 "illegals" at Waltham and Wolvesey. But he couldn't place either of them on the map in his head. Yet—much more to the point—the A34 Winchester to Oxford road couldn't be far ahead, and that would take him fast to the westward-bound M4 and M5.

But it was no use fretting (Farnham was an interesting site, which he'd always intended to measure: the *motte* there had been revetted with a buttressed shell-wall allegedly comparable with the Crusaders' keep at Acre in Israel; although that hadn't prevented good old Henry Plantagenet from demolishing it in 1155). He was going to be late, bringing them together, but that wasn't his fault—so it was no good fretting.

"You were saying, David—?" The brief intrusion of Henry of Blois and Henry Plantagenet, eventual Lord of England, Wales, Ireland and two-thirds of France, and of their great works, restored his sense of proportion, as always: the two Henrys, and David Audley and Nikolai Panin and Tom Arkenshaw, and all the ants in all the ant-hills, engaged in great works. But it would all be the same in the end—always the only question was *sooner* or *later*?

"Yes." Audley had been quite content for him to go ahead in search of the bright lights of the Three Pigeons public house. "Did you ever meet Basil Cole? Or was he before your time?" Once committed, Audley perked up. "Probably not, even if he wasn't. Because he worked for Fawcett—Victor Fawcett—? Who worked for 'Digger' Wilmot . . . I don't think he was still *in post* when that clever bugger Jaggard came into his inheritance."

Tom felt Audley's eyes on him as he searched in vain for bright lights ahead. "No." But if they were into name-dropping, he'd better drop one or two. "'Digger' Wilmot took me on—he was at school with my father. And I've met Henry Jaggard since, of course." That was the truth—even if it was the truth naked and ashamed. "But I work for Frobisher, David."

"Yes. And he approves of you, too." Audley spoke derisively. But, to give him the benefit of the doubt, that might be because he didn't wish to patronize Danny Dzieliwski's son too obviously. "At least, that's what he gave Jack Butler to understand. He says you're a straight-shooter—is that true?"

There were lights ahead. And, because Jaggard had obviously foreseen that Audley would never obey orders exactly, it was so much the opposite of the truth that he couldn't bring himself to give it a straight lie. "Not with that damn thing they gave me, David." He felt the discomfort of the police Smith and Wesson, and remembered that he had lied to Cathy Audley too. "If we meet your sniper again, for God's sake don't rely on me—I'll most likely shoot myself in the foot."

"Hah!" Audley chuckled, but then pointed suddenly. "Turn left by the pub—see the sign?"

Tom hadn't time to read the sign, only to see that the road was empty behind as they swerved into a narrow side-road. So now, even if there was an unmarked police car behind them, it would end up heading for Winchester and disappointment.

"I had a driver in Normandy—he was a damn good driver, too . . . *He* tried to shoot himself through the foot . . . purely by accident, you understand . . ."

Now they really were lost, thought Tom. Except that there was a church and another pub somewhere ahead now.

"Not that I blame him. We were in the *bocage*, you see—" Audley sat back, oblivious to his surroundings, as Tom strained in the half-light to see where he was going "—because I have three nightmares in my old age . . . One is of taking examinations, on subjects about which I know damn-all . . . But the other is about the *bocage*—every two or three years some damn fool asks me to go back to Normandy, to meet the old people whose houses we demolished, and the priests—I demolished a church in Normandy. That was probably my main contribution to winning the war —demolishing a church at point-blank range with 75-millimetre HE." Audley nodded. "It's quite simple: you just knock the corners out, and the tower falls into the chancel then, with a bit of luck—" Another nod "—and it was a fine old Norman church too, mine was, I think." Sniff. "There was a sniper in the tower, who'd just shot a friend of mine. He must have been a brave bastard!" Pause. "There's our church—do you see it?"

"Yes." Tom caught a glimpse of a squat tower.

"He missed me." Audley dismissed all churches from the conversation. "We were the last surviving tank in the troop, that night. And my driver also missed his foot."

The church came into view. And there, sure enough, was another pub. So *turn sharp left now*—

"Shot himself in the boot instead—missed his toes by a whisker." Another nod. "So we didn't have to court-martial him, thank God!"

They passed the pub, which Tom thought looking uncommonly inviting, now that the light inside it was stronger than the evening blue outside.

"So he was killed later on, after I'd left the regiment." Audley shook his head. "But . . . Basil Cole, I was asking—?"

There was still a third nightmare outstanding, in Audley's old age. But *Basil Cole*, who had worked for *Victor Fawcett*, in some Old Testament progression—*Someone* begat *Someone*, and *Someone-Else* begat *Someone-Else*—was more important than Audley's nightmares, from the Normandy *bocage* of forty years ago. Only, what mattered now on the darkening road, was that they were only "a step or two" from where Audley wanted to go. "Basil Cole—?"

"Yes." Audley rallied under pressure. "'Old King Cole'—you'll like him, Tom." Chuckle. "Drunken old bugger!"

Drunken old bugger? thought Tom. "Basil Cole?"

"Uh-huh." Audley sounded sure of himself now. "It was Old King Cole who sounded the early warning signals on Burgess and Maclean, before you were born—even almost before *I* was born, professionally speaking . . . Why are you slowing down?"

"I caught a glimpse of a church, I thought. Up ahead."

"You did?" Audley sat up, then gestured irritably. "Go on, go on!"

The church came into view. If Basil Cole dated from the early days of Burgess and Maclean then '*Old* King Cole' was right, thought Tom. "Here's the church, David."

"I said a church *and* a pub. I see no pub. You just drive—I'll tell you when. Okay?"

Tom accelerated. What he had to get used to was crossing England from pub to pub. "Okay."

"Okay. So . . . where was I? Go on, man—don't dawdle . . ."

"You said Basil Cole was a drunken old bugger."

"*Is*—not *was*." Audley corrected him. "So they put him out to grass eventually—Fawcett did. Gave him his wooden foil and niggardly pension. Fortunately his wife had a bit of money—nice woman. But hardly enough to keep him in his favourite tipple, you see."

Tom didn't see. But he needed to keep his eyes open for the next pub, so he decided not to admit it.

"And that was where my old boss came in—I take it that *he* will not be unknown to you, Tom?"

"Sir Frederick Clinton." Clinton was the near-legendary architect of Research and Development. "Colonel Butler's predecessor?"

"Correct—Fred, no less. And he was another animal who dated back to when the Ark came to rest on Mount Ararat. So he and Basil Cole were by way of being old shipmates. And he knew that in spite of Old King Cole's heavy-laden cargo of years and empty whisky bottles there was nothing wrong with his brains—they weren't so much addled as preserved. Which says a lot for the properties of Islay peat."

Tom concentrated on the road ahead.

"Also . . ." Audley twisted sideways ". . . you know, we've always run R & D on a derisory budget, you see. Old Fred liked to recruit people like me, with private incomes—he always said it was partly to save money, and partly so that they could indulge their own esoteric tastes without recourse to some third party. But actually it was so that he could divert our legitimate expenses into his slush fund, is what I know now—" He shook his head "—which I only know now because Jack Butler, who inherited that fund, is a friend of mine . . . or, a friend of a sort, anyway." Pause. "Huh!" Another pause. "He was a downy old bird—or half-downy, half-foxy—was Fred! We were always bloody nonplussed by how much he knew . . . Whereas the truth was that he had this private 'Black Economy' of his—paying selected pensioners of his own in used banknotes in little brown envelopes, to keep his private files up-to-date, and then feeding our main files with what he wanted us to see. Huh!" Another pause. "That's not the way Jack plays it now—*now* they have to come in once or twice a week, and feed the computer—beastly damn thing . . . But at least we have access to it, even if Jack always knows who's doing what now, more's the pity!" He half-chuckled, half-grunted. "Although he still slips 'em their brown envelopes, just like Fred. And you know why—?"

Tom didn't know why. What he knew was that they were at last coming to another scatter of houses in the half-light. "Why?"

"Custom and practice, Tom—custom and practice." The half-and-half sound was repeated. "His father was a printer—Father of the Union Chapel, before he became Composing Room Overseer, and then Head Printer. So Jack's a union man at heart. And he knows a thing or two about 'old Spanish customs'—like little brown envelopes with no names on 'em. Huh!"

There was a church coming up—and a public house—Tom strained his eyes to read the badly-illuminated sign outside it. "Is this where we turn left, David?"

"What?" Audley sat up. "Yes, of course it is—didn't I tell you?"

The turning was narrow and awkward, with the brickwork on each side testifying the failed efforts of those before him who had found it too narrow and too awkward. "So Basil Cole works part-time for Research and Development—is that it?"

"That's right. M to R, to be exact."

He wasn't going to make it—not because there wasn't room, but because there was a black-and-white mongrel dog in the way, sitting in the road.

"M to R?"

"Uh-huh. Fred had four old Moscow-watchers. Dorothy Marshall handles A to F, and Frank Hodgson G to L, and my own Sheila Ellis has S to Z—she feeds me directly now, every Wednesday, does Sheila—" Audley sat up again "—what's holding you up?"

"There's a dog in the road—M to R—?"

"Uh-huh. So including P . . . Run the bloody animal over, then . . . So Old King Cole is the expert on Panin—*go on, man!*"

Jesus Christ! He revved the engine angrily. "But I thought you were the expert on Panin—" He caught himself too late.

"Did you, now?" The silky satisfaction in Audley's voice confirmed his failure. "So you're not just a high-grade minder, then? Not that I ever really thought you were, of course—*run the bloody animal over—go on!*" Audley turned away from him. "Well, there's no one on our tail, anyway—at least, not from the other side, whichever side it may be . . . But you're here to report back to whoever it may be, anyway—'What the devil is that swine Audley up to?'—but it could hardly be Frobisher . . . because he can't be interested in anything I do . . . can he?"

Tom rolled the car forward. Everything Harvey had said was true, and he had betrayed himself. "I'm just here to get you to Panin, David . . . Which I'm not doing very well at the moment, actually. Because we're ninety minutes behind schedule already—" The headlights picked out trees and more brickwork ahead "—so how far to Basil Cole, then?"

"Not far. But do you have to be present when I exchange confidences with Nikolai Panin? Or do you merely deliver me to some agreed rendezvous?" Audley waved ahead. "Which is it?"

Tom put his foot down. "They have someone with him. We have someone with you. Those are the agreed terms."

"Ah! That's what Fred Clinton termed 'Mutual Agreed Internal Distrust'. Which he used to codename '*Orleans*', because Joan of Arc was the 'Maid of Orleans'—M-A-I-D, you see—?" He waved again. "Keep going."

The houses fell away, the headlights catching only the canopy of trees above. "But I was told you were the expert on Panin—"

"*An* expert—but not *the* expert. Keep going."

"But you are old—acquaintances?" Tom conjured up the material on the desk in the study, and added it to what Audley had just said—*"My own Sheila Ellis has S to Z—she feeds me directly every Wednesday"*. "So you're not researching him, then?"

"I am not," agreed Audley. "And, to be exact, I am doubly not researching my . . . 'old acquaintance', as you put it so diplomatically, Tom."

"Not far" was stretching itself. But then, if he had learnt anything this afternoon and evening, it was that Audley seldom meant exactly what he said. "'Doubly not'? Is that some sort of algebraic lie, David? 'Minus times minus equals plus'?"

"No." Audley thought his own thoughts for a moment. "Actually . . . it just means that we're studying the possible new men in the Kremlin . . . and in the KGB, which amounts to much the same thing . . ." Suddenly he raised himself again. "On the left, about three hundred yards—you'll see a big copper beech . . . And a rather *chi-chi* carved house-name-plate attached to it . . . No—we're into the *new* men, not the geriatrics—the *has-beens*, whom Comrade Gorbachev is busy kicking upstairs . . . or downstairs into the cellars, as the case may be."

Now he could slow down legitimately. But then he began to remember the pink-stained names in Audley's cuttings, which had included *Chebrikov* and *Aliev* and *Lomako*, as well as *Shevardnadze* and his own *Shkiriatov*. "And you're just studying S to Z, anyway . . . not Panin?"

"Well . . . yes, you might say—" Audley sat up "—just there! Do you see it?"

Tom applied the brake. "Not Panin?" What those cuttings told him was that Audley had never learnt to obey orders exactly: and that was also what Jaggard and Harvey had both said. And now he believed what Harvey had said.

Audley twisted round to look behind him. "Aren't you going in? Go on—there's nothing behind, so far as I can see."

The driver's privilege was to drive, or not to drive, as he chose. "Not Panin?"

"Not Panin?" Audley echoed the question as he untwisted himself. "You see where I mean?" He pointed towards the great beech tree illuminated in the headlights. Then he looked at Tom. "No, not Panin, as it happens."

Tom met the look. "Because he's a geriatric? A has-been?" He folded his arms deliberately. "He must be as old as your Basil Cole."

"Yes. So he is." A freak reflection from the dashboard glinted redly in Audley's spectacles, as though hinting at fire behind them. "But I wasn't referring to him. He's a very different kettle of fish, is Nikolai Panin." He moved slightly, and the red fire vanished. "Basil Cole will tell you."

It was the moment to confirm Audley's perhaps erroneous suspicion that he was more than a superior bodyguard. "But I want you to tell me, David."

"Now you're being difficult."

"Not difficult—"

"Obstinate, then—"

"Not obstinate, either." Tom switched off the lights. "Say . . . I want to hear what you have to say about him first—" He lifted one hand from the other to cut Audley's reply off "—because someone shot at you, David. Not at Basil Cole. Okay?"

"Well . . . if that's what you want . . ." There was just enough half-light to convey the shrug of resignation, no more than that. "Panin is not about to defect, if that's what you're thinking, my lad—not in this age of the world!"

It would have worried him if he'd thought of it, Tom realized belatedly. Because defection was always a killing matter on the Other Side. But neither Jaggard nor Harvey had even hinted at it; and to be allowed to go so far outside the London radius by his own side laughed that suspicion out of court, in any case.

"He's an *old* Communist—an old *Red* . . . from when 'Red' meant something more than buying privilege in the Party's duty-free shops." Audley's voice was scornful out of the shadows of his face. "There aren't many of them left now—thank God!" The half-grunt, half-chuckle came from deep down inside the man again. "Do you know what an 'Ironside' is—*was*, anyway—?"

Out of nowhere, in the gathering dusk, Tom realized that he was learning about something from the past at first hand, which was out of his more recent experience. "An Ironside?"

"Cromwell's Ironsides: they fought for what they loved, and loved what they fought for. Or maybe it was the other way round." The dark outline of the head, not close-cropped but just short of hair, nodded. "Or maybe old Nikolai didn't love what he knew—I don't know . . . But he fought for it all the way from Stalingrad, or whatever they call it now—'Volgograd', or something? But I'll lay you even money it'll be *Stalingrad* again, one of these days . . . But from *there*, anyway, all the bloody way to Berlin, in '45—and *bloody* is right; across twenty-five million Russian dead. And I wouldn't defect after that—not even if I was commanding the Devil's Armed Forces, with the Hounds of Hell ready to slip!" The dark head shook again. "I remember first checking him in '69—staff officer in Khalturin's division, in Chuikov's army, all the way to Khrushchev's Twentieth Congress, and afterwards . . . It took us one hell of a long time to pin down Nikolai Panin—in fact, I'm not sure that we ever did . . . But I only studied him because he happened to cross my path, anyway. It was purely accidental—or incidental, if you like. He's never really been *our* meat. And we haven't been his either, so far as I'm aware."

The slaughterhouse image reminded Tom too vividly of Beirut realities, the blood and entrails of which were far removed from metaphor. But also it hardly fitted what Jaggard had said. "Not your . . . meat?"

"He's not a bloody First Directorate man, is what I mean. He doesn't run networks—doesn't control illegals, or recruit traitors, or anything like that . . ." Audley trailed off. But then his face came round again. "What's the biggest thing the KGB does—you tell me, Tom? What is it?"

Answering trick questions was a mug's game. "You tell me, David. I'm just a promoted minder."

"It's internal security first." Audley hadn't even wanted an answer. "Then it's disinformation—fucking up our foreign policy—when we have one . . . And now it's also probably pinching our higher technology." The old man sniffed in the darkness. "I've got a cold coming on, damn it!" He sniffed again. "Panin has always been disinformation or internal security—none of your vulgar spying for him!" Another sniff. "The first time I met him, he wasn't trying to screw *us*—he was quietly and murderously engaged in making sure that the great Red Army didn't step out of line. We weren't worth a damn—we were just there to be deceived and used . . . Or *bribed* and used—huh!" Grunt-chuckle. "I did him a favour. So, a few years later, he did me a favour. Which makes us quits, in his book."

And in yours, thought Tom. "But he wants to talk to you now."

No reply. Which made Tom glance at the dashboard. But he had switched off the lights, so he could only guess how far they were falling behind schedule.

"And he's an expert on you, David."

No reply again, for a moment. "Yes. And that's another thing that worries me." Another grunt-chuckle—but this time more grunt than chuckle. "The first time, I studied him and he repaid the compliment. Which is fair enough." Another long breath. "And we also have some reason to believe that he's taken a certain non-specialist extra-mural interest in Research and Development ever afterwards. Which is really none of his business."

"Yes?" Audley hadn't really stopped there, Tom sensed.

"Oh . . . I rather thought he tried to damage me last year." Audley shrugged.

Tom waited. "Yes?"

"Oh . . . we lost a man . . ." Audley bridled ". . . here in England, too."

"Yes?" Tom remembered what Jaggard had hinted at.

"Actually, it wasn't my fault."

He would have given good money to see the old man's face. "No?"

"No. Not that it matters whose fault it was." Audley was silent for another brief moment. "But we did a bit of research afterwards, just to find out who we owed one to, for the future."

"It wasn't a suitable case for . . . reciprocal action?"

"No." Audley took up his moment of silence again. "He didn't have red tabs on his lapels. He was just a poor bloody field officer." He looked at Tom in the darkness again. "If you catch a bullet in the line of duty they won't avenge you, Tom. If I do . . . then they will. You better bear that in mind for the next few hours."

"There's no justice in this world." But it did make horrible sense, thought Tom sadly: in Lebanon, the biblical eye-for-an-eye payment had reduced local life to a murderous all-comers chaos.

"Never was, and never will be," agreed Audley. "But we've got long memories in Research and Development—like old Fred Clinton used to say, 'the baked meats of revenge are best eaten cold'. So . . . we've got a name or two on the red side of our tablet now, anyway. And we'll dish the buggers one day, you can depend on it." He sniffed. "Killing isn't our style, we don't have the resources for it, never mind the permission. But there are others we can use who think quite differently—the French, for example—" He stopped abruptly. "But you're making me digress. Because, the point is that I got Old King Cole to check up on Panin then, because he's the resident Panin-watcher—right?"

"'M to R', you mean?"

"Just so—M to R, right!" Audley nodded in the darkness. "And he said that so far old Nikolai was still busy keeping an eye on his own side . . . That he might have given the First Directorate a bit of advice, as a consultant, but nothing more." He sniffed. "Actually, to be heart-breakingly honest, he rather put me in my place, did Basil Cole. Huh!"

"Oh?" It took an effort to imagine such an occurrence. But the lightly self-mocking admission both established Cole as someone to be reckoned with and accounted for Audley's present action satisfactorily. "How?"

"He said that Panin had bigger fish to fry than me, in his own home frying-pan. And he also said that I wasn't part of the man's job—just his hobby." Another sniff. "Somehow I find that neither flattering nor reassuring, you know." Then he sat up suddenly. "But now I'll make the old swine eat his words: he can tell us why Nikolai Andrievich is poaching in my coverts again after all these years. Right?" He rapped the dashboard sharply. "So not another word, not another question—*in with you*"

Tom engaged the gear, and turned the big car cautiously past the huge beech tree into an overgrown rhododendron drive, still thick with unswept winter leaves.

They were still a long way from Panin, but he felt better now. Or, anyway, he understood why Audley was doing what he was doing, even if it also suggested that Jaggard was unaware of a real Panin-expert in their midst, who knew more about the Russian than Audley did. But then (to be fair to Jaggard) Cole might have acquired his expertise in retirement service for Research and Development, not in his previous existence.

The headlights picked up the red reflectors of a parked car, and then Tudor black-and-white half-timbering.

"Pull round to the left," said Audley.

More piles of decaying leaves; and the house wasn't genuine Tudor, but minor stockbroker's mock-Tudor, with only just enough room for him to squeeze the Ministry Rover past the elderly Ford which was jammed against its garage doors beside the darkened house. (And he had learnt something about the arcane workings of R & D, too; about which Harvey had been half-scornful, yet oddly envious: that killing wasn't their style, but that they had long memories when there was a name to enter in the ledger of unpaid accounts.)

"It doesn't look as though anyone's home, David." He scanned the unimpressive house again: its most notable attribute was the circle of huge beech trees which surrounded it, embracing it with their enormous limbs and cutting out what was left of the last faint remnants of daylight above them.

"It wouldn't—the sitting-room's at the back." Audley opened his door. "He'll be in, don't worry—he never goes out." He started to get out, but then stopped. "He's somewhere inside a five-year drink-driving disqualification . . . not that I've ever noticed any difference in him, drunk or sober." He started to move again, and then stopped again. "Don't kid yourself, Tom—drunk or sober, he's *good*, believe you me. Fawcett was a fool for retiring him, and old Fred Clinton was nobody's fool—I wish I'd known the game he was playing, years back, in fact—" Then he grunted, and did at last lever himself out of the car.

Tom switched off the lights, and for an instant it was prematurely night. Then the half-light seeped back through the beech trees, slightly reassuring him, with Beirut as well as this afternoon in mind: this was close country, with no high-rise buildings or distant ridges allowing long-shots; and neither the Russian nor the American-Israeli night-sight image intensifiers were much use in these conditions, if he had not been quite as clever and careful in shaking off any pursuit as he thought he had been.

All the same, he was uneasy: in full daylight one could expect the worst, and plan accordingly. But after that it was a case of *negotium perambulans in tenebris*. "Let's go and meet your Basil Cole then, David."

"Okay." Audley stretched himself, oblivious of any danger, and then took three steps to the mock-Tudor door, and thumped it with his fist. "Open up there!"

Tom cringed from the battering-ram challenge: Stephen of Blois hadn't hammered on the gates of Ranulf of Caen's *motte* at Theckham more noisily than that, but half of England had heard him. Or Baldwin de Redvers certainly had—and the Bishop of Salisbury too . . . and probably Robert fitz Herbert, and Henry fitz Tracy, and William fitz Odo . . . and probably the unspeakable Earl of Chester too—

"Open up there!" Audley hammered on the door again. "Basil Cole, you drunken old bugger!"

The porch light flashed on, dousing them both in a sudden pool of yellow light which made Tom skip back out of it instinctively. (Nobody turned on lights in Lebanon: rather, if there were any lights anywhere, they turned them off, inside as well as outside; and then they didn't open the door until supplied with some very different and less offensive pass-words.)

But this door opened wide suddenly, regardless equally of insult and danger. "Yes?"

There was light inside the house, innocent of all precautions. And whoever it was in the doorway, it wasn't Basil Cole, drunk or sober—it was a woman. "What do you want?"

Audley drew himself up to answer, obviously put off by the woman, and by the coldness and unexpected question.

"Ah . . . Good evening, madam—" Then he seemed to flounder.

The wrong house? thought Tom. But that was impossible!

"Mr Cole—?" The great shoulders squared, ambushed but not defeated. "Mr Basil Cole—?" Audley's voice travelled from doubt to greater certainty. "You wouldn't be by any chance Mr Cole's daughter-in-law—?"

No answer. But there came another sound from inside the house, as of a squeaky mock-Tudor door opening.

"What is it, dear?" The new voice followed the mock-Tudor sound, not so much quavering as uncertain. "Who is it, dear?"

"It's all right—it's nothing." The younger woman in the doorway threw back her answer harshly, almost dismissively.

"My name is Audley." Now there was nothing soft about Audley's own voice: being dismissed as "nothing" was plainly not to his taste. "David Audley—"

There was a fractional pause. "David—?"

"Margaret!" Audley threw the name past the younger woman.

"Mother—" The woman tried to hit Audley's reply back at him, and away out into the evening, but she was just too late.

"David Audley!" Now there was someone else inside the doorway. "Why, David—how very kind of you!" The someone bobbed up and down behind the pearls-and-twin-set obstacle between them.

"Mother—"

"Christine, dear—you remember David Audley?" The woman-behind was not to be denied. "Come in, David—you remember Dr Audley, dear!"

"Mrs Cole—" Audley offered his hand to the obstacle "—actually, I don't think we've ever met. But Basil has told me about you, of course."

The obstacle winced, but still stood her ground obstinately, and without taking Audley's hand. "Mother, I think it might be better if—"

"And this is my colleague, Sir Thomas Arkenshaw, of the Foreign and Commonwealth Office, Mrs Cole." Audley swept the unaccepted hand round to indicate Tom, like a general revealing a hitherto masked battery of heavy guns. "Who has come all the way from London to see—"

"Sir Thomas—" The obstacle had just started to frown incredulously at Tom, but now suddenly cut Audley off "—Dr Audley, *of course*, my mother-in-law has spoken of you, as one of my late father-in-law's *oldest* friends—do *please* forgive my bad manners, Dr Audley—I *simply* didn't recognize you—but I'm sure you'll understand, in the circumstances—*in the circumstances*—" The younger Mrs Cole had to draw breath there, but she drew it so quickly that Audley only had time to open his mouth, not to speak, before she plunged on "*—in the circumstances*—my father-in-law's death was so *sudden*, I'm *sure* you'll make allowances for us—you *do* understand, *don't* you?"

"Ah . . ." Andley opened his month again, but then closed it. And then he nodded. "Yes, Mrs Cole. Believe me, I *do* understand."

"Thank you, Dr Audley." The younger Mrs Cole stood aside at last, to allow her mother-in-law to get a clear view of their visitors.

"David! And Sir Thomas—" The elderly Mrs Cole peered at Tom through smudged spectacles "—it is so good of you both to come down so soon after poor Basil's dreadful accident." She shook her head. "I still can't believe it's true—that I'm not dreaming some awful nightmare."

"Mother—"

"It's all right, dear. I'm not going to embarrass you, or disgrace myself."

"I didn't mean that, Mother. I'm here, is what I was going to say."

"And so you are, dear—and I'm very grateful." The old lady smiled at Tom with her mouth as she blinked at him. "Having family is a great comfort, Sir Thomas. And now I know that his old friends and colleagues care too—enough to come all the way from London so quickly . . . when I know how busy you all are—" She transferred the smile to Audley "—although there really isn't anything you can do. My dear daughter-in-law—who is more like a daughter—has been so good. So you see, you've really had a wasted journey, David. I'm quite all right."

"I'm sure you are, Margaret," agreed Audley gently. "And you won't need to worry about anything at our end. Colonel Butler and I will deal with everything there. But . . . if there *is* anything—?" Audley rolled an eye at Tom. "I suppose there are formalities here . . ."

"There isn't anything—" The younger Mrs Cole stopped suddenly. "But if you'd like to take Dr Audley through to the sitting room—the coffee's just percolated—perhaps you would carry the tray for me, Sir Thomas?'

There was an edge of command in her voice. But more than that, she was deliberately splitting them. "I'd be pleased to, Mrs Cole."

"Yes . . ." The old lady blinked at Audley. "Or perhaps you'd like something stronger, David?"

"Coffee will do, Mother." The cutting edge flashed. "Dr Audley is driving, remember."

"Yes, dear . . . of course. Do please stay, David. And I'll tell you all about it—no, it's all right . . . It'll be good to talk to someone—" She gestured Audley onwards "—it was all so silly—so *unnecessary*—"

"Yes." The younger Mrs Cole watched Audley and her mother-in-law cross the hallway, to disappear through a mock-Tudor doorway. "So unnecessary—you can say that again!" She addressed the closing door with cold venom before turning back to Tom. "This way, Sir Thomas."

Tom followed her meekly in the opposite direction. Audley was about to get it all. But he, also, was about to get something. Only his share might not be so palatable, he suspected.

The woman touched the light-switch as she entered the room. For an instant nothing happened, then an overhead strip-light flashed, and flashed again before coming on, reminding him quite inappropriately of the flashing gunfire in the hills above Beirut.

It was just a kitchen: a rather tatty kitchen, styled in the last-word fashion of 1935, with all the attendant mess of a sudden and unexpected bereavement in the house: unwashed breakfast crockery, and innumerable coffee cups on the draining-board.

The woman turned on him in the harsh light: a handsome, yet utterly unfeminine woman, altogether different from his own dear Willy—*Willy-on-the-town now, probably with that damned naval attaché*—

Mustn't think of Willy. Must look innocent. "Coffee cups—?" At least he could smell the coffee percolating.

"Damn the coffee cups!" she blazed at him. "You aren't the old swine's 'very kind' colleagues, are you? You haven't any idea of what's happened —have you?"

"No. We haven't." It was no good lying to this woman, any more than it was any good lying to Willy. And it was particularly no good because she'd obviously heard Audley's unwise exhortation to his '*drunken old bugger'* and her *'old swine'* through the thinness of the mock-Tudor front door.

"Who are you?"

He was used to this sort of doubt, because he didn't look like the 'Sir Thomas Arkenshaw' people expected. But it was beginning to become irritating, that disbelief. "You are Mrs Cole, are you? Basil Cole's daughter-in-law?"

"Yes—"

"Then I am Sir Thomas Arkenshaw, of the Foreign and Commonwealth Office, Mrs Cole." He reached inside his jacket. "And this is my identification."

She examined his warrant card carefully before returning it to him. So she had guts. But he knew that already.

"Thank you . . . *Sir* Thomas Arkenshaw." She watched him return it to its place. But then she waited.

And she wasn't scared, thought Tom. So he had to be brutal. "How did he die, Mrs Cole?"

"He fell out of a tree."

She wasn't scared. But there was more to it than that. "He did *what*—?"

"He fell out of a tree." She repeated the statement so obstinately that he was all the more certain of its inadequacy.

"What the devil was he doing up a tree, Mrs Cole?"

"He was cutting off a branch." She grimaced at him. "All these old trees round the house . . . the copper beeches . . . they were planted back in the 1930s, Sir Thomas. And the fool who planted them stuck them too close to the house." She reached to turn the percolator off, on the working-surface beside her. "So there was this big one, at the back . . . He had put a ladder up, to get at it. He should have got a professional tree-feller to do it."

Tom was unbearably reminded of an Irish joke about "tree-fellers", the punch-line of which he couldn't remember, except that it had something to do with "three fellas" and "tree-fellers". But that had nothing to do with the fixed expression on her face.

Her nerve broke as he tried to remember the end of the joke. "When he cut the limb, it knocked him off the ladder . . . so it seems." She uncoupled the coffee percolator from its plug. "At least, that's what the policeman thought . . . Apparently, people are always killing themselves, messing about with trees."

Not good enough! She was a fine-looking woman, high-breasted and with a high IQ to match the lift of the twin-set under the pearls; and she had quite properly defended her mother-in-law from their blundering ignorance in the doorway, when they hadn't known what was happening.

"But there is something you can do, Sir Thomas." She recognized his doubt, and faced it honestly, breasts and IQ lifting together. "I never imagined that I'd ask such a thing. But it seems I can."

Tom watched her reach towards a line of cups hanging on hooks under an old-fashioned glass-fronted cupboard and then search for matching saucers. "Ask what thing, Mrs Cole?"

She looked at him. "There'll be an inquest, of course."

He wondered how much she knew about her father-in-law's work. Or, if she didn't know, whether she had guessed. "Yes. But with an accident like this, it'll be pretty much a formality."

She moistened her upper lip. "It may not be, I'm afraid."

He could legitimately frown now. "Are you suggesting it wasn't an accident, Mrs Cole? But you said . . . the policeman said—?"

"I'm not suggesting anything. But . . . my father-in-law worked for the Ministry of Defence, I believe—even after his retirement. I am presuming that you have influence. Isn't that the way the world works?"

Tom frowned again. "What do you want, Mrs Cole?"

She stared at him, her mouth primly compressed. "It would be better . . . for my mother-in-law's sake, it would be better if certain questions weren't asked at the inquest. It won't hurt anyone if they aren't asked—no harm or injustice will be done." She drew a deep breath. "You see, Sir Thomas, I know exactly how he fell out of the tree—and why."

Well, that was something! thought Tom gratefully. But then his gratitude evaporated as he realized that what he'd been thinking and what she evidently thought no longer matched at all. And one of them had to be wrong.

V

"WELL?" SAID AUDLEY.

Tom caught a last glimpse of the two Mrs Coles in his rear-view mirror: they were standing together in their doorway in a pool of yellow light. Then the dark mass of the rhododendron bushes erased them.

"Well?" Audley stabbed the word at him again. "What did she want to say to you which she couldn't say in front of the widow?"

The digital clock registered 7.30, and Tom's stomach confirmed its accuracy. But now there were more pressing matters than hunger. "She wanted me to nobble the coroner before the inquest."

"Indeed?" Audley pointed. "Go back to the village and stop at the pub. I want to make a phone call or two. There's a call box just opposite."

That was convenient. "Okay." But a little honest curiosity would be natural. "May one ask to whom?"

"One may. When one has answered my first question more adequately."

"The old lady didn't tell you, then?"

"That he fell off a ladder, do you mean?"

"No. That he was drunk when he fell."

"Ah . . . No, she didn't add that ingenious embellishment." Audley shifted slightly. "But, since he only fell this morning, just how has that been so quickly established beyond a peradventure?" Audley sniffed. "Although I can now well understand why Mrs Cole *junior* might not wish such choice circumstantial evidence to be emblazoned in the local paper." Another sniff. "But don't tell me! He smelt like a distillery and had an empty bottle of Johnnie Walker stuffed in his pocket—right?"

"Substantially right. Except it was twelve-year-old Bunnahabhain malt, and it was only half empty. And it was in his garden shed, complete with a half-full tumbler." Tom could see the lights of the village ahead. And there was nothing behind. "Christine Cole says it'll make her mother-in-law very unhappy, if that comes out."

"Bunkum! The old girl's used to what's always been the truth—it will make Mrs Christine Cole, who is teetotal, and the Reverend Brian Cole, her husband, unhappy . . . although they might equally have taken the view that the poor old devil ought to be held up as a horrible example of the evils of drink in death, just as he had been in life. That would be what I would have expected, actually—hmmm . . . In fact, I would have bet on it even, now that I come to think about it. *Damn!*" Audley thumped the dashboard. *"Damn!"*

"What?" The man's sudden vehemence took Tom by surprise.

"I was just being mildly ashamed of myself for being flippant. He was a drunken, difficult old devil. But—" He pointed again "—the pub's just ahead, on the corner—remember?"

"But what?" They were back to the awkward turning, and there was still nothing behind. "But what?"

Audley ignored him.

He negotiated the corner and swung the car onto the pub forecourt.

Audley still didn't reply, and made no effort to move. *"Damn!"*

Very well! Tom decided. "But that didn't give anyone the right to kill him, were you going to say?"

Audley turned slowly towards him. "Evidence?"

"I hardly think there'll be any. Not if it was professionally done. Is that what you think, David?"

Audley opened his door. "What I think is that I want to make a couple of phone-calls. Have you got any change?"

"No." Tom knew that his pocket was full of coins. "Don't use the call-box. Go and phone from the pub. They'll give you change."

Audley stared at him. "Is that minder's rules?"

"Just a precaution, nothing more."

"Okay. Come in and have a drink. I need one."

Tom shook his head. "I'll mind the car. Just another precaution—okay?"

He waited for two agonizingly long minutes after Audley had disappeared into the pub before going across to the call-box himself. Only two minutes was a risk, he knew. But more than that opened up a risk later on, depending on how quickly the old man managed to make his own calls. But both risks were now outweighed by a greater one, in any case.

He dialled and fed in plenty of money.

"Consolidated Slide-Dimmers. Can I help you?"

"This is Thomas Arkenshaw for Henry Jaggard. And I'm in a public call-box, and I'm in a hurry." He had to trust Garrod Harvey's promise. "Put me through."

"Putting you through directly, Sir Thomas."

The only trouble was that Jaggard might well expect him to be phoning from halfway to the West Country, thought Tom. But if Jaggard didn't ask, then he wouldn't say.

"Hullo, Tom!" Jaggard sounded almost genial. "All well?"

Tom changed his mind. "I'm in a call-box in Hampshire, just off the A34. And I've got maybe three minutes."

"What the hell—" Jaggard stopped. "Yes?"

"Do you know of a man named Cole? Basil Cole? He used to work for one of your predecessors."

"What's—" Jaggard stopped again. "Go on."

"Audley wanted to talk to him, about his old comrade. He said Cole was the expert now, not him. Only as of this morning Cole isn't talking to anyone ever again."

"How?"

Well, at least Jaggard was getting the message. "He fell off a ladder and broke his neck. Apparently he was drunk at the time."

"So—?" Jaggard evinced neither surprise nor regret. "Is that true?"

"No one saw it happen. Audley doesn't believe it. And neither do I."

"Why not? He was always a drinker." Jaggard pressed on. "Have you talked to the police? What do they say?"

"Everyone thinks it was an accident." Easy was not going to do it, decided Tom. "Christ! We've already been shot at! What else do you want?"

"Steady on, Tom! We'll check on Cole—"

"The hell you will! Audley's in a pub across the road from here doing just that, for a guess. If your people run into his people he'll know I've blown the whistle on him." Tom stared uneasily across the road towards the lights of the pub. "I want back-up on Exmoor. Because I can't guarantee satisfaction on my own, not now."

There was a fractional pause. "Does Audley want help? Has he asked for it?"

The welcoming lights of the pub mocked him. Audley might just be asking for just that now. But somehow he doubted it, after the way the old man had dismissed his police escort—and, for that matter, after he'd been so outraged that anyone should dare to take a shot at him. "I don't know what Audley wants. But *I* want back-up, I'm telling you. Give me back Harvey, at the very least."

"No. Harvey was only marked to take you to Audley—and he's busy now. But in any case . . . this is strictly a Research and Development matter now."

"Is it?" *Steady on Arkenshaw!* Tom admonished himself. "Then what am I doing in the middle of it?"

Jaggard made a snuffling sound. Or maybe it was the line. "You've been seconded, Tom. Didn't I tell you? Just temporarily, anyway—Frobisher's agreement. And Colonel Butler's . . . So if Audley wants help, or you want back-up, the request must go to Butler through Audley. I'm sorry, but that's the protocol. Is that clearly understood?"

Tom didn't think it had been the line. "So I don't have to report to you any more?" *Clearly understood.* "Yes." Or maybe, on second thoughts, *not so clearly understood!* "Just order me who I have to protect: Audley or his old comrade—if it comes to the crunch, and they start throwing punches at each other? Just give me that order."

"Panin isn't after him. He wants to talk to him." Jaggard's tone softened. "Look—"

"Someone's after him." Then Tom came to a much greater fear. "And someone already knows too much about what we're doing."

The third pause turned him back towards the pub: he had to be on borrowed time now.

"Who knew you were going to see Basil Cole?"

Jaggard was taking him seriously at last. But now he had only a useless answer. "No one. Or . . . no one except Audley."

"Right. Then Cole may actually have had an accident. Because drunks do have accidents. But we'll check up on that—and don't worry, because we'll check very circumspectly. Right?" But again Jaggard didn't wait for an answer. "And as for that bullet of Audley's . . . don't you worry about that."

Oh, great! Tom opened his mouth to swear. But then he knew that he was too late.

"Listen, Tom: Audley's made a fair few enemies in his time. So we don't think it came from the Other Side. There are lots of other candidates—"

It was a million years too late: Audley was outside the pub, peering into the car. And in another half-second he would be looking across the road.

"Are you listening, Tom?"

He turned his back towards Audley. "I'm putting the phone down now —I'll call you again when I get the chance." He cut the line, while still holding the receiver to his ear, and stared at the dialling instructions. Then he saw the spare coins he had piled up, which he had told Audley he hadn't got. But then, that was a minor lie compared with the phone-call itself: he could always have said he'd reversed the charges—

Reversed the charges—!

As the memory came back to him he knew he hadn't time for arguments. All he could remember, as he fed the coins into the box, was all those reversed charges he had made in his student youth.

The ringing note sounded in his ear. It was a long-shot, but he hadn't had any luck today, so he was in line for some now. And at least Audley hadn't seen him put the phone down and then pick it up again.

The ringing sound stopped as the phone at the other end was lifted: now he had time only for two quick questions, and two quick answers, and then one quick tapestry of falsehoods which he must hope would be believed—

He opened the door of the phone-box and beckoned across the road. "David! Come over here!"

Audley looked up and down the darkened village street, in which the main illumination was from the pub itself. Which was fair enough, since he'd been warned off the phone-box once already.

"Over here, David!" Audley's caution gave him time for a few more words. And then—"Hold on—here he is now—" The look of naked and unashamed suspicion on the old man's face (which his face was well-battered to demonstrate) encouraged him to shout for both of them "—my mother would like a word with you, David—" He thrust the receiver at Audley "—here she is now—"

He withdrew a few yards from the call-box, out of pretended tact, but actually because there was nothing he could do now. It all depended on her wits—

("*Yes?*" She had addressed the phone peremptorily, as she always did, as though it was an inadequately-trained servant who had disturbed her rest.)

("*Mamusia?*" That hadn't been the first question, but it came out automatically, from his enormous relief, now that he had a chance. "*Do you remember an old boyfriend of yours named David Audley? A big chap—?*")

("*Darling boy—! How lovely! Who did you say?*")

(If there was anything he hated, but about which he could do nothing, it was being addressed as "Darling boy!", like a character out of a play written even before her time. But this wasn't a moment for recrimination: it was the moment for *Question One*, repeated.)

("*Mamusia—do you remember David Audley? Answer me quickly!*")

("*David—David!*" At the first "David" Tom hung on a thread. But at the second one he was on a ship's cable. "*Darling—of course I do! From long before you were born, darling boy! From Cambridge—before I met your father . . . Or . . . perhaps not quite before—*")

(Audley was moving now—)

("*I once went to a ball with him—David Audley . . .*" Question Two started to become redundant before it was asked. "*Darling—I went as 'Beauty' . . . and he went as 'The Beast'—how could I forget him! Where did you meet him?*")

(*Scratch Question Two!*)

("*Mamusia, he's here now, waiting to talk to you. And he's my boss. So just tell him I've been talking to you for the last five minutes—don't argue just tell him that—okay?"* No more time. "Hold on—here he is now—")

In the end he dawdled back to the car, plagued by the same old mixture of love and exasperation and admiration and doubt which he had always —or, not always, but at least latterly—shared about her with Dad: she was gorgeous undoubtedly (and what she must have been like in Audley's youth, and in the full flush of her own, taxed his imagination beyond its furthest limits); but she had always—no, not always, but sometimes—seemed to him the best and worst of mothers, by turns affectionate and uncaring, tactful and tactless, and intellectually brilliant and embarrassingly feckless: all he had ever known was that he could never be sure of what he knew about her—that he could never be sure of anything. And that had often been good fun, but not always. And now was one of those not-always times, although now he had only himself to blame—

But Audley was coming back now—

Audley got into the car, breathing heavily. "That was an exceptionally low-down action." The old man fumbled for his safety-belt, and fumbled even more before he snapped it home. "'Darling Boy'—'Darling Boy'?" He looked at Tom in the darkness. "But I thought the phone-box was out-of-bounds—?"

But he didn't sound angry, thought Tom. In fact, he sounded foolishly at ease, even happy, after that "low-down action". So perhaps, just this important once, she had been not only at her most affectionate, but also tactful and brilliant—not (as she always had been with Willy's predecessors) the other way round.

"Yes—I'm sorry, David." That was true, and even doubly true: he had said that, but more than that he was vestigially sorry that he had played so very dirty; because, if *calling* her had been a fearful risk, *using* her against the old man hadn't been cricket in Dad's Cambridge definition of the game; but, then again, in his own definition—and in Mamusia's—*and, for that matter in Audley's*—in all of those, Dad's definition didn't apply: none of them had played Dad's Cambridge game for a long time, if ever.

"Sorry?" Audley wasn't so happy now. "I thought you Diplomatic Protection people were more into 'safe' than 'sorry'?"

"Yes." Now he really was sorry, as he realized he must be more careful with Audley. "But I didn't call her until I was sufficiently sure the road was clear. And I really don't think my mother's London line is insecure —not unless your old comrade is much better informed than he has any right to be, David."

"No?" Audley was even unhappier. But at least he had been safely diverted from the true truth. "No, I might grant you that, Darling Boy. Or . . . I might, if you can tell me who *is* better informed—eh?"

They were far from the truth, safely. But they were right into the middle of a much more worrying truth.

Tom backed the car out, and started to drive. "Yes." He needed the fastest road to the M4 now, to the West Country, when Audley would be taking the M3 to London as his objective. But he wanted a lot more out of the man before that deviation became apparent; so Audley's attention to road signs and sign-posts must be diverted for the time being.

"Yes." The trouble was that Audley was quite right, whatever convenient possibilities Jaggard chose to imagine: *someone* had got to Basil Cole, and very efficiently, even before *someone* had got to David Audley, even though their cruder solution to that assignment had failed disgracefully. "Maybe you should talk to Colonel Butler." The road was dark ahead, and dark behind: it was the hour when the early evening drinkers were drinking, and the rest of the world was settling down for its night's television, or putting its children to bed, or having its supper. "You might even ask him for some more protection, while you're about it. In fact, that's what I'd advise now, professionally."

"Even though we're not being followed?" Audley sat back comfortably, more relaxed again. "Darling Boy?"

"Yes." If Audley thought he was going to rise to Mamusia's dreadful term of endearment he was much mistaken. "But if they already know exactly how you think, they hardly need to follow us, do they?"

"Very true. And *rather* disconcerting, I agree." Audley fumbled down beside his seat. "How does one put oneself into the reclining position, Darling Boy?"

"You're not going to go to sleep on me, are you?" The thought of Audley snoring beside him during the long drive to the West Country was off-putting.

"I thought I might shut my eyes for an hour." Audley found the seat adjuster and sank out of sight. "We elderly persons . . . we don't need so much sleep, but the occasional cat-nap works wonders . . . Just wake me up on the edge of London. Then I'll make a phone-call."

"To Colonel Butler?" In return for getting his own way Tom was prepared to put up with the old man's snoring. "For back-up?"

"No. He can't spare anyone . . . Research and Development doesn't carry assorted minders on its payroll, we all work for our living . . . And I don't want anyone. Especially not any of the unemployed hoodlums Jack would have to hire." Audley sneezed explosively. "You will make the phone-call actually, Tom—to inform Nikolai Panin that we are changing the rendezvous, wherever it may be that has been agreed. Okay?"

"What?" The A34 advance warning sign flashed up ahead.

"You're quite right . . . somebody is too damn-better informed." Audley's voice was starting to get sleepy. "So we'll start out by meeting him on *my* chosen ground, where you won't have to have eyes in the back of your head . . . Then we won't need any of your 'back-up' . . . And too many people already seem to know too much, that I do know. So then we can start putting a stop to that. So . . . just wake me up between Chertsey and Sunbury, there's a good fellow, eh?"

Audley thought he was heading for the M3 to London, to the east, not the M4 to Bristol, in the west, and the M5 and distant Exmoor after that. And there was a lot more also that the poor old devil thought which was just as much in the opposite direction, most of all regarding his Danny's Darling Boy, who had somehow become one of Henry Jaggard's hoodlums—

"In Research and Development our job is to *think*, not to risk our probably over-valued necks protecting even less-valuable necks in foreign hell-holes . . . like you, Tom . . . 'poor Tom' . . ." murmured Audley. "*Thinking's* much more agreeable than *worrying* . . . You tend to enjoy a better class of life that way . . ." he trailed off into what was more likely oblivion than thought.

Tom realized that he had just begun to fall into the error of being slightly sorry for Audley, even while he had at the same time been beginning to savour the thought of the old man waking up on the other side of England from suburban London and whatever ground he'd chosen for his rendezvous with the Russian. But suddenly he became aware of a greater error—or not so much an error as a hideous mistake: he might no longer be sure where his duty lay in relation to Audley and Jaggard, but nagging regrets and minor gratifications paled into nothing beside the need to keep this man alive. And, after that bullet and Basil Cole's untimely death, his duty was inescapable.

"We're not going to London, David. We're going to Exmoor."

"What?" Audley swallowed the word.

"I said 'We're not going to London'—"

Tom hit the foot-brake to jerk Audley into wakefulness.

"*What?*" The old man tried to sit up, but couldn't "To . . . *where?*"

"To Exmoor, David. Panin's meeting us at Holcombe Bridge—the Green Man Hotel, Holcombe Bridge, on Exmoor." He glanced at the digital clock. "Actually, we should be meeting him about now. So I will have to stop before long, because it's going to take me all of three hours to get there. Apart from warning Panin that we're going to be late I need to make sure they don't let our rooms to someone else."

Audley was struggling to readjust his seat, fumbling and mumbling at the same time.

"It's a good hotel, anyway," continued Tom with false cheerfulness as the old man's mumble deepened to a thunderous growl. "It's in Egon Ronay and Rubinstein, and the Good Food Guide." Harvey had been envious, indeed. "So we shall at least be comfortable, David."

"Bugger that!" Just as he seemed about to resort to brute force Audley was jerked upright. But then, somewhat to Tom's surprise, the thunder died away into a silence which made him more nervous. Because now at last he had somehow pressed the button, and he sensed the man's thoughts rocketting up, silently because they had left sound behind. And once that rocket went up, no one knew where it would come down—Jaggard and Harvey were agreed on that. And that, of course, was why he was here.

"I'm sorry, David—"

"Don't be sorry." Audley's voice was in neutral now, neither angry nor friendly. "Let me get things straight: your job is to look after me, and get me to Nikolai Andrievich . . . and to learn, mark and inwardly digest whatever may pass between us—have I got that right?"

The rocket was up, and in orbit. "Well . . . not quite. I only have to be present because they've got someone with Panin—because that's the deal." Shrugging in the dark was useless. "They don't trust his loyalty as much as you do . . . of course."

"Of course. Whereas *my* loyalty is beyond suspicion . . . of course. Like yours?"

"What?" Just as he had shrugged unseen, so Audley must have nodded ironic agreement unseen.

"So who are you working for, at this precise but nebulous moment, Tom Arkenshaw? To whom do you report back, at regular intervals?"

At least he had an answer to that now. "I'm seconded to Research and Development—Mr Frobisher and Colonel Butler have both agreed to that." The half-truth of that chained him fast. "I have no instructions from Colonel Butler. But maybe I should have. Next time you call him you might ask him if he'd like me to—what was it?—'learn, mark and inwardly digest'? But isn't that a misquotation? Isn't it 'read', not 'learn' —?" But maybe it was a mistake to be clever. "But I am sorry, David: I should have told you about Exmoor before. Just . . . things got in the way, that's all."

"Yes." The ensuing silence suggested that Audley had noted what he'd said, but without either agreeing with or accepting it. "So . . . they've let him run free. And so have we." Audley spoke to himself.

"Panin?" Tom decided to accept the question. "I gather he has some sort of diplomatic status. *Cultural*-diplomatic status, anyway."

"Oh yes?" Audley perked up, as though his brutish minder had shown an unlooked-for vestige of intelligence. "Cultural—of course!"

That had been another nod-in-the-dark. "Something to do with an exhibition there's going to be in the BM next year, I think." Tom gave him a matching nod. "The ancient Scythians, would it be? He is a genuine scholar, I believe. Or he was, in the dim and distant past, wasn't he?"

"Uh-huh. Weren't we all?" Audley sniffed. "In the dim and distant past . . ." He trailed off into silence again.

"I never was." Tom had to break the silence.

"No?" The old man came back to him abruptly. "Don't languages count as scholarship? Manchester University, wasn't it? Russian and French there? And English and Polish before. And how many more now? Plus Latin at Waltham School, of course—they'd never let a linguist go without a dead language in his knapsack, would they! So how many is that then—seven? Eight?"

With the question of his present allegiance unresolved, he was being reminded that the old man had done his homework on *Arkenshaw, Thomas Wladyslaw Archibald*. "Give or take a couple." He remembered the *Caesar* on Audley's desk. "But my Latin's a bit rusty now, like yours, David. So if we meet one of the *arcani*, or the *frumentarii*, sniffing around Exmoor, just don't rely on me as an interpreter."

"Don't knock your talent, Darling Boy. 'The gift of tongues' is more of a negotiable asset than a nodding acquaintance with medieval history —or Ancient Scythia. If you blot your copybook with Frobisher, someone will always give you a job." Sniff. "Come to that, Jack Butler certainly would! He's always on the look-out for people who can read between the foreign lines, not just translate them. Especially if I put in a good word for you."

There was something odd here. "Are you offering me a job? Or merely bribing me, David?"

"Do you need bribing? Didn't your late father do rather well with his merchant banking? Wasn't he in on the Great Singapore Miracle—and a good friend of Lee Kwan Yoo?" The old man's inside information was offered sardonically. "Or has your dear mother got all the loot? But then . . . she sounded most affectionate. And you are the only son of your house—?"

The old devil was laying it on a bit thick. "Money isn't everything."

"Isn't it? Now, that is a great untruth beloved of those who have never been short of a buck. Because there's always a bill for what you want . . . always supposing you're wise enough—or lucky enough—to know what's good for you, apart from what you want . . . But there's always a bill—like self-respect, or honour, or peace of mind, or some such little thing . . . or talent wasted, even . . . Believe me, I know, Tom. Because I have been poor—or briefly embarrassed, anyway. And I may well have lost something then, while I was busy *disembarrassing* myself . . . before I got lucky again—" Audley caught himself quickly. "But that's ancient history, before your time. So . . . *no*, I'm not bribing you. Because Jack Butler won't make you rich. At least . . . not unless you would count plenty of spare time in which to study those exceedingly esoteric *mottes* and *baileys* of yours—huh!" Audley chuckled throatily. "Now, if *that* isn't scholarship . . . But have you published anything yet, Tom? Wasn't there something just recently?"

Christ! These weren't defences! thought Tom. *Somehow, Audley had reversed their roles, so that now he was the besieger, softening him up with mangonels and ballistas and trebuchets and belfreys—*

"I had an article in *History Today* not long ago—" Short of a clever answer at short notice he was only able to defend himself conventionally and inadequately "—on Ranulf of Caen's adulterine castle-building." He felt his defences weakening under Audley's well-informed probing, much as Ranulf's own had so quickly crumbled at Thackham under King Stephen's lightning assault.

"Ranulf of *Caen*?" Audley pondered the name for a moment. "Now, Ranulf of *Chester* I know . . . Interesting man, that. But really rather before my own prime period, of course . . . But Ranulf of *Caen* . . . He wouldn't by any remote chance be the double-agent in Stephen's army at Oxford in '42? The one who fixed it so that the Empress Matilda could escape—when the old harpy shinned down the castle walls in a white sheet in the snow, in '42?"

Audley knew too damn much. "It could have been him, yes."

"Uh-huh?" Audley pretended to be pleased. "You know, I've always had a weakness for King Stephen. A weak and foolish man, I know—always making the wrong decision if it was the easy one. And always good at starting things, but never finishing them properly. *And* he had a shifty streak, I know . . . But not *really* a bad chap—probably would have made a good fast wing three-quarter on a club rugby tour. And good value in the pub afterwards . . . although I certainly wouldn't have let him organize the tour, I agree." Sniff. "But if that's your period, Tom, the man you ought to study is John Marshall, the father of my great hero, William Marshall—John Marshall goes right the way through the whole Stephen-and-Matilda anarchy-period. Right down into *my* period too, actually. Because he turns up at the Council of Northampton in his old age, as a back-room fixer in Henry II's showdown with Thomas Becket. It's a bloody marvel someone hadn't topped him by then—he was a bad bugger—a *real* Norman . . . Whereas my William was the best knight in Christendom." Sniff. "An interesting thing, is that our own dear Jack Butler is the living and actual reincarnation of my old William. Which is why I dedicated my little book on William to our Jack, of course."

Now *that* was curious—and in a much more real way. Because, according to Harvey, Colonel Butler had got the director's job in Research and Development a few years back, when Audley himself had been in line for it. Yet Audley's affection for his rival was evident.

"Yes." Audley paused as the motorway warning signs flashed in the headlights, offering them *London* or *The West*, among closer and homelier advice, plus the mileage information that Bristol and Exeter, and therefore *Nikolai Andrievich Panin*, were still a long way away. "Yes, the great comfort of William Marshall— 'the best knight that ever lived', was what Archbishop Langton said of him after he died, Tom; and Langton knew him pretty damn well, too—the great comfort is that, quite contrary to the custom-and-practice of the age . . . the Norman Age, and our age too . . . William always played a straight bat—kept faith, was always loyal to his salt, and his King, and his God—but came out on top of the heap, nevertheless!"

Tom was still thinking of Colonel Butler: to inspire this sort of affection in a devious old devil like Audley, he must be something special.

"But I still have a sneaking admiration—or a *sneaky* admiration—for William's father, who was generally thought to be a right blackguard: 'a limb of hell and the root of all evil', is how he's described in *Gesta Stephani*. Do you recall that, Tom?"

Tom was saved from having to reply by the problem of filtering off the almost-empty A34 on to the racing westwards traffic of the motorway, which was escaping from London all the faster because its drivers were already late for their weekends at this hour of the evening.

"He was a good soldier—and a brave one . . . Left for dead, minus an eye from molten lead, covering Matilda's retreat to Ludgershall . . . Maybe he did change sides a time or two—like your friend Ranulf of Caen . . . And he certainly wasn't very fatherly to young William, at the siege of Newbury—Newbury, wasn't it?" Mercifully, Audley didn't expect an answer now, but merely sniffed his characteristic sniff. "I reckon he knew Stephen was far too kind-hearted to execute his hostages . . . But then Stephen is a good example of your fundamentally *decent* chap who is also a *fundamental* idiot, when it comes to politics . . . So perhaps John Marshall wasn't so unspeakable at Newbury, when Stephen threatened to hang little William before the castle wall—you remember? And John said he had hammers and anvils to forge a better son than William—? 'Hammers and anvils', indeed! Dirty devil!"

Was that in *Gesta Stephani?* Tom put his foot down, irritated by his inadequacy. "I'm more into fortification than politics, David . . . actually."

"Ah . . . yes . . ." Audley settled himself down. "Now . . . that is a rather impressive *motte* at Oxford, isn't it? Just opposite that architectural monstrosity of Nuffield College—'the spirit is willing, but the flèche is weak', don't they say? With Oxford Gaol in the *bailey*—and St George's Tower at the back? Is that Matilda's Castle?"

Was he being tested? "There were shell-walls in the Oxford *motte*. And *Gesta Stephani* says there was water all round, plus marshes—the *Gesta* says Stephen swam the river under fire, to take the city . . . Doesn't it, David?"

"Does it? But he didn't take the castle . . . Would his siege-works have been roughly where Nuffield College is now?" For a moment Audley sounded genuinely interested. "But then the water-table at Oxford must have been very different then—to get a wet-moat up round the mound, surely? Don't you have to go uphill, towards the appalling Westgate shopping centre?" Then his voice faded. "Not that it matters . . . since Matilda got away, down her rope, in the snow, to Wallingford Castle—didn't she—?"

Wallingford had been the key strong-point on the upper Thames, the great strategic medieval honour of the region—

Damn! What the hell was Audley up to?

"In the snow . . ." Audley murmured the words to himself, but with a different emphasis, as though they had reminded him of some other White Christmas in Oxford, long after the Empress Matilda had contested Oxford and England with Stephen of Blois ". . . in the snow in Oxford? But now we have Russians, with snow on their boots, on Exmoor . . . But why on Exmoor, Tom?"

Audley had got there simultaneously, though in a different way. "I don't know, David. But that's where he wants to meet you."

"I believe you. Because, for the time being . . . and maybe for your dear mother's sake . . . I choose to believe you. But also because I don't really have much choice, at this moment—do I?"

They were settled in the fast lane now, with uneven lines of red rear-lights stretching far ahead of them, to be overtaken, while a matching line of yellow-white headlights whipped past them on the oncoming lanes to the right. So there was the twentieth century and sudden death a few yards away; but there was the twelfth century, with all its very different, yet nonetheless human, calculations of ends against middles, and loyalties and affections, still in the background of both their minds. And he had nothing to say about that.

"Which leaves me with four questions, Tom." Unlike the Empress Matilda and King Stephen, and even unlike the Marshalls, John and William, and even Ranulf of Caen, poor old David Audley had no strong *motte and bailey* into which he could prudently withdraw: he was out in the open, committed to a *parlay* with the enemy in unknown territory. But at least he knew it now.

"Only four?" Yet, as a good medievalist, the old man would have known better than to put his trust in stone and mortar, never mind an earthen rampart and a wooden palisade: there was no strong place couldn't be taken, whether by force or guile or treachery: "the stronger the keep, the stronger the prison", Stephen of Blois had once warned Ranulf of Caen.

"Four to start with, anyway." Sniff. "Like . . . *why you*, Tom Arkenshaw? for a start—eh?"

"Me?" Tom flashed the car in front out of his way. In the medieval analysis he represented Jaggard's guile rather than the enemy's treachery. But it might yet amount to the same thing, near enough. "I thought we'd dealt with me: I'm just a slightly superior minder, aren't I?"

"Are you?" Audley waited until the car ahead had surrendered its illegal 90-mph to their dangerous 100. "Well . . . time will tell—eh?" At last he found his handkerchief, and blew his nose comprehensively. "'*Times levelled line shews man's foul misdeeds*' – Euripides?"

Nasty! thought Tom. "Very true, David. And – '*Somewhere behind Space and Time . . . Is wetter water, slimier slime*'—Rupert Brooke?" But as that didn't really mean anything, better to press on before Audley came to that conclusion also. "And Question Two, David?"

But Rupert Brooke stopped Audley in his tracks; and now there was a terrifying clot of heavy vehicles playing Grand Prix with an express coach making up lost time for Bristol, and shuddering the car with their slipstreams as he tried to reach the relative safety of open motorway beyond. "Question Two, David?"

"Yes . . ." Audley waited until they had broken through. "*Why me?* is next. But I suppose I can't expect you to attempt to answer, if you really don't know the answer to Question One—or even if you do . . . or you think you do." He sniffed again. But then he found his handkerchief and blew his nose at last. "But maybe one answer to 'Why Audley?' is quite simply 'Panin'. Only that rather begs the answer to the third and most important question. Which is *Why Panin?*" He tried for a moment to return his handkerchief to his pocket, but then gave up the struggle, against the restriction of his seat-belt. "But at least he gives us a clue, does old Nikolai: with him at least we know who we're dealing with."

Better just to drive (and hope that there weren't any unmarked police speed-traps), and listen (and just listen). "But I thought you needed Basil Cole, to tell you about Panin?"

"So I do—or, so I did . . . But I've got someone else looking into that now . . . How long have we got, before you get me to wherever it is?"

Tom looked down at the little green numbers on the dashboard. "Not very long—unless we get stopped for speeding." The thought of a dilettante crew like Research and Development extending itself over the weekend was far from comforting. "You've got someone good on him, have you?"

"Yes. I have." The old man became lofty. "How long?"

Tom glanced at the time again, and estimated it against distance; and that was no problem for nine-tenths of the journey, for all great roads were the same at night, motorway or autobahn, autoroute or autostrada. It was only that last tenth, in the wilds of Exmoor somewhere beyond Tiverton, which was imponderable. "Maybe three hours." The darkness was a pity, as well as the lost time: no chance now of taking in Robert de Bampton's great *motte*, which King Stephen had besieged in '35, just north of Tiverton. "Who, David?"

"Who—what, Tom?"

"Who have you got checking on Panin now?"

"Ah . . . now, you tell me why you need to know. And then I'll tell you . . . maybe."

"Too many people seem to know too much already. I've said it—you've agreed with it. But you've already told someone else. So I'd like to know who."

"Good try. But not good enough." Audley started fumbling with his seat-adjustment again. "At least I can get a good sleep for three hours."

"You really don't trust me, do you?"

"Don't fret yourself. I don't trust anyone. Except maybe old Nikolai Andrievich—him I *can* trust."

"I see. You can trust Panin . . ." He noted that Audley hadn't sat back yet; so the old man was waiting for him to react ". . . but not me?"

"Exactly right. But I told you before: he gives us a clue, maybe—remember?"

Gives—not *will give*, Tom remembered: he had dismissed the wrong tense too easily. So now he could only crawl. "What clue does he give us, David?"

"Clues, actually . . . or possibly, anyway." Audley's voice was lazy on its surface. But Tom felt a prickle up his spine which he recognized suddenly as something he'd felt earlier, though without accepting it consciously, whenever Nikolai Andrievich Panin had been mentioned. That calm surface—even the deliberate cosy reduction of the KGB veteran to "Nikolai Andrievich", or "Old Nikolai", for all the world as though he was truly an old and trustworthy friend—that calm surface was a sham. The truth was that the old man was scared.

"Clues, then?" Now that he had recognized it, he understood it: the sea above the Great White Shark might be as calm; but the unseen horror beneath was such that it had to be belittled, otherwise it would be too frightening. And, after their bullet and Basil Cole, that was fair enough.

"Possibly." Audley rocked slightly, from side to side. "You're still rather an equivocal character, Tom—to me, anyway. Because I know that you're on *our* side . . . but are you on *my* side? *No* . . . no, don't answer!" He waved a hand halfway across the car. "You are a minor equivocal consideration, compared with Nikolai Andrievich, who is a major *un*-equivocal one—do you see?"

He had done the old man wrong. Because being scared might be part of it, but it wasn't all of it: the old war-horse was also champing at the bit at the prospect of meeting this Russian again, after all the years in-between since last time. "You mean . . . whatever side I'm on . . . at least you know for sure whose side Panin is on, David?"

"*Ah* . . ." Audley breathed satisfaction, real or simulated, in the soporific warmth of the car-heater. "Perhaps that is what I do mean. Or . . . at least I mean that Nikolai Andrievich is a simple Russian—KGB, but *Russian* always . . . 'KGB' is merely a set of initials: Holy Mother Russia, all the way from Stalingrad to Berlin long ago, was his education. So after that, no crime is any problem for him. Whereas I am a simple Englishman—good, solid Anglo-Saxon, with only a small tincture of Norman blood . . . So I have complicated hang-ups about killing people, which he wouldn't even begin to understand. Even killing Germans, during the war . . . most of the ones I actually met seemed perfectly decent chaps—there were one or two exceptions of course . . . But there were exceptions on our side too. *Notable exceptions*, in fact: better dead than alive, certainly. Only that worried me, because we English haven't suffered the way others have—like Panin. So we English are not good haters. Except perhaps of the French . . . but that's really a sort of love-hate, flavoured with admiration . . . And there are some foolish middle class children who try to hate the Americans, out of ignorance and frustrated envy . . . Not that I blame them, mind you: it must be hard to be one of a post-imperial generation—poor little things!"

God! The old man was rambling! "And you're not . . . 'Post-imperial', David?"

"Lord no! My eighth birthday cake had a model of HMS *Hood* on the top of it: the biggest warship afloat, in the biggest navy of the greatest empire the world had ever seen—all pink, the map of the world was. And I saw Portsmouth in '44, before we went across the Narrow Sea—the *English* Channel—that last time, ignorant as I was—

> *'Our King went forth to Normandy*
> *With Grace and Power and Chivalry.*
> *And there, for him, God wrought marvellously—'*

"Ignorant as I was . . . But I saw it all, the whole D-Day armada, from the crest of Portsdown Hill, on top of one of old Palmerston's forts—the whole shebang, Tom: from Portsmouth to Gosport, with the barrage balloons overhead, in the same anchorage where the Roman *Classis Britannica* rode off Portchester, and Henry V's fleet before Agincourt, before he 'went forth'—and Nelson's, before Trafalgar, too. Though I can't honestly say that God wrought marvellously for the West Sussex Dragoons in the Normandy *bocage* thereafter, because Jerry bloody massacred us . . . However, that's another story." He stopped suddenly. "And *you* are also another story. Or the Polish half of you is, anyway."

That took Tom aback. "The Polish half?"

"Yes." Audley shook himself. "We had a Polish armoured regiment near us in Normandy . . . 1st Polish Armoured Division, attached to the 1st Canadian Army—mad buggers, they were! We were psyched up to fight Jerry all the way to Berlin, but they weren't stopping there . . . One of them said to me—and he said it in broad Yorkshire, or maybe Lancashire . . . Because he'd been stationed there, and he'd married a Lancashire girl—or maybe she was a Yorkshire girl, I don't know . . . But he had a Yorkshire/Lancashire accent anyway. And he said to me: 'We fook the fooking *Germans* first. And then we fook the fooking Russians—okay, *English*?" Audley sighed. "Poor bugger!"

"Poor bugger?" But it rang true, all the same: that was what Father had said about Mamusia's countrymen, exactly: they were all mad buggers, the Poles.

"Aye—'poor bugger'," agreed Audley. "Most of his lot were killed up beyond Caen, closing the Falaise gap . . . Killed a lot of Germans too, I shouldn't wonder. But never got to kill any *fooking* Russians therefore, to their great and enduring sorrow." Pause. "But . . . but, anyway, that was how your dear mother felt about it, to come back to the point: 'The only good Russian is a dead one', is how she felt. The way General Sheridan felt about Red Indians." Pause. "So is that how you feel, Tom? About Nikolai Andrievich?"

Once again Tom rearranged his thoughts. Audley was speaking lightly again, but the inquiry beneath was heavyweight. And, by the same token, he hadn't really been rambling on, like any old soldier: Panin was *now* for him, too. But how then should he reply?

Well—

Somebody flashed him from behind suddenly—mercifully with no accompanying flashing-blue police-light, but just to overtake him in the overtaking lane even as he was himself shaking in the slipstream of an immense Euro-lorry going flat-out in the fast lane; so he could pretend for a moment to attend to the mundane matters of life-and-death on the road.

"Just let me get out of the way of this other mad bugger behind us, David—"

Well . . . it was certainly true that Mamusia hated and despised all Russians and everything Russian with all the intensity of a natural-born hater-and-despiser; in fact, if she'd been a man she probably would have been one of Audley's "mad buggers"; and it was small wonder that the old man still remembered that fierce passion, which would have burnt even more hotly in her youth, when Katyn and the great betrayal of the Warsaw Rising were still raw gaping wounds, not hideous old scars.

He pulled over to let the other mad bugger get ahead—not an English mad bugger, but a mad American bugger secure in his diplomatically-plated Cadillac immunity—

Well . . . with the way Mamusia felt, he had always had to conceal his own inadequacy in the matter, which (if Audley's theory was correct) must be his paternal inheritance: Father's amused tolerance of almost everything had been a sore trial to Mamusia, even though it also embraced her extravagance, her admirers and her never-explained absences.

Father—

"Well, Tom?" Audley was a good passenger, oblivious to everything around him and only concerned with what was going on in his mind. But that was where his patience was exhausted now. "Well, Sir Thomas Arkenshaw?"

But Tom was momentarily inside his own thoughts, in the desolate grey country of wasted opportunities and lost might-have-beens, among the ghosts of all the things he had never shared with one person he'd loved most and admired most in all the world, the memory of whom always made him a counterfeit, rather than an inheritor, of the Arkenshaw name.

"Yes." He watched the brake-lights of the Cadillac brighten, already far ahead, as it was slowed-up by someone else who wasn't breaking the speed limit sufficiently. What Mamusia always said about Father was that he hadn't an enemy in the world: there were only his friends and the people who had never met him. But now he was neither his father's nor his mother's son, he was only himself. "I don't give a damn what you do to Panin: you can kick him, or shake him by the hand, for all I care. My job is to see you safe home, that's all." The trouble was that *only himself* was a liar. "That's all, David."

Audley digested the lie for a moment. "All right. Then, for a start, you'd better decide when to put me in my place, and not take bullshit from me."

Tom held the wheel steady. "Such as?"

"Panin is my problem, not yours. But that doesn't mean you have to let me patronize you. So . . . when you feel like it, you just tell me to go to hell—okay?"

"Okay." Tom steadied the car and himself. The old man was full of surprises, arrogant and humble by turns. But then . . . but then, because of Mamusia . . . and, damnably, because of Jaggard too . . . their relationship had an extra dimension which might confuse them both. "Go to hell, then!"

"Or go to sleep, and let you get on with your job?" Audley began to fumble with the seat-adjustment again. "Okay!"

"No!" Tom recalled himself to his duty, shutting out all other distractions. Jaggard expected more from him; and, even to do the job Audley at last seemed to be accepting as genuine, he needed more than that. "Tell me more about Panin. You said 'clues'—remember?"

"I also said 'need to know'—remember?"

"Yes." He preferred Audley sharp and nasty to Audley kindly and fumbling. "If I'm to watch your back I need to know what I'm up against —and who. Every last damn thing you know about Panin, I need to know, David."

Silence. So, although that was the truth, it was not good enough. So he would have to play dirty.

"And there are three other reasons. I wish there weren't." That, also was the truth, even though it was a truth which dirtied him—which didn't set him free, but chained him in a dungeon forever. "But there are."

"*Three* . . ." Audley stared at him in the dark, altogether perplexed, his face faintly lit on-and-off by the headlights of the oncoming traffic from the other side of the motorway ". . . three reasons? I can't even think of one, Tom—*three*?"

The bolts on the dungeon-door crashed into their sockets, and the iron key turned in the lock, and the chains rattled, echoing *forever*.

"Someone took a shot at you today, David—and missed." He couldn't go back now, even if he wanted to. Because it would still have been the truth. "I'm never going to be able to face your wife . . . *and* Cathy . . .

and my mother . . . if the next shot is a bull's-eye, David. What am I going to say? I don't think '*Sorry*' will be quite enough."

Silence again. But this time it was a different silence.

The road ahead was suddenly dark, as they crested the last rise before the descent towards Bristol, and the motorway exchange to the West, and the South-West, and the North-West. But there would be no choice there, either: he couldn't go back. And even if he could, Willy would be well into her *steak au poivre, very rare*, by now, with a good Burgundy and a Lieutenant-Commander USN. So there was nothing to go back to, anyway.

"Nikolai Panin is an interesting man. Even . . . in some ways . . . an attractive one. Although he does look a bit like a sad sheep." Sniff. "But he does his homework. So he'll know *you*, Tom, I shouldn't wonder—so don't let him catch you off your guard, eh?"

That was about as unreassuring as he'd expected. So it required no astonished reaction.

"But he's a bad bugger, all the same—make no mistake." Pause. "So, if he wants to talk to me, it isn't for the good of my health, or the good of the United Kingdom of Great Britain and Northern Ireland, or for the benefit of the Common Market and the North Atlantic Treaty Organization . . . or because he admires the Princess of Wales more than Mrs Gorbachev."

A sign came up, advising them that Bristol was close, but the next motorway service area wasn't.

"Either he wants something so badly that he's prepared to make a deal. But I doubt the deal will be much in our interest, even if it looks that way . . . Or he's going to screw us somehow—like he's the cheese in the trap." Pause. "And possibly a trap designed for me. Because he knows me. Like the back of his hand."

That was decidedly unreassuring. Except that presumably Audley and Panin both knew what the other was thinking.

"But there is another possibility. Which the traumatic events of this day suggest, actually. Though we must be careful not to 'make pictures' . . ."

Now they were coming to it. Because anyone might have followed Audley so far—or even preceded him. But this would be pure Audley.

"That pot-shot at me . . . it was quite outrageous—altogether monstrous." Disappointingly, the old man seemed to go off at a tangent suddenly, speaking almost to himself. "Yet—I cannot say that I was overwhelmed with surprise."

"No?" That was true, for Tom's recollection was of a blazing rage rather than surprise. What was surprising now was that Audley sounded like nothing so much as an elderly vicar musing sadly on an outbreak of hooliganism in his hitherto peaceful rural parish, for the benefit of his innocent curate.

The Reverend David Audley sighed. "There are some very violent types around these days. But then there always have been, I suppose."

Tom remembered what Jaggard had said on the phone. "And you must have made a few enemies in your time, David."

"Yes. Haven't we all?" The Rev. David sounded properly philosophic. "However, as I recall, I *was* surprised that the blighter missed me."

"Not to say also gratified." Tom couldn't resist the curate's murmur.

"Eh? Yes—of course." The old man had only half heard him. "So that was either gross incompetence . . . But often people *are* incompetent, it has to be admitted. Yet it could also have been a deliberate act, just to frighten me, or warn me . . . or even to encourage me to get my skates on."

There was perhaps the faintest orange tinge to the night sky ahead, which could be either the westwards motorway junction or the city of Bristol itself. "But you didn't think it was Panin, David."

"No. Or . . . if it was, then it has to be a deliberate miss. Because *his* man wouldn't have been incompetent. But that, in turn, means that he's running very scared, and he needs me—*me*, of all people!—very badly, for some reason."

"Some reason?" It wasn't fear in the old man's voice now: it was something more like satisfaction. "What reason?"

"God knows!" It *was* satisfaction. "Interesting, though, isn't it!" He fell silent, and Tom decided to let the silence work itself out without rising to it with fool questions.

"Yes . . ." Audley nodded eventually. "It was a long time ago . . ."

Tom waited for two miles, watching the red-orange glow in the distance. Driving towards Hell would be like this, he thought. And then wished he hadn't thought such an ill-omened image. "What was?"

"Eh?" Silence again. "When I first met Panin, Tom. We knew so little about him . . . But then, of course, he was an *internal* security man: he'd never really messed us around. He really wasn't particularly interested in *us* even then . . . Though it seems he became quite interested in *me* thereafter . . ."

Another silence.

"Knowing people is really what our work is all about now—who's who leads to what's what. Machines can do most of the donkey-work now: spies-in-the-sky can do the damned spying . . . It's who they are, and what's in their minds, that matters." Audley sniffed. "I remember . . ." But then he trailed off.

Tom was equally grateful that he dropped "Darling Boy" and his irritatingly friendly "Nikolai Andrievich" as the memory of that first meeting came back to him. "You remember?"

"Yes." The old man's voice was suddenly cautious. "It was about the time I met my wife . . . But tell me, Tom: did your dear mother remember me?"

"What—?" The sudden change in direction caught Tom unprepared. "She remembered you very well, David." Obviously, the memory of the woman who had said "yes" to him had drawn him back to an earlier memory, of the woman who had said "no".

"She did?" On its surface Audley's tone was exactly right. But there was something beneath that casual self-satisfaction.

"Yes." Or . . . perhaps he had seen Tom put the phone down and then pick it up again. "Yes." But he couldn't have seen that. But he could still be checking. "She particularly remembered a fancy dress ball. She went as Beauty. And you went as . . . The Beast, David—?"

Silence. And what was coming up ahead now was the M32 exchange to Bristol City, with the larger M5 interchange to the West, and to Wales and the North, promised just beyond.

He didn't want to know about Mamusia's youthful love-life, anyway. Or, anyway, not at this moment—at this moment he wanted to know more about Panin.

"It seemed a good idea at the time," said Audley. "We'd just seen Cocteau's *La Belle et La Bête*—the film. That was what gave us the idea."

He didn't want to know about old films, either—

"Jean Marais played The Beast. I can't recall the girl's name, who played Beauty. But Danny—your dear mother, Tom—she was far more beautiful."

Audley seemed to have forgotten Panin altogether, never mind that bullet of his. And never mind Basil Cole, too.

"She had a superb dress. Cobwebby lace and pearls, and floating gauze." Audley's voice was dreamy. "And I had a superb mask, for The Beast—"

He didn't want to know about fairy stories and fancy dress balls—

"But I never got to wear it—"

It had happened in the wrong order—the thought came to Tom from nowhere—*Basil Cole's accident and then Audley's bullet.*

"I got kicked in the face playing rugger that afternoon. Broken nose and two black eyes, and lips like a Ubangi tribesman. It was so painful I couldn't get the mask on."

"David—"

"So I had to go as I was, without it—"

"David—why did they kill Basil Cole in the morning when they were planning to kill you in the afternoon?"

"But we still won the fancy dress competition. Apparently—all too apparently—I was the beastliest Beast anyone had ever seen," concluded Audley. "You're absolutely right, Tom."

The M4/M5 spaghetti junction loomed ahead. "I am?"

"Yes. That's the contradictory fact. But only if you look at it from the wrong point-of-view. Plus the fact that Panin's *internal* security. Plus ancient history repeating itself, even against the odds." Sniff. "But then, there are some damn queer things happening over there, now that young Gorbachev's come to the throne. So maybe that's not so unlikely."

The interchange traffic was heavy and fast, racing to reach its weekend destinations and forcing Tom to concentrate for a moment on finding a place in it even as Audley's words sank in.

Damned traffic—

And those other, earlier words—

Damned traffic! It was like this all the way to Exeter—

Earlier words—

He found a slot in the overtaking lane at last. "You think Panin's maybe gunning for someone on his own side?" He frowned as he spoke. "But over here? And you got in the way somehow?"

"I think maybe he wants me to do the gunning. Like before. And maybe someone else doesn't like the idea. Also like before. At least, it's a working hypothesis, for a start."

"And Basil Cole?"

"He's part of the hypothesis." Audley sat up. "Slow down a bit, there's a good fellow—you're beginning to frighten me."

"We're going to be very late if I don't get a move on."

"Let the bugger wait. Or go to bed, for all I care. I'd rather be very late than *the* late. Just take it easy."

Tom shifted lanes. "Basil Cole?"

"Oh . . . *that*, I think, was Panin." Sniff. "The bastard."

"Even though he wants you to help him?"

"Even though—yes. Just because he wants help, it doesn't follow that he wants me to know what I'm really doing . . . which poor old Basil might have had a lead on. So Panin will tell me just enough, but mostly lies."

Two enemies, thought Tom. One was usually enough. Plus Henry Jaggard at his own back. "While someone else is gunning for you?"

"Ye-ess . . . Nasty prospect, isn't it?" Audley sat back again. "Still, after Lebanon you must be used to this sort of thing. And we'll get old

Nikolai Andrievich on to my would-be executioner, anyway . . . in return for our services."

"You're going to help him?"

"I'm going to sleep, actually . . . Wake me up on Exmoor, Tom."

Not yet, you're not! "You're going to help him?"

"Yes, I'm going to help him." Audley drew a deep breath and snuggled down in his seat. "And I'm also going to pay him back for Basil Cole, Tom. In full."

VI

TOM STARED UP incredulously at the thin sliver of light which showed through a narrow gap in the curtains of the main window of his bedroom in the Green Man Hotel, Holcombe Bridge.

Not my room? The night wind blew cold on the back of his neck as he forced himself to question his judgement. He had been given the best room in the hotel, the bridal suite no less—the *Princess Diana Suite*, with dressing-room and sitting-room and palatial bathroom as well as oaken-beamed bedroom with a bed the size of a rugger ground; and nothing surprising there really, from past experience of hoteliers presuming that *Sir Thomas* expected his titled due if it was vacant, and could pay for it; and, in this case, nothing surprising that mere *Dr Audley* (attendant physician to *Sir Thomas*, perhaps they'd thought?) had a small room under the eaves nearby.

The thought of Audley made him run his eye along the low bulk of the hotel, darkened now against the starless and soundless night which pressed the Green Man into its fold in the invisible moorland all around. But Audley's little window was unlit; so Audley, like Panin in the annexe, was taking his rest while he had the chance, it was to be hoped.

His eye came back to his own window *(no mistake: this whole end of the Green Man, above the silent stream by the bridge, belonged to Princess Diana and Sir Thomas this night!)*. And, as it did so, the curtains shivered suddenly, confirming his fear and his certainty beyond further question and shrinking him back against the wall's safety, out of sight if they were wrenched open.

But they weren't. Instead the sliver of light was extinguished, and night was complete again in front of the Green Man. But there was someone in his room now.

It didn't make sense—

The solidity of the wall at his back was comforting, but it was the only thing that was. Because everything else was incomprehensible now.

It was his room, and someone was inside it now. But the key was in his pocket, and it couldn't be any visiting chambermaid or under-manager, looking to his creature comforts at this hour, close to midnight—

Even, it had almost seemed a foolish conceit, to make this present night-round after he had seen Audley safely locked into his little room, with such precautions advised as could be made, and Audley contemptuous of them, replete as he had been with the late-night smoked salmon sandwiches and profiteroles which had been all the hotel had offered, together with the hugely expensive wines Audley had chosen to go with them (which had perked up the hotel management almost comically, but which had at least confirmed their estimation of "Sir Thomas" as he'd ordered them, which had taken a knock when they'd got their first sight of Sir Thomas as he was)—

"They're offering Beaumes de Venise by the glass, Tom. But if they bought that at Sainsbury's, or M and S, or wherever . . . that's a bloody rip-off, isn't it? So . . . if we had that nice Château Climens instead, maybe?"

Tom had wondered for a moment what Henry Jaggard would make of the Green Man bill, as a departmental expense, with Thomas Arkenshaw in the *Princess Diana Suite* and David Audley into the Château Climens; and then he'd thought *the hell with Henry Jaggard!*

And, later on, he'd thought: *I'd better make some sort of night-round, to check the lie of the land, after I've put Audley to bed; although, for all the good it will do in total darkness, and with no one else watching our backs, it will be no more than giving me a breath of air before I turn in—*

And he'd said to the barman/under-manager, who'd been hovering: "*I'll just take a walk outside, for a few minutes . . . to blow away the cobwebs before I turn in.*" And the barman/under-manager had said: "*Well, you'd better take a torch, Sir Thomas. It's very dark outside—or, it will be when I switch off the outside lights . . . And I'd better give you a key to the outside door, too.*"

And now he felt the solidity of the wall at his back, which had been built, stone and mortar and rough plaster, before Lorna Doone had met John Ridd, back in the deeps of fictional Exmoor. And, with no back-up out there in the night—no back-up because neither bloody Henry Jaggard nor bloody David Audley appeared to have any interest in professional protection—the bloody wall at his back was all he had, in the way of safety, now.

But, more to the point, *it simply didn't make sense—*

Because this wasn't the moment to search his room, at this time of night, when the room would be occupied (and when there wasn't anything in the room worth looking at, anyway)—*that didn't make sense—*

And . . . *maybe there was back-up, out there in the night, which Henry Jaggard hadn't told him about: the ceaseless watch-and-ward of the old Royal*

Navy, of those storm-tossed ships which the safely-guarded English never saw, but simply took for granted—because Jaggard's attitude didn't make sense otherwise, by God!

He pushed himself away from the wall, suddenly irritated by his own crass irresolution, to stare again at the darkened façade of the hotel. The only thing he knew for sure about Henry Jaggard was that he was a tricky bastard—almost as tricky as Audley. But the only thing he knew for sure about his present situation was that *someone was in his room, and this was no time to make pointless pictures about anything else—*

Mercifully, the night-key turned easily in its well-oiled lock, with only the slightest of clicks.

He closed the door carefully behind him and then stood still, listening to the silence. After the pitch-blackness of the night behind him the reception area had seemed bright at first, but now the feebleness of its minimum lighting returned. More pronounced after the clean moorland air were all the stale night-smells of the hotel, dominated by tobacco and alcohol from the bar on his right and the more acceptable hint of wood-smoke from the huge open fire in the residents' lounge on his left, where the last log of the day sat on its huge pile of ash.

Tom exhaled the smells and was conscious also that he was mixing them with a self-pitying sigh. He knew that he was tired now, and that he had a right to be tired after so long a day, which had started so fairly and had developed so foully, and which had nevertheless kept its last, more dangerous moment to its very end, when he felt least able to cope with it.

Then, from his hidden reserves, he summoned up self-contempt to drive out self-pity. Looked at from the opposite direction (and, just for this final moment of reflection, forgetting Willy), this had been a damn good day—even a lucky one: because Henry Jaggard, faced with an emergency, had chosen Tom Arkenshaw to handle it; and Audley's would-be assassin had *missed*; and now someone, up in his room, had been *careless—*

He reached inside his coat, to settle the .38 in its holster, letting the weight of it comfort him: *now someone had been careless—but this time Poor Tom wasn't defenceless!*

Two tip-toe steps to the left, and he was off the flagstones and on thick carpet, and on his way silently—

Memory flowed smoothly. The under-manager had led the way, through that door in the corner—*this door*—up the narrow (but still carpetted) private staircase to the Princess Diana suite—*this stair, these stairs, two at a time and soundless now—*

The short passage above was empty, and five silent steps took him to the door, back safely to the wall and the .38 in his hand, pressed to his chest.

There would be no sound inside, but he would listen anyway—

Sound—?

He straightened up again, back to the wall, frowning.

For Christ's sake! That was . . . ? Radio One—Radio Three—whichever was the all-night pop music station—?

Ear to the door again, to confirm the impossible truth that someone was listening to pop music in his room, after midnight, in the Green Man, Holcombe Bridge—*for Christ's sake!*

All inclination to wait vanished in that instant. And, as his free hand hovered for a second over the room-key in his pocket, that inclination also evaporated. Instead, the hand tried the door-handle, and felt the door yield, inviting him to face the music and the uninvited music-lover—

The smell hit him first, in the first milli-second of entry, out of that most ancient of human senses, which must once have made all the difference between being the hunter and the hunted, but which had already been activated down below by stale beer and tobacco, and woodsmoke, and a menu full of faint cooking smells garnished with a hint of floor-polish—

But—not so much a *smell* as a *fragrance*—an unforgettable, unforgotten fragrance—Chanel, Lancombe, whoever—

"Darling honey—where the hell have you been?" Willy raised herself on one elbow, all honey-gold and freckled and frilly silken white on the brocaded rugger-field of the great bed.

Tom felt the warmth of the room on his face, registering another sense, after sound and smell and impossible sight as she flexed one slender leg at the knee, cascading the cobwebbed silk down in a movement so characteristic—so well-remembered from last night, and other nights—that it tore his heart with its reality.

"Willy—?" He heard his own voice try to make a question of her, although he knew she was unquestionable—although he knew, as he knew that, that she was real at last, and that everything that he had had before had been an illusion. "Hullo, Willy." He wanted to keep the defeated unsteadiness out of his voice, but he couldn't. "Well . . . this is a . . . a very pleasant surprise, I must say."

"Uh-huh?" She moved slightly, letting the thick glossy page of her magazine spring back, brushing one perfect breast as it did so, and closing both the magazine and their friendship at the same time. "Is it, Tom? Is it?"

Grasping at a straw of comfort, he started to read sadness and regret into her expression. But that was a luxury he could no longer afford: he had to reject the past, as resolutely as that last log on the fire had refused to burn in the fireplace below. Henceforth he must lie on the ashes of their relationship, charred and scorched, but still substantially unburnt. "Well, maybe not pleasant, Miss Groot." Certainly not pleasant; because there were still things he couldn't work out, in that relationship, now that her cover was off. But they would have to wait until he had better and sharper weapons to hand. "But a surprise—I must admit that—" Simultaneously, he felt the weight of the weapon in his hand and saw her eyes fix on it. "I was expecting someone else . . . I'm not quite sure who, to be honest . . . But not *you*, Miss Groot." He slid the .38 back into its holster, settling it comfortably with elaborate unconcern under his own breast as though to emphasize that he could see very clearly that she carried no such weapon under hers. "Not *you*, Miss Groot."

Then he looked round the room. Its three other doors were all ajar, but he somehow felt that they concealed no back-up, either CIA or KGB. And there was really very little point in confirming his instinct, anyway.

So he came back to her, with the best smile he could manage. "Or, as you would say, Miss Groot . . . 'I sure as hell took him—you should have seen his face when he came in'." As he looked at her, and saw a muscle twitch on her cheek, he had to force himself to believe that the smile wasn't hurting her. Because, whatever else she was, she was damn good at her job, he must believe. "Okay. So you took me, Miss Groot. So what next?"

She reached across herself to adjust the too-revealing lace. "It's no good my saying that you're one-hundred-per-cent wrong, I guess—?"

No!

"Not the slightest good, my dear." What made it worse—or *worst*—was that he had never been taken like this before. "You take me once . . . that's because you're good at your job. But you take me *twice* . . . then that's because I'm stupid. So please don't insult me by pulling the other one—okay?"

She considered that for all of half a minute before replying. Then she felt under her pillow and threw a little automatic pistol on the green brocade. "Okay, Tom. So you put that somewhere on your side, and come to bed—okay?"

It was one of the new .22s he'd heard about, but had never seen. "I get a freebie, do I? For old times' sake?"

Now she was beginning to hate him. And he liked that more than anything since he had caught that treacherous fragrance. "Okay. You get a freebie. Just this once."

He wanted her to hate him, he realized. "I'm not sure I'm in the mood. Crawling round Ranulf of Caen's ditches . . . and trying to look after David Audley . . . and driving all the way down here." A weird thought struck him suddenly. "You didn't come down in a big black Cadillac, by any chance—? With CD plates?"

The dead look behind her eyes flickered questioningly for an instant, enabling him to turn away victoriously towards the hanging cupboard. With his back to her, he took off his coat, and then the harness of the .38, and then his tie, hanging each up in turn. Then he began to unbutton his shirt.

"Did you?" The quite appalling truth was that he was in the mood, in spite of everything: he wanted her with an anger and a self-loathing which ought to have revolted him but didn't. "A black Cadillac?" He moved slightly so that he could see her in one of the dressing-table mirrors. She was still on that same elbow, but was busy adjusting one shoulder-strap as though to make herself halfways decent, as she had never thought to do before. "Was that yours?"

She looked up suddenly, straight into the mirror. "Uh-huh."

Strangers in the mirror, thought Tom. *Last night we were lovers, but now we're worse than enemies, we're strangers.* He moved again, staring at himself. *And here's another stranger, too!*

He sat down on the dressing-table stool and began to take off his shoes, half-fearful that he might find cloven-hooves in them, with the toe-caps filled with devil's oakum, as in the old Polish fairy-tale Mamusia had told him years ago. "But it isn't in the hotel car park, is it?"

"They gave me a Metro, Tom."

They? "Yes. I suppose a Caddy would have been a bit obvious, at that." Now he was down to his trousers. But, very strangely, the brutal stranger inside him was embarrassed, as the old Tom had never been—just as the stranger on the bed had been embarrassed about her slipped shoulder-strap.

"You've been checking out the place, then?"

It was a curiously innocent question, delivered in a voice which had suddenly become curiously shakey. "Not well enough, apparently." There had been a Metro in the car park: a silver MG Metro, B-registered. But there had been no *Wilhemina Groot* in the hotel register to match it, of course.

"W-what took you . . . so long?"

He remembered his pyjamas—the pyjamas he hadn't worn last night.

Mamusia's Christmas-tree present from last year, still in their festive wrapper: Christian Dior, Midnight Blue, finest silk. They were the natural partners of the thing the blonde stranger on the rugger pitch was wearing. And they were in his case in the dressing-room. "I was checking the place out—not well enough—" He threw the words over his shoulder as he found Mamusia's unopened present "—I just told you."

They? he thought again. The odds said CIA, but he couldn't take that for granted. All he knew was what Audley had already concluded, that too many people already knew too much.

"I mean—" She threw the words back at him, out of the bedroom "—what took you so long to the hotel, Tom honey?"

He ripped the wrapper savagely—ridiculous things—

("They're lovely, Mamusia dear. But you know I don't wear pyjamas.")

("But you should have them nevertheless, my darling. Whenever you go away . . . if there is a fire. Or a husband knocking on your door. Or . . . on your wedding night, my darling . . . there is a moment of delicacy—")

"There was a pile-up on the motorway, just before the Taunton intersection, Miss Groot." Mamusia cherished a long love-hate relationship with the idea of her only son's hypothetical marriage: she didn't want to be a mother-in-law, but she wanted a daughter-in-law to dress and dominate; and she didn't want to be a grandmother, but she dearly wanted a grandchild to mould, having failed with Tom himself. "We were held up for an hour or more." What twisted his heart now, as the silk slid up his legs, was that of all the possibles, Willy Groot (the former occupant of the stranger on the rugger pitch) would have resisted Mamusia best, both as a wife and a mother. But that was water under the bridge, now and forever. "As a matter of fact, I wondered whether it was your Cadillac which had piled up." The memory of Mamusia's ambitions and his own was swallowed up in the more recent and far more horrific image of obscenely mangled metal, and the false fairyland of flashing blue and red lights, as the fluorescent-coated policemen had at last flagged him from one clogged motorway lane to another with angry urgency on the edge of the disaster area. "Because you came by me like a bat out of hell." The coincidence of the Cadillac vanished as he thought about it: there was only one road westwards, so they had both taken it, quite naturally; the only questionable unresolved coincidence was Willy Groot's relationship with Tom Arkenshaw, which now must be questioned and resolved. "If that was your Cadillac, Miss Groot, I take it?"

No answer. So he surveyed himself in the full-length Princess Diana bridal mirror in the emptiness of her silence—

Yes . . . well, in Mamusia's custom-built pyjamas, at least he looked like he was taking the bridegroom's role, if not Hamlet's father's—

'Such was the very armour he put on—'

It was like Peter Beckett had said in Lebanon, that last time: everyone knew the big Hamlet speeches, but the part most people knew, and the lines, were those of Horatio—

'So frown'd he once, when, in angry parle,
He smote the sledded Polack on the ice—'

"It probably was." Her voice came to him almost in a whisper from the bedroom. "We had a Marine captain driving us, from the embassy guards, who said he'd driven in the Indianapolis race."

At least it hadn't been that bloody USN fellow! thought Tom. Not that this poor frowning Anglo-Polack needed to worry about that now.

"He did drive rather fast," the small voice concluded.

Tom dismissed himself from the mirror. Whichever self that was, it didn't matter—it didn't matter any more than who had got her here, Navy man or Marine, one jump or two ahead of him. Why she was here, and to what CIA end, was all that mattered. And it wasn't one of Mamusia's "moments of delicacy" now, either.

He switched off the dressing-room light and re-entered the bedroom, squaring his shoulders in preparation for what had to be done.

She had moved, but only slightly, to face him from her pillows. The glossy magazine had disappeared, but the disgusting little pistol still lay where she'd thrown it. And now she was biting her lip, as though readying herself mentally for that *freebie*, with which they'd each insulted the other. And she also looked much smaller, and heart-rendingly less confident, than the tough Wilhemina Groot he'd left this morning on Ranulf's defences.

"Okay, then." The old Tom would have been into that inviting bed faster than light. But Tom the Stranger had other fish to fry first, and merely sat on the end of it. "So why was I one-hundred-per-cent wrong, Willy?" Almost to his surprise, he discovered that Tom the Stranger wasn't stupid.

She stopped biting her lip, but he could see that she hadn't expected him to go back to an answer he'd already scornfully rejected: she looked as though she'd expected to get raped while thinking of America, and George Washington, and the Statue of Liberty, and whatever else good little patriotic American girls thought of when Queen Victoria had been thinking of England in the same missionary position. So now it required one hell of an effort to adjust her thoughts to a more demanding intellectual challenge, as opposed to the less demanding physical one for which she'd arranged herself.

Or, alternatively, she was damn good, he reminded himself quickly.

Finally (or maybe craftily), she seemed to come to a decision. "David Audley, Tom—"

"David Audley—yes?" Better to assume that she was damn good. "David Longsdon Audley, CBE, Ph.D, MA—" He parroted Harvey's snide encapsulation of the old man's official career "—sometime Second Lieutenant, temporary Captain, 2nd West Sussex Dragoons, latterly attached Intelligence Corps . . . Rylands College, Cambridge . . . the King's College, Oxford . . . Civil Servant, Department of General Research and Development, 1957 to date." The rest had been out of *Who's Who*, Harvey had admitted, including parentage, and publications and hobbies; but he couldn't remember it all now. "David Audley—right?"

"He's here, with you, Tom—"

"You're damn right he's here!" Need and desire coincided: he had hit back and he wanted to. "But how, as a matter of academic interest, did *you* get here—into my bed?"

She squirmed slightly against her pillows, and that shoulder-strap slipped again. "I had help, Tom—"

"*Had*—?" It was hard to keep his mind on the job: the former Willy had been a wonderful companion, naked and unashamed; but this one, in courtesan's frills and ashamed, was something else. "Or *have*?"

She swallowed. "He's in big trouble, Tom."

"*He's* in big trouble?" Tom tore himself away from that alabaster curve. "For Christ's sake, *Miss* Groot—I think we're *all* in big trouble, aren't we?" The whole unacceptable truth opened up before him. "Someone took a shot at David this afternoon—or yesterday afternoon, as it is now . . . And there's a man dead now—have you heard about him, Miss Groot, eh?"

"Tom—" She tried to sit up, with what would have been delectable consequences in another world, but not now.

"So *I'm* in trouble too, Miss Groot." He hated her and himself equally. "And *you* are in trouble, right now . . . And, I shouldn't wonder, Comrade Professor Nikolai Andrievich Panin, in Room Five in the annexe at the back—*he's* also in trouble, I shouldn't wonder, eh?" On balance, even while trying to allow that she was a two-faced bitch, he felt himself weaken. So he hardened himself against his weakness. "But I'm sure you know all about that. So what's new, then?"

She ran her hand nervously over the flowered sheet. And he had seen that same hand, mud-encrusted, hold his measuring rod only this morning. But now it was clean and treacherous, with pearly nails on long fingers. And he still had his freebie to come.

The thought of that brutalized him. "Just who the hell are you working for—tell me that?"

The hand grasped the sheet. "Who the hell do you think I'm working for—damn it! And damn *you*, Tom Arkenshaw!"

That was more like her! "You were an embassy secretary in Grosvenor Square when I last knew you, Miss Groot."

She drew a deep breath, and drew herself up as she did so, regardless of what all that did to what was on view. "Tom . . . you call me *Miss Groot* just once more—just one more time . . . and you can all go screw yourselves—you, and Dr Audley, and Professor Panin—*and Colonel Sheldon, too!*"

Well, that was nailing the Old Glory to her mast, and no mistake, thought Tom. There had been a routine flimsy waiting for him on the subject of that certain Colonel Sheldon—*Sheldon, Mosby Robert, Colonel USAF (ret)*—just a few weeks back. So, as befitted a blue-blooded All-American CIA girl, Miss Wilhemina Groot was starting her name-dropping at the top.

But now she was staring at him defiantly as the name dropped, and it was maybe time for a different approach to his problems.

"I'm sorry, Willy darling." Perhaps, in fact, this was how he should have started. "The truth is . . . I've had one hell of a day since this morning." That was so much a genuine understatement of the truth, that it made him grin sadly at her. "And you did rather catch me by surprise."

She continued to stare at him, but the defiance had been drained by his apology, it seemed. "I'm sorry too, Tom. And I haven't had such a good day either—that's the truth, too." She sighed. "Not that you're ever going to believe it . . . oh—*shit!*"

He wished he could remember more about *Sheldon, Mosby Robert*, from the flimsy. But all he could recall was his thought that the personnel and hierarchy of the CIA's London Station had had little relevance to his own line of business then. But Audley would know, anyway: Audley had always been very thick and buddy-buddy with the Americans, Harvey had said. And . . . and, come to that, maybe that just might account for the presence of *Groot, Wilhemina Maryanne* at Holcombe Bridge, if not in his bed.

"Tom . . ." she trailed off uncertainly.

He realized belatedly that he'd been frowning at her, thinking of Sheldon and Audley. But she had related his face to her last statement. "Yes, Willy?"

She plucked ineffectually for a moment at her revealing neckline, then let go of it. "I haven't been on your back, these last few weeks—can you believe that, Tom?"

It would be an agreeable belief, Tom realized: it would take the metallic taste of betrayal out of his mouth for a start. And it wouldn't make him feel quite such a simpleton. But agreeable beliefs were always unwise and often dangerous. "Does it matter—now?"

She nodded. "To me it does." Another sigh. "But I don't blame you."

Either she was very sad or she was very good. But it was just remotely possible that she could be both. And, anyway, he owed these last few happy weeks a gesture. "It matters to me also, Willy." He shied away from the truth of his gesture. "Where will I ever find another girl to join me in muddy ditches?"

She looked as though she was about to burst into tears. "With stinging nettles and brambles? Don't forget the stinging nettles and brambles."

Or . . . not just very good. Better than that, even? "Stinging nettles and brambles—okay." It didn't really matter what he believed or disbelieved. But this way he could at least apply mutual regret like a soothing ointment to his wounded self-esteem, half believing its efficacy. "But now you are on my back as well as your own—okay also?"

"Not on your back, Tom." She shook her head. "They're very worried for your Dr David Audley—that's why I'm here."

'*They*' again? "Colonel Sheldon, you mean?" He accepted her nod. "Well, that makes two of us, my love. And I bet I'm more worried than he is!"

"Don't joke, Tom honey—"

"I'm not bloody-joking. Someone took a shot at him this afternoon. And I'm supposed to be looking after him. And *that* isn't a joke, by God!" He stared at her. "You know about the shot?"

She plucked the sheet again. "Half London knows about it. The Russians have been quizzing all the Warsaw Pact embassies, like the wrath of God—"

"The Russians—?" It was no surprise to him that the Americans had picked up such panic-signals: it was common knowledge that they had contacts inside those unwilling allies' intelligence-gathering operations. But . . . if this turn-up for the book wasn't deliberate disinformation . . . then it complicated everything quite appallingly.

"And they've been reading the riot act to their IRA liaison group—the Provisionals and the INLA—" Willy stopped suddenly. "What's 'the riot act', Tom? Because that's what Mosby Sheldon said: 'the Riot Act'—?"

So Sheldon knew his nineteenth-century English history. "It means they've got to stop whatever they're doing, and pack up their bags and go home. It's . . . it's what used to happen in the old days before plastic bullets and petrol bombs and policemen with riot shields and face-masks: after the Riot Act was read the military took over, with drawn swords and fixed bayonets." He frowned at her. Because, if Sheldon had it right, that meant the Russians really were on Audley's side, even if somebody else wasn't. But where did Basil Cole come into it?

"Uh-huh?" His frown stopped her for a second. "Well, they all say they've got nothing to do with it, the word is. And that's the very latest information, of about an hour ago—not long after you'd arrived, Tom honey." She regarded him questioningly for an instant. "But you said . . . you said someone was dead—*dead*?"

So the Americans didn't know about Basil Cole. And maybe the Russians didn't either . . . Or maybe one or other of them *did* know . . . or *both* knew? But the possibilities were infinite, so to hell with that, then! "So David Audley's in trouble." He sank down along the foot of the bed. "If that's all you've got to tell me, Willy darling, then it's right neighbourly of Colonel Sheldon to want to tell him—'right neighbourly'?" The damn bed was as soft as a wedding bed ought to be, but it only served to remind him of how tired he was, and of how quickly the remains of the night were draining away beneath him. "But we do already know that—all too well, we know that, actually."

She pulled herself upright. "Who's dead, Tom?"

He shook his head. "You ask Colonel Sheldon, my love—not me. I'm just a bodyguard—" Quite dreadfully soft, the damn bed "—a 'high-class minder', as I have been *re*minded myself, more than once, today: mine '*not to reason why*', in fact . . . Ask Colonel Sheldon, Willy love." The bed invited him backwards, and he found himself staring at the beamed ceiling suddenly, waiting for her to react to his refusal to tell all.

It was a beautifully beamed ceiling, with its eight radius-beams converging on a boss in the form of a carved wooden face in its centre.

God! It was *The Green Man* himself! He would have known that even without the knowledge in the back of his mind: the acanthus leaves grew out of the face quite naturally, from brow and nose, eyebrows and upper-lip and chin—acanthus leaves, not the vine-leaves he might have expected.

He felt her stir in the bed, under the covers beneath him.

The Green Man himself, indeed! And, although the face wasn't quite directly above him, the deep-carved black holes of the Green Man's eyes were not looking straight down, at nothing, but slightly obliquely, into his own eyes, and perhaps into his own soul, with ancient wisdom.

"How much does Audley know about Professor Panin, Tom?"

Her voice came from nowhere, above him. Indeed, except that it was her voice, it might have come from that foliate mouth, with its classical leaves but northern-pagan imagery, which was neither cruel nor hostile, but knowing.

"How much should he know?" *Green Man*, or *Jack o' the Green*, or *Green Knight* from *Sir Gawaine*, or *Wodwo, Wild Man—if I knew what you know I wouldn't need to ask! Because you know it all!*

"He's in bigger trouble than Audley is—you're right, Tom." She waited for only half a second, as though she didn't expect him to react. "Do you know? Or were you just guessing?"

That had been why Basil Cole had died, the Green Man told him. "I was guessing." *But not guessing, all the same. Because Basil Cole's death hadn't really been silent.* "Just guessing, Willy."

She didn't reply to that, and he guessed also that it annoyed her, that he was lying on his back, staring up at the Green Man. But then the Green Man hadn't been a woman's god in any of his incarnations, either before or after the coming of the White Christ.

He rolled sideways, on to his elbow, and raised himself to look at her. "I was just guessing, Willy darling. But I think he wouldn't come here if he didn't have to, so far from his home ground—eh?"

Still she said nothing, and he saw too late—much too late—that the Green Man had betrayed him, coming after his refusal to tell her about Basil Cole. So he must exert himself now.

"Why are you telling me all this?" (She hadn't told him anything yet; but no matter!) "Why don't you tell Audley himself?" He nodded past her bare pale pink-white-gold shoulder at the brocaded headboard of the great wedding bed. "He's in Room Two, just a yard away." (He could imagine Audley snoring now, in his own esoteric dreams.)

Still not good enough. "Or why isn't Sheldon telling me this, anyway?" Should he make it nastier? "Or are you expendable—like me?" (She must answer that, out of loyalty, if for no other reason!)

A shadow crossed her face, but he couldn't read her expression: either she hadn't wanted to see him again, or she had—it was one or other of those two extremes. "Dr Audley doesn't know me. But you do."

Very true! thought Tom. *I know you from that first English-Speaking Union meeting—from that first traditional kindred-spirit eye-contact across a crowded room, like in 'South Pacific'; and later in bed, and in many a motte-and-bailey afterwards: I know you socially, Willy—and biblically, and in every other way except one . . . which in our business is the only one that counts, eh?*

"Yes." '*Wilt thou have this woman—?*' "I do."

"And I'm not official—" She shook her head against the pillow "—my darling Tom . . . if things go wrong . . . and I think *they* think things are going to go wrong, I'm afraid . . . then I'm just a junior cypher clerk, working in low-grade traffic, who shacked up out-of-school with a middle-grade FCO Brit—" She closed her eyes for a moment, and when she opened them again they were dead "—a Brit who happened to have a handle to his name. Which they reckon puts me safely in a fine old American tradition, from Consuelo Vanderbilt onwards." She paused for a moment, watching him. "They know all about you, of course. And more than I ever told them."

"Of course." As an embassy employee—even as a secretary, never mind an intelligence cypher clerk—she had had to put her private life on the record. But he'd taken that for granted, because he had done the same.

"Of course." The mouth twisted. "So . . . I've got the right clearance for running errands. But if things go wrong I'm not Company talent—I'm just your 'bit of crumpet' . . . 'Bit of crumpet'—okay?" The twist became more pronounced. "That seems to be the British term for me."

The room was hot, he could feel its warmth on his face. But there was a cold area spreading up his back which came from inside him. Because, if Audley's friends in Grosvenor Square were concerned to keep this sort of distance from Holcombe Bridge, then Holcombe Bridge was no place to be.

"What sort of big trouble is Audley in then, Willy?"

She relaxed slightly. In the ruins of their relationship, coming back to Company business took her mind off personal desolation. "His own side's gunning for him, Tom."

"Why?"

"He's been playing politics. Political politics—with politicians."

"*Audley?*" Audley had never been political—even Harvey had said that the old man disliked all politicians equally. "Never!"

"You're wrong, honey. There's this guy he doesn't like—who is a top politician."

"He doesn't like any of them, Willy."

"He doesn't? Well, I don't know about that . . . but he seems to have set this guy up, by leaking some dirt about the insecurity of his department. And that seems to have been a big mistake."

He wanted to ask *Why?* again, but then he decided to limit his interruptions. If she was just passing on Sheldon's message without understanding it, questions would only confuse her.

"The guy's very close with their intelligence brass—*your* brass, I mean, Tom honey . . . There's a man named Jaggard, who's very smart—and who's on our side, pretty much—*our* side including the US of A . . . But he owes this politician some favours. And he wants to owe him some more favours—"

Sweet Jesus Christ! thought Tom. *Now he really was in the middle of it!*

"So he's ready to throw Audley to the wolves—even to Russian wolves, maybe." She blinked at him. "Are you with me still, Tom honey?"

Nod. He was with her, all too well. Nod again.

"Uh-huh?" She looked at him as though surprised that he had nodded so readily. "Well . . . Colonel Sheldon likes this fellow Jaggard, but he doesn't trust him—Commodore Jaggard, is it?"

"Air Commodore." Jaggard had been so perfectly pin-striped civilian that it was hard to imagine him pioneering the P1127, which had transmogrified into the Harrier, more than twenty years ago. But at least it hinted why Colonel Sheldon *USAF* might be on his side, emotionally. "Royal Air Force, Willy. Once upon a time, anyway."

"You've met him—Commodore—*Air* Commodore—Jaggard?"

"Briefly." That was strictly true: even that last time, when Henry Jaggard had blinked the rain out of his pale-blue eyes on the top of Ranulf's ditch—that had been a brief meeting. "But Colonel Sheldon likes David Audley too? At least, enough to warn him?"

"Oh yes—he surely does." She nodded back at him quickly. "He knows Audley from way back—he even calls him 'David' . . . And he did a job with him, over here, once. He has a high regard for him, Tom. And the work Audley is doing is too important to be screwed up, he says."

Here was a pretty tangle of Anglo-American loyalties! thought Tom. Because, if Jaggard needed his political allies, Sheldon also needed his British allies—and Audley too! So Sheldon was in trouble now, too.

"But not important enough to come and talk to him now?" He saw from her expression that she had thought the same question, even if she hadn't asked it. "So what does he advise, anyway?"

She licked her upper lip. "He says you should both cut and run, Tom."

That certainly sounded like good, friendly, special relationship advice, even if it was useless. "He won't do that, Willy." He shrugged helplessly. "So I can't—even though I'd like to."

"No." She nodded again. "He said Audley wouldn't run." Nod. "Not even after what happened yesterday." This time, no nod; merely curiosity. "He said Audley wouldn't run—and wouldn't trust anyone except himself."

He might as well feed her something, to take back to her boss. And, after he'd let it slip, the CIA would pick up Basil Cole's accident soon enough, anyway. "He's also lost an old colleague, from yesterday morning." The memory of Audley's anger came back to him. "So it's personal, as well as professional. I think he wants blood for blood now."

The words seemed to push her back into the pillows of the great bed, making her look smaller and, for the first time, a little frightened. For an instant, in spite of himself, he almost believed what he wanted to believe, even though he knew she wanted him to believe it too: that she wasn't really Company talent, but just a cypher clerk whose private life had come in useful to her bosses.

But then his credulity snapped, and he grinned at her. "So . . . you see, I wasn't altogether guessing when I said that Professor Nikolai Andrievich Panin was in trouble, Willy darling. Because your boss, Colonel Sheldon—he's damn right about David Audley: he may be an *old* man, but he's a tough old bastard. And he's in a nasty frame of mind right now, I rather think—a nasty *revengeful* frame of mind. And not just because some foolish fellow took the liberty of shooting at him in his own home. And he doesn't regard that as cricket . . . But some other foolish fellow has terminated someone he values." He couldn't hold the grin. "So if this was your home-state, back in the old days, you'd be watching the smoke-signals in the hills, and hearing the war-drums in the distance. Because these are *his* ancestral hunting-grounds, Willy. So maybe you should be giving Colonel Sheldon's advice to Comrade Professor Panin, not to me."

"Uh-huh?" She had got her cool back, and she was almost his old lost Willy again. "But you haven't talked to him yet—?" She busied herself suddenly with plumping up the pillows alongside her, shifting from her almost-central position.

"The Comrade-Professor?" In another moment she was going to invite him in beside her. But he wasn't ready for that: from beside her, he wouldn't be able to see her full face—her beautiful, golden-freckled, treacherous face. And the rest of her would play hell with his concentration, too. "Hell—you know we haven't!" (An incongruous recollection of the motorway accident scene returned, when he had wanted to pull rank over the police, to get ahead, and Audley had rejected the idea out-of-hand: *'But we'll be here an hour, David!'—'So I get another hour's sleep, then. Let the bugger sweat, wondering what we're up to. I'm not at his beck-and-call, keeping unilateral engagements, anyway, damn it all!'*) "I'll phone ahead, to say we'll be late." *(That had been when Audley had animated himself for a moment: 'Tell them I want two rounds of smoked salmon sandwiches, cut thin but with the crusts included . . . and a bottle of good White Burgundy (they won't have a decent Graves, they never do) . . . And I shall want a pudding—something with chocolate—milk chocolate . . .*

and their best Sauternes or Barsac, on ice—on ice, mind you, not in the bloody fridge: tell them that, Tom.')

"But he left a note—?"

And I'll bet you've read it, too! "Yes." *(That neat, meticulous, grammatical note, traced by a hand accustomed to Cyrillic, if not classical Greek, he had thought.)* "He said that he'd had a long day, with the flight and all the boring formalities, and the long drive." *(And meticulously formal, too: 'My dear Doctor Audley . . .' and 'this long journey which we share . . .' down to 'With respect and sincerity'—huh!—before that elaborate signature.)* "He wants to meet us tomorrow, somewhere in the open, but somewhere safe, Willy."

She pretended to chew on that, as though it was news to her.

Jezebel! She wanted to ask him where, but that was too obvious even for her.

But, instead of answering straight away, she reached across and twitched open the covers on what had to be his team's side of the rugger pitch. "Come inside, Tom."

He mustn't be that easy. "You said he was in trouble—'big trouble'. What sort of trouble?" He ignored the unbeatable offer, as though he hadn't heard it. "Bigger trouble than Audley is—?"

"Yes." This time she pretended that she was recalling what had been said to her—a mere cypher clerk suddenly briefed beyond her competence, on matters which she'd never decyphered or encyphered. "They say he's out of favour, in Moscow. They said he was almost ready for the scrap-heap, Tom. They were surprised he'd even been let out, to talk to your Dr Audley."

Was that what his Dr Audley had hinted at? But he had said more than that. And she was fishing now—and she was bloody good at it.

So he could fish back, equally innocently. "Do they think he's open to offers?"

"No." She shook her head so quickly that a golden tendril flopped down, across the rise of one breast. "Colonel Sheldon said that was why he was let out—because he never would defect, he said."

So Colonel Sheldon agreed with his old pal, David Audley. "So what exactly does he want with David Audley, Willy?"

"We don't know, exactly." She smoothed down his half of the pitch. "But they gave me three names, to tell you—to tell Dr Audley."

Maybe not-so-good. Because, if they'd discussed the possibility of Panin's defection in front of her, they would have talked about a lot more than that. But he must let that pass, for the time being. "What names, Willy?"

She took a remembering breath. "Zarubin, Gennadiy Ivanovich—"

She might just as well have said Smith, Peter John, with a couple of hundred million to choose from. But maybe Audley would know better. "Yes?"

"Marchuk, Leonid—Leonid—" The rest of *Marchuk, Leonid* got away from her for a moment "—Leonid *Nikitich* Marchuk."

Another bloody *Peter John Smith*. "Marchuk. Yes—?"

"Pietruszka. Adam Pietruszka—" she breathed out her relief at remembering the alien name "—Adam Pietruszka."

Tom got up, and set himself to walk round the end of the bed. The curtains in the big window overlooking the road, through which he had seen that tell-tale sliver of light, were properly drawn now, he noted.

"Marchuk?" *Pietruszka!* "Pietruszka? Zarubin?"

"Colonel Sheldon said he'd know the names." She spoke in a small voice, diffidently, as though she knew that her Anglo-Saxon-American accent left something to be desired when she tried to wrap it round Slavonic names.

He came back to her at last, round the last right-turn. *Pietruszka!* Big smile. "Then I'm sure he will."

Pietruszka, for Christ's sake! Pietruszka—Piotrowski—Wolski—Chmielewski—Pekala!

But if she was expecting him to react to that last name, then she was going to be disappointed. Because instead he sank into the bed, and took her into his arms, enfolding her softness even as that treacherous fragrance also enfolded him, mixed with her own unique Willy-smell, unforgettable and unforgotten, warm-and-female; and hated her and himself as he did so, in a mutual betrayal.

Pietruszka—that bloody - cowardly - murdering - Red - fucking - bastard - treacherous - swine!

But she pushed at him—tried to push him away, almost convulsively, turning her face from him.

"You're so cold—God!" She pushed at him again, turning her head quickly left and right. "God! I'm just crumpet now, aren't I! I'm just a sodding freebie now!" She stopped shaking under him, and became boneless and defenceless, staring up at him accusingly. "Just a freebie!"

Pietruszka! he thought, as he let himself be repulsed.

She stared at him as though she didn't know him. And they hadn't known *him* either, when he'd been taken out of the Wloclawek reservoir: his own brother had only identified him from a birth-mark on the side of his chest, they had beaten him so badly—

Audley was right: blood for blood!

Everything came together in that instant, and he knew exactly where he was. And, better than that, he was at last where he wanted to be—which was more to the point!

He pulled back from her. "I'm sorry. You're quite right—" Pull back further: go sideways, away from her "—I think I want you more than I've ever wanted you . . . Because I *need* you . . . But if I'm cold it's because I'm scared too, Willy."

"Tom . . ." That great lie, which was also not a lie, weakened her and confused her ". . . I'm sorry, too."

He sat back on his heels, in the midst of the great disordered bed. At least they were both agreed on something. But she mustn't know why he agreed with her. And, anyway, it wasn't a great lie, actually, at all: he was scared, and he did need her . . . and only a blind idiot wouldn't have wanted her, the way she was now.

But, beyond David Audley and Nikolai Panin there was *Adam Pietruszka* now. And that changed the priorities—

Blood for blood! But he must control himself, too.

"Don't be sorry." He sank back into the bed. And, the irony was, he would be warm now that he was in control of himself again. "Don 't be sorry, Willy." He reached out for her. Then he stopped, and reached up instead for the light switches, even as he re-inserted himself into the bed.

Darkness—

He reached out for her again, and this time she didn't reject him. Rather, she melted into him.

Darkness and silence. And he could almost feel the high folds of the moorland outside, protecting them.

But then she stirred uneasily, in the crook of his arm. "Shouldn't you tell Audley those names, Tom?"

Zarubin—Marchuk . . . Pietruszka?

He looked up into nothingness, as she snuggled against him, knowing that the Green Man was up there above him.

Pietruszka—Piotrowski—Wolski—Chmielewski: no doubts about those names! *And Pekala, too!*

The Green Man was still looking down on him, with that ancient inscrutable wisdom of his, dark and clear: his green leaves had once been symbolic of the pleasures of the flesh, but he also understood the necessity of sacrifice too, as part of regeneration: so his understanding was part of Father Jerzy's, pagan and Christ-like and complete.

"Tomorrow morning will do—" He had surrendered to exhaustion, and there was no going back on that white flag now; because sufficient unto the day was the evil thereof . . . and *blood for blood* was for tomorrow "—let Audley get his night's sleep—okay?"

She sighed. But then she snuggled again, without knowing what she'd accepted . . . which maybe Jaggard didn't know . . . and maybe Panin didn't know, either . . . But Audley would know, as Tom Arkenshaw knew now—

Pietruszka—damn *his black soul to hell!*

Tom felt himself divide, into his English half and his Polish half, as he held the woman he still loved in his arms, and deceived her.

Yet it was not a complete description: Father's gentler English half had once demanded blood-for-blood, the old Anglo-Saxon *wergild*—but that was long ago . . . so that half could cherish Willy now. It was Mamusia's side which wanted blood—

Somehow, he must preserve David Audley tomorrow, and yet he must exact *wergild* for Father Jerzy also—

"Tom, honey . . . hold me tight, Tom—"

Like Audley, Father also had Norman blood in him. And Norman blood had a pragmatic virtue: it attended to first things first.

So that was what he would do now, then.

VII

AUDLEY BLEW HIS nose noisily, and with evident self-pity, and surveyed the elderly Ford Cortina with distaste, and muttered again under his breath.

Out of the corner of his eye Tom observed the garage man bestow the crisp new bank notes into a back pocket, and the garage man caught his glance and nodded ingratiatingly. "She's a good runner—you can take my word for that, sir," he added quickly, in support of his nod. "An' I'll put your car under cover."

"If you'd just get in the car, David." Tom moved into the pause before Audley could explode into disbelief. "Then we can talk."

Audley opened his mouth, but another sneeze caught him before he could pronounce on the garage man's word; and, before he could recover, Tom had ducked round to the other side of the Cortina and was into the driver's seat; and, with commendable prudence, the garage man followed him as far as possible, bending down and tapping on the window, leaving Audley isolated.

Tom wound down the window.

"I know she don't look much—" The man massaged his pocket, as though he couldn't believe his luck "—but that engine there . . . that's sweet as a bell! You just start 'er up, an' listen to 'er."

There was 95,000 on the clock, and the state of the bodywork suggested that this was the second time round. But Audley had surrendered to the inevitable and was climbing in on the other side, so he turned the ignition key quickly.

The engine roared—and roared louder as he revved it to drown out what Audley was now saying.

"What did I tell you?" The garage man's reaction was a masterly overlay of gratified confidence above relieved surprise. "That's a good engine, that is—sweet as a bell . . . An' two new tyres on the back . . . You just want to watch the hand-brake—best to put 'er in gear when you leave 'er on a hill . . . I still got a bit of work to do on that—like I told you, didn't I?"

"Yes—thank you." It wasn't stopping, it was getting away that mattered now, and the road was open and the way was clear. "I'll be off then." He engaged the gear and released the defective hand-brake to suit his words. "Goodbye—goodbye—"

"Goodbye, sir—" The Cortina's movement sloughed off its proud owner, but not quite "—don't forget what I told you about the hand-brake —*the hand-brake, sir*—"

They were moving. And there was a surge of 2-litre power under his foot now, and a clear road ahead and behind, for the time being.

Audley muttered again. And then sneezed again, and blew his nose again, to demonstrate that his cold was much worse this morning, as well as his tempter.

Tom put his foot down, listening to the sound of the engine above the other assorted rattles from all sorts of places around him, inside and outside and underneath "the good runner".

"If there's one thing I hate—" Audley managed to speak at last, and with cold concentration "—or two things . . . or maybe even *three* things—" A paroxysm of sneezes engulfed all the things he hated.

Still nothing behind. Which was reassuring, even if it also shamed Tom a little for all the proper precautions he had wished on the poor old bugger this morning, before and after their hasty breakfast.

"What do you hate, David?" Still nothing. And what made him feel worse was that he felt better himself: better after last night (which had been better than better); and better because there still wasn't anything behind, as they climbed up on to the high shoulder of Cherwell Down, into open moorland, where anything behind would be nakedly following; and best of all (although that was treacherous to Willy, to think it best), because he had always wanted to see Mountsorrel—(to hell with them all —Jaggard and Audley, Panin and his po-faced Minder . . . even, almost, with Willy herself!)—*he had always wanted to see Mountsorrel!* "What do you hate, David?"

Audley emitted a growling sound, half hate and half common head-cold. "I hate Ford Cortinas—and particularly two-tone brown Cortinas!"

Now *that*, thought Tom happily, was *irrational*, in the circumstances. "Two-tone Cortinas, David?" There was nothing behind, for a mile or more.

"My wife bought one once, fourth-hand—" Audley caught himself suddenly, as though he realized at last what a fool he was making of himself. "Damn it, Tom! What the hell are we supposed to be doing at the moment?"

That was fair enough. "We're just taking precautions, David. That's all." But he mustn't sympathize with Audley too much. "What other things do you hate?"

"Huh!' Audley was getting back his cool, in spite of his cold. "I'm too old to enjoy your precautions—if that's what you mean by all this bloody cloak-and-dagger business."

Should he count "cloak-and-dagger" as Things Two and Three? "But I'm your Minder—remember, David?"

"Remember?" The old man slumped down resignedly. "How could I forget?" He sniffed against the cold. "Although it's a bloody long time since I've been professionally-minded . . . But no—I remember . . ." Then he gestured towards the battered dashboard, with its gaping hole where the radio had been. "This is a precaution, is it?"

They came to the cross-roads on the top. "This is a different car. The one we had yesterday was in the hotel car park all night. So I couldn't watch it absolutely." *So I was busy last night—okay?* "So now we've got a clean car."

Grunt. "Metaphorically speaking." Grunt—*sneeze*—

Poor old bugger! "It was the first place that offered cars for hire, David."

End of sneeze. "So you're into not trusting anyone, then? Even here?" Audley considered his handkerchief with distaste, much as he had surveyed the Cortina. "Or do you know something I don't know?"

He mustn't think "*Poor old bugger*" again. "We're meeting Panin this morning—'in the open', like he wants . . . And someone took a shot at you yesterday, David—and you didn't think that was *his* doing, I know. But that doesn't matter, because if it wasn't him then it was someone else . . . In fact, I'd rather it bloody-well *was* him—at least we'd know it then, wouldn't we!" He put his foot down again, and began to think better of the garage man in spite of the body-rattles. "But, in any case, there's also poor Basil Cole to bear in mind: *somebody* knows too damn much—you said so yourself. So a bit of cloak-and-dagger is fair enough. Okay?"

Audley said nothing for a few seconds. Then he *harumphed* chestily, and fumbled again for his handkerchief, and finally blew his nose again. "You're saying someone—*somebody*—may have bugged that big black monster of yours last night? To keep tabs on us today? Someone—*somebody*—who managed to follow us all the way to the Green Man last night?" He paused, to let the memory of the M4/M5 drive speak for him. "Like Superman, perhaps?"

It was time to poach Audley to rights. But it might be as well to do it circumspectly. "It could have been bugged when I left it outside Basil Cole's house last evening, David—they could have been watching and waiting for us . . . So I was careless there: we should have changed horses somewhere down the line yesterday, instead of here . . . just in case." And now was the time to frighten him. "Or . . . alternatively . . ."

He didn't have to drive far before Audley cracked. "Alternatively—?"

They were already coming off the high moor, down into one of those ancient valleys where prehistoric men had grubbed a living of sorts: and, in the case of this particular valley, where Gilbert of Mountsorrel had briefly been king of his castle in King Stephen's short days.

"Come clean, Tom, damn you!" snapped Audley.

Tom frowned at the long downhill road ahead. They had come back too quickly to Audley's *"Do you know something I don't know?"* when he had thought he'd headed the old man off the question. "Come clean—?"

"Huh! Or as clean as you know how, anyway!" Audley shifted, to fix a direct eye on him. "Last night you were pissed off . . . You didn't know what the hell was happening, Tom—*I* know the signs . . . because *I* have been there before myself—in no-man's-land, with one hand tied behind my back, and one foot in a bucket, and some silly fool to look after . . . *I have been there, so I recognize the symptoms* . . . so don't fuck me around, eh?"

This was bad, thought Tom: once again, he had underestimated the man, and he needed more time to sort out the *how* and the *why*. "What—?"

"I said—" Audley stopped suddenly as the road narrowed and fell away steeply between high earth-banks. "Watch your speed, man, watch your speed!"

Tom was already doing just that, with the garage man's warning about the brakes suddenly ringing in his ear. The old car could certainly show a clean pair of rear wheels to its peers on the straight, he had established. But it wasn't good running he had to worry about now, it was good stopping. And, from the way he was tensed up in the passenger's seat, Audley was sharing his fears.

Slowly, under insistent pumping of the foot-brake, the car agreed to decrease its speed to the point where he could enlist the gears to help him. "I'm sorry, David. I was thinking of other things."

"So was I." Audley sniffed and hugged himself. "This bloody *bocage* —it always gives me the creeps."

"'Bocage'?" Then Tom remembered Audley's ancient history as a teenager yeomanry tank-commander in 1944, and seized on it gratefully. "You mean, this is like Normandy, is it?"

Audley didn't reply, but sat hunched up and silent until Tom himself recalled out of his subconscious the long lines of graves in the Polish war cemetery on the road from Caen to Falaise, so many of which marked the last resting place of tank crewmen who had died half a continent away from home, for their country's freedom and in vain.

"Yes—" Audley sat up suddenly "—yes and no. Like and unlike." Sniff. "Funny thing, memory: it goes away for years. Then it comes back." He sniffed again, and turned towards Tom. "Now, young Thomas Arkenshaw . . . *alternatively*, you said. And, *alternatively* . . . someone didn't need to follow us yesterday because that someone already knew where we were going, hey?"

Tom nodded. Over the next ridge, then Mountsorrel would be somewhere down the other side, to the left. "It's possible."

"Yes," Audley agreed harshly. "Our side knew. And Nikolai Andrievich's side knew. And neither of those sides can be trusted, for a start. But there's more to you this morning than that deplorable truth. Which, for another start, wouldn't cheer you up—"

"David!" Old memories of blazing tanks, more often British and Polish than German in the *bloody* bocage, had given Tom more time, and more time advised him to come clean. Or, at least, fairly clean. "Let me—"

"No!" Audley cut him off. "Don't attempt to deny it—or explain it . . . at least until I have finished thinking aloud, anyway." Sniff. "Yesterday you were unhappy . . . and, as you have admitted, somewhat careless. Today, you are happy, but careful . . . And you refused to talk business until we were away from the Green Man and in a safe—huh! *relatively* safe—car, in the middle of nowhere. Right?"

Tom managed to open his mouth, but Audley forestalled him. "And I do not think—I do not *believe*—that your happiness is simply the product of youth and a good night's sleep." A handkerchief appeared from nowhere and the old man blew his nose on it. "Whereas I had a dreadful night, full of fly-blown nightmares . . . But that is because I have heard the chimes at midnight too often, and now I like to have my own true woman within reach beside me, and my own true mattress beneath me . . . But now the fresh air has blown the cobwebs from my brain and I can see clearly again." The old man balled up the damp handkerchief and stuffed it into the pocket of his pale expensive raincoat, and flourished a fresh one from another pocket. "So—I tell you this only for your dear mother's sake—so if you are about to deceive me, I caution you to do it well. Because, for her sake, I have decided to trust you this morning until I think you are playing me false. But then, *also* for her sake, I will pack you back to that pen-pushing paper-hanger Frobisher, and you can make your peace with him as best you can." Audley wiped his face with the fresh handkerchief. "Is that crystal clear, now?"

They breasted the new ridge, and Tom caught a glimpse of heather-dark moorland away to his left, with its sharply treeless skyline under the rainclouds. But he knew that he couldn't see so far into Audley in spite of Jaggard's calculations and the man's own admissions—even in spite of that once-upon-a-time special relationship with Mamusia. Because Audley had his own true woman now; and, anyway, Audley was also not to be trusted, in his own right.

"Crystal clear, David." And yet, in spite of that mistrust (and perhaps because of Mamusia; but more, perhaps, because he had never met anyone in the service like this strange, garrulous, dangerous old man), he felt himself drawn to him, and into the game. "If I double-cross you, then you'll shop me. Right?"

"Hmm . . ." For the first time, Audley was taking notice of his surroundings. "Just tell me one thing then, Tom—"

"One thing?" They were going down again. But this time he had the right low gear in advance; because, although he could see nothing as the high Devon *bocage* banks reared up again on each side, he knew that Mountsorrel must be down there somewhere, just ahead and to the left, on its own spit of land above the ancient river crossing.

"Yes." Audley's tone was casual, but his big hands were squeezing each other nervously on his lap, again as though his *bocage*-memories of well-sited German 88s and lurking *panzerfaust* infantry had returned with the earth-banks. "One simple question to start off with, anyway. Now that we know where we stand, as it were."

The road twisted, and then straightened again so that Tom could see clear down to the parapets of a narrow little stone bridge at the bottom of the hill. So there had to be an opening of some sort on the left before that. "Go on, David."

"Yes." The hands continued to work. "Just where the devil are we going?"

"Ah!" There was a gap ahead, in the high bank on the left; and, although it looked small . . . and it was unsignposted (but then Mountsorrel wasn't National Trust, of course) . . . it was the only gap he could discern in this last hundred yards, before the bridge. *"Ah!"* He pumped the foot-brake furiously, debating whether to overshoot and then back up the hill rather than attempt the turning on his first run. "*Here*, as it happens, is where we're going . . . I think—" *The hell with it!* he thought, swinging the wheel.

The old car creaked in every metal bone and sinew, and canted over dangerously as it slithered in slow motion into a sharp left-hand turn, so that for a moment he feared that it would slam broadside into the bank which rose up again on the lower side of the entrance. But, by the grace of God, it accepted his change of direction, and then stalled in a final protest.

"Indeed?" Audley had lurched against him, swearing under his breath, as they had taken the turn. But now his voice was only mildly incredulous. "And *where*, pray, is *here*, Tom?"

He might well ask, thought Tom, surveying the unpromising vista up the muddy rutted track ahead between future luxuriant banks of stinging nettles.

"That is to say—" Audley amended his question suddenly "—does Panin know how to get to Bodger's Farm?"

"Bodger's Farm?" Tom followed Audley's pointing finger. On the passenger's side, on the wreck of a five-bar gate propped against two oil drums, a crudely-painted board bore that legend.

"Is this where you wanted to go?" inquired Audley politely. "And, if it is, will he be able to get here?"

Tom's confidence weakened. But then long experience of similar places reanimated it. "He has my Ordnance Survey map with the rendezvous marked. I gave it to his escort this morning, before breakfast."

"His escort? His *minder*, you mean?" Audley grinned wolfishly at him. "What was he like?"

Tom turned the ignition key, and the engine purred sweetly at the first touch. "He didn't look the part." He grinned back at Audley. "He seemed a rather inoffensive little fellow, actually." He engaged first gear cautiously. "Very polite, he was, David. In barely adequate English."

"Is that so?" Audley looked around him curiously. "Well, I'm sure appearances are deceptive . . . We're going on, are we?"

The wheels squelched and spun, and then took hold. "For a little way. Then we shall have to walk across the fields, I expect."

"You expect? You haven't been here before, then?"

"No." Tom caught a glimpse of a grey roof through the straggling hedge on his right, down the side of the hill.

"You didn't see Panin himself?"

"No." More roofs, and a hint of yellowish-grey stone. And, in the left foreground, the ruin of an antique farm-tractor half-sunken on the verge beside the track, with the remains of last year's dead nettles still entwined in it.

"I see—" Audley stopped suddenly as Bodger's Farm presented itself to them at last, in all its agricultural squalor.

Tom decided against entering the farmyard morass, even though that would take him closer to what must presumably be the farmhouse itself, for lack of a more likely parking place: any vehicle with less than four-wheel drive attempting that yard might find itself a permanent resident—like the abandoned Rover, old but not yet vintage, which lay wheel-less on one side, to serve now (judging by its present occupants) as a chicken-house.

"You did say . . ." Audley's tone was gently hopeful, looking for confirmation rather than information ". . . that we weren't actually meeting . . . *here* . . . didn't you?"

"Yes—no—" Tom caught a flicker of movement at one curtained window in the blank face of the house "—I'll just go and get directions,

David. Okay?" He opened his door, observing what seemed to be the farmer's domestic refuse pile, which included non-biodegradable washing-up liquid containers among other unspeakable material which was already sodden and well-rotted. "If you'd like to go up there, towards the field—by that gate?"

He stepped out gingerly, into the mud in preference to the domestic midden; which, from its smell, included fish-heads as well as cabbage leaves; and thought, as he did so, that a high, dry summer might not be preferable on Bodger's Farm, because this would be the kingdom of flies, and blow-flies, and all manner of winged insects then. But he must move, now that he was moving, before Audley could protest.

A large dominant cockerel, with bright red upstanding comb and jaunty tail-feathers, eyed him sidelong from its vantage-point on the roof of the Rover with bright reptilian certainty, regretting only that he was too big to be edible, then turning away and defecating nervously on the stained and pitted metal, which had once been some Sunday driver's pride-and-joy.

Tom searched for something just slightly better than filth on which to place his good clean shoes, wondering as he did so what Audley was wearing (and, for God's sake, what shoes Comrade Professor Panin and his minder might have laced up this morning, in all innocence!). But long before he reached the flagstones set in the overgrown grass in front of the farmhouse door he gave up the attempt, and walked through the muck regardless.

(The trouble was, he decided, that the farm was huddled into the hillside, halfway down on its own platform across which all the rainwater from the top evidently made its way, unregulated by anything so outrageously Roman or modern as a drainage system, so it seemed.)

There was no bell or button on the door, which had last been painted when King George VI (or maybe his father) had been on the throne. But there was nothing to push or pull, so he rapped on it with his knuckles instead.

No answer—no sound from within. But he had seen that movement at the low window on his left, with its half-drawn faded curtains. So he knocked again, more sharply than before.

(The incongruous ambience of this squalid place, he thought, was its clashing colours: against the old natural greens and red-browns and greys of grass and mud, and roof and wall, there was the garish yellow of the ranks of plastic drums outside the barn and the vivid orange of the plastic sacks he could see inside it; and the bright red of the brand-new tractor also inside it, beside the sacks—all probably paid for by the EEC, yet as out-of-place and unnatural as the empty *squeezee* Fairy Liquid and

Palmolive pressure containers on the cabbage-stalk-fish-head garbage heap through which he'd walked just now.)

The door-latch snapped behind him, making him jump just as he had reached Audley in his survey *(Audley stamping through the mud, oblivious of it!)*. But the door didn't open, it only shivered as he turned back to it; but then the bolts inside cracked, and the key inside clicked, and the door began to open, scraping on the floor beneath it.

Tom composed his face into a mask of obsequious inquiry even before he could see anyone in the opening.

"Good morning—" (Could the farmer be Mr Bodger? But could *anyone* be Mr Bodger?) "—sir . . . I'm sorry to bother—" (or should it be *bodger?* he thought insanely) "—to bother you, so early in the morning, sir."

No answer, not even a grunt. Only the shadowy presence of someone taller than his own ceiling, therefore stooped under it, and a waft of smell composed of innumerable elements, in which damp walls predominated but paraffin and unwashed clothes and fried bacon fat also played their parts, among other things which he could not even guess at.

Tom tried to continue without breathing in too much of it. "Do you mind if . . ." The incongruity of the request enveloped him, like the smell ". . . if I go to see your castle, sir?" The incongruity increased beyond his imagination as he thought of Gilbert de Merville riding to Mountsorrel Castle this way, on his iron-shod *destrier*, eight hundred years ago—*eight-and-a-half hundred years ago*—in this same mud, if not this same world.

The presence shook itself. "Cross the fields. Follow the track. 'Bout 'alf a mile. You can't miss it—church is on t'other side, opposite."

Tom was overwhelmed by gratitude and relief, so that he felt in his pocket willingly. "There is a charge, I presume?"

"No charge." The presence also seemed relieved, as though he had expected someone worse, in direct descent from Joscelin himself, demanding money rather than offering it. "Jus' make sure you shuts the gates . . . 'cause I've got beasts up there, that way."

"Of course." Tom remembered Panin, and offered what was in his hand nevertheless. "I have two friends—two foreign gentlemen—who are also coming shortly . . . If you would be so good as to direct them . . . This is for your trouble, sir—"

The door started to close, with the banknote ignored. "No trouble. Jus' so they closes the gates, that's all." The words just managed to escape as it snapped shut, and as Tom turned away he heard the key click in the lock and the bolts rattle back top and bottom.

He crossed the yard diagonally, through a mixture of what looked like one part of Exmoor mud to three parts of cow-dung, to where Audley stood unconcernedly in a clump of dead nettles beside another antique farm-gate which was secured to its post by a loop of bright orange plastic rope.

The old man regarded him quizzically. "This is the right place, then?"

"Yes." As he unhooked the gate he observed that Audley's shoes were only slightly less mud-and-dung encrusted than his own. But they were stout heavy country shoes, and Audley didn't seem to mind, anyway; if anything, he sounded much more polite and friendly than earlier, when he'd been in relative comfort. Perhaps the sight of all the piles of refuse reminded him of his beloved compost heaps. "This way—about half a mile."

"Indeed?" Audley waited while he closed the gate. "Now, tell me, Tom . . . what gave you the idea of this particular rendezvous? Rather than any other?"

Tom winced. It had seemed an innocently interesting idea, both in his head and on the map, after reading Panin's note the night before. "I was rather hoping you weren't going to ask that." He studied the deeply-rutted track with distaste. "Shall we walk on the grass?"

"Yes. That would be the sensible thing to do," agreed Audley. "I rather approve of it, that's all."

"Approve of it—?" Tom failed to avoid a rich new cow-pat, and slid dangerously in it for a second before he regained his balance.

"Ye-ess. In the open, and nice and private, like he wants. But make the bugger suffer a bit for his privacy. Yes . . . I *like* it, Tom." Audley beamed at him. "So now you tell me why you're so happy—or why you *were* so happy first thing, if not now . . . Right?"

They had already topped a minor corrugation in the side of the valley, so that now a small lateral re-entrant lay below them. But there was no sign of Mountsorrel on the spur ahead. "I had a visitor last night, David."

"A visitor?" Audley was striding out on his long legs, his pale raincoat flapping, as though he knew where he was going. Or as though, even if he didn't know, he was confident of getting there.

The memory of Willy cheered Tom, restoring his happiness in that instant. "A girl I know. A very pretty girl, too."

"Well, well!" Audley didn't miss a step. "Now *that* is cunning such as I love to hear. Or uncommonly good management, anyway . . . Or quite exceptional good luck—which will do just as well." He sniffed, and then chuckled throatily. "Give me a minder who's lucky—then I'm truly safe, by golly!" He threw a grin over his shoulder. "Perhaps that fellow yesterday really was aiming at me. But with you beside me he never had a hope, eh?"

The old man was in good shape, in spite of his cold, thought Tom, lengthening his stride. And in good heart now, apparently. Or was this just an old war-horse—on this track an old *destrier*—snorting at the prospect of what he'd been trained for, with his iron-shod hoofs?

"Not any of those, I'm afraid—" The ground at the bottom of the re-entrant was boggy, with grass mounds standing out of water; but it might have been Trafalgar Square for all the notice the old man took of it: he splashed through it regardless "—she works for the CIA, David."

"Ah!" Audley checked and turned as he reached firmer ground beyond the bog. "Now, that'll be the new chap, Sheldon—Mosby-Something-Sheldon? *Major, USAF* when I first met him, but always 'Doc' to his associates. And 'Mose-honey' to the girl he had in tow last time I met him . . . and *she* was a very pretty girl too—and she worked for the CIA too, as I have good reason to recall." He cracked another grin, but this time it wasn't a real one. "He's quite a good chap, actually. Sound Virginian Confederate stock, is our major."

"He's a colonel now."

"Is he so? Well, they would have had to promote him." Audley turned away, up the hillside. "He's a dentist by profession—one-time profession, anyway. Which proves his patriotism, if nothing else. Because I'll bet he could make a lot more money 'hanging out his shingle', or whatever they do, and building expensive bridgework, than hanging out the flag . . . and sending pretty girls to visit you late at night." He gave Tom a sidelong look. "So what did she have to tell you? And what did she want in exchange?" Sniff. "And what—w-what did you give her—?" The sniff turned into a giant sneeze, which occasioned a desperate search for the reserve handkerchief. "Or shouldn't I ask?" The old man blew his nose. "Damn blasted cold!"

Tom blessed the cold for giving him time to straighten his thoughts and his face. "She says you're in trouble."

"Huh!" Audley tossed his head and breathed in deeply. "That's nothing new. What have I done this time?"

"You've offended some politician or other, she says."

"Oh . . . *that?*" Audley shrugged. "It wasn't anything personal. He just needs to tighten up his department, that's all. Serve the bugger right!" He gave Tom another sidelong look, but this time he winked as well. "I've got any number of enemies in high places, boy. But I've got one or two friends as well—and maybe in higher places, too. So no need to worry about *that*." The eye which had winked became fish-cold. "What else?"

"She said Panin was also in trouble." It was no good passing on the "cut-and-run" advice: Audley would just laugh at that. "The Americans are quite surprised he was let out to talk to you."

"Ah . . ." Audley stumped up the hillside in silence for a moment or two ". . . now *that* is interesting. Even if it's hardly surprising." He grimaced at the grass beneath his feet. "Although that's the sort of thing, properly elaborated with chapter and verse, which Basil Cole could have explained . . . ye-ess . . . But now he can't, can he?" He stopped suddenly, and turned again, stone-faced to match the cold eyes. "So we shall have to live on my fat, pending nourishment from elsewhere, for the time being." The eyes looked through Tom, and then past him, but not at anything, quite unfocused. "If *he* is in trouble, so you say . . ."

In spite of himself, Tom had to turn, even though he was close to the crest now. But there was nothing behind them: Audley was looking at things inside his head, which pointed from the past into the present. "*She* said, David."

"*She* said—yes . . ." The look continued ". . . and I said 'friends'—so *I* said." The old man blinked, and snapped back to him. "Perhaps I delude myself when I say I have *friends* . . . So perhaps we are both in trouble—as *she* says." The corner of his mouth twitched. "But what we have to remember is that Panin lives in a different world from ours, in which 'trouble' has a different meaning."

It was a statement, not a question. But it seemed to be looking for an answer, nevertheless. "His trouble could be terminal, do you mean?"

Another twitch. "It's hard to say now. Basil Cole could have told us." It was the right answer, all the same, the twitch suggested. "But *he* has no friends—not even with a 'perhaps'. He just has success or failure—and then a fresh lease or bankruptcy, as the case may be." He nodded suddenly. "But you're quite right, Tom: he has the advantage on us because we're only playing games, but he's playing life-and-death, maybe. So he plays harder, always."

Tom thought of Basil Cole. "And he kills people, maybe?"

"Without a second thought—" Audley twisted away, up the hillside again "—or without investigative journalists, or questioning civil servants, or inconvenient questions in Parliament, anyway . . . *if he pulls it off, boy—if he pulls it off!*" He stepped out again, leaving Tom behind.

Tom opened his mouth, wanting to stop the big man reaching the crest before he could, because Mountsorrel ought to be visible from there and he wanted to be the first to make sure that it was. But Audley's legs were too long and he had too much momentum, and the first words that came into his head were useless, anyway: if Panin was already "in trouble" they both knew the KGB's unforgiving attitude to failed overseas operations mounted to restore a waning reputation.

"David!" Even as the right Audley-stopping words occurred to him he saw that it was too late: Audley had stopped of his own accord at the top. "She did give me something else—"

"Well!" Audley was staring ahead, hands on his hips. "I might have known!" He squared his shoulders and shook his head. Then he turned back to Tom abruptly. "What else did she give you, Sheldon's woman?"

Willy described as "Sheldon's woman" cut deep, and the accuracy of the description turned the knife in the wound. But at least Mountsorrel must be in view at last, and that made him stand firm where he was, down the hillside. "What might you have known, David?" he inquired innocently.

Audley tossed his head. "What did she tell you?"

All the pleasure of Mountsorrel was gone before he had set eyes on it. "She gave me three names, David." He paused deliberately. "Does Zarubin ring any of your bells?"

"Zarubin?" Against his backdrop of grey rainclouds Audley looked huge above him. "Yes—he rings bells . . . albeit discordantly, Tom." He gave Tom back an equally deliberate pause. "He's a 24-carat KGB *shit*, is Colonel Gennadiy Zarubin . . . If that's his real name. Which it almost certainly isn't, because only God and Central KGB Records know that." Sniff. "But yes, he certainly rings bells—a whole bloody peal of them, with umpteen thousand changes: KGB Triple-Cross Major, that might do for him . . . And I can maybe think of a few people who'd like to see him hanged—or 'hung', should it be, in this context?—but . . . *strung up*, anyway. And there'd be some jostling in the queue to pull on his rope too, by God!" He nodded. "Gennadiy *Ivanovich Zarubin*—" He stopped suddenly, frowning at Tom as though he'd remembered something.

"Yes, David?"

"Mmmm . . ." The frown was edged with calculations. "But you said *names*, didn't you, Tom? So ring another bell then—eh?"

It was no good: he'd been too slow. "Marchuk. Leonid Marchuk."

No surprise. Rather . . . satisfaction? "Yes." Nod. "That's a good name."

"Good?" The old bastard *had* remembered something.

"Yes." Audley showed the edges of ivory-yellow teeth, which were damn good imitations if they weren't his own. "'Good' in the General Phil Sheridan sense, of the-only-good-indian being a dead one." He stopped again, but this time raised an eyebrow. "But you don't know that—?"

"He's dead is he?" Tom relaxed slightly. Because if Audley *knew* . . . then that was really rather reassuring, on balance. "Marchuk's dead?"

The eyebrow lifted again, but disbelievingly now. "On the Czestochowa road, to Katowice, was it?" Audley murdered the Polish place-names, as every good Englishman always did. "Another tragic accident—like Basil Cole's? Except that poor old Basil fell out of his tree, and poor Leonid lost control of his KGB-issue Mercedes—?" Audley *tut-tutted* insincerely. "All these tragic accidents! *'In the midst of life we are in death . . .'* It makes me quite grateful that I didn't take my own car out this morning —or climb one of the trees in my garden . . . One can be so *accidental*, can't one?"

On the Czestochowa road? Willy hadn't known that detail, so Audley knew more than the CIA did about Marchuk's death. "Perhaps he didn't have a minder, David. Or maybe he didn't do what his minder told him?"

Audley acknowledged the message with the very slightest of bows. "Perhaps." Then he dropped the shutters on casual pretence. "Three names. So give me the Third Man, and stop pissing me around, Tom—right?" He turned, to take another look at what lay beyond, and then came back to Tom. "Right?"

Not right. Because (as always), the more he let himself be bullied, the more he would be bullied: but the lesson of King Stephen was that when one was in the weaker position it might be safer to let oneself be bullied than to antagonize someone who was not yet an enemy. "You tell me, David." Instinct strengthened him. "You tell me who your Third Man is—after Zarubin and Marchuk—" Instinct pushed him further "—after them, but before Panin, David? *You tell me—right?*"

Audley smiled, and Tom hated the thought that he might be remembering *Danny Dzieliwski* as he cocked his head. "Fair enough!" Shrug. "And we're short of time, anyway." Another shrug. "So, for size, let's say . . . *Piotrowski*, Tom?"

Wrong—but close enough! "Or *Pietruszka*—"

Audley gestured dismissively. "Same thing. Does it matter?"

"To me it does." A knot of anger twisted in Tom's guts. But then the dominant Arkenshaw half of him, descended from a long line of cold-blooded Englishmen, warned him that that particular length of gut was unreliably Polish. "What same thing, David?"

The old man watched him thoughtfully. "They're both doing time in some Polish jail, aren't they? Officially, anyway, if not actually. And . . . twenty-five years each, wasn't it?" Sniff. "Isn't there a typical Polish joke about that—about Piotrowski and Pietruszka getting twenty-five year sentences for murdering Father Jerzy Popieluszko? One year for the murder—and twenty-four for getting caught?"

The knot twisted again, even though it was a typical Polish joke. "I didn't know you were an expert on Polish affairs, David."

"I'm not. Although I did learn quite a lot of Polish history when I was pursuing your dear mother so unavailingly long ago, when I cherished the foolish belief that the way to her heart might be through a profound knowledge of the Jagiello dynasty, and Sobieski's ride to the relief of Vienna, and Pilsudski's tactics against Trotsky." Audley smiled disarmingly again for a second. Then his face blanked over again. "But the murder of Father Popieluszko did rather interest me for historical reasons as well as professional ones, you see, Tom. Historical analogies always interest me, particularly as they bear on the conflict between the 'Accident' and 'Conspiracy' theories."

Tom's Arkenshaw 51 per cent restrained his Dzieliwski 49 per cent. "What historical analogy?"

"My dear boy!" Audley seemed genuinely surprised. "*You*, with your special hobby shouldn't ask that! Don't you remember when Henry Plantagenet cried 'Who will rid me of this turbulent priest?', or words to that effect? So Fitz-Urse and the other three knights instantly caught the next cross-Channel ferry and murdered Thomas Becket in his own cathedral just as messily and incompetently as the Poles and the KGB murdered your Father Jerzy. And Henry threw up his hands in horror, and promptly disowned them?" Audley's lip curled cynically. "And he did penance for it. And his Thomas—your patron saint maybe, Tom?—*he* got his sainthood wings . . . But then Henry Plantagenet of England didn't have to worry about his turbulent priest anymore, did he? And *your* General Jaruzelski—"

"Not *my* General Jaruzelski, damn you!" snapped Tom.

"I do beg your pardon, Tom!" The old man raised his palm. "I mean, of course, *their* General Jaruzelski—agent for Messrs Comrades Brezhnev, Andropov, Chernenko, Gorbachev and Company Limited, registered in Moscow and Warsaw and other places too numerous to mention—*their* good General . . . *he* didn't have to worry about *his* turbulent priest again, either. And neither did they, eh?"

"You're wrong." In spite of his Arkenshaw self, Tom couldn't leave it at that. "People come from all over Poland to pray at his grave, David. And there's always a mound of flowers on it. And men from his Warsaw steel plant stand guard there, night and day."

"Oh yes!" Audley cut through his words. "And, in God's good time, as interpreted by the Vatican, he'll be Saint George Popieluszko, just like our Saint Thomas Becket—you can bet on it! And they'll go on coming to—where is it, Tom—?"

"St Stanislaw Kostka, in Zoliborz." The words came out stiffly.

"St Stanislaw Kostka, in Zoliborz." Audley just about managed to parrot the pronunciation. "Just like Thomas Becket's shrine in Canterbury, only without so much gold and precious stones—

"*'Thenne longen folk to go on pilgrimages—'*

"—just like we all had to learn for School Cert, out of Chaucer . . . or it would have been 'O-Levels', for you, presumably—

> "*'And specially, from every shires ende*
> *Of Engelond, to Canterbury they wende,*
> *The holy blisful martir for to seeke,*
> *That them hath holpen when that they were weeke.'*

"Remember?" Again the lip curled. "I've always thought that that was the one big mistake Marx made—not incorporating the Opium of the Masses into his formula somehow . . . Or Lenin might have managed an interpretative footnote or two, just to keep the non-party peasants quiet, like the feudal Church and State did, with a 'treasure-in-heaven' clause . . . Just for the time being, anyway, before they were likely to get anything much on earth, while they were very obviously getting the rough end of the Revolution."

That was enough. In fact, with Panin at their backs (maybe even now getting his feet muddy in Mr Bodger's farmyard), it was too much, even disregarding its casual blasphemy.

"How does Zarubin fit in with Father Popieluszko's murderers, David?"

Audley beckoned him. "In the most obvious way. Can't you guess—if you really don't know?"

Tom felt the soft hillside under his feet holding him back, in spite of the image of Panin at his back. "It was a KGB assassination?"

Audley looked surprised again, momentarily. "You really don't know?" Surprise warred with suspicion. "Of course . . . you are just . . . Damn! That sounds too damn patronizing for words, when I don't mean it that way—"

"Just a minder?" If Audley wasn't being honest now, then he was good. But then he *was* good. "A high-class minder?"

The old man's face suggested that he found himself where he didn't want to be. "I suppose . . . if I said that I wouldn't like that job, because I don't think I could do it—?" Audley shook his head. "But the hell with that! Because . . . the truth is, I don't know whether it was a KGB hit, or whether they just agreed to it." He drew a deep breath. "Maybe Basil Cole could have told us more—I don't know that, either—whether Jaruzelski was in on it, or not . . . Or whether he was in on it, but he was just obeying orders—*I don't bloody-well know, and that's the truth!*"

He cocked his head over his shoulder, towards Mountsorrel. "Which is why we're going in half-blind now, I'm afraid, Tom."

Tom's feet shifted under him. "But the KGB were in on it?"

Audley half turned as Tom started to move. "Of course they bloody-were! Zarubin and Marchuk were the contact-men, with Piotrowski and Pietruszka. And, although I never asked old Basil about Marchuk's road accident—whether it was genuine old-fashioned *accident*, or genuine old-fashioned Polish-revenge *conspiracy*—" Audley cut off as Tom reached him, on the crest of the ridge.

Mountsorrel, Tom saw and thought the same thing, while trying to listen to what Audley was saying at the same time.

"So now we have to guess," said Audley.

At least neither of them had to guess about Mountsorrel, thought Tom, hugging the view to himself: it was a perfect *motte-and-bailey* fortress for his collection, built up on its spur of land above the river-crossing below with unerring Norman offensive-defensive insight; and then abandoned, either after King Stephen had put down Baldwin de Redvers at Exeter, or after Henry II Plantagenet had taken firm hold of his kingdom a few years later: a bloody-perfect *motte-and-bailey*, with its wooden pallisades fallen and rotted-away eight-hundred years ago and only marked now by the prickly furze which grew on the earth ramparts which still rose from the green spring cow-pastures of its hillside.

God! If only he had his measuring-kit, and Willy here beside him, like yesterday, to hold the other end of the tape-measure, and to crawl among those prickly furze-bushes!

"So now we have to guess—?" Even though David Audley was a bad joke when compared with Willy Groot . . . And even though he would never come here again, *via* that muddy yard, with his lost Willy, now . . . Even, in spite of all of that, *he would come here again, to measure Mountsorrel!* And that made him smile the question at Audley.

"But that's why you're happy, isn't it?" Then Audley looked at him strangely. "Isn't there a chance now . . . now that you've got a vague idea why Panin's here . . . that you can maybe settle your Polish score, while I settle up with him? Isn't that it?" Audley cocked that knowing eyebrow of his. "Don't we both have a score now? Or . . . what else did your young Sheldon-woman have to say—?"

The old man was going for the big fish, and Tom could see no reason now why he shouldn't pass on the rest of Willy's pillow-talk, which he had been husbanding. "Zarubin was recalled to Moscow in January, David." As he spoke Audley turned back to Mountsorrel, and he thought *maybe the old man's not got it wrong, after all: it would be agreeable, next time he kissed Mamusia, to know that he'd done something to settle that score, even though he could never tell her; for she had wept for Father Jerzy, and had worn black for him.* "Did you know that?"

"No. Zarubin's none of my business." Audley continued to study Mountsorrel. "But . . . that would be prudent to get him out, if Marchuk's accident wasn't accidental. Which, I suppose, we can now assume it wasn't . . . So—?"

"The word is that he's gone 'diplomatic'." He wanted to study Mountsorrel too. But there would be time for that later. "At the time of the murder he was officially a cultural attaché in Warsaw. Although his main links were actually with the church affairs section of the Ministry of the Interior—Pietruszka's department."

"Uh-huh?" Audley nodded at Mountsorrel. "This is one of your pristine *mottes and baileys*, I take it, Tom? 'Adulterine', would it be?"

"Very likely." Tom decided to drop Pietruszka and play the game. Because, if Audley wasn't worried about Panin, why should he be? "Professor Fraser thinks it's Gilbert de Merville's 'Mountsorrel Castle', which surrendered after Stephen took Exeter from Baldwin de Redvers in 1136. Gilbert certainly was one of Baldwin's men, and he held land in these parts."

"Mmm . . ." Audley nodded again. "And Gilbert was a bad bastard, wasn't he? Wasn't he the one who hanged his hostages—including the children? Which good old Stephen never had the heart to do?" Another nod. "So what's Zarubin doing now, then?"

He had been right to play the game. "The word is that he may be coming to England very shortly. Like . . . any day now, David. Or he may even be here already."

"Is that so?" Audley shifted his gaze slightly, to consider their own approach line to Mountsorrel, along the deeply tractor-furrowed track. "You know, I rather think this must be the original road to your castle, Tom—" He pointed ahead "—see how the ridge is deeply cut there? That's not some old Devon farmer's spade-work: that's peasant sweated-labour, that is, or I'm a monkey's uncle!" Satisfied nod. "So why is he coming? Because it's safer here, between Exmoor and London, than it is between Czestochowa and Warsaw . . . at least for him, if not for me? Or has he got work to do?"

Tom listened to Willy's whisper, editing out the added endearments and the warmth and softness of her in the crook of his arm. "It all depends on the progress they make, to get Reagan and Gorbachev together in the autumn, Sheldon thinks."

"Ah!" Audley looked up and down the track again. "If there isn't a road on the other side of that ridge ahead, where the castle is . . . then this just *has* to be the one . . . if that's the main entrance there—" He pointed "—in that gap in the gorse, right?" He lowered his hand. "If they don't meet, he's certainly not going to be able to detach our revered Iron Lady from her favourite film star, not even after her happy meeting with Tsar Mikhail . . . Not with our commitment to Cruise and Trident —" The hand came up again "—do you see that gap? Is that the main *bailey* entrance, Tom?"

The higher *motte* was diagonally on the far side, away from them; and it would be interesting to find out how deep the ditch was on that far side, and whether it cut down into the beginning of bed-rock there. "I think it probably is, David." That would fix the *motte* high above its river valley too, where he would expect it to be; because, when they had half a chance, the Normans never made a mistake, with their eye for ground.

"Yes. I think you're right." Audley gave him the undeserved credit for the insight. "So you just keep your eye on that—right?" Pause. "So his brief could be . . . if Mr President and the Tsar don't meet . . . to give aid and comfort to poor old CND, surreptitiously, contributing generously to the collections, like my darling wife does." Sniff. "That's what I'd do, anyway, if I was calling the shots." He gestured forwards. "Shall we go then—where glory waits, Tom?"

Something held Tom back on the crest, beside Audley, all his certainties and half-certainties suddenly hedged by doubt and half-uncertainty as he stared at the gap in the ring of prickly gorse which encircled and overran both the outer rampart and the *motte* itself. Because there were suddenly too many imponderables—too many conflicting bloody-minded interests, like the brackets and incomprehensible symbols of some mathematical equation which he lacked both the skill and the intelligence to unravel: Jaggard was playing his own game against Audley, as well as Panin; and Audley and Panin were each playing their own games too, probably against someone else as well as each other. And he was in the middle of all their games, hog-tied not only by his vengeful thoughts about Father Jerzy's murderers, but also by his last-night memories of Willy, which broke every rule in the book because sexual encounters of the closest sort were still the commonest form of betrayal, still out-performing cash and ideology across the world.

But then, mercifully—mercifully, while he was still havering—Audley reached towards him, to grasp his arm above the elbow.

"*There*, Tom—" The grip tightened painfully "*—do you see—?*"

He had already been told where he had to look, in that gap in the rampart out of which Gilbert de Merville had ridden for the last time in 1136, when he'd surrendered Mountsorrel to King Stephen's man, who might have ridden past Bodger's Farm to this very point, to make sure of Baldwin de Redvers' castellan's surrender.

There was someone in the gap—

Audley's fingers squeezed his arm. "I told you—I should have known!" After that final squeeze, the hand released his arm. "To get ahead of Nikolai Andrievich you have to get up very early in the morning—I should have known better!"

Now there was another figure, beside the first one. "That's Panin, is it?"

"Huh!" Audley grunted. "At this distance, with my eyes, it might be Jack Butler . . . or Henry Jaggard . . . or the Archdeacon of Truro, for all I know, Tom. But I'll give you ten-to-one—or a hundred-to-one, if you want to put your money down—that *that's* Nikolai Andrievich . . . and that *that* little one – the one that's twitching around, like he's got ants in his pants . . . that *that* one is his minder . . . his own Thomas *Arkenshaw*, all the way from Dzerzhinsky Square?"

Dzerzhinsky Square cut deep, as it always did: the historical truth that Dzerzhinsky had been a Polish aristocrat, who had founded Lenin's secret intelligence and simultaneously betrayed his class and his country, was a wound which never healed—which certainly didn't heal now, above Gilbert of Merville's *motte!*

Audley waited, but again mercifully. "Okay, Tom?" The merciful pause extended. "So let's go and zap the bugger, eh? *Let's go and do it—eh?*"

VIII

AUDLEY HAD BEEN right about Professor Andrievich Panin, and quite cruelly right: he looked like nothing so much as an elderly sheep, with his queerly bent nose and an inadequate lower jaw at the bottom of his elongated face; or, anyway, he didn't look like what he was, and so much so that Tom had to look at Audley himself to accept his "I-told-you-so".

But Audley himself was no comfort, for he didn't look the part either, quite disconcertingly; and then, just as he was type-casting Audley once again, the little Russian minder whom he'd met so briefly before breakfast ducked out from the bushes again, with what was obviously his habitual expression of mild bewilderment, but also buttoning up the old-fashioned fly-buttons on his trousers quite openly.

So here we are! thought Tom: *The Elderly Sheep, who must have seen a hecatomb of human lambs go to the slaughter, so that blood couldn't worry him now, innocent or otherwise; and the one-time Fairground English Pugilist, who looked as though he had let the young hopefuls hit his face while he delivered the killing body-blows (and who looked so beamishly happy now, at the prospect of slugging it out with an old friend); and this little KGB Stan Laurel, from a hundred tragi-comedies, minus only his bowler hat; and, not least incongruous, Sir Thomas Arkenshaw, the dead ringer of Count Waldemar Osinski, Mamusia's mother's brother, who had led his lancers to victory against Trotsky's machine-gunners against all military reason and elementary commonsense: altogether a most incongruous quartet, to meet in the entrance of Gilbert de Merville's forgotten castle!*

"See that—?" The Pugilist touched his elbow. "You don't often see those now, Tom."

"What?" *This was the main entrance to the Mountsorrel bailey*—he could see that now, at a glance. "What?"

"Fly-buttons. There must have been a shortage of zip-fasteners when that suit came off the peg in the good old USS of R, Tom lad—" Audley hissed his opinion from the corner of his mouth "—*Professor Panin—Nikolai!* It's been a long time . . . in fact, more years than I care to remember, eh?" But he advanced through the gap in the ramparts with all the confidence of King Stephen's favourite baron accepting the surrender of Gilbert de Merville's castellan in 1136 *anno domini*. "But . . . good to see you, anyway, Nikolai."

"Dr Audley—*David!*" The Sheep's accent was classless and stateless, and all the more curious for its lack of origin. "A long time is true." The Sheep stopped on his full stop, and took Audley's hand and gave it one formal shake. Only then did he look at Tom officially, although Tom had been conscious of a long preceding scrutiny as they had approached Mountsorrel's entrance.

"May I present Sir Thomas Arkenshaw, late of the Foreign and Commonwealth Office, who is here to see that I don't make a perfect fool of myself?" Audley rose to the occasion. "At least, in so far as I am ever capable of perfection, anyway."

The Sheep's hand was small and dry and smooth and warm, but not soft: it was like shaking a skin-tight glove. But The Sheep also registered his own disadvantage, which Tom sensed from experience of those before him who couldn't make the age and the Polish face fit the English title. "Sir . . . Thomas."

"Baronet, Nikolai." Audley sounded as though he was about to enjoy himself. "Tom hasn't rendered Our Sovereign Lady—or *either* of my sovereign ladies—any signal service himself. Or not yet, anyway. Or not signal enough to be tapped on the shoulder with a sword, and told to 'Rise, Sir Thomas!' He's not 'Sir Thomas, *knight*'—he's a hereditary 'Sir Thomas, *Baronet*', with no damned merit attached to it, do you see?"

"Ah!" The Sheep stopped trying to reassemble Tom from his constituent parts. "A *lord*—"

"No." Tom was tired of being mocked so early, before the pubs opened. "But one of my ancestors made too much money, Professor. It was just a way of making him pay extra taxes, that's all."

"Is that so, Sir Thomas?" The Sheep's deeply-lined and pock-marked face remained effortlessly inscrutable. "And that was long ago, truly?"

"Yes." The Sheep was playing the Pugilist's game, Tom decided. So maybe he'd better play too. "About midway between Tsar Ivan the Terrible and Tsar Peter the Great, actually."

"Which is to say, about three-hundred-and-fifty years before Tsar Mikhail Gorbachev, Nikolai," said Audley pleasantly. "Who is your problem at the moment, I take it?"

"My problem?" Panin hardly looked at Audley. "Sir Thomas—may I present Major Kazimierz Sadowski?" He spread a hand towards Stan Laurel. "Dr Audley—Major Sadowski—Major, you have heard me tell of the unique Dr Audley? Well, this is he, in the substantial flesh." The face-lines cracked their customary grooves into a travesty of a smile. "The

Major was formerly a tank officer, David. I have told him that you were also once the same, in the Great Patriotic War. So he is now probably trying to think of a British tank large enough for you in those far-off days —was it perhaps a 'Churchill'?"

"No." Audley didn't offer his hand to the Major, only his deepest suspicion. For which Tom was truly grateful, since it at least partially covered his own surprise. "It was a 'Cromwell', actually. Which was probably a lot more comfortable than a T-34. But a bloody-sight less safe." As he spoke he frowned horribly at the Major, who also hadn't attempted to take the hand which hadn't been offered. "But that isn't a good KGB name, is it—*Kazimierz-Whatever*—? It sounds decidedly . . . Polish, would that be?" He stared belligerently at the Major for a moment, but then turned back to Panin as it became obvious that he was no more likely to get an answer than a hand. "Polish, Nikolai?"

Panin managed to shrug without moving. "You once said to me, 'In my father's house there are many rooms'—?"

"'Mansions'—not 'rooms', Nikolai." Audley faced Panin squarely. "The Gospel According to St John, chapter fourteen. And John also said '*Other sheep I have, which are not of this fold*', I do agree! And he also said a few other things, which are perhaps even more apposite to this morning —like, '*Ye are of your father, the devil*', Nikolai, for a start!"

Panin turned to Tom. "I have made an error, Sir Thomas: I have quoted at him from his own Book!"

"So you have." Suddenly Audley's voice became cold and hard. " '*It is expedient to us, that one man should die for the people!*'." He turned to Tom, just as the Russian had done. "Sorry for the blasphemy, Tom. But this bugger owes us a life, and I'm damned if I'm going to pretend that I don't know that he knows that he does." He fixed Tom only for a half-second before returning to Panin. "Tell me about Basil Cole, Nikolai. Because, if we're going to do any business at all, that's one expediency I need to know about first."

Panin stared at Audley. "Basil Cole." Then he frowned. "Basil Cole?"

"Don't tell me you've never heard of him." Sniff. "He cut his teeth on you, I shouldn't wonder—the late Basil Cole, Professor."

Panin gave Audley three seconds, then he looked around, up and down Gilbert of Merville's ditches, left and right. "I do not like this place. It was your idea—one of your historical ideas, David?"

"It was *your* idea, Professor—outside, in the open?" Audley nodded at Tom without looking at him. "Your idea in general. And Tom's in particular." The old man looked down at Panin's feet. "Too dirty for you, is it?"

Panin stared at Tom interrogatively.

"I think it's a good place." Audley continued before either of them could speak. "An appropriate place, anyway."

That got Panin back. "Appropriate?"

"Yes." This time Audley quartered Gilbert of Merville's long-forgotten work. "The mid-twelfth century in England happens to be Sir Thomas's hobby, and that was when this pile of dirt was thrown together. But I take it you don't know about the mid-twelfth century in England, Professor?" Audley smiled at the Russian. "In the great days of Kiev, that would be, I suppose—when Moscow was a muddy frontier settlement?" The smile broadened. "But, of course, you're safe in the days long before that! Ancient Scythian archaeology—I remember, from the old days . . ." He shrugged apologetically. "I'm afraid this isn't sufficiently archaeological, in your meaning of the word, old friend. But not inappropriate, no."

"No?" Panin studied his surroundings for a moment before continuing; and (thought Tom) he didn't need to be a genius either to understand its function or to guess that Audley was somehow lying in wait for him back in history. "But it would also be *your* period, my dear David—would it not? Those essays of yours which I so assiduously read before we last met, in those same old days—on the crusading Kingdom of Jerusalem . . . That was the twelfth century, wasn't it?" Having finished with the *bailey* rampart, he scrutinized the *motte* itself. "They were . . . if I may say so without giving offence . . . not altogether *un*scholarly." Now he was relating the position of the *motte* to the *bailey*. "In fact, if those crusader castles had not conveniently crossed every frontier from Egypt to Turkey I might almost have thought that you were following Lawrence's footsteps, and not misusing your scholarship in the service of your country's needs." He completed his survey, but did so facing Major Stan Laurel Sadowski, not Audley. "Major . . . I do not like either of these ridges, as I have already said. But that across the valley is masked by the mound if we take but a few steps. So I would have you upon the ridge above us, while we transact our business?" He pointed up the hillside.

Major Sadowski indicated that he understood the English language not with a nod, let alone a word or any variation in his permanent expression of surprise-verging-on-tears, but simply by moving to obey Panin's request without question or delay.

Panin watched him depart through Gilbert of Merville's *bailey* gateway. "The advantage of having a Pole is that he does what he is told," said Panin to the Major's back. Then he came again to Audley. "And, of course, my dear David, the poor creature has been over-awed by your presence. And by our medieval crusaders of the twelfth century. And I'm sure he doesn't know your T. E. Lawrence from D. H. Lawrence—do you think *Lady Chatterley's Lover* has ever been translated into Polish? I would think not, eh?" He continued to stare at Audley, but so fixedly that Tom felt that he himself was very deliberately *not* being looked at, even though his reciprocal dismissal was now presumably what the Russian required.

"Oh . . . do you think so?" Audley cocked his head, frowning slightly, as if the question was of importance. "*Lady Chatterley* must have been . . . mid-1920s? And it must have been one of Lawrence's last books, because he died in 1930. So Poland was still a free country then." Then he nodded, still frowning. "But the Catholics might have banned it, I agree." He drew a sudden breath and then sneezed explosively, and began to search for his handkerchief. "So you may well be right, at that." He buried his face in the handkerchief. "I do beg your pardon, Nikolai."

"You have a cold?" inquired Panin sympathetically.

"I have a cold." Audley nodded. "And Sir Thomas stays, Nikolai."

Now Panin glanced at Tom, but then quickly returned to Audley. "They do not trust you even now, David? Even less than they trust me?"

Sniff. "Nobody trusts me." The thought seemed to brighten Audley. "Not even my dear wife."

The two old men considered each other in silence, and Tom decided it was time to hear his own voice again. "I think what Dr Audley means is that I'm not so good at doing what I'm told, Professor—unlike Major Sadòwski—" He realized too late, as he pronounced the name, that he had made the mistake of inflecting it correctly "—even though I am equally overawed by meeting the celebrated Professor Panin, naturally."

"Hah! And so you'd better be, Tom," agreed Audley. "Not every day do you get to meet an old Central Committee man who was dandled on the knee of Vladimir Il'ich Lenin as a baby, and given a revolutionary blessing! Or is that just a story, Nikolai?"

"It is just a story." Panin was giving his whole speculative attention to Tom now. "Vladimir Il'ich did not dandle babies on his knee."

"No—of course!" Audley nodded agreement. "Only poor devils who have to win the proletariat vote have to dandle babies—of course! And your old dad fought with the White Army in any case, didn't he? In the Semenovski Guards, was it?"

Panin continued to stare at Tom. "And I am no longer on the Central Committee." He ignored Audley's flippancies. "This place was a fortress, Sir Thomas. Correct?"

Tom had just registered the *Semenovski Guards*: they had been among the Imperial guards regiments of the Tsar himself. So Audley was playing dirty, as was his custom. "Yes, Professor." He was tempted to leave it at that, but found that he couldn't. "It was probably built by a man named Gilbert de Merville in the mid-1130s, who was a supporter of a great baron named Baldwin de Redvers. If it is, then it's Mountsorrel Castle."

Panin turned away for a moment, to the gorse-and-bracken covered line of *bailey* ditch-and-rampart again, and then to the higher *motte* across the few yards of cow-hoofprinted and cowpatted expanse of coarse pasture which separated the *bailey* gate from the ditched *motte* overlooking the river crossing below. But when he came back to Tom there was something in his face, or behind his eyes, which betrayed an insight into what it had once been, before it had been trodden down and demilitarized by eight-and-a-half centuries of time and cows.

"So how is Mountsorrel Castle appropriate to us now, Sir Thomas?"

"Ah!" Audley burst back into the conversation like a Cromwell finding its gap in the *bocage* at last. "Now . . . now what I *meant*, Nikolai . . . was not so much related to *place*, you see . . . Although this particular place is also *not* inappropriate—" He gave Tom a quick sidelong glance "—it is an adulterine construction, is it, Tom?"

The question caught Tom off-balance. "I'm not sure, David—"

" 'Adulterine'?" The word unbalanced Panin too—quite understandably, thought Tom.

" 'Illegal', Nikolai." Audley didn't want to be interrupted. "In the days of our strong kings, you couldn't just put up a castle when you felt like it—you had to have a licence to build and crenellate . . . Although 'crenellate' is a bit later, I suppose—like, to put up battlements and loopholes; so this was probably no more than a stout pallisade, like an old US cavalry stockade, to keep the native English-Indians out, eh?" Because he didn't want to be interrupted he didn't wait to be understood. "What I meant was the *timing* of it, not really the *placing* . . . do you see?"

Tom didn't see. But, nevertheless and loyally, he looked towards the Russian as though he did.

"The timing?" Under their combined scrutiny Panin had to ask the question, even though he must know he was walking into some prepared ambush. But then, instead, he gestured towards the *motte*. "Shall we walk a little way? I feel . . . a little over-looked here, is the truth—?"

Quite suddenly Tom remembered Audley's terrace, and the flesh up his backbone crawled at the memory, so that his feet moved before his brain stamped their movement order, taking him towards the protection of Gilbert's earth mound.

Panin moved with him. And Tom felt a breath of wind on his cheeks, and the topmost growth of gorse and bracken and old winter bramble shivered on the mound ahead of him, in the same breath of moving air, which had a decided hint of rain-to-come in it, sweeping up the Bristol Channel between Lundy Island and the Gower Peninsula from the distant Atlantic Ocean.

"Timing—?" Panin reached relative safety, but turned to find Audley still rooted to his spot behind them in the entrance, snuffling into his handkerchief again. "David—?"

"Coming . . ." Audley took his time, even adding to it with a scrutiny of the nearer hillside, on which Major Sadowski was now presumably doing his invisible guard-duty. "Coming . . ."

Willy! thought Tom, staring into the junction of the *bailey* ditch with that of the *motte*. At this point on the Mountsorrel spur the topsoil had been thin, but Gilbert's forced-labourers hadn't been allowed to skimp their ditching: the outer edge was still an eight-foot vertical rock-wall, overhung with trailing brambles growing over it from the top, *and he would have liked Willy to have seen that ruthless Norman attention to essential detail—*

"I'm sorry!" Audley strode up, with that long, purposeful stride of his. "I was busy sneezing again. And then I was thinking." He looked around, up at the mound, then again at the Major's ridge, and finally back to Panin. "Is this safe enough for you, then?"

Panin sighed, but seemed to accept that Audley had taken the lead again. "What were you thinking?"

"I was thinking of my dear wife again, actually." Audley peered at the rock-cut ditch. "That's a good piece of work there, Tom—do you see—?"

"Yes." A bit of Tom was irritated at being taught to suck eggs. But he also admired the old man's powers of observation and his determination at least to pretend that the shared memory of the terrace didn't frighten him.

"Yes." Panin watched Audley peering into Gilbert's good work. "I trust that Mrs Audley is well?"

"Uh-huh. She's very well . . . Are you sure this is 'adulterine', Tom? This ditch must have taken a hell of a lot of digging." Suddenly he turned back to Panin. "She's well. But she's not happy, Nikolai. And neither am I."

"Yes." Panin nodded. "That I can understand."

"You can?" Audley waited for more.

Another nod. "I too am not happy, David."

This time Audley nodded. "Yes. That *I* can understand, also."

The lines in the Russian's face were like dry wadis in a stony desert, in an enlarged satellite photo. "Someone made an attempt on your life yesterday, I have been informed."

"You have been informed?" Audley repeated the words mildly. "It wasn't you, then?" he raised his hand quickly. "No—of course I didn't mean that, old comrade. I never thought for a moment that it was you. And Tom will bear me out there—eh, Tom?"

"I am most relieved to hear that, David." The Russian gave Tom no time to bear true witness. "But—"

"Because if it had been you—" Audley cut him off "—then I wouldn't be here now, would I?" He gave Panin his Beast-smile. "And you, old comrade . . . *you* would have been looking for a very deep hole, somewhere east of Nizhni Novgorod. Although you would know, because Jack Butler is a stickler for etiquette—and the son of a good trade unionist too, who knows his Rule Book backwards, and his 'Custom and Practice', which covers what isn't actually written into the book . . . and what maybe *can't* be written into it—" He switched to Tom, with a glint of mischief in his eye "—old Jack's dad was a printer, so Jack was brought up on 'Old Spanish customs'—" The mocking eye returned to Panin "—so *you* would know, Nikolai, that there wouldn't be a hole deep enough, not even in Holy Mother Russia—not even in the little monks' cells in Zagorsk Monastery—where Jack wouldn't find you in the end, if he thought it was your finger on the trigger, eh?" The slow Beast-smile became almost loving. "Right?"

Panin's immobility impressed Tom. "About Colonel Butler . . . I bow to your superior knowledge, David." Then the dry wadis twisted. "But about me . . . of course, you are also quite right: if I judged you better dead, then you would be dead. But the rest . . . that is irrelevant, because we both know that we are concerned with the perceived welfare of our respective mother-countries. And we are both on 'borrowed time' now, I think."

"For God's sake!" Audley interjected the blasphemy hotly. "Are you trying to frighten me?"

"I am stating a truth, David—" Panin cut back at Audley. But then he inclined his head stiffly, as though uncharacteristically. "It's forty years now—forty-one, for you . . . more than forty for me—since we both saw too many better men killed in a good cause—dead, and rotten, and forgotten . . . But we are both still here: that is all I mean."

"Okay!" Audley raised his hand again. "Okay, okay, *okay!*" The hand came down. "So it wasn't *you*, Nikolai! But it was *someone*—" The last vestige of the Beast-smile was long-gone "—and it was also *someone* with Basil Cole yesterday. So let's start with him. Or not at all."

"As you wish." Panin studied Major Sadowski's ridge again. "About your . . . experience, of yesterday . . . I have been told, of course, David."

"I should hope so!" Audley followed the Russian's gaze. "And that's why the loquacious Major is on guard-duty, is it? Or did you just want to get his little pocket tape-recorder out of range?"

"About Basil Cole I do *not* know." Panin came back to them. "That is to say . . . *of* him I know. But that was in former times. And he never worked for you—for either Colonel Butler, or for Sir Frederick before him, to my knowledge." The mournful sheep-face expression betrayed nothing. Only the pale brown eyes hinted at life behind the mask. "Also he is retired. Or would 'dismissed' be the correct word?"

"No. 'Murdered' is the correct word." The cold matter-of-fact tone of Audley's correction somehow emphasized the anger it concealed.

"Of that I know nothing, my friend."

Audley winced visibly at what he clearly took to be another incorrect word—so visibly and so clearly that not even Panin could ignore the reaction.

"You do not believe me?" The Russian countered that banked-up rage with an asbestos-covered curiosity.

Audley sniffed. "I tell you what, old *comrade*—" he sniffed again, and began to search for his handkerchief "—old *comrade*—" he found the handkerchief, but waved it at Gilbert de Merville's overgrown strongpoint above them before applying it to his nose "—I said this place was appropriate . . . you remember?" He buried his face in the handkerchief.

Panin studied the *motte* for a moment, then waited until Audley had completed his noisy "having-a-cold" ritual. "Yes. And you also said 'timing', equally mysteriously—I do remember, David."

"Good!" Audley spread a hand round the *bailey*, proprietorially. "*Place*: Gilbert de Merville's cosy hideaway, Mountsorrel Castle. And I suppose you could say Gilbert had the instincts of a Lebanese war-lord plus the military know-how of an Israeli tank-commander . . . *Timing*: mid-twelfth-century England, give or take a few years—mid-Civil War, anyway. King Stephen: played 20, won 5, lost 5, drew 10; the Empress Matilda; played 20, won 5, lost 5, drew 10." He shook his head. "Not so easy to assess Gilbert's score, because he probably changed sides half-a-dozen times. The only side he was on was Gilbert de Merville's side—"

"David—"

"Uh-huh! Haven't finished yet." Audley wagged a finger. "You may have diplomatic privilege, old comrade. But you're on my patch now, so I get to do the talking when it suits me—right?"

Panin closed his mouth and battened down his face, reducing his vision to reptilian eye-slits. Or . . . *feline*, if not *reptilian*, Tom amended the image, recalling the look in the eyes of Mamusia's vile old neutered tom (*"My other darling Tom!"*), which always gazed at him with a thwarted malevolence hinting at a very different relationship if their sizes had been reversed. But then he sensed the eyes catch his own scrutiny, and the hungry glint behind them was extinguished, and the terrifying old man was giving Audley a slow, almost stately, nod.

"Right!" If Audley had received the same frightening signal he showed no sign of it: he seemed to be enjoying himself again. "Very interesting century, the twelfth, Nikolai. The Gothic cathedrals were on their launch-pads—from Chartres and St Denis, and Sens, all the way across Europe, even to the Middle East—the ideas, and the style, and the geometry . . . Well, as far as Poland, anyway, if not Russia . . . And nothing like that has lifted off into the heavens until you and the Americans lifted off, but much more disagreeably, back in the fifties." Sniff. "More technology, but less spirit—?"

Panin held his peace, without difficulty, even though Audley paused very deliberately, as though to allow him the Right of Reply, knowing quite well that he would not exercise it. And Tom's mixture of fascinated fear and curiosity moved further up the gauge, even though it was already well into the red in the knowledge that these two veterans of an on-going war, which had started long before he was born, were consumed with old men's hatred for each other, in spite of their elaborate politeness.

"Marvellously good things." Audley agreed with Panin's silence. "And marvellously *bad* ones too. And Gilbert de Merville was almost certainly one of those . . . like, there was this Peterborough monk, who wrote up the *Anglo-Saxon Chronicle* for those times, which I learnt by heart as a young lad come up to Cambridge fresh from laying waste Normandy, and sacking Germany, and buying the *fräuleins* for a few packets of Lucky Strikes: '*Every strong man made his castles . . . And when the castles were made they filled them with devils and evil men . . . And then they seized those who they supposed had any riches—*'—and I don't need to tell *you*, of all people, the sort of riches we were after in '45, because you were after the same bloody things, pretty much—'*—and they tortured them with unspeakable tortures, so that I neither can nor may tell all the horrors and all the tortures that they did to the wretched men of this land, but it was said that "Christ and His angels were asleep".*' " Audley gave the Russian his purest and sweetest Beast-smile. "And you may not be able to recall the Monk of Peterborough on the 'Anarchy' of Stephen and Matilda, but you were in Khalturin's Guards Division, so you surely remember what you did in Germany. And afterwards, eh?"

"Yes." Panin couldn't duck so direct a challenge. "And I remember the Ukraine also, before I was transferred to the Berlin front at the last—"

"And Poland?" Audley didn't look at Tom. "You remember the Warsaw Rising? Did you hear the sound of our planes trying to drop supplies to them, when you were just across the river there—? When you bastards wouldn't give us landing rights, so we had to make the round trip—do you remember that sound, too?"

Every Pole knew that story, thought Tom. And not a few Poles still remembered the names of the Polish Lancaster bomber crews who had died on those abortive mercy trips, delivering half their loads to the Germans. But if that was designed for his benefit it was a crude and unnecessary reminder of unsettled scores, of which he needed no reminding . . . But then, at times, Audley *was* crude—

"What are you saying, David?" Audley's sudden obsession with Polish history seemed to confuse the Russian. "I was a staff officer with the Guards—"

"Huh!" Audley tossed his head like a two-year-old.

"A *staff* officer—" Unbelievably Audley had drawn blood from Panin, the momentary emphasis suggested "—and I thought we were in the twelfth century—? Or . . . the *mid*-twelfth century?"

"So we were!" All Audley wanted was that tell-tale stain through those very old bandages, apparently. "And . . . what I mean is that they built their marvellous cathedrals, which took them closer to heaven than anyone's ever been since . . . but then, the other half of their time the Normans were *beasts*—just like the little girl who had a little curl right in the middle of her forehead:

When she was good
She was very, very good,
But when she was bad she was horrid—

and, in fact, if you want a really good example of that, then who better than King Henry II Plantagenet himself, who came after Matilda-and-Stephen, eh?" Audley shook his head sadly at the Russian. "A great king, Henry —knew his Latin and his Law. Ruled half of Western Europe. Made short work of bastards like Gilbert de Merville, and his like . . . Loved the Fair Rosamund—married the fair Eleanor, and all that . . ." He shook his head again, and trailed off with a sigh.

Panin waited, not patiently but nonetheless well-contained within himself again now and not to be drawn. And in that moment of silence Tom knew exactly what Audley was about, and what was coming now.

"So there he was, keeping Christmas like a good Christian in his own private two-thirds of France—" Audley flicked a glance at Tom "—in Chinon, would it have been, Tom—in 1170—? Somewhere like that, anyway—" He transferred the glance back to Panin "—when this news arrived from England, about this damned inconvenient priest, who'd been shooting his mouth off again, because he reckoned the Church was above the State. Which drove Henry right up the wall, naturally. So he shouted —shouted supposedly to no one in particular, but to everyone in general—'Is there no one here among all you skunks, who owe me everything—your horses, your lands and your castles and your *droits de seigneur*—'—or, as it might be in your set-up today, Nikolai, 'your Mercedes cars, and your *dachas* and Black Sea holidays, and your pretty ballet-dancers, and special shopping privileges'—'*Is there no-one who'll get rid of this priest for me, with no questions asked?*'" He drew a quick breath which was only half a sniff. "So Fitz-Urse and a few of the lads jumped in their Mercedes—on their horses—and took the next cross-Channel ferry and chopped up the priest right in front of his own altar." This time he grimaced quickly at Panin. "A proper bungled job, it was—they didn't even bother to silence the witnesses. So Henry had to throw them to the wolves officially, the murderers—" He cocked a frown at Tom "—but what *did* happen to Fitz-Urse and the other three, Tom? I really ought to know, but for the life of me I can't recall at the moment—?"

"I don't know." Tom, for the life of Tom, couldn't look at the Russian in that moment. "I expect they were excommunicated and banished."

"Ah . . . yes, I'm sure they were!" Audley agreed readily. "But, of course, you probably know the story, Nikolai, old comrade—the martyrdom of Archbishop Saint Thomas Becket at Canterbury? It's all in Churchill's *History of the English-Speaking Peoples*, which you've read—it's just the sort of good story he revelled in." He grinned. "But, although he made the right noises about King Henry getting his comeuppance in the end, when those appalling sons of his made war on him—'*Such is the bitter taste of worldly power. Such are the correctives of glory*'—I've always thought he had a sneaking sympathy for Henry. I know I have—I think Thomas Becket was wrong, and got what he asked for . . . And, of course, after the 1945 Election, which corrected old Winston's glory, no one knew the bitter taste of worldly power better than he did." Another grin. "And I was one of those who voted against him in '45, too—I voted for Clem Attlee and Labour. Even though Attlee was an Oxford man."

By this time, although still for the life of him, Tom couldn't *not* look at Nikolai Andrievich Panin, to see how he was handling Archbishop Saint Thomas Becket, and Henry II Plantagenet and Winston S. Churchill, not to mention Father Jerzy Popieluszko.

"An Oxford man?" Panin was handling them all well. "And you, of course, are a Cambridge man?" The sheep-face was like a visor, worn and pitted with time on the outside, but betraying nothing of the man within. "A Cambridge man who remembers his quotations well!"

Audley shrugged modestly. "Oh . . . that's just what my old Latin master beat into me, to help me pass my exams. Examiners love quotations. The trick is to throw the Latin ones into the History answers, and the History ones into the English ones, and the English ones into the bloody Latin, he said. Because that way they all think you know more than you're telling. Or . . . even if they aren't so stupid, at least they know that you've been well-taught, at any rate."

Panin nodded. "I see." He stopped the nod with his sheep-face at an angle. "So you have been well-taught. But do you know less than you are telling now . . . or more?"

"Hmmm . . ." Audley considered the proposition, or pretended to do so. "Well now . . . be that as it may . . . and you don't know, and I'm not about to tell you . . . there are *two* things that you do know—and one more that I am willing to tell you. That is, if you haven't listened properly so far, anyway."

"Two things?" Panin accepted the test. "You have been shot at—"

"And missed. So I'm giving you the benefit of the doubt there, for reasons of Mutual Assured Destruction." Audley accepted Panin's first answer. "And I've also come across a friend of mine who has been put down like an inconvenient dog . . . for which I have agreed *temporarily* to give you the benefit of the doubt."

" 'Temporarily' will do." Panin nodded. "In the circumstances I can ask no more than that, I agree. But . . . this third thing, which I have missed—"

Audley raised his chin and sighted Panin down his big broken nose. "This is my patch, Nikolai. Shooting me in my own house isn't cricket, to say the least. But Basil Cole . . ." Nose, chin and face became Complete Beast "—I draw my wages to make sure that sort of thing doesn't happen here. You can do what you bloody-well please in your own backyard—you can murder the important ones, or exile them, or put them in psychiatric hospitals, if that's what turns you on . . . And you can make the little ones disappear, and Amnesty International won't even know their names when you put the muzzle of the gun to the back of their necks. Because that's *your* 'Anarchy', and Christ and his saints haven't gone to sleep in your benighted Socialist heaven—because they've never even woken up there, by God! But that's *your* patch, and there's nothing I can do about it—not even if it was my job. Which it isn't." Sniff. "But this is *my* patch. So when you try to extend your Anarchy here it has to cross my dead body in the ditch first—" The old man pointed to Gilbert de Merville's "good work"—"do I make myself clear?"

Panin had been listening intently from behind his mask. But now he was looking directly at Tom. And what chilled Tom to the bone was that he seemed to have accepted everything Audley had said—every last ounce of capitalist insult, and scorn, and slight regard—without offence.

Audley picked up the look. "You're worried about him, are you?"

Panin took the direct look back to Audley.

"Can you trust him?" Sniff. "Can *I* trust him?" Another sniff, followed by a sickening swallow. "With the family silver, I can. And with my wife I can . . . because younger men don't turn her on." Another swallow. "And with my own daughter, for the time being, I suppose." Audley joined the Russian's scrutiny with his own at last. "And my ox, and my ass, and my life, and such minor impedimenta . . . yes, undoubtedly I can trust him." He nodded, and then turned the nod into a half-amused shake. "Don't look so outraged, Tom—the Comrade Professor hasn't lived to see old age here by trusting his own people, never mind us! He had no Jack Butler at his back—no, nor a Fred Clinton either, in the old days—to take the rap when things don't go quite according to plan." He transferred the shake to Panin. "And things aren't so easy on the other side just at the moment, are they, old comrade—under the New Management? A lot of redundancy and retirement, would there be?" He waited for a moment. "Perhaps that's what Basil Cole would have told me. Among other things."

This time Panin almost spoke, but again controlled himself behind his defensive silence, as though waiting for Audley to exhaust his armoured cavalryman's instinct for probing tactics.

"Well, anyway—" Audley gestured dismissively towards Tom "—Sir Thomas Arkenshaw just happens to be the son of my very oldest girlfriend. Or *second* oldest, actually; although the other wench is dead, and in a foreign country . . . My *second* oldest girlfriend: once a great girl, now a great lady." The brutal face lifted, and Audley used all his inches to look down on his "old comrade". "Indeed, one might say that, but for certain juvenile miscalculations on my part, mediated by a mischance on the rugger field perhaps, this Thomas Arkenshaw *junior* might have been David Audley *junior*—will that do for you?"

As though to avoid being looked-down on, Panin himself had found something quite absorbing among the muddy hoof-prints at the bottom of Gilbert de Merville's ditch. But now he came out of his absorption. "Things are not so good for you, either."

"What?" The statement took Audley aback.

"You are not in good smell—no, that should be 'odour', for some reason, I think . . . good *odour*—?" Panin paused, but only for half-a-second now that he was clear of his trenches at last. "You have offended too many of your politicians, and now one too many, I think—with your games. So that not even the so-very-good Colonel Butler can protect you. Because there is a point where even the so-very-good-and-noble Colonel must protect himself, I think—yes?"

"Yes?" Audley frowned. "No! Stuff and nonsense!"

"No—*not* nonsense." Panin shook his head slowly. "You are right to say that our circumstances are different. But this time do not interrupt, if you please!" But, to Tom's surprise, the Russian did not instantly continue himself, but waited for Audley to bite him.

But Audley didn't bite.

"Very good!" Panin savoured Audley's silence, sniffing at it approvingly. "When I first encountered you I thought you were much more . . . much more in rank—a colonel, but almost a general—than you really were. I did not understand what you were. And that confused me."

"Is that a fact?" Audley brightened. "Well, actually, you confused me a bit too. So that was when we both started doing our homework, eh?"

Panin ignored Audley's pleasure. "You are clever, David. But you are an amateur."

"No." Audley had forgotten the "Don't interrupt" admonition while it still echoed in the still air between them. "You've still got it bloody-wrong, Nikolai—the word is *'Gentleman'* not *'Amateur'*! And, what you mean, is that . . . I don't *have* to give a damn, if I screw up—but *you*, poor old comrade . . . *you* have been scared half out of your wits every time you've farted without permission these last thirty-forty years, if you haven't got written authorization . . . Unless, of course, you've turned up on the hundred per cent winning side—like after Mironov had that unfortunate accident in Yugoslavia, after Khrushchev was outvoted? And you were deep in a trench in the Altai mountains—?" He turned as though for support to Tom. "It was an *archaeological* trench, I hasten to add! Because when in doubt the Comrade Professor always goes to ground in ancient Scythia, never in Dzerzhinsky Square. It's a sort of return-to-the-womb thing he has. Even this latest cover he's got—the Scythian Exhibition at the BM next year . . . *that's* a subconscious going-to-ground instinct, I shouldn't wonder—"

"But we are not talking about me, David." Panin wasn't interested in Tom now: he had accepted Sir Thomas Arkenshaw as a hypothetical Audley offspring apparently, and that was enough. "Over the last twenty-five years you have been going too far—not all the time, but too often . . . Over the last fifteen years, to my certain knowledge—how many times? How many times?"

Audley shrugged. "I'm still here. That makes no times, to my reckoning."

"But Colonel Butler has not Sir Frederick Clinton's influence."

"Maybe not. But Jack is very well-regarded in high places, Nikolai. In fact, in the extremely unlikely event of any change of government, centre-right or centre-left, Jack's the lad who'll get the majority vote."

Audley's voice was smug. "You're on a loser if you think otherwise."

"Indeed?" The eye-slits opened again fractionally; which was probably as close to a registration of surprise as Panin allowed himself, Tom decided. "A man for all parties? You make him sound truly remarkable."

"He *is* remarkable." Audley warmed to his subject. "There's no one like our Jack—not in this black age, anyway." He glanced at Gilbert de Merville's mound thoughtfully for a moment. "You can't lay a finger on him."

"I'm impressed." The eyes slitted again. "Perhaps I should have studied him more carefully, and not you."

"Wouldn't have done you any good. You wouldn't begin to understand him." Audley shook his head. "He'll always catch *you* by the heel. You'll never fathom him out."

"You think not?" Even Panin couldn't resist that challenge.

"Not a chance. I've been trying for years." This time the sniff, unlike all its predecessors, was cheerful. "Got nowhere—like the Raj trying to fathom Gandhi . . . Except that Jack's not what you'd call non-violent." Shrug—happy shrug, like the sniff. "That's the trouble with men who are instinctively and logically *good*: the rest of us, who are ordinarily, and instinctively, and logically *bad*—and in your case, old comrade, *worse*—can never get inside their minds. At least, not the way we can sometimes get inside each others'—do you see? Like now, for instance, eh?"

Panin considered Audley's insults without any sign of offence. "You surprise me more and more, David—"

"Not half as much as Jack would, if you'd invited him here instead of me." Audley frowned suddenly. "And, come to think of it . . . why the blue blazes *did* you invite me here—?" Somehow he caught Tom's eye in the middle of the question. "By which I mean not *here*, much as I approve of Sir Thomas's quaint choice of rendezvous—I mean *down* here—up here, out here? The West Country, Nikolai?" He shook his head. "Not your country, Nikolai. Definitely not your country. Not since John Ridd put down the Doones hereabout, anyway."

"No, not my country." The latest insult went the way of all its predecessors. "There is something you don't know, then?"

"Ah!" Audley refused to be mocked. "You got the Thomas Becket analogy! I was beginning to fear it had all gone to waste. Jolly good!" He gave Tom a "So there!" nod. "But . . . *yes*, in answer to your question. Only I'm a quick learner, and I can hardly wait to be taught." Sniff. "Teach me, Nikolai, teach me."

Tom was drawn back to Audley suddenly, as all the banter and facetiousness went out of the old man's voice in that instant. And he saw that the face matched the voice, with no hint of Beast-bonhomie any more; and that that was the true face and the true voice of the man who had been blinding and bluffing them both with the twelfth century only to get himself where he wanted to be in the twentieth.

"Gennadiy Zarubin, David," said Panin, pronouncing the name with something of Audley's unconcealed harshness.

"Major-General Gennadiy Zarubin." For that lack of surprise Audley owed Tom, and Tom owed Willy and Colonel Sheldon. But, considering how very recently *Gennadiy Zarubin* had been added to the mixture, Audley handled the name well. "It had to be him, of course."

"Of course." Panin agreed readily enough, but then looked sidelong at Audley. "Of course?"

"Simple arithmetic." Audley shrugged. "The poor bloody priest himself—whose memory I won't insult by trying to pronounce his name—*he's* safe in heaven. And Marchuk's doing a long stretch in hell. And your four obedient Poles . . . who were just about as incompetent as Henry Plantagenet's obedient knights . . . *they're* doing time in some holiday-camp, is our latest guess. Although hell will get them too, in God's good time, I shouldn't wonder."

"So?" The sidelong look was oddly frozen. "I didn't know you were a religious man, David."

"I'm not. I'm just an old-fashioned High Days and Holidays Anglican, seeing as it's not respectable to worship Mithras these days." Audley smiled one of his smiles. "But your Poles were probably brought up as good little Catholics, so it's hell for them in due course—" The smile curdled suddenly, as though the old man had smelt something more like the charnel-house. "Or are they there already? Just to be on the safe side, eh?"

The sidelong glance became full-face. "What?"

"Oh—come on!" Audley made a vaguely-insulting gesture. "If it's one thing your lot is good at, it's killing inconvenient Poles. Like at Katyn, remember—?" The hand waved some more. "Or even letting the Nazis do your dirty work for you . . . like Warsaw in '44?"

Panin tensed, so it seemed to Tom. "That is a lie—"

"No, it bloody-isn't!" Audley's vaguely-waved hand clenched. "I had some good mates in the 1st Polish Armoured, '44 to '45. And they had fathers and uncles in '40, at Katyn and elsewhere. And—*and, Christ! They had younger brothers and sons, some of them, at Warsaw in '44, where you let them die!*"

"It is a lie!" As he spoke, Panin squared up to Audley, and the old man matched him, on the very edge of Gilbert de Merville's rock-cut ditch, each with one elderly fist visible to Tom—ridiculous old fists, clenching and unclenching now, as though in preparation for a pensioners' punch-up, regardless of age and diplomatic protocol.

"It's the truth—and you know it!" sneered Audley, fixing his big feet squarely in the muddy grass.

"*David!* For God's sake!" exclaimed Tom, simultaneously terrified and aware that Audley was not only the aggressor, but would certainly be the victor, with size and weight on his side, if the two old men came to blows here.

Audley twisted a grimace at him, without taking his eyes off the Russian, but relaxing slightly. "Maybe not Katyn. But he knows damn well what happened on the Warsaw front in '44, when they wouldn't give the RAF landing rights, to drop supplies to the Poles—never mind not helping the poor bastards themselves, the buggers. Because he was *there*, by God! Sitting on his arse on the other side of the river!"

Panin spluttered slightly. "You dishonour me—!"

"If I could—I would!" Audley's hand came up. But at least it was a finger now, not a fist. "You-were-there—" He rounded on Tom without warning "—and *you* should know what happened there, of all people, Tom!"

Panin looked at Tom, and Tom himself was astonished at Audley's indiscretion—so astonished that for a moment all he could think of was the Russian's description of Audley as "*amateur*". "I thought we were discussing Gennadiy Zarubin—? Not . . . not ancient East European military history, anyway—" He looked from one to the other.

The Russian composed himself first; although that, thought Tom bitterly, was composure born of suddenly-renewed interest in Sir Thomas Arkenshaw, who could not only get his tongue round a Polish name but was also apparently an expert on the Warsaw Rising of '44, it seemed. "That is true." The momentary change in the man's aura, which had somehow hinted at the presence of a ravening wolf within that elderly sheep, had already vanished so completely that memory queried its existence. "You must forgive me, Sir Thomas. But I, also, had good comrades in '44. And before that, and after that. And also brothers. And I also remember them." He drew a slow breath. "But I should not. And you are right to draw us back to pressing matters." He considered Tom for another five slow seconds before returning to Audley. "Thank you, Sir Thomas."

Audley shrugged, no longer truculent but quite unapologetic. "I was only doing my arithmetic. Two dead, four jailed, equals six. Six from seven equals one. One equals Zarubin. That's all." It was Audley who was battened down now. "But you were about to do the rest of the sum for me."

This time Audley got the five seconds. "How much do you know, David?"

"Uh-uh." Audley shook his head. "Gennadiy Zarubin, you were saying—?"

"You know that he's here, of course." Panin waited in vain for Audley to answer. "Of course you do!"

Audley looked into the ditch. "It isn't really very hard, the rock here—is it, Tom?" He looked up at Tom. "Not like the rock ditch on the Roman wall between Carrawburgh and Chesters, by Milecastle 30, where they had to bore holes and split the stuff with boiling water—or vinegar, was it? And they never did finish the job, at that . . . Jack Butler showed me the place, long ago—oh, it must be thirteen years ago, about." He nodded. "All of that, because I think Faith was pregnant at the time . . . But this doesn't look nearly so hard."

Tom rolled an eye at the Russian, as speechless as Panin himself was.

"It's still good work, for a rush job." Audley bent over the ditch, hands on knees. "But not a *great* work, is what I mean—not with this crumbly red sandstone . . . Is that what it is? Or is it—what the devil is it?" He started to reach down below the lip of the ditch, but then abandoned the attempt.

"They are going to kill him." Panin found his voice at last. "Zarubin, David."

Audley found a suitable tuft of grass on which to kneel. "Uh-huh? Who's 'they'?" He reached over the edge. "In Zarubin's case there must be a fairly long waiting-list for that honour—" He wrenched at something out of Tom's view "—but presumably these would be Poles, of course . . . eh?" He gave the unseen bit of rock another wrench.

"Terrorists," said Panin.

"Terrorists—naturally . . ." Another wrench ". . . freedom fighters, partisans, guerrillas . . . *franc-tireurs*, Robin Hood's 'Merry Men', UNITA, IRA, ENOSIS, Weathermen, ETA—join the bloody club:

> *'He crucified noble, he scarified mean,*
> *He filled old ladies with kerosene;*
> *While over the water the papers cried,*
> *"The patriot fights for his countryside!"'*

—it's all old hat, Nikolai. We're used to it, long before from our own late imperial past, even before these more indiscriminate times. And so were your Tsarist predecessors, actually—" He twisted towards Tom suddenly "—it's tougher than I thought, this rock—*Poles* is what he means, I suspect."

"Poles, yes." Panin surrendered. "They call themselves 'The Sons of the Eagle'."

"Do they now!" Audley abandoned his efforts, straightening up and brushing the dirt from his hands, though still on his knees. "Boh Da Thone, in Burma in the '80s—the *1880s*—*he* killed under the Peacock Banner. At least, according to Kipling he did. But with the Poles the bird would have to be the good old-fashioned eagle, of course." He stood up, shifting his attention from his grubby hands to the damp patches on each knee of his trousers. " 'Sons of the Eagle'? Can't say that I've ever heard of them, though. Have you, Tom?"

"No." It occurred to Tom that Audley hadn't been indiscreet, he had deliberately set out to establish Sir Thomas as his Polish expert as part of his frontal attack on Panin. Indeed, he no doubt assumed that Tom *was* an expert, just as Jaggard had probably done. But there was nothing to be done about that now. "No, I haven't." He looked at Panin questioningly.

"They are the violent element in what remains of Solidarity, Sir Thomas." The Russian's voice was flatly matter-of-fact. "They are terrorists."

Tom felt Audley's eye on him. "Solidarity has no violent wing. It never has had. Neither Walesa or the Church would allow it, David." He shook his head. "No way."

"I see." Audley pursed his lips. "So Marchuk was an accident, then?"

"I didn't say that." Tom wished he felt more confident. "I said that Solidarity is non-violent, that's all."

Audley rubbed his chin thoughtfully, leaving a smear of dirt on his jaw-line. "Of course. But it's all academic, really—"

"Academic?" Tom had to control his Polish half. "What d'you mean?"

"Yes. Where state violence is institutionalized there can be no distinction between violence and non-violence in anti-state activities: they are either treason or criminal lunacy—you either get the bullet, or regular injections down on the funny-farm." Audley returned to Panin. "But that's in *your* backyard of course, Nikolai. So . . . *academic*, as I say. Whereas your present problem is *here*—and definitely *not* academic, obviously."

This time the Russian gave not the slightest hint that Audley's latest insult had touched the wolf inside the sheep's armour; if anything, he seemed more relaxed. "Your problem too, David."

"My problem?" Audley feigned theatrical surprise. "My dear fellow, now that you have most economically explained to me what is about to happen, I can descry no very great problem. Your masters, in their wisdom, have posted the unspeakable Zarubin here—presumably because they regard London as a relatively safe billet. Or maybe it's a genuine promotion—? As a reward for presiding over the elimination of that poor unpronounceable priest—'Father George', shall I call him? Though, on second thoughts, it can hardly be that, for the work was *not* well-done—" He pointed a dirty finger at the ditch "—not like that—*that* is a damn good ditch!"

"No—"

"*No*—I agree! But, nevertheless, we shall bend every thew and sinew to save Zarubin's unworthy hide, now that you've warned us. And, in my case, all the more so because of yesterday's traumas—or should it be 'traumae'—?" Audley switched to Tom without warning, and caught him in the midst of another bout of incredulity.

" 'Traumata'," he answered automatically. What this last mock-flippancy reminded him was that Audley hadn't forgotten Basil Cole, as for a moment he appeared to have done. But the old man was still set on goading Panin, of course. " 'Traumata', David."

"Ah! From the Greek, of course!" Audley fielded the word happily. "To my shame I only did Latin, so I'm really only half-educated. Or altogether *un*educated, as my old classics master always maintained." Back to Panin "But yes . . . we shall of course do our best. So when your 'Sons of the Eagle' liquidate Zarubin, we shall catch them, and put them away for life." He shrugged. "Of course, you will get some damn bad publicity, during the trial, when all the dirty laundry about Father George comes out . . . The newspapers will have a ball with that, tut-tutting hypocritically about wickedness begetting wickedness. But it'll only be a nine-days' wonder, and everyone will soon forget again." He cocked a shrewd eye at Panin. "And, anyway, a mad dog like Zarubin is probably best put down—won't your masters be secretly quite relieved to be disembarrassed of him? Won't it actually make things easier in Poland, in the end—?" Audley's mouth twisted, in support of his eye. "Not your cup-of-tea, Nikolai? Better heroically-dead in foreign parts, with two columns of lies in *Pravda*?"

Panin's face was a picture of nothing. "I am here to prevent that thing, David."

"Right." Audley's hand came up. "So we'll both do our best. And you can always blame me afterwards. But I can live with that."

"No." Far beneath Panin's picture of nothing there was another picture, but Tom couldn't read it. "It will not be enough for me to do that—I cannot afford to do that. And neither can you, David, I think." The Russian shook his head slowly. "Because I am already living on what you call 'borrowed time', David—that I know." The head stopped shaking. "And . . . with all due respect . . . I believe you are in the same position. Which is why I asked for you, David." This time it was the Russian's hand which came up, and Tom noticed for the first time that there was a thick gold ring on one of the fingers. "No, do not interrupt me—"

"I wasn't going to—" There was a ring on Audley's finger, too.

"General Zarubin is not here for his own safety. He is here to arrange an important visit, David. Because, if the Geneva talks fail, we shall be appealing directly to Europe, David." Panin lowered his hand. "And that is what Basil Cole would have told you, I think. So perhaps that is why he died, David." Another slow shake. "Not merely to discredit me."

That sent Audley back on his heels, Tom sensed. Or at least it stopped his mouth for once, anyway.

"We have to stop this thing. It will not be good enough—not *safe* enough, for either of us—to catch the assassins afterwards. Because if all that happens, and then there is no meeting because of it . . . then my head will roll. And yours too . . . and even perhaps Colonel Butler's, David. Although your heads are of no concern to me—I will admit *that*, if nothing else." Something almost changed in the Russian's face. "I might even enjoy that thought . . . if we were not in the same cart—cart?" Something *did* change: the depth of the deep creases on each side of the mouth deepened slightly. "Or should it be 'tumbril', since we are talking of heads dropping into the basket?"

Tom had to watch Audley's reaction now. And, as he watched, it came to him perversely again that everything Audley had done so far—all the insults, and the pretence to greater knowledge than he actually possessed—had been geared not only, or not so much, to avenging Basil Cole as to deriving this profit (indeed, his own words, "*doing business*", had suggested that, exactly, from recent memory). But now the Russian had turned the tables, and almost contemptuously so, by combining mutual survival with co-operation—even, he had twisted the knife, by putting Colonel Butler in the same cart with them both.

And he could see, at a glance, that Audley didn't like what had been done to him, because the big old man's ugly face wasn't sheep-inscrutable: it might be beast-like, but it was rarely expressionless, and it was prey to an alphabet of emotions now.

"You are a perfect *shit*, Nikolai—aren't you!" Audley sniffed, and then wiped his big nose on the back of his dirty hand. "You never were going to make a deal, were you!"

"Not with you, David—no." Panin nodded. "We happen to have drawn the same card from the pack, this time." The creases deepened. "Not like last time."

"Uh-huh?" Audley was already adjusting to defeat, and putting it down to experience. "You've got a long memory."

"I think we both have." Panin shrugged off the past, wisely adjusting to victory. "But the important thing is that I have a deal for the enemy this time, David. But I need you for that. And that is why I am here."

Here suddenly registered with Tom. Because they had all used the word, or accepted it in its widest sense; but it had always had another and a more exact and geographical meaning—they had even left a precise question about that *here* behind them, unanswered and mysterious: *"Down here, up here, out here—the West Country, Nikolai"*—

"Here?" The same word had registered with Audley, simultaneously.

"Yes." Panin looked from one to the other of them. " 'This is not your country', you said?"

"Yes." Audley was instantly as battened down on Exmoor as he had ever been in his Normandy *bocage*. "And you agreed that it wasn't—?"

The Russian cased Gilbert de Merville's long-overgrown fortress for an answer—the whole open space of the *bailey*, from left to right, and then finally the mound of the *motte*, alongside which they stood, on the edge of the ditch, before coming back to Audley. "How far are we from the sea here?"

"Not far." Audley admitted the truth cautiously. "No place on Exmoor is far from the sea. No place in Devon is far . . ." Even that wasn't cautious enough, but geography was against him ". . . from the sea. So what?" He tossed his head arrogantly. "But you wouldn't understand that, of course, would you! All you've got is a sea of grass, or snow and frozen pack-ice, eh?" Only then he seemed to understand that he could no longer sting an answer, and didn't even need to do so. "He's coming here, is he? Zarubin—*General* Zarubin?"

"Yes. He's coming here." Nod. "Here."

"Why?"

"Because this is *his* country, David. His father was an 'AB'—is that right? An 'Able Seaman'?"

"A *what*?" Audley's jaw dropped.

"Yes. With 'Dunsterforce', David. Before either of us were born, but I think you'll remember '*Dunsterforce*', nevertheless?" Panin nodded. "He 'jumped ship'—'ran', is perhaps the correct term? Or maybe he fell . . . fell, or jumped or ran, anyway . . . to us. So this is his son's country, and he wants to see it before he dies."

Audley had tightened his jaw, but it had fallen again. " 'Dunsterforce'—? You're joking!"

"Before he dies." Panin nodded. "But our job is to see that he doesn't die, David."

IX

AUDLEY DIDN'T SAY a word as they trudged back the way they had come, until they reached the top of the descending fold from which they'd first spotted Russian-occupied Mountsorrel Castle. Then he turned and waved across at Panin, who was already halfway up the main ridge, and murmured darkly to himself.

Tom watched the Russian acknowledge the wave. "What was that, David?"

Audley lowered his arm. "I said 'You crafty son-of-a-bitch'." He turned away and started walking again without another word.

Tom accelerated after him. "Can it be true?" he shouted at the big man's back.

"Can what be true?" Audley returned the question over his shoulder while lengthening his downhill stride.

"About Zarubin—" Tom broke into a trot "—Zarubin's father—?"

"Oh yes . . . *huh!*" Audley was already on the edge of the boggy ground again, and as regardless of it as before. "*Anything* can be true of that swine Zarubin. He's ex-Special Division, Second Directorate, from way back —" He sneezed suddenly, but didn't miss a splashing step "*—from way back—*" Another sneeze "—COMECON-Warsaw Pact expert . . . *I* first caught a whiff of Zarubin in '68, in Czechoslovakia, but he dates back to Budapest in '56, when he commanded a snatch-and-exterminate squad as a young captain . . . So he must be a man who loves his work . . . Could be anything from forty-five to fifty-five, I suppose . . . But a natural for post-Solidarity Poland, anyway—got exactly the pedigree for that sort of dirty work. No bloody surprise there, by God!"

There was water in Tom's shoes, he could feel it squelch between his toes as he tried to catch up with Audley beyond the bog. "But, David—"

"Surprising over here, though—at least, to me." Audley stopped with so little warning that Tom overshot him, and had to turn to face him. "What about these 'Sons of the Eagle', so-called? Who the hell are they, Tom?"

"I don't know." It was useless to pretend. "I've never heard of them."

Audley frowned. "But you're the bloody expert—" The frown deepened "—aren't you?"

"I'm not an expert on Polish affairs, David."

For an instant Audley stared him out of countenance. "Then why the hell did they give you to me?"

Only the obvious answer presented itself. "To guard your back."

"That won't do. Any plug-ugly could do that." Audley shook his head. "You're still too much of a coincidence, Tom—that's what you are!"

The obvious and official answer lay between them like a dead fish on the deck, past its last gasp. "Then I honestly don't know, David. You can believe me or not—" An alternative answer came to him "—but if you thought I was an expert . . . just because of my mother . . . then you're wrong. So maybe someone else made the same mistaken assumption—?"

"Hmm . . ." Audley's mouth twitched "That, at least, has the ring of incompetence! But it also means that someone on our side is engaged in some convoluted nonsense—" Another twitch "—which also rings a bell, eh?"

Tom felt his brain race even as he put his face into neutral and let his mouth lie. "I don't know about that either, David. But my job is to look after you, as best I can." Yet the trouble was, while he could remember exactly what Jaggard had said, there was that part of him which was asking again, and more insistently, *whose side are you on, Tom Arkenshaw?*

Audley found a grin somewhere. "Well, if you do that I guess I can't grumble. And if Panin's telling the truth, then you don't have too much to worry about."

But that only reminded Tom of his own unanswered question. "I mean, is he telling the truth—about Zarubin's father, David?"

"Hah!" Audley wiped his nose with the back of his hand. "Well, at least *that* could be true—yes!" Audley started to swing away from him again. "Let's go! He's going to get to the next rendezvous before us as it is, damn it! How far is it—to this place of his, where the Eagles have landed—?"

"I don't know—" Audley was past him already "—until I see the map in the car . . . But, David—*'Dunsterforce'*—what was that?"

"Huh! You may well ask, boy!" Audley half-chuckled, half-growled over his shoulder. "That's a thing of beauty, that is—fact improving on fiction, and heaping irony on the top of it: the only reason no one remembers *Dunsterforce* today is because no one combines all the talents of Kipling and Buchan and Le Carré . . . God! But I'd have loved to be there!" Sniff. "Or probably I wouldn't, with the way the Cabinet chickened out—chickened out after Wilson chickened out, admittedly, in spite of Cabot Lodge doing his best . . ."

"Wilson?" Tom was half-breathless again. "Harold Wilson—?"

"Jesus Christ, no!" Audley's stride lengthened again. "*President* Wilson, I'm talking about—1919, 1920ish . . . 1920, it would have been. The idea was to get the Americans into the Black Sea, after the Russian Revolution, rather as we got them into Greece after the last war . . . Bryce—Lord Bryce—put it to Cabot Lodge, and Cabot Lodge swung the Senate. But Wilson wouldn't play. So poor old General Dunsterville was left out on a limb down in the back of beyond, on the Caspian Sea. Which, of course, he'd always expected to be—lovely man, Lionel Dunsterville! Spoke even more languages than you do, Tom . . . But I suppose I can hardly expect you to know anything about his romantic little fiasco—not while your Polish ancestors were beating the daylights out of Trotsky outside Warsaw, anyway."

Tom's confusion increased. Panin's parting aside about "Dunsterforce" had gone over his head, and now Audley's "Dunsterville" merely followed it.

And he was falling behind again—

"David—"

"It's all true, though—'Dunsterforce'—" It was as though the old man had five-league boots "—however unlikely it sounds. In fact, that's almost certainly where the Navy story comes from, which sounds apocryphal but is probably just as true—about the fish jam . . . long before my time, or yours . . . Long before my father's time—more like my grandfather's time!"

Tom had just managed to reach his shoulder, but breathlessness and fish jam left him speechless.

"The trouble is . . . yes, the *only* trouble is—" A growling note entered Audley's voice "—that that bastard son-of-a-bitch back there knows all too-damn well that I, of all people, am most likely to swallow any Dunsterforce story—fish jam and all—" He pointed ahead. "But there's the car, anyway." Once again he stopped without warning and faced Tom. "So what do we do, then? No time for your beloved back-up now, not even if I agreed to it. Which I don't." He grinned unhelpfully.

A memory came to Tom, but equally unhelpfully, of Willy's golden head on the pillow next to his. Willy had "had help", she had said, in getting into his room last night. And the Company would never have sent her so far from home alone, that wasn't their way—that way, at least, they were careful. So Willy and her Help were maybe ten miles away, and maybe half-an-hour, from Farmer Bodger's farmyard at this moment; and that was the nearest thing he had to any sort of back-up. But neither Audley nor Jaggard would thank him for calling the 7th Cavalry out on Exmoor.

"Panin hasn't left us any time, David. I'm not sure that I like that."

"Hmm . . . But then he wants to keep everything low key and strictly non-violent . . ." Audley moved his head in a curious circular motion, which was neither a shake nor a nod. "And in his state of professional health that has a certain logic to it. Because he can no more afford a scandal than I can . . . not to put too fine a point on the situation." Audley wiped his nose thoughtfully.

"Yes." Tom hid behind unwilling acceptance of the old man's own logic while actually noting that for the first time Audley had conceded the truth of what everyone else had been saying: that he himself was no longer invulnerable. But then he also saw the flaw in the logic. "But yesterday wasn't non-violent, was it?" And . . . better to be brutally explicit. "Your bullet and Basil Cole weren't low key, David."

"Hmm . . . My bullet certainly wasn't." Audley sniffed. "And I wish to God I had Old King Cole at the end of a phone now—we'd know what we were about then—you're damn right there, Tom! Topping Basil was just too-damn neat . . . it *smells* of Panin, no matter how many times he swears to the contrary." Nod. Then a succession of small nods. "Yes . . . in the Great Patriotic War he might have been an NKVD hood, but he was also a working staff-officer. So he'd know how blind the front-line is when they can't get any intelligence briefings about what's ahead and on the flanks . . . So I'll bet he knows I'm running blind as well as scared now, in spite of all the bull-shit I've fed him to the contrary. Huh! But we still go on, eh?"

Once again, in spite of all the other bull-shit which he'd received, Tom warmed to Mamusia's ancient Beast. Because, for all his pride and bloody-mindedness and plain awkwardness, the old Beast was scared underneath, as he had every right to be. But, in spite of all that, the old Beast intended to go ahead—that was obvious. And in that the old Beast wasn't disappointing; even, he could see how Colonel Butler might be tempted to return the trust and loyalty which he had received this day—even if it was Audley's own peculiar variety of trust-and-loyalty—in exchange for such cavalryman's courage.

"Huh!" The old man had completed his logic-versus-flawed-logic process. "But we don't have any choice in the matter, young Tom: there's always a risk, but we're in the risk-taking business—we're the poor-bloody Hotspur nettle-pluckers—

'Out of this nettle, danger, we pluck this flower, safety'

Are you game for that, boy?"

Tom didn't like being called "boy", any more than "Darling boy". But one half of him (and maybe Mamusia's half, too) shrugged off the diminutive. "Yes." Only there was still the other half (which was Father's cautious English half, but in which Jaggard also still had the controlling interest). "But I'd like to make a phone-call first, David."

"A phone-call?" Audley frowned at him, then at the car, then back at him. "To whom?"

"I want to know what they've got on your bullet, from yesterday." It was reasonable, but there was no harm in making it more so, so he grinned at Audley, and knew to his shame that it was a boyish grin. "Besides which . . . they'll be expecting me to phone in. But don't worry: I won't tell them that we're about to behave stupidly—I agree that we don't have any choice." Instinct and inclination suddenly combined. "You would have done okay in my grandfather's regiment, David—in . . . my mother's father's regiment, the Ulyani Lancers: they never could resist charging the machine-guns, when it came to the crunch."

"Hah!" Audley was plainly delighted with the insult. "And you would have done well enough in the old Wesdragons, Tom: The West Sussex Dragoons . . . Because they were thick as two planks too!" Nod. "In fact, my old CO . . . 'Kit' Sykes—or *Bill Sykes* to his friends, of whom I was never one—*he* used to say . . . rather like Marshal Foch, of whom he'd certainly never heard, because he boasted that he'd never opened a book in his life, and he hated all Frenchmen as a matter of principle . . . *he* used to say, *'Don't worry about the flanks—God only knows where they are, and they aren't your business anyway. And don't worry about the rear, because I shall be breathing down the back of your unwashed neck, and there's nothing behind us except cooks and bottle-washers, anyway. Just go and find out whether there's anything up ahead between us and the cocktail bar in the Adlon Hotel in Berlin, there's a good fellow! And if there isn't, then order six bottles of their best Champagne on my account—understood?'* " The old man's pleasure in his old soldier's memory was like a hot bottle in a cold bed in mid-winter. "Understood, Tom?"

"Understood, David." Only he needed to take his speculator's profit on a favourable market. "But I still need to make my phone-call—I want to know what the cooks and the bottle-washers have been doing—okay?"

Audley shrugged, and started to move again. "No harm in that, I suppose . . . just so as you don't tell 'em anything. No point in worrying 'em—old Jack particularly. He worries about me a lot when I'm out of his reach, you know—" The rest was lost, half-mumbled at an increasing distance, leaving Tom momentarily rooted to his spot by an onrush of sympathy for Colonel Butler, who must surely be as long-suffering as he was remarkable in other respects.

Then he remembered *Dunsterforce*, which he would need very soon to explain to Jaggard. The trouble was . . . getting any sort of straight answer out of the old man in his present elliptical mood (or probably in any mood, come to that) didn't lend itself to speed; and the last thing he wanted was a lecture on post-World War One Anglo-American policy in the Near and Middle East—he'd had enough of the 1985 results of that old impossible tangle, for Christ's sake!

Besides which—

"Wait for me, David!" But Audley took not a blind bit of notice.

Besides which what *was* he going to tell Jaggard? (Audley was already half-way to the car, his raincoat flapping around him like a pair of pale wings; and that reminded him of his original job, and also that he was getting careless: because that almost-white raincoat stood out too much for safety against the faded green of the landscape; and because Henry Jaggard hadn't told him the half of it—because Henry Jaggard was up to something, and Henry Jaggard couldn't be trusted!)

He had no time to tell Jaggard about Willy. And could he tell Jaggard what Audley was doing, when Audley himself still didn't really know what Panin was up to?

Bloody Dunsterforce! First things first. (Audley, large and white, had reached the car—and the sooner he was safe inside it, the better. That ought to have been ahead of first: that was more carelessness!)

He broke into a run, forgetting everything for a moment—

Audley gave up trying to wrench the car door open and stood waiting for him, getting larger and whiter by the second.

He reached the car himself finally, breathless and careless, and happily ridiculous. "Sorry, David. I locked it." The gun under his arm felt huge.

"I know you locked it. But do you really think anyone would steal a heap like this—from a muddy farmyard?" The old man regarded him pityingly.

"Just habit." *Beirut habit*, thought Tom, and it was disturbing thought. But it was a thought he had unthought too easily until now. "Go and stand over there, by the end of the barn."

"Just unlock the door, there's a good fellow."

Tom sighed. "Just go and stand by the barn—round the corner of it."

"What the devil—?" The old man's shoulders slumped suddenly. "For God's sake . . . you don't really think . . .?" Then he straightened up again. "Or are you trying to frighten me? Because you're succeeding, you know."

"Good." Tom pointed towards the barn. "Don't be difficult, David. I won't take long."

"I should hope not! I have wet feet and a cold. And I'm past my prime." Audley held up his hand and started backing away. "All right, all right

—just don't do yourself an injury. Your dear Mother would never forgive me . . ."

Tom waited until the old man was out of sight. "Actually, this isn't going to be very difficult—can you hear me?"

"Yes—" Sneeze "—no?"

"We parked on nice mud . . . just hoof-prints and our footprints, I think—nice distinctive prints, too!"

"Of course," agreed Audley. "Like Shakespeare said."

Tom opened the passenger's door gingerly. Then he leaned across to the driver's. "What d'you mean—Shakespeare?" He unlocked the bonnet. "Shakespeare?"

"Henry V, dear boy. The night before Agincourt."

Nothing anywhere there. Look in the boot. Look under the seats. "The night—" Nothing anywhere: false alarm? "—before Agincourt?"

"Uh-huh. Like young Harry said: *'Every subject's duty is the king's; but every subject's soul is his own.'* " Sneeze. "Joke, Tom: sole, not soul . . . Not very good, but the best I can manage in the circumstances: you said 'footprints', and I said 'sole'—okay?"

"Very good." Check everything again, was the rule.

"Not really. Not in these circumstances, actually, it occurs belatedly to me—*bad* joke, in fact. Is there a bomb in our car?"

"You can come out now." Tom drew a deep breath. "False alarm, David."

Audley squelched across the yard. "But with good intent."

"Yes." Tom knew he was smiling like an idiot. "It was a good joke."

Audley shook his head, unsmiling. "Not if you remember the bit that comes before, where the soldier says that the king has a heavy reckoning to make *'when all those legs and arms and heads, chopt off in battle, shall join together at the latter day, and cry all, "We died at such a place".'* " He shook his head again. "Bad joke. Forgive me, Tom. I apologize.'

"No need to." He had never seen the old man so serious, not even after the news of Basil Cole's death. "I have been getting careless."

"And I have been worse than careless: I have been playing my little games maybe a little too thoughtlessly of late—Panin's right. And that gives him the edge on me now." He looked at Tom sadly. "It's like my wife has said on occasion: 'How can such a clever man as you so often end up being too clever by half?' " Sniff. "My trouble is . . . as you get older there are things you can't do any more, Tom. So sometimes I get a little bored. And then I make a little excitement for myself. So . . . now I am justly served, perhaps. But you are not."

Poor old bugger! Getting older was something Tom had occasionally thought about. But not *being* older. But now he didn't know quite how to react. "It's okay, David." He patted the Cortina. "In Beirut I used to do this all the time, pretty much. It's all right."

"It isn't all right. Being too clever by half is bad enough. But not being clever enough is worse. People get killed when I'm not clever enough. And I'm not being clever enough at the moment, I suspect."

That could really only mean one thing. "You think Panin's up to something—apart from protecting Zarubin?"

"Hmm . . . I'll tell you something about Comrade Panin, Tom—one of the things we *do* know about him. He was the pupil of a man named Berzin, who was a professor of psychology in the Dzerzhinsky KGB Centre in the old days. We've got a whole book of his lectures in our archives, which some thoughtful person presented to us. Lots of theories, old Berzin had—some of 'em simple and old hat, some of 'em devious as hell. 'Get your enemy to do your work for you', was one . . . and one that Panin likes, too. But there was another one I recall, because it's pricking my thumbs at the moment. Berzin called it his 'Benefit Maximization' theory, or some such jargon—he liked jargon. What he meant, though, was that having a main objective in any operation should never preclude subsidiary objectives. In fact, he even referred to 'the single objective heresy': '*the successful operative must balance caution and calculation with daring, risk-acceptance and greed for windfall benefits in what may seem unrelated sectors of activity . . .*' Or something like that—I'm not sure of the translation of 'windfall', but 'greed' is the exact word, straight out of the Bible in Russian, apparently." Audley nodded. "And our Nikolai is nothing if not greedy. Apart from which . . . if, as he says and I very much suspect, his present position is as uncertain as mine is . . . he needs to ride home with a whole lot of severed heads attached to his saddlebow."

It was a chilly metaphor, as cold as the metal under his hand, thought Tom. "And yours may be one of them, you think?"

The brutal mouth twitched upwards. "Well, apart from Zarubin, I'm the only target around." Another twitch. "But it does occur to me now that if the 'Sons of the Eagle' just happened to put a bullet through me . . . then no one could blame *him*, could they? That would have the virtue of neatness." The twitch became the old familiar Beast-grin. "It just occurred to me out of the blue. And it's probably quite fanciful."

The metal was almost burning-cold. "We don't have to keep his next rendezvous, David. We could let him go it alone—"

"Cut-and-run? For *him*?" This time the sniff was worthy of the nose. "Not on your nellie, Tom! The day I do that for Panin . . . then he doesn't have to worry about me ever again. And right now he still does, I tell you."

It was useless to argue with him, because his pride certainly equalled Panin's greed.

"Besides which . . . I'd never know what he was up to, would I?" The Beast-grin softened. "And I couldn't abide that—it would make me bully my wife and beat my daughter." Audley shook his head almost cheerfully. "And we couldn't have that, could we! So let's go, then—where glory waits."

Maybe the car wouldn't start, hoped Tom. But he had just looked at the engine under the bonnet, and it had looked the way the garage man said it would—almost as good as the beaten-up Chevvy he had used in Beirut.

"What are you waiting for?" Audley stopped halfway into the car. "What do you want now? Wasn't it a phone—?"

"I'd prefer you not to wear that raincoat, for a start." Better anger than despair.

Audley raised himself, huge and off-white. "Why the hell not?"

"It stands out like a—like a fucking sore thumb, David."

"What?" The old Audley sparked again. "You want me to die of pneumonia, then?"

"Pneumonia would suit me fine." He preferred the old Audley, actually. "No one's going to blame me for that. And it isn't usually terminal these days, anyway. But . . . suit yourself." He ought to have known that the direct approach never worked with the old man.

But Audley was nevertheless obediently taking the coat off. "I shall put it on again if it rains." He balled the coat up and threw it into the back of the car. And then looked aggressively at Tom. "Which it looks like doing any moment now. Is that all?"

Tom got into the car, And, of course, it started at the first twist of the ignition key, as he knew it would do. But what he needed, short of the protective back-up he had always wanted, was bloody *Dunsterforce*, before some bloody telephone.

He toyed for a moment with the idea of three-point-turning into the farmyard, and bogging down in it. But the thought was beneath him—and it was par for this course that the Cortina wouldn't bog down, anyway. When inanimate things were against one, it was useless to fight them.

"Yes." He reversed savagely down the track towards the road, knowing that he would stop carefully at the junction, even though there wouldn't be anything to delay him: if God intended David Audley to rendezvous again with his old comrade, then he would clear the road. "Tell me about this fish jam of yours, David."

"Ah . . ." Audley was making a dog's-breakfast of safety-belting himself up as always, oblivious of all nuances when it suited him. "Ah! Now what you really need to know, young Tom, is the story of Major-General

Lionel Dunsterville, who was indirectly responsible—if not *ultimately* responsible—for serving up the jam . . . Which, of course, was good Beluga caviare, as the Comrade Professor well knows—and knows well that I know too, of course. Which is the problem—"

The car bumped and lurched over the pot-holes. And even if it hadn't it was going to be a bumpy ride, because the old bugger was already playing his games again, in spite of everything—

But it wasn't, somehow. Not even though they came to a tatty, old-fashioned (but unvandalized) phone-box on an impossible blind corner on the upper edge of a hillside village only five or ten minutes away from Bodger's Farm; which must therefore have been well within the range of Gilbert de Merville's forced-labour net, when he'd been raising Mountsorrel.

And, even, it was Audley who broke first, trying to snap the thread of his own inconsequential tale, out of fish jam (which the sailors had hated), and the long-dead, far-flung past, from Devon to the high passes of the North-West Frontier, and back to Devon again, and on to the equally distant Caspian Sea, off Enzeli in Persia, and Baku in Transcaucasia, and Astrakhan on one of the mouths of the Volga.

"Aren't you supposed to be phoning?" The old man found his wrist-watch with difficulty, on the inside of his wrist. "They'll be there by now, almost—?"

He had to find the number, and reverse the charges, with his imagination still ablaze.

And do the necessary: "This is an open line—" It had sounded like the dreadful Harvey on the other end, sweating out his Saturday as duty-creature to Jaggard "—the number is—"

But finally Jaggard came on, irascibly. "Arkenshaw! Where the hell have you been?"

Jaggard wasn't to be trusted, he thought. But then—*but neither am I now!* "I'm in Devon, on Exmoor. I'm at—" He squinted at the name and number again, where he was.

"I know where you are, damn it! What the devil's happening?"

So Audley's bullet and Basil Cole had fully worked themselves through the system since yesterday. "We should abort this operation, sir, I think."

Pause.

"Just tell me what's happening, Tom." Jaggard had his cool back now.

"Do you know who the 'Sons of the Eagle' are, sir?"

Another pause. But he could imagine what Jaggard was doing, out of his earshot; and then what Harvey would be doing. "No."

Well—let's see how good Harvey is! "They are a Polish dissident group. Panin says that they're terrorists, subsidiary to Solidarity."

"You've talked to Panin?"

Keep to the truth while you can. "Audley has. I've just listened in. Panin's down here with a Polish minder, by name Sadowski. Major Kasimierz Sadowski." *Wait, and let him feed that also to Harvey.*

"Yes?" The pause was just long enough to confirm Tom's suspicion that Harvey wasn't monitoring the call on an extension line: this was Jaggard's privately-taped exchange. And, of course, he knew about Sadowski.

"Panin says he's here to stop the Sons of the Eagle from killing General Zarubin." Tom gave him only half a second. "You know about Zarubin?"

"Go on."

So Jaggard didn't need to put that through either. "Zarubin masterminded the murder of Father Popieluszko." Tom gave the dead priest's name every last Polish inflection, to the point of incomprehensibility. And then waited.

"Go on. Go on."

"Do you know where Zarubin is now?"

Fractional pause. "Don't keep asking me questions. Just tell me what's happening."

"Zarubin's on the way here. At this very moment." Tom shivered helplessly at the meaning of his own words. "He'll be here any time, in the next hour or two. Here on Exmoor, sir. And the Sons of the Eagle will be waiting for him."

This time it wasn't so much a pause as a silence while Jaggard digested this disquieting intelligence. But finally he came to life again. "Panin told you this?"

Audley was watching him from the car. "Yes, sir."

"How does he know?"

Fair question. "He's not saying. Presumably they've got someone inside the Sons of the Eagle."

"And how do they know—the Poles—about Zarubin?"

Another fair question. "He wouldn't say that, either. He just stated it as a fact, and stuck to it. But . . ."

"But what?"

Tom nodded gratefully to Audley. "Dr Audley thinks, if Panin's got someone on the inside, then maybe he's set the thing up himself."

"What?" Jaggard sounded irritated. "Set up Zarubin as a target? Why the blazes should he do that?"

"Zarubin is a target already. The Poles have already killed his deputy —a man named Marchuk. Leonid Marchuk—"

"Spell it." Tom's pronunciation invariably floored native Englishmen.
"M-A-R-C-H-U-K. L-E—"
"I've got that. Go on."
"That was in Poland." It wouldn't take long for the computer to confirm that. "Zarubin was posted back to Moscow after that. But now he's in England, and Panin probably reckons he can't be protected properly here. So he's taking the initiative instead."
"The initiative—" That rocked Jaggard somewhat. "What initiative?"
"He says he doesn't want any trouble—not with what Zarubin's doing over here at the moment, especially. He says that'll be bad for both sides."
"He does? Well, he's going about it in a damn funny way! What does he propose to do, for heaven's sake?"
"He wants to make a deal."
"A deal—?" Jaggard stopped suddenly. "Hold on."
Tom waited, focusing on Audley again. He mustn't forget to ask about Audley's bullet and Basil Cole's death to give himself some sort of cover story for all this chat.
"Arkenshaw?" Jaggard came on the line again. "I have confirmation on Marchuk. A suspicious road accident . . . Not a nice man, Marchuk. But then neither is Zarubin, by all accounts. But we haven't got one damn thing on your 'Sons of the Eagle'." Pause. "But you knew about them, did you? But . . . never mind. What deal? With us?"
"No, sir. With the Sons of the Eagle." *Put that in your pipe!* But he could improve on that. "With a man named Szymiac."
"With—? Shimshe . . . ack?"
"That's right. S-Z-Y-M-I-A-C—one of their top men. Szymiac. Panin knows exactly where to find him. He's rented a house at East Lyn, just outside Lynmouth. In preparation for welcoming Zarubin to Exmoor." Tom wondered what the computer would make of that. But then, if it had fluffed the Sons of the Eagle it was unlikely to throw up Szymiac from its electronic stomach.
Jaggard growled unintelligibly. "What sort of deal can Panin possibly make with Sh . . . Ssshhim-shak? Are you—*is he* serious?"
"A very obvious deal." For an instant Tom heard the wind whistle round his cosy phone-kiosk. It was a cold east wind, which had freshened in the last hour, possibly blowing all the way from the Urals to Exmoor, across the prostrate body of his mother's country.
"It isn't obvious to me, I said," said Jaggard sharply. "Are you there?"
"Yes." Tom saw that Audley was holding up his wrist and tapping his wrist-watch meaningfully. "Jaruzelski's got a whole lot of Solidarity activists under lock-and-key. All he has to do is throw away the key—or worse. And that gives Panin pretty good bargaining power."

Pause. Then pause-into-silence. And now Audley was shrugging at him. "I'm running out of time, sir." If Jaggard had forgotten Exmoor-realities it was time to remind him. "Dr Audley is waiting for me. So I also need to know what you've got about everything that happened yesterday . . . *sir*."

"Yes." Was that an in-take of breath? "What does Audley say about all this? Does he accept it?" Only half-a-second. "But you want to abort—?"

"I do." This was where the truth became too complicated. "He doesn't."

"Why not?" Jaggard ignored what he wanted for the second time.

"He wants to find out what Panin is really up to." Even as he answered, Tom knew that he was on a loser; because Jaggard could no more resist that challenge than Audley could; and also because Jaggard was sitting safe and comfortably, while they were at the sharp end.

"Panin's up to something else?" Jaggard's question was hedged with caution.

"Yes, sir. I think he is."

"The hell with what you think! What does Audley say?"

He should have expected this. "It relates to why Zarubin is coming here, sir." He had thought to enjoy this tall story, but Jaggard had ruined his enjoyment.

"Ah . . . yes . . ." Jaggard temporized, as though he'd been untimely switched back to another outstanding question, which had already occurred to him but which he'd decided was relatively unimportant in his scale of priority questions. "What the blazes is he doing down there, where you are? Apart from risking his neck—?"

It would have been better to have reached this point earlier on, when Audley wasn't making faces at him from the car. "What do our records say about him—about Zarubin?"

"About Zarubin?" Jaggard had been expecting an answer, not a question—and particularly not after his express order to the contrary. So, for a moment, he was close to answering. "What the hell are you playing at, Arkenshaw?"

"I'm not playing at anything. What have we got on Zarubin?"

"What—? Man, we've got what you'd expect: he's officially a senior officer of the Red Army, ex-Warsaw Pact headquarters secretariat, seconded to the Foreign Ministry with effect from January 1985. With a list of decorations to match." Jaggard's cool bent, but didn't crack. "He's career KGB, Second Directorate, with the rank of general, dated December 1984."

"We don't have the name of his father?"

Pause. "We don't have the name of his father. Or his wife. Or his wife's father. Or his wife's uncle's second cousin. Or his mother's aunt—" Caution suddenly "—what's his father got to do with him coming to Exmoor?"

That was an unlooked-for gift. "Just about everything, according to Panin. Because Zarubin's father was born in a fisherman's cottage on Brentiscombe Head. On the day Mafeking was relieved. Mafeking Day —May 17, 1900." Tom resisted the temptation to add that Audley himself had supplied the exact date after Panin had supplied the event. "Brentiscombe Head is up the coast from Lynmouth, towards Ilfracombe. Zarubin's father's name was *Roberts* . . . Or maybe his christian name was *Robert*—Panin's not too sure about that . . . at least, not as sure as he is about the cottage on Brentiscombe Head, anyway. Because Zarubin took his grandfather's name—" He could allow himself this satisfaction, anyway "—that's to say, his mother's father's name . . . Do you understand?"

No hint of understanding came down the line. Which would have been gratifying if Audley hadn't wound down his car-window to draw his attention to time's winged chariot. So he nodded at Audley and re-applied himself to the telephone. "What he says is that Zarubin's father was an Englishman—that he joined the Royal Navy straight from school, in 1914. And he served in HMS *Goliath*, in the Dardanelles in 1915. And then, finally, he fell overboard, from HMS *President Kruger*, in the Caspian Sea in 1920—"

"*Where—?*" Jaggard gagged on the Caspian Sea, without ever reaching HMS *President Kruger*, as well he might, thought Tom; even Audley had done a second take on that—as well *he* might, too: a child born in 1964 could have been sunk by the Argentinians in the South Atlantic in 1982, but it took too big a stretch of the imagination to have him fall off HMS *Adolf Hitler* the year after, in any conceivable war, never mind in the landlocked Caspian Sea where the Royal Navy had no obvious business.

"Yes, sir. In the Caspian Sea . . . serving with the Royal Navy Caspian Squadron, in support of Dunsterforce." He couldn't resist playing *Dunsterforce* for all it was undoubtedly worth. "We had a combined operation in Iran—in *Persia*—after the First World War, to keep the Turks first . . . and then the Bolsheviks . . . away from India, sir. And it was commanded by a man named Dunsterville—Major-General Lionel Dunsterville. But it all came pretty-much unstuck, because of lack of support. Typical Foreign Office foul-up, probably."

An indeterminate sound came down the line. "What the hell are you talking about, Arkenshaw?"

You may well ask, sir! "Zarubin's father was taken prisoner by the Bolsheviks . . . somewhere off Astrakhan, at the mouth of the Volga in

1920, after he fell overboard. Or, Audley says he may have deserted . . . because there were some mutinies in the navy, about that time. That would account for the Bolsheviks not shooting him, anyway. Or maybe he was just a fast talker." He couldn't repeat Audley's theory that *Able Seaman Roberts* had developed an upper-class taste for caviare which only membership of the Communist Party could satisfy.

Another strangled growl reached him. "This sounds like Audley talking. Is this what he's saying?"

"No, sir." The lie came quickly, because he was half-ready for it. But there was also half-truth in it. "He's extremely suspicious of the whole story: he says it could be all true, but he doesn't like it. That's what I've been trying to say, sir."

"Why doesn't he like it?" Jaggard couldn't avoid the obvious question.

"He says it's just the sort of damned cock-and-bull story Panin would dream up for him."

"It's all hogwash, is it?"

"Some of it's true, apparently—about 'Dunsterforce', and HMS *President Kruger*, anyway." He had to avoid even looking towards Audley now. "But he says Panin would expect him to know about it. Because everyone knows he's dotty about Rudyard Kipling—Panin included."

"Rudyard Kipling?" The sudden growl in Jaggard's voice, which overlaid its incredulity, suggested that everyone included him. "What the blazes has he got to do with Zarubin—or his father?"

"Just about everything, sir. 'Dunsterforce' was commanded by Lionel Dunsterville. And Dunsterville was Kipling's best friend at the United Services College at Westward Ho!—just down the coast from here, outside Bideford—Dunsterville was Kipling's actual model for Stalky in *Stalky & Co*—"

(" *'Your Uncle Stalky is a Great Man'*." He heard Audley's voice inside his head. *"And Dunsterville was, of course: eight languages, including Chinese and German and Persian, never mind all the Indian dialects. Crammed into the Indian Army from the United Services College—dreadful place . . . But crammed by Cormell Price, who was a great headmaster. And not an imperialist, even though USC only existed to supply the Empire with dedicated servants —he was 'Prooshian Bates, the downy bird' in 'Stalky', Cormell Price . . . Friend of Swinburne, and William Morris, and Dante Gabriel Rossetti, and Burne-Jones . . . Kipling should never have been in that school—he wasn't going into the army. But Cormell Price was the perfect headmaster for him, nevertheless . . . But the hell with that, Tom! See how that son-of-a-bitch has ambushed me again! I'll bet he bloody-well knows I'm wasting time telling you about Cormell Price!"*)

"All right, all right! I get the drift, man. Panin claims Zarubin is half an Englishman, by blood if by nothing else. And Audley knows that this could be true—and we haven't got anything to say that it isn't . . ." Jaggard trailed off for a moment. "But Panin can't know for sure that we don't know about Zarubin, or what we do know. So maybe it *is* true, damn it! So where does that leave us?"

"It's why Zarubin's coming here." Tom shook himself free from Kipling and Cormell Price. "He's always wanted to see his father's birthplace. He's never made any secret of it, apparently. And this is the first time he's had the chance."

"Hmm . . ." The silence at the other end suggested that Jaggard was running through Zarubin's *curriculum vitae* again. "There's nothing in his record to suggest filial piety. Or any other kind of piety, come to that—he's a bloodthirsty Dzerzhinsky Centre-trained honours graduate, with a lot of scalps hanging outside his tent. Including your Father Jerzy's, Arkenshaw, among all the others. In fact . . . he's the sort Gorbachev shouldn't be promoting now . . . if anything, that's rather surprising. Except he's the right age, I suppose." Pause. "What does Audley say?"

"Maybe it's just curiosity—on Zarubin's part."

"Well, it's damn dangerous curiosity, if there's a hit-squad waiting for him down there," growled Jaggard. "It's full of holes. It stinks, Arkenshaw, it stinks."

"Yes, sir—I agree. And that's why I think we should abort." Tom's heart lightened. "If you can intercept Zarubin . . . then I can warn Panin off. After all, he is playing games on our ground."

Another growl. "Oh yes? And then someone puts a bullet into Zarubin outside the Dorchester one night? Is that it?"

"We can send Zarubin back home. And Panin with him. Let them solve their own homegrown terrorism and leave us in peace." But Tom felt his argument weakening even as he made it: sending Zarubin home would be an unfriendly act, never mind an admission that the UK couldn't protect a fully-accredited diplomat in her own backyard, even though that was sadly true.

Again the silence lengthened, as Jaggard made the same connections. "What does Audley say? Is that what he wants?"

The son-of-a-bitch has ambushed us, thought Tom bitterly, knowing what he must say, and then exactly how Jaggard would come back to him. "He says that either Panin's up to something nasty, or Zarubin is. But he wants to find out what it is." He glanced towards the car, but the old man looked as though he'd given up and gone to sleep. So probably he was dreaming of Kipling and Dunsterville arguing about the pre-Raphaelites with Cormell Price on the windy beaches of Westward Ho! in the 1880s, before fame and Empire and the Caspian Sea overtook them. "But what about that shot someone took at Audley yesterday? And what about Basil Cole?" This time, as he spoke, he decided to get stroppy, with desperation cancelling Jaggard's huge seniority. "Someone has to have come up with something there, for Christ's sake! Or am I on my own down here, and no one gives a damn what I'm doing—?"

No answer. And the old man in the Cortina across the road was settling himself more comfortably, no longer worried either about time or Panin—or even that he was parked on a blind corner; which only served first to increase Tom's sense of desperation and isolation as he thought *either he's stupid or he trusts me; but he isn't stupid, so he trusts me: but if he trusts me, then he is stupid—*

"Apart from which Dr Audley is waiting for me," he continued harshly. "And that's what he thinks I'm finding out. So I have to have something to tell him . . . *sir.*"

"Yes." After *no answer* the answer came smoothly now. "Don't worry about that business at Audley's house. We have that in hand, and it has nothing to do with what you're engaged in, Tom."

So it was *Tom* again now. "What d'you mean—?" A hideous thought struck Tom between the shoulder-blades, coming appropriately from behind and stopping him in mid-protest. "I mean . . . what about Basil Cole, then? I've got to tell him *something*, damn it!"

"That's not so straightforward. Because . . . the accident seems fair enough, on the face of it. Because, with all the trampling around there, there wasn't much evidence left. But he wasn't really very drunk at the time, it seems. Or not morning-drunk, from the stomach contents." Pause. "And it appears someone got the wife out of the house on a wild-goose chase, at the material time. Which would have given someone else a free run there, when she was away." Pause. "So that does look like murder, we think." Pause. "Though whether it was your 'Sons of the Eagle' or the Other Side, we don't know yet." Pause. "So you just give him that, and embroider it a bit . . . Cole's wife helps out at a hospital there, running relatives to visit their next-of-kin when it comes to the last rites. And she was given an urgent address by someone—someone they can't trace, at the wrong address. That's the strength of it, and we're working on it. But . . . for the rest—" Jaggard's ingratiating tone dropped away from his voice, like a drop-tank from an old-fashioned fighter-plane as it zoomed into combat "—if that's what Audley wants, then he's in charge, Arkenshaw. And your job is simply to keep him in one piece. How many times do I have to spell it out for you?"

How many times, indeed! But then, even beyond the recurrent memory of his promise to Audley's wife and daughter, Jaggard's crude image conjured up the man himself squelching through Farmer Bodger's yard not half-an-hour previously—Audley sobered by his own responsibility for Tom Arkenshaw as he thought of blown-up legs and arms and heads *joining together on the latter day*. "You're going to have to spell it out every time you talk to me. Because I didn't like the odds yesterday, and I like them even less today. I think we're going to be in trouble before we've finished down here. And I want to put that on record."

Silence.

Tom took a deep breath. "Someone tried to kill Audley yesterday. They may try again."

"Oh . . ." It sounded not so much like anger as exasperation ". . . oh, all right, Tom—have it your way, then! Let me think, now . . ."

Tom didn't require the order, he was surprised enough not only with Jaggard's second thought, but also with this almost-confirmation of that knife-thrust of suspicion.

"All right, then—" Now Jaggard was his old self again "—I'm not going to call out the anti-terrorist squad, or the Special Branch, to line every hedgerow. There probably isn't time, and we as good as promised Panin's people that we wouldn't interfere with his business with Audley . . . Apart from which we might scare off these 'Sons of the Eagle' of his, which would only make matters worse, undoubtedly."

That sounded suspiciously like "any aid, short of actual help". Indeed, it sounded even more like Jaggard covering his flank against awkward questions in some future inquiry. But what else could he expect? "Yes, sir?"

"But I'll do what I can for you—I'll put what I can scrape together on the road. They'll be just over your skyline in a couple of hours. And you've got the contingency number."

"Yes." *Not good enough*. "Yes." Tom came to a decision. "I'll call you as soon as we've got anything." He had the contingency number. And he also had another number. "Goodbye."

Audley was mercifully still wrapped in dreams, or day-dreams, as he dialled the other number.

"Green Man Hotel—can I help you?"

I hope so! "Room 12, please."

"Room 12—putting you through, sir."

Tom's conscience pricked him, but only slightly.

"Hullo there?"

The conscience-pricking sharpened, and he was suddenly aware that his hand was sweaty on the receiver. "Listen, Willy—"

*

Audley yawned, and stretched against his seat-belt. "You've been a most unconscionable time, dear boy. What *have* you been doing?"

"I'm sorry, David." Of course the car started at the first touch once more, with malignant obedience. "Everyone was busy saving the world."

"Oh yes?" There was only the merest hint that the unconscionable time had re-aroused the old man's suspicions, which the episode in Farmer Bodger's yard had momentarily allayed. "Since the weekend is with us, I'm surprised you found anyone at all there."

Better to counter-attack, as though from a clear conscience. "I didn't think you were worried." He put his foot down as the road opened up ahead. "I saw you snoring."

"I was not asleep!" Audley sniffed, and wiped his nose on the back of his huge dirty paw like a geriatric schoolboy. "I was thinking of Kipling and Dunsterville . . . and fact imitating fiction, actually. Because he must have written *Puck of Pook's Hill* . . . oh, all of thirty years before Dunsterville got the dirty end of the stick on the Caspian—just like Parnesius got the dirty end defending the Roman Wall, and de Aquila did at Pevensey—one of your few good Normans, Tom, defending England for bad Normans against worse ones!" He studied Tom for a long moment. "You're not married—? No, I can see you're not! But when you are, and your union is blessed with a son or a daughter . . . and preferably with a daughter like my Cathy . . . I shall then present one of my First Edition *Pucks*, suitably inscribed, to your offspring . . . In the remote hope that she—or even *he*—may accidentally read *Puck's Song* in it, and then get some faint idea about what it's all about—

> *'As for my comrades in camp or highway,*
> *That lift their eyebrows scornfully,*
> *Tell them their way is not my way—*
> *Tell them that England hath taken me!'*

"But *no*—I have *not* been asleep, in answer to your fairly insulting statement. Because, if I looked as though I was snoring, then that is only because I can no longer breathe through my nose."

Tom felt chastened. But he also wondered whether the old boy had a secret and medicinal hip-flask; only he couldn't smell anything suggesting that. "You weren't thinking about Panin, then? Or Zarubin?" Another road-sign, sprouting out of a Normandy-bocage-high bank, indicated that *Lynmouth* and *Lynton* were now dreadfully close, with Willy still far behind. "Don't they rate ahead of Kipling, at the moment?"

"Oh, they do—they do!" Audley had seen the same sign, but it didn't seem to frighten him. "I thought of them first off, when I made those silly signals to you, Tom—for which I really must apologize . . . when you were busy, too. But that was when I came back to Kipling, from our previous conversation. And I must admit that I found him much more interesting to think about. And more relevant too, by God!"

"Relevant?"

"That's right. Because he's already said it all. The way it is, the way it always was. And the way it always will be, Tom—"

There were houses ahead, just the first irregular scatter of them here and there, half-hidden on a steeply-wooded hillside.

"—which, of course, you know all too well, as you demonstrated back in that farmyard. But which, sitting in my comfortable research department, protected by my great age and seniority, I keep having to remind myself:

> *'No proposition Euclid wrote,*
> *No formulae the text books know,*
> *Will turn the bullet from your coat,*
> *Or ward the tulwar's downward blow.'* "

There was a sign up ahead: *East Lyn ½*

Audley grinned cheerfully at him. "I always find Kipling relaxing. It's such a pity they don't make children learn poetry by heart nowadays. We had reams of it dinned into us. In the end it becomes . . . not so much easy—although Kipling and all the other good old rhyming stuff *is* easy . . . but not so much easy as a habit . . . And, do you know, my feet are almost dry. Must be the car heater, I suppose, eh?"

Tom followed the sign uphill. The old man *was* blethering. But then, the old man was frightened, and this was merely the sign of his fear. But also, the poor old bugger had every right to be frightened in these circumstances, with Panin and the Sons of the Eagle ahead, and the tricky, treacherous Tom Arkenshaw at his side. Even, very likely, the older one got, the more one had to draw on one's diminished reserves of courage in such situations. And old men must know better than young ones that they weren't immortal, so their "borrowed time" must seem all the more valuable.

"Well, there's old Nikolai, waiting patiently for us." Audley pointed suddenly. "But I don't see the talkative Major. And I don't see their car, either. So they must have tucked that round the side somewhere, I suppose . . . Still, the Comrade Professor doesn't seem very nervous. And that's reassuring."

Panin certainly didn't appear worried: he was watching a hooligan crowd of small birds fighting over something edible in the middle of the road. But otherwise Audley was still blethering about the obvious.

As Tom scattered the birds the Russian looked up and saw them, but gave no sign of having done so. And in that instant Tom decided whose side he was on.

He drove fifty yards before stopping, and then watched Audley release his seat-belt.

"Listen, David—" As he put his hand on the old man's arm he realized that this was the first time he'd touched him. On the terrace yesterday they hadn't shaken hands because Audley's had been dirty from his bonfire-making—about as dirty as they were now. "Listen, David . . ."

Audley regarded him inquiringly, his battered features suddenly scrubbed clean of all other emotions. "Aren't you going to back up?"

Panin was standing still and the birds were back in the road, Tom observed in the rear-view mirror. "He can wait. Do you know who I'm working for?"

Audley's face didn't change. "I did rather wonder. From time to time."

"Henry Jaggard, David. I have to report everything you do to him."

Still no change, but a tiny nod. "Ah . . . well, that's also reassuring. He's a sharp fellow, Henry Jaggard—very clever. But at least he's on our side." Then a slight frown. "Jack Butler doesn't know this, I take it?"

"No. Not as far as I know."

"No." The frown vanished. "That's reassuring too. One doesn't like one's idols to have clay feet. But . . . you don't by any chance know what Henry Jaggard is up to? Apart from securing the defence of the realm and furthering his own career, that is—?"

Tom flicked a glance into the mirror again. Panin was still waiting patiently, and there was still no sign of Major Sadowski. "No." He shook his head at Audley. "My job is to protect you. And to obey your orders, David."

Audley's eyebrows lifted slightly. "That doesn't seem too outrageous. But, since I don't know what the hell I'm doing, he must be having a rather frustrating time." A hint of the old Beast-grin. "So what's your problem?"

"If I had my way we wouldn't be here. Or . . . we'd have a lot more back-up right now. But he won't have that."

Nod. "He's quite right. A troop of heavy-hoofed Special Branch men in clean black Rovers would frighten the natives. And they wouldn't turn a bullet from my coat, either—not if it's got my name on it, Tom. Or, put another way—it would be my friend and colleague Paul Mitchell's way, because he's into 1914-18 poetry . . . and so, to a quite remarkable extent, is Jack Butler, too:

'Nor lead nor steel shall reach him, so
That it be not the Destined Will.'

Not Kipling, that. But it could have been. So not to worry." He reached for his door handle. "We just have to keep our powder dry, that's all."

"No—" Again Tom touched Audley's arm "—that's the point, David . . . That bullet yesterday . . ."

"Yes?" Audley nodded. "I did rather wonder about that, too." The eyebrow cocked again. "Henry Jaggard too—? To galvanize me into urgent and furious activity instantly?"

"He isn't as worried about it as he ought to be."

"He isn't, isn't he?" Audley twisted in his seat to gaze out of the rear window. "Well, I suppose that could be quiet confidence in himself . . . and in you . . . however misplaced." The old man's tone hardened with each word. "Or . . . it could be Henry Jaggard or one of his minions leaving nothing to chance, as you suggest . . . But here's the Galloping Major now, anyway. So let's go and join the bird-watching party then, eh?" Audley straightened himself and opened his door.

Tom felt ridiculously anti-climaxed. He had burnt his boats—perhaps even, subconsciously, he had burnt them for Mamusia's sake, too. But Audley had been there, or nearly, before him, so he might just as well have kept his options open.

A gust of wind, damp with fine cobwebby rain, caught him full in the face as he frowned across the top of the car at Audley.

The old man was smiling at him—not grinning the Beast-grin, but smiling an old maid's almost hesitant smile; which, since his face was so dirty, made him look foolishly-beastly. "I really need my raincoat now, dear boy. But, since you say I mustn't wear it, I'll chance pneumonia instead. Because I am vastly obliged and obligated to you now." The smile twitched. "And because I also know the difference between betrayal and keeping faith in the fine print at the bottom of the contract, you see. Because I've been there too . . . So let's go and do it again, then."

Tom watched him walk away, with the walk instantly lengthening into that characteristic long-legged stride. Then he bent down into the car and reached for the cast-aside raincoat in the back, using the required contortion also to ease the Smith and Wesson out of its holster into his hand to hold under it before he backed out again.

Audley had already reached Panin and Sadowski, and was nodding in answer to the Russian. Tom dropped the car key into his pocket *(who would steal a heap like this?)*, and settled the coat untidily over his right hand. Mercifully, there was a lot of raincoat; but then, any raincoat made to cover Audley had to be tent-like.

"Tom—" Audley called across the decreasing yards as he approached them "—Tom—" Now the raincoat received half-a-glance, and Tom's guts twisted; but then the old man ignored the coat "—of course, they've cheated, as you would expect!"

"Cheated?" Tom let his outrage at the word further cover the coat's untidiness. "How?" He looked accusingly at Panin. "What?"

"Not exactly . . . *cheated*, Sir Thomas." The Russian lifted a hand quickly. "As a precaution we have had men watching this place, to see who has come and who has gone, you understand?" The fingers of the hand opened, and the hand shook defensively. "With General Zarubin so close there is no margin for error, Sir Thomas. We cannot afford to be careless."

"Which, translated, means that they've counted all the Poles out, and then they've counted them all in," snapped Audley. "And there are only two of them."

"That is correct." Panin took a confirmatory nod from Sadowski before nodding himself. "One is Szymiac, the other we do not know. But they operate in two-man cells, we do know. And Szymiac will have scouted the ground, and will drive the car. For he is the brains, and not an assassin—it is the other man who will fire the shot." He fixed Tom through his eye-slits. "Small units, quickly in and quickly out, regardless of everything after proper reconnaissance: they learned that from us, I suspect."

That hadn't been how it had been with Father Jerzy, thought Tom. But then, they had used Polish scum for that, because only scum would work for them, and scum was reliably stupid. But these men were patriots, however deluded now. Or . . . maybe not so deluded?

But he must not think Polish thoughts now: *England had taken him, and their way was not his way now, and that was the end of it!*

"So they're both inside." He looked up at the houses above him: a well-spaced row of very English houses, rather gimcrack-1930ish, each detached from the other behind its garden, which rose up the hill from the road. "Where?"

"There." Panin pointed to one further on from where they were standing. "And we must act now, this minute, because our time is running out . . . Szymiac has already brought out their car from the garage . . . Dr Audley?"

"Suits me." Audley shrugged. "Let's get it over with. Tom—?"

Time running out wasn't to Tom's taste. But then nothing since Ranulf of Caen's ditch yesterday had tasted right. And the nasty little Major—*more Polish scum!*—was already accepting his orders, like the little obedient swine that he was.

They walked the few yards of respectable pavement, then turned up the drive to the house, between rock gardens which had once been lovingly well-tended, when the house had been private and not for hire, but which were now tended just enough to keep them respectable.

And Panin and his watchers had been right: there was a car parked ready, outside the peeling cream-and-brown front door; and, by the coincidence of successful mass-production, it was also a Ford Cortina—and one which matched the front door, near enough, in common milk-chocolate-brown, with a pale beige hardtop, like a million other cars and doors.

"So what do we do, then?" inquired Audley politely. "Just knock on the door and ask for Mr . . . Shim-she-ack?"

Panin half turned towards him. "That is exactly what we shall do, Dr Audley. We come in peace, to preserve the peace." He nodded to the Pole. "Major Sadowski, if you please—?"

The Pole slid by him and flattened himself against the wall of the house on the left of the door. And, as he did so, he drew a short-barrelled revolver from inside his jacket, holding it flat against his chest.

"Some peace!" murmured Audley.

"A precaution, no more." Panin turned towards the door. "Have confidence, Dr Audley—David." He reached for the heavy black door-knocker.

Audley sneezed explosively as the knocker banged, while Tom stared helplessly at the weapon in the Pole's hand, which was a kissing cousin of the one he held in his own. All he could do was to remember that peace-keeping forces the world over were usually and prudently armed to the teeth, and hope that the Pole knew his business.

The echoes of Panin's knocking died away into silence. But then there came an indeterminate sound from inside the house, part scraping, part slithering, followed by a footstep.

"But first a moment of play-acting." Panin nodded to Sadowski again, who seemed to flatten even more against his wall, dead-faced.

The door opened slowly, first only a crack, then somewhat more.

"Good morning, sir—" The Russian's habitually-drooping shoulders had squared, but his voice had stiffened and deepened even more unnaturally. "—I wish to speak to Mr Sizzeemeeack. And my name is *Smith*—Chief Detective Inspector, CID, Exmoor Division, West of England Police Authority—and I must *advise* you, sir, that I 'ave a warrant to search these premises, which are surrounded by my officers, acting under my orders." Panin lifted one foot as he spoke, and placed it firmly in the opening of the door.

Audley sneezed again, as a kaleidoscope of bright unreal thoughts and images burst inside Tom's brain: *Professor Nikolai Andrievich Panin's foot-in-the-door (like an encyclopaedia salesman who didn't intend to take "no" for an answer) was as heavily caked in red Devon mud as his own: and the Russian's stage-policeman's voice, even down to its one carefully dropped "h", was as unnatural as a two-pound note or a three-dollar bill: and maybe Audley's sneeze hadn't been a continuation of his self-pitying common cold, but the beginning of a shared hysteria—*

But then Panin added his hand, placed flat against the door in support of his foot-in-the-gap, and his flattened Polish scum edged his shoulder along the wall, closer to the door, with the weapon in his hand aching to be used, not for peace-keeping but for argument-settling if the door started to close. And then it was no kaleidoscope, and the Smith and Wesson under Audley's raincoat was huge and heavy, and it was no joke—

"So we don't want any trouble now, do we?" Suddenly Panin's voice also wasn't funny, as he caught his breath: it was maybe a travesty of the falsely-friendly, deceptively matter-of-fact policeman's voice in every tight corner, when the unarmed representative of The Law in all its majesty had to humour some mad bastard who was long past law and reason. But then Panin adjusted this position slightly, spreading the hand suddenly towards Audley while keeping his foot in the door. "And I have with me . . ." The hand passed Audley ". . . Sir Thomas Arkenshaw, of the Home Office—" The hand came back from Tom to Audley "—and also Dr David Audley . . . who wish to talk with Mr Sizzeemeeack . . . So, if you would be so good as to inform 'im of our presence . . . then that would be to our mutual advantage, *sir*—"

Tom struggled against the weight of the Smith and Wesson and his sense of unreality again, knowing that he would nevermore be able to address Jaggard, or anyone else, with such old-fashioned deference: after Panin, with this poor damned anonymous murderous fool, no one could ever be "*Sir*" again!

But . . . *it was working, it was working*: the door was opening, and Panin was moving into it—and . . . and even Sadowski was dropping the kissing cousin back into the holster inside his coat—

"Excuse me, David—" He pushed past Audley in Panin's wake, out of the way, ahead of the unwinding Major, too "—Minder always comes first—sorry!"

A last breath of rain-sodden wind hit him again, just as he entered the hall: *one door dead-ahead, with half a lavatory-pedestal in view, glimpsed between Panin and his victim; closed doors each side, left and right, with a small table on the left and an old-fashioned hat-and-coat rack on the right, hung with coats; coats under which two cheap, well-worn suitcases and what looked like a golfing bag were inadequately concealed—they had been the source of that scrape-and-slither he had heard before the door was opened, piled ready for departure in the centre of the hall, he could even see the tramline marks they had left on the dirty linoleum on the floor—*

But Szymiac's man was moving again—crabwise and hesitantly towards one of the doors on the left now, where previously he had backed up unwillingly before the advance of the bogus Chief Detective Inspector Smith of the probably non-existent Exmoor Division; and the man's smooth unhealthy face was as obsequiously blank as Major Sadowski's—maybe that was their joint stock-in-trade expression for survival on both sides of the law in their native land.

"*No!* You stay where you are!" Now that they were inside, Panin's hold on Chief Detective Smith's voice was already slipping: where it should have been a bark it came out as a biting snap. "Zzz—" But he just managed to catch Sadowski's name before it completed the slip "—Major!"

Sadowski brushed Tom's shoulder, as he must also have brushed Audley's in getting ahead of him after Tom, also in the exercise of his minder's prerogative.

"Watch this man." Panin didn't take his eyes off this Son of the Eagle. "He's in here, is he? Mr Sizzeemeeack?"

Tom was half-aware of Sadowski on his right, somewhat entangled with the hat-stand-coat-rack and the pile of luggage, but was equally unwilling to take his eyes off the Son of the Eagle, who merely nodded confirmation, as voiceless and obedient as Sadowski himself.

"Good!" Panin caught Tom's eye now, and nodded, almost as though he knew what was under Audley's trailing raincoat, as he raised his hand and rapped sharply on the door with his knuckles.

Tom stared, transfixed in the first fraction of a second by the action and the sound; and then, in the next fraction, by Panin's hand as it grasped the door-knob; and then, in the last and almost simultaneous instant of time, by the unwilling acceptance of the thought that Panin was as brave as Audley, when it came to the crunch of actually risking his skin in the front line—

"Mr Sizzeemeeack—?" Panin turned the knob. "I am Chief Detective Inspector Smith—and I am coming in—do you hear me?"

The thought amended itself slightly as Panin threw open the door: the knock and the challenge were a calculated risk, that the Poles weren't about to challenge the British police, whatever they might want to do to General Gennadiy Zarubin; to which might be added the Russian's confidence that Szymiac was the brains, not the brawn of the operation —the brawn which even now was covered by Major Sadowski's pale eyes behind them. But then the memory of the Russian's last nod, which had deliberately appealed to him, activated his own reflexes as Panin stepped over the threshold into the room.

"Mr Sizzeemeeack?" Panin confirmed his suspicion by taking his second step to one side, after the first one had been forward, to give him something like a clear field of fire.

Again, Tom had the sense of photographing everything, in that split-second.

Insanely, even as he saw the man himself, the room summed itself up for him: it had come down in the world, just as the man himself must have done to be here inside it, far from home and in a foreign land and doing a dirty patriotic job—

"Shim-she-ack!" Panin snapped the name accurately in Polish.

(In its better days, the room had had pictures on the wall, and other furniture which had left empty ghost-marks behind on the wallpaper; while the man himself was also a shadow, more like the men outside, Sadowski and his charge, but unreal compared with the menace of Panin and Audley.)

"You know why I am here, don't you?" snapped Panin, utterly himself now, in his accentless English. "I represent—"

The deafening explosion outside the room which cut him off seemed, in its own fraction of time, more than the gun-shot it was: it was almost a physical concussion of shocked surprise inside Tom, wrong-footing him mentally even as the second shot followed it almost instantaneously.

Ever afterwards he saw the next seconds in slow motion, fragmented frame by frame: *the man Szymiac is staring at Panin, with his mouth open: the mouth is framing a word, but the ringing echoes from the hall, together with a splintering-crashing-thumping all-in-one sound blot out the word; Panin himself is throwing his shoulder against Audley, away from the door on the very edge of his vision: the man Szymiac is also moving, so fast even in slow motion as to be a blur, clawing as he moves inside his buttoned-up jacket; and the sound and jerk of his own Smith and Wesson are overtaken by another and much louder explosion in the doorway behind him; and, finally and somehow always strangely in the slow motion progression, the man Szymiac stops in his sideways movement and is thrown backwards, slammed against the wall by his own and Sadowski's bullets.*

But the slow motion itself ceased then, as he whirled towards the doorway, flinging aside Audley's raincoat to face Sadowski and then freezing as the Major slowly lowered his revolver, two-handed, until it pointed at the floor—at, in fact, a single coat-button with a long thread attached to it which lay midway between them on the threadbare carpet.

Tom sniffed, and smelt burnt cloth; which perplexed him for only a moment, as his eye caught the edge of the tangled wreckage of Audley's coat, through which he had fired; which made him think, with a touch of hysteria, *Mrs Audley won't like that—poor old David'll never be able to explain all those burnholes as a carelessly thrown away cigar butt, because none of us smokes—the best thing he can do is say he lost the whole coat somewhere—*

"You . . . bloody . . . *bastard*," breathed Audley. "You . . . *bastard!*"

Panin looked away, to where the man Szymiac lay tumbled awkwardly against the wall, in an unhumanly uncomfortable position and quite without dignity, reminding Tom of Beirut scenes he had been working to forget. Then Panin was looking at Sadowski, who returned the look without the least sign of emotion, let alone apology, before he turned away back into the hall.

"You bastard." On his third repetition Audley sounded almost conversational "You never intended to talk to them—did you?"

Panin faced him again. "A most unfortunate accident, Dr Audley. Major Sadowski was obviously forced to protect himself. And—" He flicked a glance at Tom "—and Sir Thomas reacted in the same manner, of course. With the most commendable speed too, if I may say so." No trace of irony: the Russian's tone was as bland as his face was expressionless. "But that, of course, was an inevitable sequel to what had gone before."

"Yes—of course." Audley blew his nose on his bedraggled handkerchief. "Do put that damned thing away, Tom."

Tom slid the Smith and Wesson back into its holster.

Audley blew his nose again. "Or, if not a sequel to a most unfortunate accident, the second part of a most fortunate and deliberate double murder?"

Panin actually produced a frown. "A . . . double murder, Dr Audley?"

"That's right: a double murder to which—as you always intended—I have just been a witness. Or practically an accomplice . . . although not even you could have expected such luck in advance. So just a witness." Audley glanced again at Szymiac's body, and then moved so that he faced away from it. "But now, presumably, I am cast as the undertaker, with no questions asked? And the First Gravedigger too, maybe? With Sir Thomas as my assistant? Is that my next role? Do let me know, Professor."

Panin started to shrug, but then stopped. "I cannot accept your alternative suggestion, Dr Audley. But . . . as to what you should do now, I would not presume to advise you what to do, in your own country."

"Ah . . . my own country!" Audley accepted the scoring point without any good loser's grace. "You're giving it back to me now, are you?"

"You misunderstand me—"

"No I bloody-don't! But do go on—?"

Panin coughed. "I was going to say . . . my Government would certainly not appreciate publicity in this unfortunate matter—"

"I'll bet they wouldn't!" With Audley, an invitation to "go on" evidently had only a five seconds' life. "And maybe you wouldn't either? Or was this massacre cleared from the start?" An edge of bitterness entered the old man's voice. "Without Basil Cole I find it a little difficult to put two-and-two together—as I'm sure you foresaw I might . . . But I shall pick up all the pieces in the end, never fear!" He grinned falsely. "So what are you offering in exchange for amnesty and oblivion, then?"

Panin seemed taken aback. "What am I offering? My good David, if *I* am in some slight difficulty *perhaps* . . . then *you* are in some much more considerable difficulty *undoubtedly*, I would have thought!" He cocked his head slightly at Audley. "A shared secret—"

"—Won't do!" Audley shook his head quickly. "You are mistaking the nature of our positions again: *my* difficulty may—or may not—be more considerable than yours. But I don't give a bugger about that: before they can sack me I'll quit, and warm my feet on my investments, and to hell with them! But *your* difficulty . . . what makes you think I'm going to sweep this under the carpet? Do you think you can just walk away from this?"

Unlike Audley, Tom didn't have his back completely to the thing that had been a surprised human being a few minutes before, but which was even now surrendering its body-heat for the last time. And that thought ran cold up and down his spine as he heard the two of them bargaining in the presence of the poor damned thing . . . Not that the poor damn thing was objecting.

Once again Panin seemed off-put to the point of almost-frowning. "You cannot be threatening me, surely?"

"Threatening you?" Audley paid the Russian back in his own coin. "Would I do that—?" But as he cut himself off he caught the look of distaste on Tom's face. "What is it, Tom?"

There was no way of expressing the truth of what he felt. So he had to lie. "I was thinking that I ought to make a phone-call." Must do better than that. "In case someone heard those shots."

Audley made a derisive sound. "No one hears anything these days. Or, if they do, they turn up the television, so as they won't hear anything else—" Then he focused on Tom. "But if you want to phone—"

Tom remembered his duty suddenly. "No." He looked at the Russian. "I couldn't bear to leave you when you have Professor Panin by the balls, David. Do please swing on them—and take not the slightest notice of me. I'm just a fly on the wall." He smiled at the Russian as sweetly as his duty-remembered face allowed.

Panin regarded him curiously. "He has me . . . by the balls, Sir Thomas?"

Duty beckoned. "Oh yes—so it seems to me, Professor. Undoubtedly."

"But . . . how?" If the curiosity wasn't genuine, it was well simulated.

"This is England, sir." *Stiffen it up: make like "Sir Thomas Arkenshaw".* "Or . . . the Exmoor Division of the West of England Police Authority?" He put a cutting edge into his voice. "We don't just lose inconvenient bodies to order, Professor Panin. We have to have good and sufficient reason for doing anything like that."

"I see." But Panin had had time to rally. "And General Zarubin is not good and sufficient reason?"

"General Zarubin?" Audley fielded the name quickly, before Tom could react to it. But then he stopped, to stare past them both.

Tom turned from them both, to find Major Sadowski in the doorway again—and armed again, too. But this time it was with a very different sort of weapon.

"Ah!" Panin gave the long rifle only half a glance before nodding at Audley. "Now perhaps you will believe me, David—eh?"

Audley reached out and grasped the rifle, but for a moment the Pole wouldn't let go of it, so that they seemed on the edge of an undignified tug-of-war. Then, either because of the bigger man's main force or because of some tiny signal from his Russian master, Sadowski let go.

"See this, Tom?" Audley thrust the weapon towards him for closer inspection. But it was not something he'd ever seen before, although he recognized it all too well: the long slender barrel, and the chunky rectangular butt (with elliptical cut-out providing a pistol-grip behind the trigger)—and, above all, the telescopic sight above—identified its purpose beyond all doubt.

"They call it 'the Green Machine', so I'm told." Audley hefted the rifle in his big hands, as though estimating its weight. "It'll be the army's new standard sniper-issue, starting in '87. They haven't had anything new for donkeys' years—nothing even as good as the Argies had, even. In fact, what they had was based on the 1914 Lee-Enfield, I rather think. But this'll do a lot better—" He canted the weapon sideways "—Schmidt and Bender sight, to correct cross-winds at longer ranges."

Tom goggled slightly, not so much at the weapon itself as at Audley's unlikely expertise.

"I only know because of accident—I hate firearms." Audley picked up his astonishment. "But there was a bit of a scandal late last year, during the testing, when they had a break-in and lost a couple of these little beauties . . . Minus the sights, of course. But Schmidt and Bender must have sold a few of those elsewhere, I shouldn't wonder. Only . . . anyway, someone thought it was the IRA. And someone else thought we might look into it, just for old times' sake. But Jack Butler wisely said that we were too busy with other things—" Audley gave Panin a sidelong look, just as he simultaneously threw the rifle back at Sadowski; who caught it, but with a fumble and only just; and rewarded the big man with a milli-second's glare of red hate before his eyes went dull again "—but *I* always thought it was a GRU job . . . I'm told they're very hot on new weaponry—is that so?" He pretended to relax. "But then you've never liked the GRU, have you, Nikolai? They're basically just brutal and licentious soldiery, aren't they? *Spetsnaz* cannon-fodder?"

Panin gave the Pole a curt dismissive nod. "See what else you can find—"

"No!" Audley recollected himself. "Better give it to Sir Thomas here —*if you please!*" He reached out again, and the same tug-of-war restarted.

Panin gave the Pole another nod. "Evidence, David? Very well!"

Audley took possession of the rifle again. "Stolen property." He presented it to Tom. "At least I shall be able to give Jack Butler something."

Tom felt the weight in his hands. But, even more than that, he felt its dreadful life-and-death power: at 500 yards, or even a thousand, with wind-drift allowed for, if this was what Audley must have been thinking of all the time since yesterday, in those throw-away lines of Kipling, then no wonder that he had been scared.

"You can give him much more than that, David." Panin didn't even look at Sadowski as he dismissed him again. "General Zarubin will give you more."

Audley waited until Sadowski had disappeared again. "I wish he'd bloody-say something—just once . . . even if it was only 'Goodbye'." He blinked at the Russian. "He isn't a lip-reading deaf-mute by any chance, is he?" Then he turned to Tom without waiting for an answer. "See what that poor devil's got in his pockets, will you?"

Tom frowned at him. "What?"

"My dear boy—we're going to be hanged, drawn and quartered for this if he was just reaching for his wallet. But if he has . . . *had* . . . a gun in there, then perhaps they'll only hang us. Besides which I should have thought it might set your mind at rest somewhat?" Audley blinked again, and then sniffed and wiped his nose with the back of his hand. "Okay?" He returned to the Russian. "You were saying, Nikolai—?"

Szymiac's coat was open now, and Tom could see the broken threads and the slight tear where the coat-button on the floor had been ripped out. And the man's shirt was bloody in two places, over the heart and lower down, near the waistband of his trousers: the spreading stains had mingled but the different wounds were still quite plain. And he could guess which Smith and Wesson bullet was which from Sadowski's evident professionalism as well as from the memory of his own unsatisfactory firing position, which for one pathetic moment now had roused the half-hope that he might have missed altogether.

He saw the shoulder-holster immediately, tucked under the left armpit, as the body slid back and down under his touch, as inanimate as a sack, the head lolling heavily forward to reveal a bald patch like a tonsure at the back. He started to think *well, a real tonsure wouldn't be inappropriate*, but then he thrust the thought away from him and concentrated on extracting the pistol delicately from its cradle. It was small and light and short-barrelled, not unlike a Makarov, but with a distinctively different grip which reminded him of a Walther.

Then he became aware that both the dreadful old men were watching him in silence, so he held it up for their inspection.

"Well, that's something," murmured Audley. "Not much, but better than nothing, I suppose." He took a step towards Tom and reached for the weapon. "Evidence, Tom." He showed it to Panin for a second, and then dropped it into his pocket.

"P-64." The Russian nodded. "Polish Army issue."

"Is that a fact, now?" Audley seemed only mildly interested. "Well, I suppose it would be, wouldn't it! But . . . you were saying—? General Zarubin wants to give me something—'to give to Jack Butler, was it? Or what—?"

Tom let the coat fall back on the blood-stained shirt, watching them both intently as they stared at each other—*two really dreadful old men!*

"You were saying?" Audley opened the bidding formally.

"He will be grateful."

"Uh-huh?" Audley nodded, then looked down at the rifle, which Tom had leant against a chair, and then nodded again at Panin. "I can well imagine that. But as we've already done his—*your*—dirty work, that would seem a somewhat devalued currency now. I've never been able to pay any bills with gratitude: the next word after 'Thank you' is usually 'Goodbye'."

"But he still has business to transact here. Which, of course, is his main business, you understand?"

Another nod. "Yes—of course." Audley gestured towards the rifle, and then patted his pocket. "This is *your* business. For which you too are grateful—of course. But if you are insufficiently grateful, and I make waves . . . then that will interfere with *his* business—I do apologize for being so slow on the uptake, Nikolai! What you mean . . . is that General Zarubin's gratitude is only just beginning, eh?" Innocent understanding did not sit well on the old man's face; somehow it only made his expression more brutal. "All I can do to you is get you on the next plane home, as *persona non grata*. And then you have to take your chance. But General Zarubin doesn't want to go home either—he's got a lot to lose too, has he?"

The Russian's mouth tightened. "You have much to lose, also—"

"That won't wash." Audley cut him off. "We've been there before, too."

"And Colonel Butler?"

"Jack will take his chance, like you." Another shake.

"And your country?"

Audley sniffed, not with his head-cold, but derisively. "Just make me your offer, and stop buggering about." He made a hideous face at Panin. "You always knew it would come to this—at least, that it would if your dumb-mute did his work properly."

Panin stared at him for a long moment. "I can't give you an offer, David. I am not empowered to do so. But General Zarubin will trade you a name, face to face. And that will . . . will perhaps clear you from this—" He pointed past Audley, towards Szymiac "—with your superiors."

"Tom!" Audley was no longer looking at Panin, and made no attempt to follow his finger. "Better make your call now, just in case, so someone can clear up after us." He fixed Tom unblinkingly. "And we'll go and see what Henry Plantagenet has to offer, in exchange for not doing penance for Thomas Becket. Right?"

X

THE ROAD OUTSIDE was reassuringly empty except for a young woman exercising her children and her dogs, regardless of the weather. But then suddenly it wasn't reassuringly empty at all, Tom realized.

Chiefly it was the children and the dogs which disguised Wilhemina Groot initially, because children were not her favourite human beings and dogs were her least favourite animals. But she was also more conventionally disguised in clothes which, to his certain knowledge, had never before featured in her wardrobe: the Willy he knew and now knew that he loved had hitherto either been a smart city girl, dressed by Bruce Oldfield and Yves St Laurent, or a *motte-and-bailey* girl, dressed in jeans and his own cast-off sports gear for lack of anything better, never a Young Farmer/Young Conservative/Sloane-Ranger-far-from-home, uniformed in Barbour jacket and green wellington boots, with her blonde hair concealed under a tweed deerstalker.

Tom cursed under his breath, recalling his precise phone instructions, which were the last element of her disguise. It had been her helper he had asked for, as an ally at a pinch, not this complication of Willy herself. But this was unarguably Willy herself now being fraternized by one of a pair of damp and over-exuberant Dalmatian dogs inadequately controlled by a pair of damp children, and he had to make the best of it.

Still, there was a plus as well as a minus in the scene, he told himself desperately: if he hadn't immediately identified her, then maybe Panin and Sadowski hadn't either, ahead of him—ahead of him ostensibly to superintend the Zarubin rendezvous, but more likely to get clear of their victims as quickly as possible; to which action Audley had all-too-readily agreed—a worryingly pre-occupied Audley (as well he bloody-might be!), but an Audley who was even now four strides ahead of him, on the way back to the parked car; and, at the very least, there was no sign of any of Panin's own watchers at the moment.

But now he was close to her, and although she had pretended to enjoy the Dalmatian's affection for Audley's benefit as he passed her she was looking at him now, and with a much greater desperation than his.

"There's a lovely boy, then!" She observed the Dalmatian's juvenile owner's momentary glance at Tom, and hit the dog hard on the jaw with her fist. "Hi, Tom!"

The dog emitted an astonished yelp of pain on discovering (as Tom himself had already done) that despite her lack of inches Willy packed a mean punch, and sprawled sideways away from her into the gutter.

The dog's owner was further diverted by the yelp, but then her spotty little brother, who had been trying to ride the other animal, fell from its back, and added his own anguished cries to the confusion as both Dalmatians set off in different directions.

"They've just gone—" Willy skipped to avoid her dog as it tried to pull the little girl away from them, in the same direction as its comrade "—your friends have gone, Tom . . . They just pulled out, like a bat out of hell . . . in a grey Austin Montego with dirty number plates—thataway." She pointed past Tom. "I only just got here. I'm sorry."

"Did they recognize you—" Tom stopped as he saw her face.

"Recognize me?" Her fuse ignited. "For God's sake, honey! You called for help, and you didn't give us much time—I told you last night, this isn't *my* league! So how the heck should I know? I didn't see them last night—if they can recognize an embassy secretary being raped by a goddamn bit-part player from a Walt Disney production—raped in the rain before lunch in the middle of nowhere—?" But then, in her turn, she also stopped. "What's wrong, Tom?"

"Nothing's wrong." In the circumstances that was something less than the truth. But at least she was right: if he himself had only just spotted her, disguised by clothes and dogs and children, then she ought not to have rated a second glance. "I was expecting . . . hoping for . . . your helper, that's all, Willy. In the front line, as it were—that's all I meant."

" 'As it were'?" She mimicked him. "My most efficient 'helper' is keeping an eye on us, don't you fret. Colonel Sheldon wouldn't like me to come to any harm—Dad wouldn't take kindly to that." But then, in spite of the typical Willy-banter, she was frowning at him with that sure insight of hers, the ignited fuse quite extinguished. "Only you didn't mean that, did you? Because I know you, Tom Arkenshaw. And this is like last night, when I dropped those names, and it was wrong then. But it's even more wrong now—isn't it? Isn't it?"

Tom looked around quickly. He couldn't see any All-American marine, but at least he still couldn't see Panin's back-up either. Only, Audley had reached the car; and although he was busy kicking one of the Dalmatians right now he could hardly be unaware that Sir Thomas Arkenshaw was busy chatting up some strange young woman when they ought both to be already on the way to Brentiscombe Point.

"I told you—don't fret! My 'helper' is what you'd call a 'pro', Tom honey." She was already grinning, at once wickedly and reassuringly at the same time, as he came back to her. " 'Big panic'—or 'SNAFU', as my boss says . . . only I'm not supposed to know what the 'FU' stands for, because he knows my uncle and my dad—is that what you really mean, Tom?" She almost reached out to him, but then restrained herself. "So what do we do now?"

She was lovely. But her helper was all he had for back-up, so he owed them both a true signal now, with no pretending. And to hell with Audley, who was looking at him. "All right, Willy darling . . . Maybe big panic, or maybe the worse is over—I don't know." Then he remembered Audley pocketing "the evidence", and knew beyond doubt that the big man had been concerned to arm himself as best he could. "But my guess is there's more to come—though I don't see how."

She struggled with that for a second only. "The worst is over—?"

She was quick, too. "We have to get away from here quickly, as well as after Panin. Because there are two dead men in the house, back up there. And even if the neighbours didn't hear the shots, then there'll be one of our removal vans here soon enough, and it probably won't be too healthy. But we have to follow Panin anyway. Because he's leading us to Zarubin, Willy."

"Zzz—Zarubin—?"

"Don't ask me how or why. There isn't time—and if there was, you wouldn't believe it, in any case. But he's made us an offer we can't refuse, apparently." Time had run out, once again; he didn't even need to look at Audley to know that. "Have you got a good map in your car?"

The *Zzz* of *Zarubin* was still on her lips, and she had to change their shape to get rid of it. "Yes, we've got a whole lot of maps—your big maps, with every goddamn thing on them . . . like every *motte* and *bailey*.

Naturally, with its funds and its forethought, the CIA always had an unlimited supply of Ordnance Survey large-scale masterpieces. "Brentiscombe Point is up the coast from here, towards Ilfracombe. There's a stream comes down to the sea there, and a few cottages. And the Devon Coast Path runs along there, eastwards—there's a 'Roman Fortlet' marked just inland from it." He could remeber Audley's voice in his ear. "It wasn't really a fort, it was a signal station. You'll find two others marked further east—this is the last of the three. On the path under the fort is where we're meeting him." He concentrated on her. "Tell your man I want back-up there." Now for the truth. "And you keep well away this time, Willy. Because if you're there I shall only worry." That was the truth, and there was no way of wrapping it up. "You'll just be in the way. Do you understand?" And, anyway, it was best unwrapped. "Do I make myself clear?"

"Oh sure! You make yourself very clear. All too clear!" She almost ignited again, but caught her temper with a conscious effort. "Okay,

Tom: message received." What she wanted to do, he could see, was look over her shoulder at Audley. But she controlled that desire also, and merely nodded. "Problems you've gotten yourself, but I'll try not to be an extra one. It's my bodyguard you want now, not my body. Message received. So off you go, then."

She was so close to him that he could see the fine moisture of the wet wind on the finer golden down on her skin. And he knew then that of all the things in the world he wanted to do, "going off" away from her was the last and worst. "Willy—"

"No, Tom!" She raised her hand, almost as though to touch him again; but then she drew it back, as if their polarities repelled each other. " 'Stand not upon the order of your going—go at once!'—I learnt that at college, when we played *Macbeth.*" She smiled up at him.

Tom goggled at her. "You played Lady Macbeth—?"

"Hell *no*! It was a *ladies'* college—so I played Macbeth . . . *Go on, Tom,* for God's sake!" The hand waved urgently at him. "But . . . just you be very careful out there, like Sergeant Esterhase says—okay?"

Almost embarrassingly, Audley wasn't fuming at the delay: he was as avuncular as a bishop at a vicarage tea party.

"I'm sorry, David!" Still no sign of Panin's man—any more than of Willy's: the road was empty enough to risk a three-point turn across it.

"Don't be." What was worse than not-fuming was the big man's unashamed interest; and, looking in all directions as he completed the manoeuvre, Tom observed Willy crossing the road ahead of him now; which would bring her to Audley's side, for further inspection. "There's no hurry, now that we know where to go—" The car's angry acceleration slammed him back into his seat as Tom put his foot down "—just take it easy! Because Major-General Zarubin will wait for us, Tom." As they reached her, Audley raised his hand in a parody of Queen Elizabeth the Queen Mother's much-loved wave; and, what was worst of all, Wilhemina Groot returned the wave. "*Yes* . . . Major-General Gennadiy Zarubin will undoubtedly wait patiently on our coming, Tom." Audley settled himself back comfortably, even folding his arms to demonstrate his equanimity. "He has a name to give us. So he needs us."

Tom became aware that his foot had the accelerator flat down; and that this was both unnecessary, because the damage was done, and dangerous, because they were already approaching the next corner too fast. "What name, David?"

"What name?" Audley jerked forward as the brakes began to do the best they could. "Now . . . would that have been Mosby Sheldon's young woman, by any remote chance, Tom?"

Tom cooled himself down, helped by the relief of getting round the bend on four wheels and on the road. "And if it was?"

"Then he's still running true to form. Because he had a very pretty woman in tow last time I met him. And *she* didn't look the part either, as I recall . . ." The old man twisted in order to observe him more closely. "But . . . what you omitted to tell me, young Tom . . . is that you already know her quite well. Or even better than that, perhaps?"

Tom forced himself to watch the speedometer. "What?"

"Oh, come on, now!" Audley's voice teased him. "I may be almost superannuated, but I still have some of my eyesight and all of my memory. And—apart from that—I wouldn't for one moment question your taste, either. For she seems to be a spirited young woman, as well as a stylish one—am I right?"

It was that damned return wave, thought Tom. But then that was Willy, to the life. "And if you are right?"

"My dear Tom! Don't snap at me so—*I* have never objected to such imaginative extensions of the 'Special Relationship'—quite the opposite!"

"I wasn't snapping." As Tom cut him off he realized that he was making a fool of himself. "I didn't expect her—not here. That's all."

"Of course!" Audley hastened to spread agreement on the subject. "But . . . what I meant to say, in my clumsy way . . . is that we take a somewhat more laid-back view of friendly contacts with friendly powers in Research and Development. Much more so than your boss Henry Jaggard probably does, to take an example. Which is not to say that he's wrong, in taking a narrower view of *his* activities . . . But we are in the business of contacts and fair trading, without too much red tape, you understand . . . So some of my very best friends—*real* friends—the ones I can rely on to play honestly with me anyway, even though we both know that we salute a different flag every morning, and when the sun goes down, are Americans . . . or Germans." The old man sniffed. "At least, so long as we are of value to each other. Which makes life more interesting. But also sometimes even makes it safer, too."

Tom had the feeling that he was tuned in to a commercial. But since Colonel Sheldon had despatched Willy and her helper to the Green Man last night it was a commercial with a demonstrably convincing sales story: because the CIA obviously cared for Dr David Audley's skin. In fact, if anything, they cared rather more for it than Henry Jaggard seemed to do.

"Hah-hmm . . ." Audley cleared his throat. "So what did your young lady have to tell you then, Tom?"

So that was the object of the commercial break then, thought Tom bleakly: the old man was trying to talk his fears away again, possibly letting the sound of his voice blot out the thumping of his heart as usual.

But he was also desperate for more information, in the certain knowledge that he was sailing much too close to a rocky shore in almost total darkness, with the boom of the breaking waves in his ears.

"Nothing more, I'm afraid, David." There was a *Brentiscombe* sign ahead on the empty wind-and-rain-swept road; and Tom could hear the same sound in his head, beneath the steady rhythm of the engine, of those cruel breakers which would accept no error of navigation. "Except they're almost as frightened as I am, I think." He took the turning, which split him on to a narrower road, and then on to an even narrower one, further splitting *Brentiscombe* from *Hunter's Inn*, which forced him to concentrate on his driving.

"Well—" Audley stopped as Tom negotiated a blind bend between high banks "—well, that makes all of us scared shitless—Panin included."

"Panin included?" Trees arched over the road, some naked, some still obstinately refusing to let go of their long-dead leaves. "Panin too?"

"Aye. And that's what scares me most, Tom." Freed from his ancient *bocage* memories, Audley relaxed again. "This bastard Zarubin must be something quite exceptional, to make old Nikolai twitch the way he did, when he said 'Follow me' back there." He shook his head. "This is another of those moments when I wish I had Old King Cole whispering drunken insults in my ear. Because . . . because your damn computer print-outs may be good, and all very well if you've time to read them. But they add two and two, and two and two *ad infinitum* . . . But they never bloody-well tell you when two-and-two equals *five*—or fifty-five, or *minus*-five . . . *Because they don't smell the difference between dead men and dead mules, Tom—it's all carrion to them . . . And, if you've ever smelt the real-life difference—Christ!*"

They had gone up and down, and now they were going up and across and down; and, although he couldn't smell the sea, Tom felt its presence. "Dead men are worse, are they?" The road wasn't so much narrow as ridiculous now, with a rocky stream on one side, and trees on the other, and pot-holes everywhere.

"God—no!" The old man lurched against him. "Men are just quite unspeakable. But . . . they ask to be buried, I suppose . . . I don't know. But horses are worse, and they take a lot more burying. And so do cows, actually . . . But *mules* . . . You ask Jack Butler about mules—he's an expert, and he says they're much worse. Because I never had to bury a mule in the war, after its guts had burst."

They turned sharply, and Tom suddenly saw the sea ahead of them in a deep cutting between steep forested hillsides, battleship-grey under lighter grey layers of rain-clouds. "You said Panin had a name for us, David."

"I didn't say it. *He* said it, Tom. Remember?" Audley divested himself from his comparative study of the smell of dead and corrupted flesh. "He said Zarubin had the name."

The road sign warned of a 1-in-4 drop, somewhat belatedly. "But what name?"

"For God's sake—I don't know!" Audley had found his handkerchief again. "But I do know that we've got someone inside their London operation." Sniff. "I'm not supposed to know, but I do. And I'm thinking . . . if *I* know, then maybe they're on to him." He blew his nose, and then he stuffed the rag back into his pocket. "If he traded that name—traded the fact that they knew it . . . and let us have the man himself, because he's no damn good to them now: the only thing worth anything is that *they* know now, that he's tipping us off—*I don't know, damn it!*" He shook his head. "But that would be good enough to trade for whatever he wants, anyway." He looked at Tom suddenly. "And don't get the wrong idea, boy. Because it certainly won't be 'Panin', that name . . . Because Nikolai Andrievich Panin isn't going to defect—not in this age of the dirty world . . . Of all men, it won't be Nikolai Andrievich: I don't need Basil Cole to tell me that—*that* I know for myself, even if I know practically bugger-all else!" He shook his head again, still looking at Tom. "If Nikolai Andrievich is scared, the only possible reason I can think of is that it's Major-General Gennadiy Zarubin who is about to make the great leap from darkness to light, boy."

There was a stream falling vertically down a moss-covered cliff, with white water splashing across the roadway, covering it with a detritus of twigs and dead leaves; but he had to steer through the mess, because there was a rocky waterfall on the other side, a foot away from his nearside wheels; and there was utter confusion in his mind.

"But—" The Cortina crunched through the barrier, with one thicker branch banging against the floor under his foot, and then scraping away behind him "—but . . . *Zarubin*—?"

"He put down your Polish Thomas Becket?" Audley neatly avoided trying to pronounce Father Popieluszko's name. "My God! That's maybe only the half of it! What if he was also the man behind that Turkish lunatic who put a bullet into the Pope—how's that for size as a bonus, eh?"

The last one-in-four descent brought them out into the floor of the combe, where it reached the sea itself between a steep wooded hill on its sheltered southern side and an even steeper hillside of rocky scree and bracken on the other, with a lush water-meadow between, secret and surprising.

Tom's mouth opened, but then closed again as he concentrated on negotiating the track's final constriction—a little bridge so narrow and scarred by previous too-close encounters with vehicles that he feared for the Cortina's rusty wings—so that for that moment the idea of Zarubin in his wider setting, as the KGB's religious expert, slipped away from him.

"Phew! What a place!" said Audley in an oddly stilted voice. " 'The Pleasant Isle of Aves', no less!"

"What?" Once over the bridge they were on a wider road, although the remains of its ancient metalling was hardly visible among its pot-holes as it led them towards a scatter of vehicles parked beside a huddle of cottages at the far end of the meadow.

"Kipling, dear boy." Audley craned his neck to take in the scene. "This isn't quite Stalky country—*Dunsterville* country, I should say . . . But it's tucked away well enough to qualify, eh?" He twisted in order to examine their line of approach. "No coaches, and precious few tourists . . . But, if old Nikolai isn't romancing us, this is where Major-General Zarubin's paternal ancestors scratched a risky and uncertain living, fishing for the fickle shoals of herring in olden times." He came back to Tom. "Herring, wouldn't it have been? Didn't they catch herring hereabouts, off Lynmouth, before they caught tourists in season?"

"Did they?" Tom noted the cars (an elderly Land Rover, scarred from the bridge; a decrepit Austin 1100, resting on its collapsed springs; a vintage Volkswagen Beetle, waiting for a collector to find it; and the same spanking-new Montego he had noted outside the *Green Man* last night, in which Professor Panin and his hit-man had kept their last rendezvous); while, at the same time, he expanded Zarubin's role: not so much an expert, rather a *removal man*—a remover of turbulent and inconvenient priests from the scenes of KGB action?

"Of course they did!" Audley sniffed, but in derision and not because of his cold. "Herring was *the* fish, in the old days: it fed the poor and it manned the Royal Navy—they ploughed it into the fields, even . . . But I don't expect you've ever eaten a herring, eh? No 'herrings-in-tomato-sauce' for you, even! Fish fingers, more like—eh?" But now he had also taken in the cars, as he freed himself from his safety-belt, as Tom parked on the end of them, beside the Montego. "But at least we're in the right place, anyway."

Tom released his own belt. "But where's Zarubin, then?"

"Huh! He'll be walking his father's old path, along the cliffs—like old Nikolai said he would." Audley gave him an old-fashioned grin, and shook his head in agreement. "I know, I know! The idea of Major-General Gennadiy Zarubin cherishing a sentimental conceit for any-bloody-thing . . . let alone for his ancestral past . . . that's not *likely*, I do agree, Tom.

But, then, most of the things people do, when they can indulge the luxury of doing those things for their own gratification . . ." He shook his head again ". . . The truth is that Panin's got us by the short hairs, and he knows it. Because even producing Zarubin for our inspection—producing him privately, face-to-face like this, away from the official embassy circuit . . . I could never resist that opportunity, just in case it offered us a dividend." He pushed open the door, and swung one leg out of it. "But offering us *a name*, into the bargain—you tell me, Tom: what would you do?" He fixed Tom irrevocably. "After what's already happened—back there, in that damned abattoir of his?"

Tom saw the ultimate conflict of interests clearly, between himself and Audley—between the minder and the minded, whose interests were more often than not fatally opposed when it came to risk-taking. But to that he also had a standard answer. "If I were you, David—that is, if I were as pig-headed as you, but perhaps a bit more sensible . . . if I were you, I'd send someone else instead of me—" He raised his hand quickly "—because it might be safer for all concerned, is why: not cowardice, but plain common sense." He shook his head. "I'm not a target. At least, not on my own I'm not. But if you are . . . then we both are at risk. So let me go instead of you."

"Mmm . . ." Audley looked down the mouth of the combe, towards its U-shaped opening to the sea. Then he smiled at Tom across the bonnet of the car. "I must admit that I did toy with that convenient get-out myself, not so very long ago. And . . . not so much because I really believe in its logic, as because I have an absurd hankering to see my unborn grandchildren one day." Only then he shook his head back at Tom. "But it won't do, I'm afraid . . . and I'm afraid that 'afraid' is right. But for two reasons, I'm *afraid*, anyway." He stopped abruptly, and pointed down the combe again. "Do you see where the path goes up the hillside, beyond the cottages—on the right there? That'll be what they call the 'Somerset and North Devon Coast Path' on the map, I shouldn't wonder—eh?"

Tom had already noted the map and observed the zig-zag line. "What two reasons?" It was useless to argue, but he must make the attempt.

"The odds are that he won't talk to you—Zarubin won't." Audley started to climb into his raincoat. "I brought an umbrella, didn't I? I put it in the back somewhere—?"

"Then he can talk to you some other time. On our terms." There was a huge ugly burn-mark on the big man's sleeve—on both sides of the sleeve, in fact; with a puncture mark in its centre—and there must be several other such marks elsewhere on the coat, for a guess. "On our terms, when you're good and ready, David."

Audley reappeared triumphantly from the car, brandishing the umbrella. "I knew it was there . . . But I am ready, dear boy. And never more so than now." He stepped away from the car. "Come on, then."

Tom watched him sniff the wind, and despaired. "That's only one reason."

"No, it isn't." As it wasn't actually raining the old man busied himself with furling the umbrella neatly, as though for a stroll up Whitehall. "That is the other reason, exactly: if I let the bastards frighten me now, I'll never walk free again—don't you see?" He stabbed the umbrella decisively into the mud at his feet, looking at Tom with a quite uncharacteristically pleading look. "Don't you see?"

Tom saw—and saw suddenly to the uttermost part, which he had never glimpsed so clearly before. But he couldn't think of anything to say.

"If they want me dead, then I am dead," said Audley disarmingly. "But if they don't . . . and I *don't* go and find out what they *do* want now . . . then I shall have to move house, and take all sorts of quite demoralising precautions—at least, until Jack Butler can read the riot act to them . . . And I'm damned if I'm going to put Jack to that sort of trouble." Another grin. "And I'm also damned if I'm going to let them make me a coward-dying-many-times-before-his-death, too! I'm *damned* if I'm going to let Panin do that to me, in fact." The grin vanished utterly. "So let's go and find out what the old devil's really got up to then, Tom—right?"

So they walked.

Their walking was unreal, but on one level of experience its unreality was no new experience for Tom: the routine precautions he had superintended in the past, even in nominally peaceful parts of the Middle East, had always been fraught with similar tension; and in the Lebanon, where each side was against itself, as well as the middle and the mirror-image extremes, unreality was the only reality within the killing-zone.

But what was different here, and more unnerving, was the far greater unreality of a landscape in which only nature and the elements were violent, with no eyeless ruins and twisted wreckage, but only a coastline beaten by the fierce winter gales and the unconquerable sea itself—the same natural path along which Major-General Gennadiy Zarubin's father just might have walked, from Brentiscombe Point to Lynmouth long ago, before he had walked all the way from the Caspian Sea to Moscow—*long ago, long ago, long ago!*

"It's amazing how the wind hits you, and then misses you, isn't it!" Audley puffed slightly, from the steepness of the path, as they completed the first zig-zag up the hillside. "I wonder whether he really did."

"Who—" Puffed or not, the old man was always difficult to keep up with "—who did? And did what?"

"But it's quite blown my cold away." Audley stopped for a moment, and drew the salt-sea wind into his lungs.

"The wind?" And, as always, Audley was hard to keep up with on another level. "Who did what?"

"Zarubin *père*." Audley nodded at the wrinkled, white-waved water, which was already far below them. "God help sailors on a day like this! Whether he was a simple sailor-lad, o'ertaken by great events—a great war and a great revolution, to name but two—and cast ashore in a far foreign land . . . And you can't get much further or more foreign than the Caspian, at the mouth of the Volga." He cocked an eye at Tom. "What a story—if it's true!"

"Yes." This time he managed to start walking alongside the old man, trying to match stride for stride. "I was thinking the same thing. If it's true."

"Uh-huh. It would be nice to think it was, somehow." Audley nodded as he walked. "Pity that we'll never know now."

"We'll never know?" Tom cocked his own eye at the skyline above them. The steep hillside wore a combat jacket of browns and greens, the russet of last year's bracken mixed with the winter-worn dark gorse and lighter grass and broken by rocky outcrops. "Won't we?"

"Panin's a careful man. If it wasn't true he'd make it so, for our benefit, just in case. He's a man who likes to mix certainty with risk, I think—or the other way round."

"But why?" Far down below, on the green floor of the combe, he could see two tiny figures in red anoraks—children at this height, but they might easily be adults—circling two toy black-and-white cows in the meadow; while above him the skyline and the whole landscape was empty. But in this well-camouflaged country the only certainty was *risk*, was all he knew. "Why, David?"

Audley said nothing for a dozen yards or more, as they followed the path across the hillside, over a stone culvert through which a stream splashed, noisy but invisible under the bracken. "Who knows? If this is really Zarubin's country, then Panin must have thanked his lucky stars, because he'd know I couldn't resist such a tale, never mind the bait. And if it isn't . . . well, the same pretty much applies, whichever way the game's played: I did the dirty on him, once upon a time. So it's only history repeating itself, with a few cosmetic variations. *He* knows—and he also knows that *I* know. And so on, ad infinitum—it's no use trying to make sense of it: it's only like peeling a large Spanish onion, which makes me weep, but never makes me sad." He half turned towards Tom in mid-stride, and patted himself vaguely in the midriff. "All we can do is keep our powder dry, like Jack Butler always says . . . and hope for the best, eh?"

Tom remembered two uncomfortable things almost simultaneously, and was further reminded of both of them by the additional burn marks which Audley's flapping raincoat revealed during the half-turn: the dead Pole's little pistol, which Audley had palmed as "evidence", would be about as much use in these conditions as a pea-shooter (even supposing the old man could still point it in the right direction, and not shoot himself in the foot); and, in these same conditions, his own Police Smith and Wesson, in his own hand and with five rounds remaining, provided only marginally more protection, if that.

"Yes." He grinned foolishly at Audley. There was no point in voicing his professional doubts now. All he could do was hope for that best of Audley's, while the stretch of path ahead of them was still empty. (Only Mad Dogs and Englishmen, and Visiting KGB Generals, went out in such wind-and-rain.) And the gorse-broken skyline was still equally empty above them. "You're right, David."

All the same, he scanned their surroundings even more carefully—only to discover instantly that the zag of the zig-zag behind them was no longer empty, however innocent: there was a head-scarfed woman there, with a child hidden in a push-chair, accompanied by a youth encased in a green anorak carrying an enormous red-and-yellow kite—clutching it with evident care, and obvious difficulty, since it was doing its best to hang-glide him into space already from the less-windy stretch of the path below.

"What's the matter, Tom?" inquired Audley.

"Nothing." If the bloody child soared into the sky-line under his bloody kite, then that would have to be a problem for his idiot mother. All Sir Thomas Arkenshaw and Dr David Audley needed to do was to get round this last bit of pathway, in order not to be able to witness the tragedy, with the wind taking care of the mother's anguished cries.

"What?" Audley was oblivious of women and children and kites.

"Nothing." Tom erased them too. "I was going to say . . . you don't really think Panin's up to more violence, surely?"

"Hah!" Audley breathed in gratefully. "No, I don't, Tom." He supported this pronouncement with another huge breath, cold-free, taken into the teeth of the wind. "Instinct tells me not. Otherwise I wouldn't be here, to be honest." Another huge breath. "Because age has made a coward of me."

"What?" Partly it was because the wind made the old man almost inaudible. But also Tom couldn't resist taking another look at the Mad

Englishwoman and her family. (And she was trying to button up the protective hood of the baby's pushchair now, while the Awful Child was wrestling with his kite.)

"What I'm depending on—" Audley almost shouted the words "—is that Panin will know that Jack Butler will hold *him* responsible if anything unpleasant happens to me, no matter how it seems. Just as—" The wind gusted strongly, carrying away the rest of his words.

And if anything unpleasant happens to us? Tom wondered momentarily, although he already knew the answer to his own fate: the doom of bodyguards down the ages, long before King Harold's household thegns had died to a man round his body, was part of the contract of service. Even if Willy Groot shed a tear for him she would still reckon he'd only got what he asked for in his line of work.

Somehow Audley had got ahead of him again. "What—?"

The old man stopped, and stared around for a second, and then turned. "I said 'Just as Jack will hold *me* responsible for whatever happens otherwise', Tom." He gave Tom a hard look. "And Henry Jaggard will hold *you* responsible also, eh?"

The wind dropped, suddenly and freakishly, so that Audley's final shout came out unnaturally loudly, as though to emphasize what had been in the back of Tom's mind ever since he had come to his decision. Then, even more suddenly, its full force hit him again at the corner of the path where it reached the coast at last, almost stopping him in his tracks.

"Yes—" Not so much the wind as the whole glorious panorama of the North Devon coastline took his breath away, with headland after headland plunging uncompromisingly into the sea, with the promise of deep-water directly beneath them: an indomitable coast against which the wind and the waves beat endlessly but in vain.

But Audley was still staring at him, partly blocking his view of the path along this coast and finally concentrating his mind at the same time. "I shall resign, of course," he said.

"Yes?" Disappointingly, the big man accepted this shock-horror revelation with only mild interest. "Why?"

It was on the tip of Tom's tongue to tell the truth, that he was fed up with the accumulated risk of being an accidental and secondary target while trying unsuccessfully to make obstinate old buggers like Audley himself take the most basic precautions. But then he saw that it wasn't quite the real truth.

"I can't work for a man I've betrayed." He liked the harshness in his own voice. "I should have quit an hour ago, and left you to get on with your damn 'Nikolai' by yourself. But I promised your daughter, in a moment of weakness, that I'd watch over you, David." Looking at Audley now was like looking at a coin with hate on one side, and love on the other, when the coin was balanced so that he could see neither side. "I'm keeping faith with her now—against my better judgement."

"Ah!" Still only mild interest. "The old thankless task! Believe me, boy—I *do* understand. Because I've been there too, myself." The old Beast-smile returned, moistened now by the fine mist of rain which was stinging Tom's own cheek, hard-driven by the wind. "So just answer me this one question, then: *who would you betray—your country or your friend?*"

As well as irritation bordering on anger, Tom felt the rain driving cold into his exposed eye. "That's a ridiculous question, David. It's bad enough to have to risk my neck for you. But I don't have to put up with humbug as well."

"No." The smile twisted downwards. "But just this once—just this *last* time . . . can't you humour your dear mother's old friend?" The smile vanished. "And then no more questions."

That Mamusia's old flame played dirty right to the last question was absurdly comforting, somehow: it made the outcome of that old, long-resolved contest between Audley and Father, in which Father would always have played a straight bat (just like William Marshall in Ranulf of Chester's day) quite astonishing. But it also confirmed every loving thing he had ever thought about Father in that same instant.

"All right." He wished Audley would get out of the way, so that he could see the path ahead; but this answer must clear that obstacle too, anyway. "Since this is my country it's no question. But if it was Poland . . . that might be more difficult. But in *this* country . . . if my so-called 'friend' was British, then he would have already betrayed me, and all my other friends, so he'd be a traitor, and 'betrayal' doesn't describe my *reaction* to that, when I blow the whistle on him. Or, if he's a foreigner . . . then he's a false friend and an enemy—I might still honour him then, but 'betrayal' still doesn't apply, just the same, when I get him in my sights—" In spite of all the wind (or perhaps because of it), a sudden tingle in his nose made him sneeze. "Is that what you want? 'My country' —*right* . . . before my 'friend'—*wrong*?"

Audley shook his head. "It was just a question." He stepped aside, leaning into the wind, which flapped his bullet-ridden raincoat around his knees, to reveal the path behind him as well as the bullet-holes. "I already had my money on the answer. And there's a place for you in R & D when you want it, is my answer to that, Tom."

The cleared path had a foreground, and a middleground, and a background, snaking round the next headland. But there was only the middleground, really. Because there, where the path cut into a cascade of dead bracken and heather and gorse which fell from the skyline above down into the invisible sea far below, three men were waiting for them.

Three—?

Instantly, he sorted them out: saw, but didn't count, *Nikolai Andrievich Panin*, muffled against the wind and dark overcoated still; saw, but dismissed, his little Major, who was better-protected in a short rainproof jacket like the Barbour which Willy had been wearing, wherever Willy might be, but somewhere mercifully safe now; and saw, and only saw, the third and last and first figure most of all, raincoated like Audley.

"You watch Sadowski, Tom." Audley shouted his whisper at close quarters. "I don't trust Panin . . . But Sadowski is a bloody hit-man! Remember?" He touched Tom's arm, propelling him forward. "Remember?"

"Yes." Tom let himself be propelled on to the foreground of the path, where a trickle of water from the hillside above had reduced the path to a morass churned up by footprints and hoofprints; although all he could really concentrate on as he squelched forward was that first figure.

The mud gave way and slid treacherously underfoot, but he could still only see Major-General Gennadiy Zarubin standing four-square on the path, in what might have been his father's country, and his grandfather's, before the two world wars had demoted and promoted his line: another tall, raincoated figure, almost as broad-shouldered as Audley himself, waiting now to make them that offer which Audley had chosen not to refuse, with the headlands behind him already fading into the rain-squall which was sweeping into them, and over them, out of the infinite greyness of sea-and-sky which filled half their world.

He lifted his hand, to keep the driving rain off his cheek and out of his ear, and also so that he might hear what Audley might say, as the gap between them decreased step by step; and, at the same time, reached across his chest and felt the weight and shape of the Smith and Wesson; and finally glanced up to scan the gorse-broken skyline above them.

Odd that there was still a scatter of yellow flowers on this sea-blown wuzzy, when there hadn't been a single flower on the gorse at Mountsorrel: and some of these were winter-browned at the edges (he saw each complex flower with a photographic clarity which surprised him); *but others were blooming freshly, defying wind and winter equally, against all the odds, while all the lower ground-hugging heather flowers were long-dead and colourless—*

"He's a big bugger, isn't he!" Audley's words, when they came, were utterly inconsequential. "I wouldn't like to meet him in a dark alley in Berlin—either side of the Wall!"

Almost as big as you are—or maybe even bigger! The thought twisted through Tom's brain, challenging him to wonder what Audley himself had been like in his own dark alleys, years ago, in the dark ages.

"He doesn't even look like a Russian." Audley hissed his final useless judgement into Tom's protected landward ear in the instant that he quickened and lengthened his stride across the last few yards, to the man himself, thrusting out his hand in a classic gesture of false friendship. *"General Zarubin! Good morning to you!"*

A shaft of light—it wasn't true sunlight, but it was something more than the murk which had shrouded them so far—lightened the two big men as they met, as Zarubin matched Audley with his own hand: it was a strange unnatural light, like the light of Limbo, between Heaven and Hell—

"Dr Audley—"

Time accelerated and slowed down, spiked on *now* and on *forever afterwards* simultaneously, as the two meat-plate hands reached out towards each other, with an empty yard separating them which would never be bridged as the Major-General seemed to throw himself forward, on to hands and knees, to stare through Audley with blank astonishment in the same *now-and-never* instant that the bright red blossomed from his white shirt on each side of his tartan tie, and the blood gushed out of his mouth like vomit—

Tom hit Audley with his shoulder, every ounce of his weight spinning the big man sideways against the overhang of the hillside, above the path, even before General Zarubin's dead body finally subsided into the mud.

"Oooff!" The sound of Audley's breath and his own mingled as they both fell, binding them together into oak-tree-and-ivy flailing together in their fall, with no thought for afterwards. But then Tom's training (never before exercised like that), and Audley's lack-of-training (still uninformed from yesterday's bullet, and still unbelieving), turned them both into a confusion of threshing legs and arms, all trying to re-establish their independence.

"For Christ's sake—!" Audley mouthed the words into his ear.

"Shut up!" Tom pushed him down as he tried to sit up, pressing his face into the stony bank below the yellow-flowered gorse. "God—!"

God was not an appeal: *God* was the sight of Nikolai Panin still standing up in the open, above the still-twitching body of Major-General Gennadiy Zarubin, as though the rest of his life had minutes to spare, not seconds. "Get down, man! For God's sake—!"

Panin threw away another precious second in shifting his surprised look from the hillside above to Tom. Then he hunched himself ludicrously, as though to make a smaller target, and sank to his knees beside Zarubin.

To hell with him! thought Tom, as Audley pushed and heaved beneath him. *He could take his bloody chances!*

"Damn you, Tom! Let me up, damn you!" Audley swore at him.

"You stay right where you are." Tom kept his elbow on Audley's neck as he watched Panin raise his comrade's body slightly, and simultaneously tried to remember the instant of the bullet's impact. Because there was a dark mark no bigger than a shilling high up on the broad expanse of Zarubin's back, just above the shoulder blade: so the high-velocity bullet had come downwards steeply, shattering flesh and bone, to blossom that huge exit-wound where the shirt had reddened—had come *downwards* from not far away, and not more laterally from some distance greater *ahead* of them—

He couldn't hold the big man down much longer—

That was right! Because the three men had been hugging this same overhang above the path, where the wind hadn't been so fierce, when he had first glimpsed them. So the killer hadn't killed before because he hadn't had a clear shot until Zarubin stepped out to greet Audley—

Christ! The next thought rolled Audley away from him, even as he cleared the Smith and Wesson from its holster. "Get down, David!"

"What the devil—?" Even in the instant of his release Audley picked up his panic signal, and shrank into the overhang obediently.

"Where's Sadowski?" Tom snarled at Panin.

"Sadowski?" The Russian let go of Zarubin's shoulder, and the body dropped back into the mud as though gravity finally had a stronger claim on death than on life. "Major Sadowski is doing his duty, Sir Thomas." He looked down at the blood on his hand with evident distaste. But then calmly wiped it off on the dead man's raincoat before looking up again at Tom. "Just as you are doing now."

The freak wind suddenly howled around them, swirling the sharp raindrops into Tom's face from a new direction, half-blinding him.

"*Tom—*" Audley's voice came from behind and below him "*—go!*"

"No!" Panin straightened up, still on his knees but fumbling into his raincoat. "Your duty is to protect *us*, Sir Thomas. Let Sadowski—"

"Shut up!" Audley's voice was level with Tom now, and it was deep-frozen with pure hate. "And if you find what you've got inside there, I'll shoot you in the guts, I swear to God—as God is my witness!" The old man's voice modulated, as though he was surprised by his own passion. "I'll shoot you in the guts, Nikolai . . . because after all these years the only thing I can remember is to shoot *low*—so I may actually shoot your balls off instead—*go, Tom!*"

Panin froze. Then swayed, as another gust shook him; but swayed like a frozen dummy nevertheless, unmoving even though moving.

"That's right." Thick velvet suddenly covered the steel. "Now the hand comes out—*slowly* . . . ever-so slowly . . . *that's right!*" Audley drew a deep breath. "God! You were bloody close then, I tell you! Because it's been forty years . . . well, maybe thirty years, give or take . . . But I never was very good with small guns. Okay with 75-millimetres, but no good with 9-millimetres . . . *Go, Tom—for God's sake, while this old devil and I frighten each other equally—go on, Tom! Go!*"

Standing up on the path, even for an instant, also frightened Tom. But then the beginning of returning logic steeled him to take a full look at the skyline above him, with the loss of precious time already also spurring calculation as he did so: *Sadowski had gone straight up into the wuzzy, somewhere behind them—but why?*

"Go on, Tom—go find out what he's up to, there's a good chap." Audley had his voice almost back to the conversational level. Yet somehow that sounded louder than a shout inside Tom's head as he moved obediently to the order.

Sadowski wasn't protecting Panin, as he ought to be doing—

The overhang, where the cliff-path had been cut from the living rock of the hillside, soon petered out. But then the gorse-wuzzy was still old and impenetrable as he searched for an opening further along as he followed the path round the headland, its sharp spikes and brown-frosted yellow flowers mocking him—

Like Sadowski, he wasn't protecting his man now, so what the hell was he doing?

There was a gap just ahead, at last—

There was something very wrong here: he had promised Henry Jaggard implicitly, and Cathy Audley explicitly, not to do what he was doing; and he was risking his own life in breaking those promises. But, in the midst of what was now a huge disaster, David Audley had given an order, because his instinct was to fight disaster, to the last gasp and the last bullet—and—and by sweet Jesus Christ!—that was his own Polish instinct, too!

Now there was the gap in the wuzzy—a gap where a summer-fire had burnt it back long ago, to let the heather and the bracken get a stronger foothold for a time until it could re-establish itself—so that was the way he would go—

The dead wuzzy and heath and bracken gave place suddenly to a crumbling stone wall, reinforced by a sheep-proof wire fence.

Over the wall and the fence: there was smooth hillside grass now, liberally sprinkled with sharp-focused sheep-dung and smaller rabbit-droppings, with the curve of the headland above him and the full fury of the wind at his back, driving him upwards towards the crest; indeed, even as he let the wind drive him, he saw real sheep away to his left, huddled against the inland line of the wall, and also the white danger-signal tail of a rabbit bobbing off to his left, into a square wall of windswept gorse—

But there was no other living thing, either ahead or left-and-right, as he came towards the high point, with the whole coastline behind him fully revealed and stretching into far rain-mist: *this, almost to the very yard, where that dimpled trench-line marked the edge of the gorse square, must have been where the old Romans had built their signal-station, with this superb view of any Irish raiders sailing up the Bristol Channel—although in this bone-cutting wind it must have been more a punishment-posting than a mere watch-keeping duty—*

Another ten yards, and he would be at the high-point of the ditch, where the ancient pallisaded-and-revetted gateway must have been, with a high watchtower somewhere inside that wuzzy, all built with timber brought up from distant inland wooded valleys with great labour and organization far surpassing anything Ranulf of Caen and Gilbert of Mountsorrel could have managed more than a thousand years later, in a less efficient age of the world—

And then he saw them: and saw them both together, on the corner of another sheep-wall-and-fence inwards from the Roman signal station, but not in those other ages of Romans and Normans safely dead, but in his own now, with his own death shouting—

Which way?

They saw him almost in the same instant, perhaps by chance, or perhaps because they were being properly careful: it didn't matter, because in his own age, if he gave that damned *Green Machine* rifle a clear sight, he was dead now—and the odds against him clogged his throat with fear even as he tried to make a decision—

Which way? Because if he went back the way he had come, the curve of the hillside would still give them a clear view as he reached the stone wall again, which was higher on this side, so that he would have to climb up it—

★

The thought became its own decision: there was a narrow band of grass between the gorse-wuzzy of the Roman fort and the steep bracken-and-heather below him, and his legs were already anticipating his brain's instructions, already running him where he needed to go, automatically twisting and jinking him like that frightened rabbit which had itself showed him how to take cover in the wuzzy.

But he wasn't going into the wuzzy like the rabbit: the gorse was old and thick on both sides of him, and even if he could break through it (which he didn't think he could, anyway), it would slow him down too much—or it might even stop him altogether. And that was all the man with the rifle needed—

("The Green Machine", Audley had called it, of course: "They had a break-in and lost a couple—": and they had one in the car now—but the other was up there on his flank somewhere! Damn, damn damn!)

He had to keep moving: so long as he was moving sideways—then he had a chance. Not even the best marksman liked deflection shooting: marksmen liked sitting targets—

But the damned wuzzy was still too high on either side, and he could feel the land falling away under his feet with each rabbit-bound. So what he was doing now was running back the way he'd come, parallel to the invisible path below him and the great grey sea itself. So this route would trap him on the very point of the high ground, on that last straight stretch after the zig-zags had brought them up from Brentiscombe meadow. So . . . *he must bear right—must take the risk that they were on an interception course above him: once down in that heather-and-bracken, among the stone outcrops, then he'd have a chance as they came over the skyline in their turn, because he still had his gun—*

Even as he changed direction the slope in front of him seemed to drop away and the whole combe sprang into view far beneath him, with its tiny houses huddled under foreshortened trees and the line of model cars parked beyond them. But in the very instant that he saw the combe a bullet cracked viciously—cracked and double-cracked—the sound was above him, yet also somehow behind him and ahead of him too in the same fraction of time before the howling wind carried it away.

As Tom threw himself forwards he already knew that he could never keep his feet on such a descent, but he managed an impossible succession of downwards rabbit-leaps towards the nearest outcrop before the ground slipped from under him on the rain-sodden bracken. Yet even then, by some acrobatic miracle, he contrived to control his slide for another twenty yards, first on his bottom and then on his back, until one foot suddenly snagged in a deep-rooted patch of heather, twisting him sideways with an explosion of pain. And then earth and sky whirled, and he was rolling and tumbling helplessly, grabbing—*grabbing*—

Christ Jesus! He'd lost the gun!

Heather and bracken tore his hands as he tried to slow his descent, but then the hopelessness of recovering the weapon opened them again, even though he felt that it was like letting go of life itself as he slid and tumbled the last few yards to drop over a miniature cliff on to the path below.

The fall jarred stars in front of his eyes for a moment—red and yellow stars, seen hazily through blurring rain and sweat. But then they weren't stars at all: they were a huge red-and-yellow kite, straining to escape from their owner up the path, a few yards away.

"Get away! Get away!" Tom screamed at the boy as he tried to struggle to his feet. "Get away!"

The kite and the boy parted company: the kite soared upwards and outwards, and the boy seemed to disappear outwards and downwards, over the edge of the track. And Tom cried out in anguish as his ankle grated and gave way under him.

He fell on his side, and for a second he wanted only to curl up into a ball and disappear. But then his brain ordered *hands and knees—hands and knees if not feet, Tom!*

He heard himself cry out again in agony as he righted himself and the broken bones of his ankle screamed at him. And then it was too late.

It seemed hugely unfair that Major Sadowski had made the same descent somehow intact: the Major should have fallen too, and lost his gun, and even broke his bloody neck, thought Tom angrily. But Sadowski hadn't. And neither had the man in the combat jacket, who swam into view—unfocused and then focused—with the white eyes in the blackened face and the rifle in his hands. And that was unfair, too.

In fact, everything was unfair—even being killed on his hands and knees on a muddy path was unfair. And his ankle hurt like hell, too—

He wiped his sweaty face with one hand, hypnotized by the muzzle of the gun in Sadowski's fist, which was pointing at him. But then, inexplicably, it wasn't pointing at him as the man in the combat jacket said something—or started to say something as Sadowski shot him at close quarters, spinning him clear off the path.

Tom frowned uncomprehending at Sadowski, watching him replace the gun methodically in its holster. Then the Major took three steps and started to reach down for the rifle, which his murdered comrade had so suddenly relinquished.

"Leave it!" shouted a shrill voice from far behind Tom.

The Major froze for a second, his hand halfway to the rifle. Then his head moved slightly, so that he was staring past Tom, up the path towards the sea.

The urge to turn himself in the direction of Sadowski's stare and towards that weird far-off imperious voice, yet at the same time keep his eyes on the Major himself, was too much for flesh-and-blood: wishing to do both taxed Tom's enfeebled powers of decision so that he attempted to do both, and ended up by doing neither as he exerted pressure again on his smashed bones and was facing uselessly into space across half an empty mile, towards the zig-zag path on the hillside on the other side of the combe, as the blinding pain and the explosive chatter of a machine-pistol confused his senses.

The distant hillside blurred and the treacherous wind took the noise and spread it into infinity, so that the echo was only inside his head instead of reverberating up and down the combe and far and wide over the high empty Devon coastline. But it froze him nevertheless, just as the strange shrill voice had held Major Sadowski for that lost moment in the past, before he had come to what Tom knew—*knew without needing to understand*—had been his final and inevitable decision, because that had always been the Major's game—

Kill, or be killed!

The far hillside became crystal-clear, so that Tom could observe with detached interest that it was steeper than his own, with less vegetation and with avalanches of rocky scree; and thought (light-headedly) *that if Major-General Gennadiy Zarubin* (who was dead) *had climbed that way, then maybe Major Sadowski* (and maybe the man-in-the-combat-jacket, with the black-face-but-white-eyes) *wouldn't be dead; but he hadn't, and they were—he was, and they were . . . so now Tom Arkenshaw—so Tom Arkenshaw, against all the odds—*

He lifted his bad ankle again. And, though it still screamed out at him, he was almost grateful for the pain's reassurance that he was still in his own world, the world of the living, as he contrived to look over his shoulder at last—

He saw the child's push-chair first, on the bend in the patch where it turned to follow the coastline a dozen yards away, almost on the very spot where he said "I shall resign" to Audley, five hundred feet above the great grey angry sea, so very recently—so very recently and so long ago for Zarubin and Sadowski and the camouflaged man . . . for them, in fact, it had been the rest of their whole lifetimes—

The head-scarfed mother detached herself from the overhang, still holding the machine-pistol stiffly at the ready, ignoring him and her empty push-chair equally as she sidled step-by-careful-step across the path—the old professionally well-balanced step, ready for anything: he had seen that before, the fluid careful body, the steady gun and the watchful eyes! But he had never really been in that class, in which preservation was not a sequence of precautions, but a violent pre-emptive action against the terrorists—

She reached the edge of the path, and took one quick up-and-down glance over it, only to confirm what she already knew while hardly taking her eye off the path over Tom and beyond him, just in case (and *just in case* was another hallmark of the pro)—

But now, at last, she looked at him, and advanced towards him. And, just as he was testing the idea that maybe she wasn't a woman after all, she smiled at him and he knew that she was, of course: it wasn't just that remembered voice, and certainly not the smile, it was everything about her which made her a woman.

"Hi there, Sir Thomas." She was late-thirties at close quarters, but not noticeably hard-as-nails. "I'm Shirley."

Tom felt at a disadvantage. "Hullo . . . Shirley." Part of the disadvantage was a feeling of intense gratitude. Which, because she had only been doing her job, made him also feel foolish. But there was also the fact that he couldn't stand up: as she moved cautiously past him and he tried to keep her in sight his broken bones reminded him painfully of his fall. "I'm afraid I've broken my ankle."

"Is that a fact?" The path was empty except for the rifle which Sadowski had reached for in vain. But she wasn't interested in that. "Is there anyone else up there, Sir Thomas?" She watched the hillside as she spoke.

"No." The pain made him catch his breath. "There were just the two of them."

"Two?" She shifted her attention to the outside edge of the path. "Hmm . . . well that surely makes two." She studied what he couldn't see for a moment, then she peered further back. "You can come on up, Wilhemina."

Tom's disadvantaged feeling expanded into embarrassment. He should have known, of course—children, dogs or kites, none of them were Willy's scene. But chiefly it was obstinate disobedience which came naturally to her.

"Wilhemina!" This time Shirley shouted the name. "Come on up!"

"I'm coming—I'm coming!" Willy sounded angry, rather than scared, in the distance. "I fell halfway down the hill, darn it, Shirl!"

Tom sat up with difficulty, holding his injured leg with both hands unsuccessfully. Not that he was about to regain much dignity, with his knuckles skinned and bloodied by his fall through the gorse, and his face not much better, by the feel of it.

"Hmm . . ." Shirley stared down at him. But there was a surprising lack of disdain in her expression. "You got the other one, huh?"

Tom hid his surprise beneath his pain. But then he realized that she must have been round the point of the path when Sadowski had killed his comrade: she must have been covering Audley when the freak wind had carried the sound of Sadowski's shot—or one of the shots—back to her; and Willy had been behind her, and therefore been closer to this point; so Willy had arrived here first—was that it?

Quite deliberately, he let the bones grate again, and cried out in genuine agony.

"Tom honey! For God's sake—!" Willy's anguished cry also came to his rescue.

"He's okay." Shirl's voice was coldly matter-of-fact. "He's just hurt his ankle—that's all."

"Tom honey!" With the hood of her anorak down and her hair out she was Willy. "I thought you were shot!"

"I'm all right." She was going to fuss over him, and he liked the idea of that because it gave him time to think. "Honestly I am, Willy."

"Oh, Tom—you're a mess!" Her eyes were dark with concern. "You're not fit to be allowed out on your own—that's the truth!"

What Tom thought first, as she brushed his own hair out of his eyes, was *—I'm the only one who knows what really happened, in all its confusing completeness—*

And then the thought betrayed him: *in the second place it wasn't quite so confusing now—*

But he looked at Shirley, with sudden knowledge conferring power greater than pain. "Is Audley all right?"

"When I last saw him he was just fine." Shirley rewarded him with a look of undeserved professional approval. "I think he was quite enjoying himself, maybe."

Tom tried to concentrate on her, to the exclusion of Willy's perfume and her soft solicitous touch. "Enjoying himself?"

"Yeah." Shirley shared one efficient minder's secret with another less-efficient minder. "Dr Audley likes winning, Sir Thomas."

"W——" Tom caught the word before it betrayed him, and turned it into a very different word. "*Willy* . . . I love you, Willy." But, as he changed the word, it became the absolute and ultimate truth. "Do you love me, Willy?"

Wilhemina Groot considered the wreck of Sir Thomas Arkenshaw critically. "I don't know about *love*, Tom honey. But someone has got to look after you—*that* I do know!"

This was what mattered, in the third place, after knowledge and power.

And, also, Willy Groot would know how to keep Mamusia in her place. "Will you become the umpteenth Lady Arkenshaw, in Debrett's, and Burke's *Peerage*, Willy?"

The wind and rain swirled round them, and Tom felt the wetness of the puddle in which he was sitting chill his backside. But that was a minor discomfort compared with the importance of Willy Groot's decision, which would decide Tom Arkenshaw's fate—and possibly Dr David Audley's fate, and the future of Research and Development, and that *preux chevalier* Colonel Jack Butler with it . . . and maybe even Henry Jaggard too . . . *but bugger all of them!* Tom Arkenshaw first—*first and last!*

"Tom honey! I thought you'd never ask—"

"Christ O'Reilly!" Shirley exploded. "We've got two dead men within spitting distance—and a Russian with diplomatic privilege just round the corner—"

"Shut up, Shirley," said Willy. "*Yes*, Tom." She turned to Shirley at last. "Being married to Tom will never be dull: He'll be a full-time job. He's half-Polish, you see—half good Anglo-Saxon-Anglo-Norman, but half Polish. It's a great mixture: half of him is steady and calculates both ends against the middle—but half is into charging the machine-guns on horseback . . . Isn't that the truth, Tom honey?"

Tom thought of Sadowski, who had charged his last machine-gun in vain. But then he thought of David Audley, who had calculated everything exactly in the end—even including Tom Arkenshaw himself.

"More or less, Willy—yes." But what he actually thought was . . . *being married to Willy Groot would never be dull either, although it might be uncomfortable at times; but then being married—professionally married—to David Audley would be much the same; but now they had both asked for his hand in marriage, and they both needed him, albeit for different reasons: so who was he to go against the vote of the majority?*

He smiled at Shirley. "I can give you a telephone number to ring, to clear up the mess. And I think I shall also need a stretcher, to carry me back to civilization."

Or, anyway, what passed for civilization, in an age as dark as that of King Stephen and the Empress Matilda. And in so dark an age the prudent man must look to his own interests with the greatest care.

"I'd like to talk to David Audley, too," he added. "There are things he needs to know."

PART THREE

Winners and Losers and Winners

IN THE EVENT, it was Garrod Harvey who began the inquiry into "The Exmoor Massacre", not Henry Jaggard himself.

However (as Jaggard was at pains to explain very quickly), this was not because the whole thing had been his (Garrod Harvey's) idea in the first place, but rather because his (Henry Jaggard's) view of Research and Development was all too well-known; so that if justice was to be seen to be done (if not actually done), it would be far more distinctly seen to be so if it resulted from a recommendation from below rather than a simple act of joyful obedience on his (Henry Jaggard's) part to a Ministerial and FCO ultimatum.

Which was the truth, up to a point.

By then the mortal remains of Major-General Gennadiy Zarubin—the victim of a tragic heart attack while *en route* to a tour of the Westland helicopter works at Yeovil—were themselves *en route* to Moscow, accompanied by his grieving comrade, Professor Nikolai Andrievich Panin. And the Gorbachev appeasers in the FCO, who knew exactly what had happened to the General's heart, had expressed "I-told-you-so" delight at the Soviet Embassy's friendly desire to hush up the whole affair, subject only to the punishment of whoever had been responsible for such lax security on the British side; which quite properly pointed to the serving up of David Audley's head on a platter, suitably garnished with a lettuce leaf, two radishes and a carrot *Julienne*, in the Nouvelle Cuisine manner.

So the outcome of the inquiry was cut-and-dried, and every prospect was pleasing on the surface. But in retrospect Henry Jaggard still shuddered at the risks he had taken in going along with Garrod Harvey's lateral thinking, for he was by nature a belt-and-braces man. And, also, he had wind of certain rumours which were going the rounds beneath the surface, which most disconcertingly combined outrageously inaccurate elements with disturbingly accurate ones; so that it was to these rumours that he turned the conversation first, when Garrod Harvey came back from his exploratory interview with Colonel Jack Butler, following his final de-briefing of Sir Thomas Arkenshaw . . .

"Yes." Harvey pushed a chair across the carpet towards the desk, and lowered himself into it gingerly, as though in pain. "Well, there are basically two of them, with variations: there's what might be called 'the Irish joke' and 'the Polish joke'." He flexed his shoulders cautiously. "The Irish joke appears to have emanated from somewhere in the Special Branch, and is simple and circumstantial, and quite amusing. But wildly wide of the mark, in more senses than one." He paused for an instant, in order to concentrate on his right shoulder. "Whereas the Polish one is much more ingenious, Henry. But not nearly so funny, because it is substantially true, I rather think."

It was reassuring that Garrod Harvey had done his home-work properly as usual, thought Jaggard. "And that's the one David Audley himself has put abroad, I take it?"

"Well . . . actually . . . *no*. I rather think his was the Irish one." Harvey stopped flexing his shoulder. "He has quite a few friends in the Branch. In fact, although he has a lot of enemies, he does also seem to have a surprising number of friends, Henry. Particularly in Grosvenor Square."

"Indeed? Well they're not going to be able to help him now." Special Branch friends or American friends, he must expect Audley to take defensive measures. "But you have the truth from Tom Arkenshaw, Garry?"

"I . . . have an undoubtedly true account of what happened." Harvey's answer carefully amended the question. "And I've had a little talk with Colonel Butler. He was really extremely affable—"

"*Affable?*" Affability had never been one of Jack Butler's faults in the past.

"Helpful, then." Harvey stretched again. "I'm sorry, Henry: I played squash with a purveyor of the Polish *non*-joke last night, and he beat the hell out of me—I've been in agony ever since . . . No, what I mean is that Butler admits quite frankly that this wasn't David Audley's finest hour. And so does Audley himself, apparently."

"He does, does he?" Now Henry Jaggard's suspicions were fully-armed, so that he was more than ever determined to settle his doubts first. "Tell me the Irish joke, Garry."

"The Irish joke? Okay, then: it's apparently a version of the Connaught Ranger's defence, when he was accused of murdering his corporal—back in the Duke of Wellington's time, during the Peninsular War: he said he hadn't *really* murdered the corporal, because he'd been aiming at his sergeant, but his musket threw the ball wide by a yard." Garrod Harvey looked a little disappointed. "That's a joke, Henry."

"Thank you for telling me. I'm laughing inside."

Garrod Harvey started to shrug, but then his squash-playing injury hit him again. "The word is that the Irish—the INLA—have had Audley on their list for years, even since that fellow O'Leary was shot, up north somewhere. And there was an old IRA man named Kelly who was killed more recently, down in Dorset somewhere—"

"Audley had nothing to do with his death. Neither did we."

"This is the *rumour*, Henry. Which is that Audley's worked his way to the top of their hit-list. So they were waiting for him when he met Zarubin on Exmoor."

"Ah!" Jaggard had heard that the Irish were being blamed for the Exmoor Massacre, but he had not picked up the exact details. "A case of poor marksmanship, do you mean?"

This time Garrod Harvey's pain wasn't physical. "Mistaken identity, actually. Because it seems that Audley and Zarubin are about the same build. And they were both wearing Burberry raincoats. So this Connaught Ranger shot the corporal instead of the sergeant, Henry. And then Zarubin's escort went after him, and also got shot. But the Americans had two of their people on hand—two *women* actually, so the story goes . . . And one of them shot the Paddy before he could correct his mistake. End of Irish joke."

It sounded like an inside story—but not quite. "Nothing about those two 'Irishmen' in the house at East Lyn, whom we had to bury? Or about their Polish passports, and all that 'Sons of the Eagle' literature that was found there? Or is that in the Polish joke—?"

Garrod Harvey didn't move his aching shoulders. "Nothing about them. Or about poor old Basil Cole, either—no! But there is some good Special Branch corroborative detail, all the same, Henry. Which isn't so funny, actually."

Actually . . . *Basil Cole* wasn't so funny, thought Jaggard. "What detail?"

"It seems . . . *it seems* . . . that the INLA took a shot at Audley just the day before, down in Sussex. And missed, so rumour has it." For a moment Garrod Harvey looked into space above Henry Jaggard's head. "It is certainly a well-known fact that there were road-blocks out over half Sussex on that day, with the police and the Special Branch as thick as bees in June . . . or whenever bees are thick." He gave Jaggard a blank look.

That was nasty. "I thought that was merely an anti-terrorist exercise, Garry?"

"Yes." The look was still blank. "But one about which David Audley might have had certain suspicions, in the end."

That was enough. "Tell me the Polish joke. Or *non*-joke—?"

"*Non*-joke. And Audley doesn't really come into it—Professor Nikolai

Panin has the leading role. And Viking very nearly has another leading one."

That was even nastier. "I can see that it isn't a joke. Go on, then."

Garrod Harvey stared at him, like a man trying to remember a joke, but afraid that he hasn't got the punch-line clear in his mind. "It begins with General Zarubin becoming surplus to KGB requirements . . . or surplus to alleged Gorbachev needs, anyway . . . ever since they killed that Polish priest so incompetently—" He focused on Jaggard "—this is still the *rumour*, Henry. It's not what *I'm* saying, you understand—?"

"Of course." But there were limits to credibility. "But I don't see how that was a KGB problem—if that's what you mean—?"

Garrod Harvey continued to stare at him, but no longer blankly. "Zarubin was Panin's problem. But he also had another problem, Henry—just as you did, actually." He cocked his head slightly. "In a way it's almost a mirror-image situation—almost exactly."

"A mirror-image?" Now that he thought about one of his worries, Jaggard could see the force of the analogy. "How's that?"

"Well . . . it seems that they knew they had a problem, in the London Embassy—just as you suspected." Garrod Harvey adapted himself to Jaggard's frown. "They knew they had a leak somewhere. So Panin decided to use Zarubin as the expendable bait in a trap: he let slip certain information at certain levels, and waited to see how it all turned out." He nodded. "And Viking picked up his bit, and passed it on to us."

Jaggard experienced his own twinge. But it was of excitement, not of pain. "But we didn't act on it, Garry."

"We didn't—you were absolutely right—" Harvey almost stuttered over his agreement "—right to give them Audley instead of Viking, that is."

That wasn't how Jaggard wished to remember his decision. "That wasn't quite what we did." It was on the tip of his tongue to remind Harvey that he'd backed Audley against Panin himself. "But go on, Garry—?"

Harvey nodded enthusiastically. "So *we* didn't tip him off. *But the Americans did—right?*" Another nod. "*Their* man in the Embassy tipped *them* off . . . And they sent down the 7th Cavalry—or the daughters of the 7th Cavalry—to look after him. And thereby blew their man—do you see, Henry?"

Henry Jaggard saw. And also saw many beautiful advantages from his vision, like a flower blossoming in slow motion, as Viking obtained a longer lease of life from the CIA's error. But, at the same time, his less-sanguine self saw innumerable predators and parasites attacking his flower. "Oh yes? And just where—where *exactly*—do the 'Sons of the

Eagle' come into this? I grant you they weren't Irishmen, Garry. But whoever they are, they are now extremely *dead*. So who were they, then?"

Garrod Harvey nodded. "Ah! That's the really clever bit—the pure bloody-minded Panin bit! Because the 'Sons of the Eagle' are the deal Panin made with General Jaruzelski's Fifth Bureau, which provided him with both his hit-men and his cannon-fodder, and all his window-dressing—like the passports and the forged Solidarity literature. Because the Fifth Bureau was only too pleased to kill Zarubin for him—the general knew too much about their involvement in the killing of the priest, and they could close that file when they closed *his* file . . . And they dreamed up the 'Sons of the Eagle' as a bonus, as well as a cover, so that they could hang a terrorist charge on Solidarity into the bargain."

"And have their men massacred?"

"Oh . . . they weren't in on *that* part of the deal, Henry: the so-called 'Major Sadowski' wasn't a Fifth Bureau man—he was pure KGB, with a Polish accent . . . a bear in eagle's feathers. All he was doing was killing Poles, which is an all-the-year-round sport for Russians. And for Panin it was merely making sure that there wouldn't be any inconvenient witnesses around, just in case we had the place staked out after all—" Once again Harvey caught a shrug just in time "—I mean, he wasn't keeping his promise . . . so why should he expect us to keep ours?"

"Hmm . . ." Jaggard was still captivated by the Viking bonus. Until this moment he hadn't given the man more than another month, before he'd have to be extricated. But now, if he was run cautiously . . . or even allowed to lie fallow for a few months . . . his working life might be greatly extended, and perhaps even all the way back to Moscow. "So the Americans have lost their man, then? A pity . . ."

"Oh, they got him out in time. I rather think they guessed he was already on borrowed time in there. But they have lost him, in effect—yes."

Jaggard felt generous. "Well, it wasn't any of their business. But we owe them one now, nevertheless." Then a thought struck him. "They weren't the originators of the Polish joke by any chance, maybe?"

Garrod Harvey shook his head and winced. "I think not, actually."

"No?" Jaggard saw that Harvey's "thinking not" was only the brown wrapping covering certain knowledge. But then he also saw that if this ingenious and circumstantial account of the Exmoor Massacre was neither Audley's nor the CIA's work . . . then maybe Viking wasn't so safe after all, damn it to hell! "You're not about to suggest that this is all KGB disinformation I hope, Garry?" He heard his disappointment roughen the question. "Yet still substantially true?"

Garrod Harvey held his head steady. "It does rather look that way, I'm afraid."

"Why—" Jaggard controlled his voice "—why should they want to give us so much?"

"It's a very good question—I agree." Garrod Harvey was genuinely uncertain now. "But what I *think* is . . . everything didn't quite go the way they planned it, you see . . ." He trailed off.

But Henry Jaggard saw once again, and all too well. Because no plan, however good, ever survived the cold plunge into reality still warm and dry.

Harvey met his scrutiny. "It's possible that the shot we took at Audley unsettled them—" He held up his hand. "It had to be done, Henry. Because we had to concentrate his mind . . . for *our* purposes. But they didn't know about that—just as we didn't know about Basil Cole. And the Americans turning up must have unsettled them even more."

Jaggard waited.

"But the real balls-up was when Audley ordered Tom Arkenshaw to go after Major Sadowski—and Tom obeyed his order. Because it seems that Panin was going to put a stop to that, only Audley threatened to shoot him on the spot, himself." Harvey drew a breath. "So Tom saw Sadowski giving the sniper a friendly 'hullo' when they should have been shooting it out." Harvey almost smiled. "The irony of which is that Sadowski was probably only trying to get close enough to make sure his bullet went in the right place. Whereas the sniper had a rifle, and didn't need to do that—so Tom knew at once how the land lay: that they were in it together. And, of course, they *both* went after him then. And finally, to clinch it, when they had him at their mercy Sadowski obligingly shot his sniper-friend first."

"Why did he do that?"

"Ah . . . well, Sadowski was a real pro, whatever else—or whoever else—he was. He hardly said a word in front of Tom, so it's possible that he recognized him from somewhere, and didn't want to risk his Russian-accented Polish in front of him. But if he was a slow talker he was a fast thinker, Tom reckons. So he wanted the sniper's bullet in Tom, and his bullet in the sniper, for the autopsy."

"He could have told the sniper to kill Tom, surely."

This time Garrod Harvey forgot not to shrug, and paid the price for shrugging. "If you want a thing done properly . . . And what Tom Arkenshaw also thinks is that the Major liked his work. And in his own line of work he's met one or two of the breed, I shouldn't wonder."

Jaggard remembered his duty belatedly. "He's all right, is he—Tom?"

"All right?" A shadow crossed Garrod Harvey's face. "Sir Thomas Arkenshaw has a badly-broken ankle and a heavy cold—for both of which

David Audley is more or less responsible. But he thinks Audley's quite a man, nevertheless."

"Yes?" That had always been a danger, on the debit side of the special connection Arkenshaw had with Audley which had made him the man for the job. "But you haven't any doubts about his report, Garry?"

"Oh, no." Harvey managed a carefully-controlled nod. "It'll be as full and honest as you could wish for, Henry—right down to Audley's continued insistence on going it alone whenever Tom advised him against it." Another controlled nod. "Audley behaved *exactly* as I predicted, in fact."

"Well, that's all right, then—" But Jaggard saw that it wasn't "—isn't it?"

"He also told Audley everything that happened, after he'd gone after Major Sadowski." Garrod Harvey's lips compressed. "And he admits that he also told Audley that he was reporting back to you, Henry."

"He—?" In that instant Sir Thomas Arkenshaw's name moved from the black to the red side of the tablet in Henry Jaggard's mind, marked now for *No further promotion*. But then he knew that he wanted to know more about the fatal admission. "How did he come to admit that? You pressed him—?"

"He volunteered it of his own accord." Something close to approval was in Garrod Harvey's voice. "Sir Thomas Arkenshaw is a medievalist, like David Audley. And I may be wrong, but . . . it was almost like a formal act of defiance—or whatever the old medieval Arkenshaws did, when they renounced their feudal allegiance, and moved from one side to the other, in the old days." Garrod Harvey didn't shrug, but rather twisted himself uncomfortably for a moment. "You also have to remember that he's half-Polish, Henry. They're an unpredictable lot, in my experience." Harvey raised an eyebrow. "Eh?"

There was something damnably not right with Garrod Harvey this afternoon. And, as Jaggard trusted Harvey more than he trusted most men, that was much more worrying than Sir Thomas Arkenshaw's medieval Polish practices. "What are you trying to tell me, Garry?"

The eyebrow came down. "Tom Arkenshaw isn't very pleased with us, for having done what we did to him. And he's also deeply humiliated—professionally humiliated—by what happened . . . '*I ran like a rabbit*', is how he put it." Another controlled nod. "And he has been trying to protect people like Audley—and Zarubin—from people like Panin and Sadowski . . . maybe for too long." Another nod. "We worry about all the killers there are loose in the world, who can pick and choose their killing-grounds at leisure. But we don't give much thought for the poor bastards who are expected to out-think the killers—or put themselves in the way of the bullet when they don't."

That simplified the message. "It's called 'battle-fatigue', Garry." Jaggard nodded wisely, without pain. "We've just got to rest him up, that's all."

"It's too late for that."

"How is it too late? Has he resigned?" That, at least, would simplify this problem. Though Garrod Harvey was right, of course, in his general thesis; and that would bear further inquiry in the future. "He's resigned—?"

The same shadow which had crossed Garrod Harvey's face before now recrossed it. "He's asked for a transfer to Research and Development, Henry."

"He's *what*—?"

Another controlled nod. "Colonel Butler knows about it. And he says that he's very ready to give Sir Thomas Arkenshaw a try. Because he's one down on his establishment, since last year." Then Garrod Harvey held his head very steady. "He already has the necessary endorsement from his Selection and Recruitment Adviser. And I don't need to tell you who *he* is."

In a perverse way Henry Jaggard felt himself warming to David Audley, and not for the first time: it would have been disappointing if the man had let himself be beaten too easily, with no unexpected tricks in his bag. Yet also he was glad because such tricks made what had to be done that much easier—because before there had always been a nuance of regret, that he had to break someone useful and loyal because cruel necessity had overtaken him. But now, by his actions, Audley had not only deprived him of any real certainty about Viking, but had also ruined Sir Thomas Arkenshaw, who had been marked for promotion. "Well, if Audley thinks that'll save him he's about to learn otherwise, Garry!"

Garrod Harvey's face was suddenly a picture. "Henry—"

"No!" He had all that he needed now. "There are five men dead—*five* dead men to account for. Which is a bloody massacre, by any standards. Or *six* . . . if you count the man Cole—"

Harvey shook his head, forgetting his back. "You can't count Basil Cole, Henry. That was Panin making sure Audley didn't get whatever advice Cole might have given him—" His mouth twisted "—or maybe it was even Panin making sure that Audley would never let go—I don't know . . . But Panin would have known that Audley would go to Cole first, in any case. And—"

"It doesn't matter what the hell he thought!" Henry Jaggard was beyond arguing the toss with subordinates. "I want Audley out, Garry. And I know Jack Butler will fight for him—you don't need to tell me that." He overrode Garrod Harvey brutally. "All the better if he does:

we need that. Because Audley's sacking is what's really going to pull R & D into line—Audley is the real heart of R & D, not Butler. If we can get Audley, then we've got it all—Glamis, Cawdor and the whole kingdom—"

"*Henry*—"

"And I know everyone admires him. *You* admire him—and Tom Arkenshaw does . . . And, damn it, *I* admire him too, Garry—*I know!*" Even now, in spite of everything, he knew that he would sincerely regret Audley's passing: over many years Audley had probably done more good for the state than either he or Garrod Harvey ever would. "But he's got to go. Because it's not only what *I* want: it's what the Minister wants, and it's what the FCO wants. And, with what you've got, it'll have to be what Downing Street will have to want this time. *Do you understand, Garry?*"

"Yes." Garrod Harvey stared at him. "But *no*, Henry."

"No—" Harvey's uncharacteristic obstinacy took Jaggard flat back. "What d'you mean—*no*?"

"I do understand." The stare was fixed immovably. "But it's not on, Henry. We can't do it."

Jaggard opened his mouth to blaspheme, but then he amended the sound. "What d'you mean—?"

"I talked to the Americans—to Colonel Sheldon, at Grosvenor Square." Garrod Harvey moistened his lips. "He asked to see me. But in any case I had to warn him—that his man inside the Soviet Embassy was at risk. And I also wanted to know why he'd put him at risk, by sending down those two women to tip off Audley, Henry."

"Yes?" Jaggard watched Garrod Harvey touch his lips with the back of his hand, as though he was afraid, and was suddenly afraid himself.

"Mose—Colonel Sheldon . . . he's nobody's fool. And he knows David Audley—they worked together ten years ago, Henry."

Jaggard pushed his fear down. "I know that. And Sheldon likes him—"

"Liking doesn't come into it. Mosby Sheldon threw away his man, and saved Audley, because the CIA rates what Audley's doing—and what R & D is doing—as of the highest importance." Nod. "The work they're doing on the Gorbachev 'Order of Battle' is considered crucial to the whole nuclear disarmament dialogue: what they're feeding the President comes from agreed joint Anglo-American intelligence. And R & D is the best part of that, according to Sheldon. Because he's one of Admiral Stansfield Turner's fast-track promotions. So he rates analytic intelligence as the most important *human* function, now that their orbiting satellites can do all the old conventional spy functions." Nod. "It's who the new men are, and how they think, that matters—not where the missiles are, and what they are . . . *Liking* just doesn't come into it, Henry."

Henry Jaggard began to feel old. Up until this instant he had thought of Audley as *old*. But now he included himself in the same condemnation.

Garrod Harvey seemed to have forgotten his bad back, too. "Sheldon knew exactly what was coming—he knew it all: Zarubin and the Poles—and that poor Polish priest—are just water under the bridge to him . . . the Thames, or the Vistula, or the Moskva—all just water." Nod. "And he'd heard all the rumours, too—the Irish joke, and the Polish joke . . . And he wasn't laughing, Henry." Nod. "What he told me was that the Americans aren't going to stand by and see Audley put down—Audley and Research and Development both. They don't want it—and they won't have it."

Jaggard waited for a moment, until he was sure that Garrod Harvey had got all his bad news off his chest, which must have been discomforting him considerably more than his squash-player's back all this time. But he also used the moment to compose himself, as he sensed the red warning signal of his own anger shining brighter even than the flashing amber of fear. "*They* won't have it, Garry? *They* won't have it?"

Garrod Harvey swallowed. "Sheldon's a good friend of ours, Henry."

"I know what he is. And who he is. But I don't think he outranks me yet—never mind the FCO . . . and the Minister—not in this, anyway." He watched Garrod Harvey for another moment. "So—?"

Garrod Harvey touched his mouth again. "He'll go above you, Henry. Or . . . the Ambassador will. To the top, Henry."

There had to be more. "To the PM?" There had to be a lot more. "To tell the PM that the CIA London Station won't have an incompetent British officer disciplined? An *elderly* incompetent officer?" Much, much more. "Who has let the KGB put one over on us, in our own back yard—to our own very considerable diplomatic embarrassment?" He had to shake his head there. "Just because the elderly—elderly *and* incompetent—officer still does useful work on his good days?"

Garrod Harvey's chin came up, reminding Henry Jaggard unbearably of his father, who had also been gutsy in a tight corner. "No, Henry—you don't understand. What I mean—"

"I know exactly what you mean." Jaggard's spirits rose again. Viking might yet be salvaged, even if only for a few more months. But, almost more than that, he liked the way Garry Harvey was at last refusing to be overawed. "The Americans value R & D. Well, so do I—and I'm not proposing to dismantle it, just to bring it to heel."

"But Audley—"

"I value Audley too, Garry. So I won't let him be disgraced. I'll do it decently—damn it, I'll even get him a 'K', if that'll satisfy all his friends: he can be 'Sir David Audley'. And we'll make him a consultant into the bargain—tell Sheldon that, Garry." But he could see even as he spoke that Garrod Harvey's bayonets were still obstinately fixed and pointing at him. "What the devil do they want?"

"They want no change, Henry."

Enough was enough. "Well, they damn well can't have it. And that's flat. Audley goes. With or without a knighthood."

Garrod Harvey cocked his head slightly. "To please the Minister? And the FCO?"

"And to please me." Garrod Harvey's change of tactics wasn't going to change Henry Jaggard's mind now: this was one time when he had to fight the Americans.

"Yes." The slight head-movement seemed to remind Harvey of his shoulder again. "And it'll please the KGB too—having you on their side, Henry."

Jaggard stared at him.

"And the Minister. And the FCO." Garrod Harvey blinked. "A pretty impressive Anglo-Soviet alliance, Professor Panin has put together; nothing like it since 1941, Henry."

Jaggard stared at him.

"Why did Panin ask for David Audley, of all people?" Garrod Harvey didn't wait for an answer. "He had a perfectly good plan—the Polish joke: get rid of Zarubin and flush out a traitor, all-in-one? He could have asked for an office-cleaner from the Foreign Office to take him down to Exmoor. But he didn't. He asked for a load of unstable dynamite, in the person of David Audley—and then he deliberately primed Audley ready to explode by murdering one of Audley's old friends?" He shook his head slowly. "That was one hell of a risk to take, because Audley may be old, but he's not stupid. So . . . asking Audley doesn't make sense, Henry. At least, it doesn't if the Polish joke was the only one he intended." The slow shake stopped. "But supposing there was also a *Russian* joke—a joke he didn't intend to tell us?"

"A Russian joke?" Jaggard wasn't laughing inside or outside now.

Harvey nodded again. "Panin needs to bring off something difficult, for his own sake. Zarubin was no great problem—and if they knew there was a traitor in the London Embassy . . . that didn't require Audley as a catalyst—*much* too dangerous, Audley." From nod to shake. "Audley's not a bit of cheese. He's not a mouse, either—he's a bloody tiger, Henry: he needs a big tiger-trap, is what he needs." Garrod Harvey watched Henry Jaggard make all the final connections. "So what happens, if you —and the Minister and the FCO—get what you want? Audley gets thrown out . . . and, whatever you say, that'll totally dislocate R & D for at least six months, and maybe even longer. Maybe even forever, perhaps? And *that* really would be a feather in Panin's cap." The slow, irritating shake recommenced. "Henry, *we* were trying to *Shibbuwich* David Audley, and R & D with him. But suppose the KGB was trying to do the same thing?"

All Jaggard could do now was stare.

"So if the American Ambassador says to the PM '*Whose side is your side on, for God's sakes?*', then what the hell are we going to say?"

Henry Jaggard felt the old sour taste on his tongue in that instant, which was all the more bitter because he knew that he was still right, even in defeat. "And you believe this?"

No nod, no shake. "It doesn't matter what I believe. All that matters is that it fits better than anything else. Plus the fact that Panin has always wanted to get David Audley." Garrod Harvey almost smiled. "Tom Arkenshaw says that they were mostly quite unbearably polite to each other—right down to the last moment, when Audley pulled a gun on Panin, and said he was going to shoot off his balls first. And Tom says Panin knew that was God's truth: he says it was like Mowgli and Shere Khan in Kipling—Tom knows his Kipling too. And that's what really makes me think it may be the way it is, Henry. I'm sorry, but—"

"Shut up!" Henry Jaggard knew that the only way to survive defeat was to face it quickly. And, with what Garrod Harvey would undoubtedly report, defeat was now certain; because Garry wasn't about to let his own head roll with Henry Jaggard's. Which, with this Prime Minister of all others, it undoubtedly would.

"Henry—"

"No!" Jaggard didn't need to hear any more, he just needed a little time to think.

"But Henry—" This time it was the look on Jaggard's face which cut Garrod Harvey off.

Audley was behind the American action, of course. As always, it wouldn't be provable, but it was nonetheless certain. But there was no use gnashing his teeth over that: they—and the Russians too—had set out to *shibbuwich* the man, only to be *shibbuwiched* themselves. And that was that. All that mattered now was to survive.

"It's all right, Garry." He smiled at Garrod Harvey, with all necessary mental adjustments no sooner calculated than made. "I'll deal with the Minister and the rest of them. Fortunately, things haven't gone too far yet. So I shall be able to recommend an informal protest to the Soviet Embassy. And you can reassure Mosby Sheldon—you can tell him that I entirely agree with him."

Garrod Harvey blinked. "I'll do that. But I was going to tell you . . . about Colonel Butler, Henry."

"Ah, yes . . ." Jack Butler would also have to be appeased, of course. "I'll have a word with Colonel Butler too." At least he understood now why Butler had been so uncharacteristically affable: once the Prime Minister learnt that R & D had been a specific KGB target (and Audley could be relied on to let that piece of information leak upwards, for sure), then Butler's stock would go even higher in Downing Street.

"It isn't that, Henry." There was a curious expression on Garrod Harvey's face; it was not embarrassment, yet he was embarrassed all the same.

"Yes, Garry?" Jaggard felt that he was ready for any shock now. "You're not about to ask for a transfer to R & D, are you?"

The expression vanished. "Good God, no!"

"Well, that's all right then." Jaggard concealed his vast relief. "Don't worry, my dear fellow. Audley has won, and we have lost. But it was my fault, not yours. It *was* a good idea . . . and we haven't lost forever."

Garrod Harvey took a breath. "That's just it, Henry. We haven't lost at all—*we've won, Henry*."

"We've—?" Henry Jaggard was so taken aback that the final word failed to arrive.

"We've won." Garrod Harvey nodded. "I said Colonel Butler was helpful." He nodded again.

" 'Affable'—" Jaggard cursed himself for interrupting. "Go on, Garry —go on!"

"Yes . . . well, he said that he felt R & D was getting too isolated— that this business on Exmoor was a good illustration of how dangerous such isolation could be, with his most valuable officer going in blind and risking his neck like a subaltern in the trenches. So he wants to integrate his work much more closely with what you need in the future."

Henry Jaggard opened his mouth. "God bless my soul!"

"Yes." The next nod was so vigorous that it hurt. "Regular meetings —joint policy briefings, the lot."

"God Almighty!"

Garrod Harvey swallowed. "There is a price, though."

Henry Jaggard came down to earth. "A price?"

"He thinks we should be a lot more accountable. So if he comes into the fold he'll be bringing the Stansfield Turner CIA recommendations with him: he says that if we don't meet Parliament half way, Parliament will come and get us."

So that was the way the land lay, thought Jaggard. "I see!"

And then he did see. Or, at least, he began to wonder whether David

Audley might not be behind this last joke also: the very obvious wheeling-up of a huge Trojan horse to the as-yet-unbreached walls of British Intelligence, with Audley himself inside it. The trouble was, he couldn't decide whether it was an attack or the last, best defence of Research and Development.

"I see." What he needed was time. "Well, I'll go and talk with Colonel Butler, Garry. We'll sort something out."

For the time being, he decided R & D was best left well alone, to its own devices.